The Bloodmoon Hunters

BOOK ONE

THE SILENT RUINATION

KYLE STEPHENSON

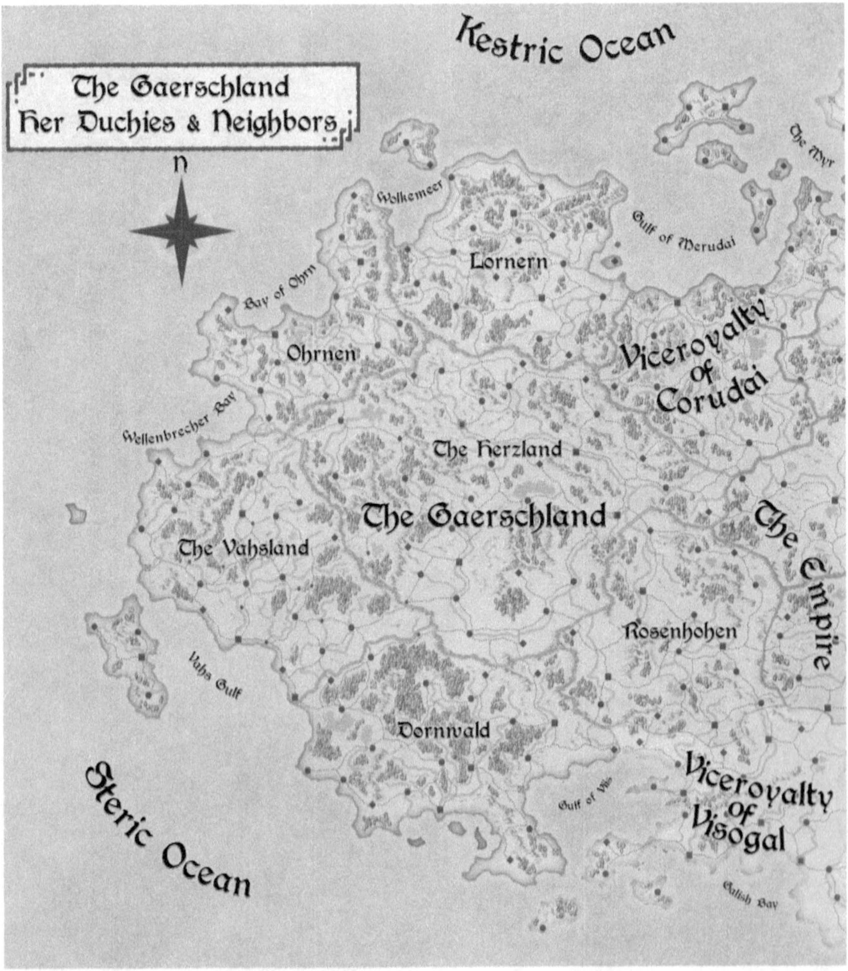

The Gaerschland
Her Duchies & Neighbors
N
Kestric Ocean
Wolkemeer
Lornern
Bay of Ohrn
Ohrnen
Gulf of Merudai
The Myr
Viceroyalty of Corudai
The Herzland
Wellenbrecher Bay
The Gaerschland
The Empire
The Vahsland
Vahs Gulf
Rosenhohen
Dornwald
Gulf of Vhir
Viceroyalty of Visogal
Steric Ocean
Callsh Bay

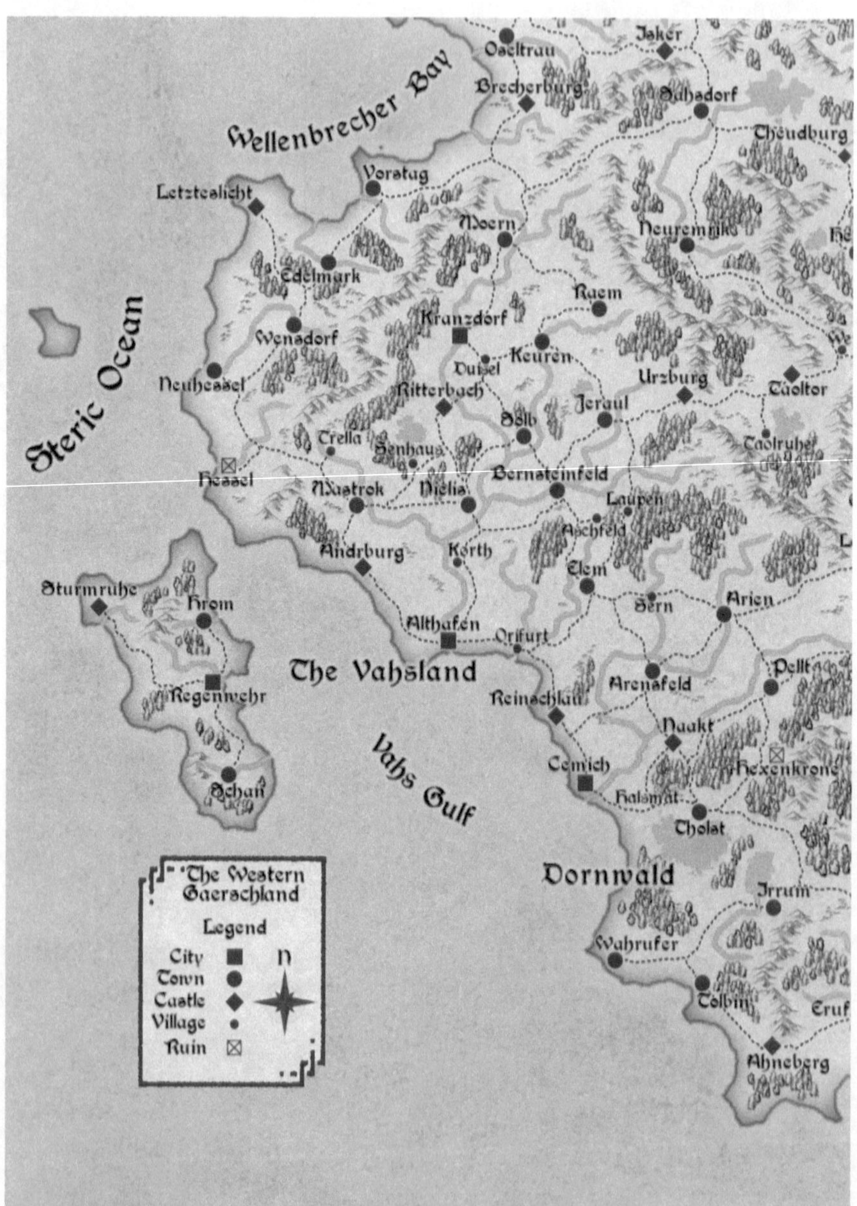

Wellenbrecher Bay
Steric Ocean
Jaker
Oseltrau
Brecherburg
Sühadorf
Theudburg
Vorstag
Letztelicht
Moern
Neuremnik
He
Edelmark
Raem
Kranzdorf
Wensdorf
Keuren
Urzburg
Duisel
Taoltor
Neuhessel
Ritterbach
Jeraul
Sslb
Crella
Taolruhe
Senhaus
Hessel
Bernsteinfeld
Wustrok
Niclia
Laupen
Aschfeld
L
Andrburg
Korth
Elem
Sturmruhe
Arien
Sern
Hrom
Althafen
The Vahsland
Orifurt
Pellt
Arensfeld
Regenwehr
Reinschlau
Naakt
Hexenkrone
Vahs Gulf
Cemich
Schau
Halmat
Tholat
Dornwald
Irrum
The Western
Gaerschland
Wahrufer
Legend
City
Town
N
Castle
Tolbin
Eruf
Village
Ruin
Ahneberg

PROLOGUE

ERIK

Carrion birds wheeled about in a sick dance overhead, singing out in grim jubilation like men and women awaiting a feast. Their harsh cries sounded like a death knell, and each call made Erik grip his hands to his ears tighter as he huddled alone in the hollow of a dead, desiccated tree. Gero, Erik's older brother, should have been back by now. He should have been back a long time ago, but he still hadn't returned, even after what felt like an hour. Erik was scared and hungry, and now that hunger was starting to bite away at his stomach like little insects gnawing on his insides.

Gero had told him to stay put, and Erik tried his best, but he couldn't do it anymore. He crawled out of the crevice and brushed off bits of dirt and deadwood, wincing each time the vultures sang to one another. Erik began to move toward the lonely farm, its fields fallow and its livestock nowhere to be found.

A cluster of buildings sat adjacent to the fields, empty and more haunting than the stretch of barren sod. That was where Gero had said he was heading, so Erik started toward it. The buildings were old, and what paint had been applied to clay-daubed walls was beginning to chip and flake. He ambled slowly toward the farmhouses, wary of whoever was inside. They must have found Gero and tied him up for trying to steal from them.

Erik stopped when he heard the faintest of scratching sounds. He looked around for the source of the noise but didn't see anything. Then a door creaked, and uneven footsteps soon followed. He ducked low and crawled toward the small stone wall that surrounded the farm, peering over the top of it to watch as a man moved out into view.

The man was dressed in dirty, loose-fitting clothes, though Erik couldn't tell if he was the owner or just one of the farmhands. Still in the shadow of the house, he stumbled forward, and Erik thought he spotted a bottle in his hands. The man took another lopsided step and then seemed to steady himself as he stepped out into the setting sun. Erik let out a yelp as he saw the sickly pallor of the man's skin and the gaping, bloody wound in his arm.

The man shook in place, almost falling over again, letting out a haunting croak as he turned lazily in Erik's direction. The cursed man's eyes were crusted over and dim. It was hard to think he could even see, but Erik fell back in fear regardless, clutching both hands to his mouth as he slumped forward against stone. The man was a Nachzehrer. Uncle Bertram had told him about them, but Erik had never seen one before now. The accursed kin, men turned into monsters bearing the stigmata of a great sin upon their souls. Erik snuck another peek and saw the thing turning away from him.

A crash tore its attention from him as a door busted open and Gero came running out. He was badly wounded; blood dripped from shallow bites and scratches, but he moved at a brisk pace. Erik caught sight of their father's dagger, light glinting off its cold silver blade as Gero spun around to slice at another of the foul ghouls trailing behind him. More of the fiends came out from the buildings, tottering on shambling, unsteady legs but from too many angles for Gero to escape.

One lunged at him and missed, Gero slitting its neck as it lurched past, but another grabbed him by the arm and pulled him down. He stabbed at it, shrieks and moans roaring from its mouth as it let him loose. All Erik could do was watch, petrified, as his brother was piled on by the slavering throng. His screams for help echoed out over the fields. Finally, the madness ended, and Erik knew his brother was dead.

Just like their father. Just like Uncle Albrecht, Aunt Vera, and all their cousins in Stenwarl. He let out a sob, then bit down on his lips, trying to silence himself as his eyes welled with tears. Shuffling footsteps began to sound, and he didn't need to peer over the wall to confirm what he already understood: he was too late. They had heard him. Now they were coming to kill him, too.

Pushing himself to his feet, Erik ran, stumbling but not falling as he moved parallel to the short wall. He kept turning his head back to watch as the horde approached the spot where he had been. Suddenly, he ran face-first into someone and fell back onto his rear. He looked up, ready to ask for help. His eyes widened as he stared into two murky, dead orbs. Dried stains of pus and tears clung to the grisly face, its slack jaw revealing a bloated tongue.

The monster reached out for Erik, but then the shooting started. It turned toward the sudden noise, and Erik used the moment to flee, jumping over the stone wall and running between the houses. He stopped when he saw Gero standing there, mouth agape like the monster he had just fled from. His ash-blond hair was caked with blood and dirt, and his flesh and clothes were ripped to shreds, yet there he stood. A glint of silver caught Erik's eye. He watched his brother raise a shaking, half-eaten hand before dropping their father's dagger.

More gunfire drew Gero's attention and Erik charged the monster that had been his brother. He screamed as a gunshot tore a hole into the Nachzehrer's side and sent it stumbling. Erik ducked down, scooped up the gore-soaked dagger, and leaped onto his transformed brother, plunging the blade into his heart just like Uncle Bertram had taught him. He heard the sizzling as the true silver tore at Gero's cursed flesh, and after a moment, the thrashing stopped.

Erik fell over, half sobbing, half laughing as he lay in the dirt amidst the grime of death. A shadow fell over him and he looked up, expecting to see another of the beasts but finding a man with thick brown mutton chops and bright blue eyes.

"Get up," he commanded.

Erik did as he was told, and the man handed him a vial full of blue liquid.

"Drink."

Again, Erik did as he was asked, uncorking the vial and downing the slimy substance within. It tasted awful and burned his mouth and throat as it went down, but he finished it.

"That was medicine to keep you from becoming like them," the man said. "Name's Ottokar. Yours?"

"Erik," he replied.

Ottokar grunted in acknowledgment and turned to look at what had been Erik's brother, raising an eyebrow.

"Gero," Erik said. He sniffled, trying to hold back tears, and Ottokar nodded. The man knelt down and pulled the dagger from Gero's chest, slowly examining it.

"True silver blade," Ottokar said. "Impressive for a child. Your father's?"

"He gave it to us before he died."

"In Stenwarl?"

"Yes," Erik said. Ottokar swore profusely in response.

"Master," another man called from the distance. "We've put down the accursed, all of them we found anyway." The man came over, dressed nearly identically to Ottokar, though he was younger, maybe Gero's age, with golden blond hair. "A survivor?"

"Heinrich, meet Erik," Ottokar said. "Boy just killed his first monster."

"Him?" Heinrich responded. "How?" Ottokar waggled the grimy dagger in the air, specks of blackened blood splattering down to the ground. "That would explain it. The partisans want your orders."

"Pile up the dead and burn them. Livestock too. We'll move on to the fields after that."

"What about the houses and the barn?" Erik asked. "They were full of them when my brother and I..." He choked on the words, but he swallowed them back down.

"Need to search them, but Heinrich and I can handle that," Ottokar said.

"Why?" Erik asked.

"Won't do if a beasty is left hiding in a basement. Might not burn with the rest and then its curse could spread. Bookworms back at the guild might be able to tell you all about how, but I never had any time for all that."

"You're taking him with us?" Heinrich asked. "You can't be serious?"

"And what would you do? Leave a child out here alone after he just dealt mercy to his own brother?"

"Take him to his family," Heinrich said. Turning to Erik, he asked, "Where did you even come from, kid?"

"Gero and I escaped from the capitol a few weeks ago."

This time it was Heinrich who swore profusely.

"But father had only taken us there to visit our aunt and uncle before the empire invaded," Erik continued.

"Well then, where is the rest of your family?" Heinrich asked.

"Vorbotenruhe," Erik said. Heinrich swore again and Ottokar started laughing as the younger man slumped over in defeat. Ottokar snapped his fingers and Heinrich turned and left, giving out orders to people Erik assumed were the partisans he had been talking about.

The next hour passed by a dazed Erik as if it were but a few minutes. Men and women in tattered clothing armed with poorly maintained rifles moved about him while Ottokar and Heinrich searched the houses.

The two huntsmen looked out of place among their helpers, well-armed with guns that Erik had only seen in the coastal markets and when he visited Uncle Bertram. Their thick coats and leather masks made them look like ghosts as they entered and exited building after building, leaving fire in their wake. The partisans set fires too, piling the bodies of people with those of cows and pigs, burning them together as if there wasn't any difference. Erik fought with one man who tried to add his brother to the mound.

"This isn't his home," he said. "Please, you have to burn him separately so I can take him home." It didn't take much prodding for them to acquiesce. They set Gero on a small pile of dead brush and hastily harvested grain and set him ablaze on his lonely mound. Scourging, they called it: burning away the impurities. Erik stared into the fire as it consumed his brother's body, the haunting screams of untold numbers of people flooding out from his memories. His breathing grew heavy and ragged, but he kept staring into the flames.

CHAPTER ONE

PETRA

A word spoken in places of silence is little good to the hearts of men in darkness. When you speak, do so in places of great clamor; raise your voice over the din of barter and battle both, for all will heed you who are worthy of the word. For it is not by deed or repute that man and woman may be made worthy, but by their willingness to put themselves aside in the tumult of their lives and simply listen.

Alaric the Confessor, Proclamations 9:3-4

The bell's deep toll rang from the belfry of the local church once, twice, then thrice to mark the hour and frighten away the worst of the monsters that lurked in the wilds. Petra looked up and watched as it swung back and forth in its perch, sending streaks of sunlight dancing off its sterling edges. Her master clapped her lightly on the shoulder, and she turned her eyes back to the crowded street in front of her. She followed close behind him, winding through the busy market where people from all the surrounding communities came to hawk their wares.

It was a familiar sight, and it brought back some of the few happy memories she had of home. The smell of grilled meats and fresh bread hung in the air, flowing up from beneath multicolored awnings and out of open windows.

"You hungry?" her master, Heinrich Taube, asked, looking back over his shoulder at her with an arched eyebrow. It had only been a few hours since their last meal, but she couldn't resist the opportunity to fill up on something that wasn't traveling rations. The look on Heinrich's face told her he was thinking the same.

"Yeah," she said. "How about some skewers? Should be easy to eat while we find our contact."

"Smart thinking, as always. And maybe if we're lucky, one of these vendors will know where we can find the Greifenflügel."

"We almost never are," Petra said.

"Can't be too hard to find with a name like that though," Heinrich said.

They approached a stall with grilled lamb skewers, and Heinrich haggled for four, undercutting his own bargaining efforts on purpose in a game he liked to play to get information. He thought it was money well spent, but most times, they only ended up with something any stranger on the street likely would have told them for free. But Petra didn't particularly care right at that moment; she was entranced by the smell of the succulently dripping lamb laden on the two tiny spears Heinrich dangled before her.

"Any luck?" she asked between bites.

"Of course not," Heinrich said, tearing a fatty chunk from one of his skewers like a vulture. "Leave it to me to find a food stall run by an imperial bootlicker."

"At least he sold you our lunch. Didn't the last guy like that throw your coins clear across the market?"

"No, he pocketed them, then threw the whole damned loaf of bread I'd just paid for across the market."

"That wasn't what you said happened at the time. You're embellishing again."

"I never do that."

"Sure," Petra said, laughing. Finishing her late lunch, she flagged down an older woman with plain clothes and brown hair in a bun. "Excuse me. Sorry to bother you, but we're new in town and need to find a tavern called the Greifenflügel. Could you point us in the right direction?"

"Of course." The older woman smiled as she explained the best course with just as many names as directions. Petra thanked her and returned to Heinrich's side.

"See? That wasn't so hard now, was it?"

"If her directions are accurate," Heinrich said.

"Well, even if they aren't, at least they were free." Petra led the way through the village until finally, they stood outside the tavern. A light blue sign with a white and gold gryphon hung from the rafters. Its intricate lettering made it abundantly clear that they were at the right place.

"Told you."

The two entered the Greifenflügel and shrugged off their travel packs by the coatrack before making their way to the bar. Petra was surprised at how many people were there so long after lunch, but then she realized that most of them were probably the hired help for the landowners who were there for market day. They would certainly have some time on their hands as well as some extra coins after spending half the day helping haul goods into town.

They would all spend the night in town along with the landowners who had hired them, though if they kept spending their wages on booze, they probably wouldn't be sleeping in the nicer inns. Because most of them were busying themselves gawking at the two Jäger, Petra figured they could enjoy their lice-ridden beds. She joined Heinrich at the bar, ignoring the odd looks as best she could, and climbed up the stool's rung to the top, which stood just barely too high for her to easily sit on.

Gradually, the conversations in the tavern returned to normal topics and volume, the too-obvious whispers about Jäger and monsters dying out as the other patrons wet their lips with ale.

"Feeling homesick?" Heinrich asked with a laugh, poking Petra in the shoulder playfully.

"Not a chance," she said, flashing a smile. "Besides, if I went back home, I'd never get to see all the different towns that look just like Wohlen."

"Oh, I think Laupen has its own unique charm," Heinrich said, his eyes following the skirt of a barmaid as she came from the back room with a pitcher of ale. Petra pretended to wretch at the thought of where his mind was wandering, barely keeping in a laugh as the woman glanced at him and blushed. "Wohlen isn't that bad."

"Try living around there," Petra said.

The nearby barkeep interrupted their conversation. "We don't get many Jäger around these parts, so that must mean you two are here to help with our bahkauv problem." The man was shorter than Heinrich but not quite as short as Petra, with dark red hair and a burn scar on his right temple. He spoke in a tired voice, though she couldn't tell right away if he was simply overworked or if he'd lost someone to the creature and was in mourning.

"Picked up that contract and a couple of others from out this way on our last visit to the guild in Kranzdorf. We'll take two pints of your weakest while we're here," Heinrich said as he took off his hat and placed it on the counter. He ran his hand through his sweat-dampened blond hair, then wiped it on his grey pants. "You take thaler or imperial coin?"

"Either," said the barkeep. "At least until the war's over."

"How much?"

"Three kleinthaler a pint, or five sesterces."

Heinrich nodded as he pulled six small silver coins from his purse, each marked with a royal eagle, and placed them on the counter. The barkeep took one and examined it closely before taking all six and pocketing them. He ducked down behind the oak slab, came back up with two tankards, and grabbed a pitcher from the shelves behind him. He poured both drinks, then returned the pitcher to its place.

"The last town we were in only charged two kleinthaler a pint. You gouging the prices because of the war or because of the bahkauv?" Heinrich asked, taking a deep sip from his mug.

"The damned beast is what's doing it. Most of my stock comes from Aschfeld. It's just a way down the road west of here, but you probably knew that bit already."

"You sure your shipments haven't been getting appropriated by soldiers?"

"Hard to appropriate booze from a pair of towns most people couldn't find on a map. I don't even think our local lord knows exactly where we are, though I know for a fact his taxman does, the slimy bastard."

"One of the many pleasures of living in the middle of nowhere," Petra said.

"I'd drink to that," said the barkeep, "but I can't afford to at the moment. How much did the contract you took say you'd be paid?"

"Shouldn't you know that, seeing as how it's your contract?" Petra asked.

"I can read, girl, but I can't write well," the barkeep said, shaking his head as he looked at her. "So lacking that specific skill, I had the local militia captain write the request to come hunt the bahkauv down, but I don't trust him with telling the whole truth. Or to have offered a fair wage, for that matter."

"Why not?"

"Kaspar doesn't think what happened to Linus was caused by a bahkauv."

"I take it Linus is the merchant who the contract mentioned got attacked," Heinrich said. "Can we speak with him?"

"Well, you could try, but you'd look quite the fool asking questions to the soil."

"So, this Kaspar guy. Militia captain, right?" Heinrich got a small nod from the barkeep. "He left that part out of the contract."

"Figures," said the barkeep.

"Have any other merchants been attacked?" Petra asked.

"No," the barkeep replied. "But that was almost a month ago, and Linus' boss won't risk sending any more barrels until we figure this thing out."

"A bit overdramatic if you ask me," Petra said. "I'm not complaining or anything, but forty kleinthaler seems a bit much for a job like this."

"Forty? Guess that isn't too surprising considering Linus was the Amtmann's nephew," the barkeep said.

"Oh," Petra said.

"He was a good kid, good with numbers, but a little spacey sometimes. Didn't deserve what happened to him. For my part, I liked the lad. He was a good sport even when you drank him under the table, which was damn near every time he drank. He couldn't hold his liquor for his life, and he knew it, so he rarely sampled the product he was moving."

"Why didn't the Amtmann write the request himself if it was his nephew who died?" Heinrich asked.

"The man's a wreck right now. He stepped in and helped me renegotiate my agreement with the brewery owners in Aschfeld. The deal was that I got to pay half for each barrel and Linus would handle transport at half the wage they were paying the guy before him."

"And now Linus is dead, mauled doing the job his uncle had secured for him," Heinrich said.

"Right. Now we've got this beast to deal with and the worry our local lord might start poking his head around wondering why his man in Laupen isn't reporting on time anymore. And everyone comes hounding my ear off about the price of booze going up as if I'm the one to solve it."

"All that aside," Heinrich said, "How does this relate to it being a bahkauv? I mean, we'll look into it, but so far, nothing you've said tells me it really was a bahkauv."

"Aye, sorry about that. It's been a long month. So, I didn't see the body myself, but Kaspar said it was bad. He described how Linus was torn to shreds, and the mule pulling his cart was gone."

"Still doesn't help prove it's a bahkauv," Petra pointed out.

Heinrich hushed her. "Were all the barrels intact?"

"All but one."

"Smashed or leaking?"

"Leaking."

"It probably was a bahkauv then," Heinrich concluded. The barkeep stared at him for a moment, unsure of what to say, his mouth opening and closing several times. Then, Heinrich elaborated. "Bahkauv don't drink beer, and they don't attack drunks to sip the alcohol from their blood." He took a nice long sip of his ale as if to make his point.

"Right, a bahkauv wouldn't attack someone because it wants the alcohol but because the smell of the boiled hops is similar to the scent they secrete to mark their territory," Petra said.

"So bahkauvs piss beer?" the barkeep asked.

"No," said Heinrich. "But if that helps you understand it, then go right ahead." He turned on his stool and leaned back, laughing in quiet, broken bursts. "Sorry," he stammered. "Sorry, I'm just remembering an old bahkauv hunt I went on when I was a journeyman. Our kader had found a fresh marking, and my friend Ludi tried tasting it because he thought if it smells like beer, it must taste like it too. He puked his guts out for three days straight. Ulla and I had to capture the thing without him."

"Wait, you captured it?" the barkeep asked.

"Of course we captured it," Heinrich said, turning back toward the bar. "Put it in a caged wagon and drove it a few miles into the wilderness on the far side of town. Splashed the area with the samples of its scent we'd collected along the way so it wouldn't think to go back."

"Why didn't you just kill it? I thought that was what you people did?"

"We kill monsters, but not everything you think of as a monster really deserves that title," Heinrich said. "We exterminate the accursed kin on sight because if we didn't, they would overrun the country. Hell, I've scourged more villages like yours than I care to remember. But when I find a beast like a bahkauv that just got too close to a village and mistook some poor fool for a threat, I try my best to relocate it because it doesn't know better."

"You will kill this one though, right?"

"Only if we don't have any other choice," Heinrich said. He finished his drink, pushing the tankard toward the barkeep. "Your church still run by one of ours?"

"Brother Traugott never bothered leaving," the barkeep said, "and we haven't had any members of the imperial church come to arrest him, either. Middle of nowhere and all."

"Thanks," Heinrich said. "Petra, finish your drink. I want to go meet Brother Traugott."

"Sure," Petra said, "but we won't need any holy water to hunt a bahkauv."

"We will need room and board," Heinrich said.

"We still have plenty of money left from the job in Uldz though."

"That won't matter with all the people here in town from the countryside. Even if we find an empty room it'll probably be too expensive, or too filthy."

"He's right. Cheapest inn in town is one called the Blauritter, and I wouldn't recommend it," the barkeep said. "Anton's not a bad sort, but he keeps his prices low by not hiring help to clean the rooms. Had more than a few customers from out of town complain about lice and rat shit."

"See, Petra?" Heinrich said.

"Fine," she said. "I can think of worse things to sleep on than church pews."

"Like sleeping in rat shit," Heinrich said.

"As if we haven't slept in worse." Petra downed the rest of her ale in a single pull, hopping down from the stool and giving a curt goodbye to the barkeep. She grabbed her pack, her rifle clattering against the cobbled floor as its sling slipped from the pack. Heinrich followed close behind, eventually coming to walk beside her as they made their way toward the church, guided by its high-reaching spire.

The church was one of the few buildings in Laupen made entirely of stone, one of the safe havens in the small village should an outbreak require it to be scourged. Stained glass windows sat nestled in shallow stone alcoves, their iconography shaded beneath the overhangs of a white tiled roof. Walking in through the open doors, they found themselves flanked by statues of the younger two Confessors, Gerlind and Clovis, their pale grey faces eternally expressing mercy. Following the deep green carpet into the main hall, on either side of the dais where a single wooden lectern stood, they found twin statues of Alaric, the First Confessor, one standing, the other kneeling.

The windows that lined the upper walls of the building's length depicted the heraldic halo, while those behind the dais showed the same three scenes every Gaersche church had immortalized in colored glass. They were Alaric among the angels at what would become the capital of Lornern in the northeast, Gerlind laying the foundation of the monastery that bore her name in the Herzland, and Clovis being burned at the stake by the pagans of the east.

Petra wasn't much for religion, but even she could appreciate the craftsmanship that went into churches. She didn't exactly consider herself to be a nonbeliever either, though. It was hard to say none of it was true when she'd seen monsters burn at the touch of holy water or recoil at the sound of a herald's bell. But the priests always talked about miracles and benedictions, of answered prayers, and she had never seen anything that matched their descriptions. She *had* seen the fetid remains of a priestess torn to shreds by monsters on the side of the road, her little, true silver bell lying uselessly in the bloody muck.

"Hello?" Heinrich called out. "Brother Traugott?"

"I'm coming!" The priest's yell came from a small door off to one side of the hall, leading into the kitchen and living quarters. Traugott came into the room with a spry gait that belied his old, wrinkled visage. His wispy white hair covered only the back and sides of his head, and he had no facial hair to disguise his drooping cheeks. The priest looked over the two gun-toting individuals standing in the middle of his church, then said, "It seems you have me at a disadvantage, Herr and Frau."

"I'm Heinrich Taube and this is my apprentice, Petra Ebner," Heinrich said. "We're from the Jäger Guild in Kranzdorf."

"Hello," Petra said.

"You don't need holy water to hunt bahkauvs," Traugott said plainly, turning to go back into the side rooms. He stopped just outside the door and said, "You can sleep on the pews, or you can use the beds in the infirmary across the way. We don't have any orphans here, luckily, nor sick, so make yourselves comfortable. Your kind always does."

CHAPTER TWO

FAUST

To those who work crafts with their hands, work well to provide your goods for your fellows. To the artist, let the works of yours uplift the spirits of all mankind. To the warriors, fight well to safeguard the people from the dangers of the world. To the rulers, guide well the nations and tribes. Last and least of these are you in the eyes of men but nevertheless moved by purpose divine. To the humble farmer and the brave but oft-forgotten hunter, may all come to honor you, for the toils of your hands and the sweat of your brow fill their bellies all the days of your life until you too are received in eternal glory.

Gerlind the Confessor, Book of Tiers 2:30-33

The soft patter of rain thrummed a steady beat across the windows as Faust sat in a well-worn chair reading an old tome in the corner of the castle library. Sparse rays of sunlight pierced through the grey clouds, and fewer still shone down through the diamond-shaped panes of the leaded windows.

Faust flipped a vellum page, careful not to leave any new damage on the worn parchment. Stylized drawings of various monsters and their lairs paired with wildly outdated descriptions covered each page, marred by stains and edged with small tears. The ink was faded from age, and it was a marvel it had survived this long.

The condition of each volume spoke of the care and concern the lords of Tholst had taken in maintaining the traditional knowledge of the past and the beautiful artistry of the enthusiastic authors who weren't quite as informed as they had thought themselves in those bygone eras. There was a certain charm in the earnestness of each long-since-disproven diatribe on bahkauv behavior or accounts of the nesting habits of lindworms.

Faust had read almost every book in Tholst covering the topic of monsters and likely half of the those that sat on the shelves in his family's library in Dorneswik, though both collections combined would no doubt pale in comparison to those of the Academy of Vaon or any of the Empire's Athenaeums. Still, there was a certain comfort in the limited, yet familiar space around him.

He leaned back in his seat, staring up at the rafters for a moment and catching the swift glint of light on a spider's silk, its weaver dangling on a lone thread. Raising a phantom pistol, he sighted in the spider as if it were one of those great preternatural beasts. He made a slight pop with his mouth and mimicked the rise of recoil from his imaginary weapon. His left sleeve slid down his arm to reveal the jagged edge of one of his pale scars.

He let his arms fall back down to his sides, fixing his sleeve to hide the unsightly mark and with it, a single foul memory. The vivid shade of a werewolf played across his mind, the shock of deep red and a phantom pain coming and going with it. He turned back toward the text, a soft smile creasing across his face as he drowned out the wayward thought with accounts from the holy sentinels who served the Confessors of old.

Almost miraculously, Meinherd chose that exact moment to snore, and Faust's eye twitched as his attention was drawn to the poorest excuse for a priest he'd ever known. This herald had done very little heralding since he came to Tholst, but he did snore quite loudly when he nodded off in naps, whose frequency would better suit a man twice his age. Meinherd sat nearly upright in a chair that was pulled close to a table a few feet away. His grey robes warped with each breath as the red-headed priest sputtered in his sleep.

Most of the clergy Faust had met before Meinherd more accurately fit the mold of the Heraldic Church's teachings. The young ones were always moving, their true silver bells ringing as they walked. They stood on street corners preaching and only quieted when they sat to eat or lay down to sleep. They were diligent to a fault, often annoyingly so, according to some, but then again, diligence was the chief virtue of the church's patron archangel, the Harbinger. How a man like Meinherd ever passed his initiation was beyond Faust.

Trying, and failing, to return his thoughts to the ancient tales, Faust sighed and shut the tome. He got up, made his way to where Meinherd slept and touched the priest's shoulder. Meinherd's eyes opened with the fierceness of a child realizing he's been caught sleeping during morning lessons. The great irony, of course, was that he was supposed to be the one teaching said lessons. "Ah, have you finished your reading for the day, Prinz Faust?"

"About an hour ago, Brother Meinherd, and then some," Faust said. "You fell asleep. Again." The priest rubbed a hand over his mutton chops and down his chin, eyeing the closed books on more practical subjects that sat on the table in front of him and then the volume of teratology. Meinherd snorted out a laugh before pushing his chair out and standing up. He almost towered over Faust with his broad shoulders, a hollow, jovial expression masking his boredom.

He moved to the chair Faust had started the evening in, collecting Alwin Dahl's *Treatises on Natural Philosophy,* Eduard Roth's *Histories of the Gaersche, Seventh Edition,* and Leonore Strauss' *Realpolitik: Trade and War as Means of Diplomacy.* One by one, Meinherd opened them to the bookmarks, checking each page with a nod. "Fine," he said.

"That's it?"

"If you want a lecture on wasting time, then go find someone else to give it to you," Meinherd said as he turned to Faust. The priest's steely blue eyes stared almost blankly into his student's. "I understand where your interests lie, my boy, but I do hope you realize the necessity of these readings. Your father and godfather both expect much of you, but I imagine you hear enough of that from everyone else."

"Thank you," Faust said with a small nod. He watched as Meinherd turned and stalked off around the upper rung of the library, one hand dancing across the tops of each table and chair he passed. Faust turned his eyes to their table and the leather-bound volumes on top of it, the three books he found to bring him halfway between bored and excited. "Brother Meinherd," he said. The priest stopped and turned his head back in Faust's direction. "I found Dahl's chapter on the biological differences between monsters and non-magical animals intriguing. Thank you for recommending it."

"Good, good, not that I understood a word of it myself, but I figured it would strike your sensibilities. Enjoy the rest of your day, my Prinz," Meinherd said, a smile pulling his whiskers up his cheeks. Without another word, the herald descended the stairs to the ground floor of the library. Faust watched as he left for some other room of his godfather's castle. The light coming through the windows shrank into pinpricks before finally vanishing behind ever-darkening clouds. The soft, prattling rain became progressively more violent, matched with flashes of lightning and the bombastic crashes of thunder in the air.

Faust had begun to leave when a sudden tinge of something made him turn around. He backtracked first to the table, then to his favorite bookshelf in the castle library. One vacant spot yawned open between thick tomes from ages past. Faust gently slotted Ansgar's *Mysteries of the Wild Hunt* back into its rightful place and started back toward the exit. He scooped Dahl's work up as he left, hastily descending the wooden staircase to the carpeted stonework floor below.

Exiting the empty library, Faust made his way through the rest of the castle to his quarters, passing only a few members of the staff as he went. Twin banners bearing his family's colors hung like curtains on either side of his door, making it nearly impossible to mistake, save for the rare occasions his parents came to visit Tholst. He pushed the door ajar and closed it behind him, entering his apartment. His family's heraldry hung over his small hearth, a shield of polished bronze always staring at him, reminding him of a home he barely remembered.

Faust left his study material on his desk among half-written letters and ambled over to the fireplace. His warped reflection peered back at him, an almost featureless face beneath a well-trimmed head of raven black hair staring out from the Heraldic halo at the shield's center. Around that halo was the von Schwarzdorn's briar crown with eight inward-facing thorns touching the tips of the eight fanning rays that shone out from the halo's disk.

Eventually, Faust stopped his staring contest with his own reflection and threw himself onto the quilted linens of his bed. The storm outside was growing ever more vicious in its assault on the castle walls, and Faust began to drift off to the rabid rhythm it created. Three swift knocks roused him from his half-sleep, and he rolled over onto his back. A second volley came as he sat up, and when he approached the door, he heard Olivia shout his name from the other side.

Faust made sure to take two steps backward as he swung open the door, dodging Olivia's fist that swung into the now-empty door frame. Irritation sat plainly on her otherwise elegant face, a strand of pale blond hair dangling down from her scalp.

"What is it?" Faust said.

"A messenger came from Dorneswik with letters for you and Father," Olivia replied.

"Do you have it with you?" Faust asked.

"Do I look like a maid to you?" Faust looked her up and down, almost to the point of exaggeration.

"Maids don't typically wear dresses imported from Kranzdorf, but I'm sure it might become a fad amongst the wealthier nobility any day now," Faust joked. He sidestepped Olivia's fist, thankful that her expensive dress limited her swing to his face.

"I jest, of course. You look absolutely stunning, as usual. I am certain Joachim von Aust's heart will flutter with delight if you wear that to your next ball."

Olivia swung at him again, a warm blush cresting her cheeks. "Do you really think so? You don't think it's too much?"

"Oh, the price tag was most certainly too much, but I'm sure his face will be as red as yours is right now when he realizes you purposefully bought a dress in his favorite color."

"I hope so," she said. Then, in a spark of realization, she turned back into her angry self, glaring daggers at his head. "You!" she said through clenched teeth. "Father has both letters with him in his study. Get there now before I wrinkle my new dress trying to maim you."

With a short, dry laugh, Faust left Olivia to her fuming and made his way through the dimly lit hallways of the castle, peering outside whenever he passed a window at the tempest-tossed sky. It worried him that a messenger braved such foul weather over a pair of letters. Glancing down at himself, he frowned and began straightening his shirt, trying to rub out the wrinkles as best he could. The Markgräfin would spare him no end of grief if she saw him so disheveled, but perhaps she wouldn't be attending such an impromptu meeting.

As Faust approached the Markgraf's study, he could hear the murmurs of a heated discussion through the thick timbers of the office door. A single guard stood to one side in a grey uniform, a purple sash with black edges wrapped around his waist and an armband of similar coloration on his right arm. His pants had a pair of purple lampasse stripes trailing from waist to calves, disappearing into his black boots. The guard turned, angling himself so he could open the door with his free hand and balance his rifle in the other. He knocked before pushing the portal ajar.

Faust strode into the study-turned-war room to find his godfather, Johann von Tollkirsche, leaning against one side of the long maple table that sat in the middle of the room. Across the corner from him, standing before the low-burning fireplace, was Ingrid Blumberg, captain of his household guards, and his men-at-arms.

"Taking a full retinue across the border will only escalate the very situation we have been ordered to help quell," Johann said.

"I understand your concerns, my lord, but we can't risk your life, or that of the young prinz," Ingrid said.

"Which is exactly what will happen if the lords of the southern Vahsland decide we are an invading force and turn to crush us," Johann said.

"They wouldn't dare, not before determining your intentions first," the captain said.

"I think they very much would. My personal positions are well known, Ingrid," Johann said.

"The Vahsland is full of dandies and merchants. I doubt they could even tell the difference between an invading army and a parading one." Ingrid rubbed her temples with a gloved hand and returned it to the table. She wore a uniform identical to the guard outside, save for three diamonds embroidered onto her armband.

"Considering the simple fact that the Vahslanders have been butchering each other for the better part of the last two years, I would suggest you spare me your jests. My mind is already made. We will take only a half dozen men."

"Do I get a say in how many men we take with us on this mission I seem to have been volunteered for?" Faust said.

"Oh, Faust, when did you get here?" Johann asked.

"He's been standing there for a minute at the least," Ingrid answered. "Please talk some sense into the Markgraf, my Prinz."

"Ingrid," Johann said.

"I have no desire to get in the middle of all this, but if we have to go into the Vahsland, why don't we take a dozen men from Tholst and gather a few more from your cousin in Naakt?" Faust asked.

He walked up to the table, where painted stones had been placed on every major settlement in the Gaerschland. He had a basic idea of the representation: red supported the imperial viceroy, blue opposed him, and white was undeclared. "Where in the Vahsland do we need to go? Wait, Olivia said something about a letter. Might it be easier to glean the details from there?"

"Right, I have yours right here." Johann handed Faust the unopened letter. "I imagine it says much the same as mine."

Faust examined his family's seal emblazoned in the wax, frowning as he reached for a letter opener and parted the envelope. He unfolded the two pages within and read:

My dear son,

I will skip the pleasantries oft used by men of letters in favor of ordaining to you a task of grave importance in simple fashion. You are doubtless aware of the civil war in the dukedom of the Vahsland, though the particulars may elude your studies. Needless to say, I have until now pursued a position of neutrality between my peer, the Herzog zu Kranzdorf, and his vassal the Markgraf zu Althafen. My decision to intercede now comes only at the news that both parties are willing to negotiate an end to the hostility between them, and the task of arbitration has fallen to our house.

Under any other circumstances, I would happily oblige them myself, but by a particularly foul stroke of misfortune, I will be unable to attend the peace talks that are being arranged in the township of Elem. As bright a lad as you are, you no doubt realize already that it is my desire for you to go to Elem and act as mediator in my stead. The second page enclosed with this letter is the documentation necessary to sanction this act.

You are almost a man by law, and I have no doubt that between the tutelage of Johann and Brother Meinherd, you will be more than capable of overseeing the negotiations. I have instructed both to travel with you to Elem, that you may leverage their experience and reputations in whatever ways you require.

Know that I believe wholeheartedly in your abilities, my son, though we so rarely have the chance to speak. I can entrust no one else with this task, least of all the two men I have ordered to travel with you. Heed their words with the same grain of salt that you would any other person alive. I will gladly await word of your success ever the more as I prepare to march our troops against a rebellion within our own dukedom, though I hope the mere show of force will be enough to settle this matter bloodlessly.

Your loving father,
Harald von Schwarzdorn,
The honorable Herzog zu Dorneswik.

Faust looked from the letter to Johann, then back to the pages penned by his father. "He cannot be serious, can he?" he asked. Faust's godfather pushed himself off of the table, teetering slightly before rubbing his own temples.

"I am afraid he is," Johann said. "Ingrid, have Ruger go outside to get Meinherd. He has to come with us, so he needs to be here for this." Ingrid gave a curt nod, moving around the table and then stepping out of the room to talk to her subordinate. "I do not like this any more than you do," Johann said to Faust.

"You told Ingrid your position was well known, but I must have missed it somewhere," Faust said.

"His lordship is well known for having sympathies toward the cause of the Volksheer," Meinherd interjected, pushing his way into the room between the dumbfounded soldiers, "A group that I am an unabashed member of."

"I thought this war was localized to the Vahsland," Faust said, watching as Ingrid reentered the room with a look of pure annoyance directed at the herald.

"The civil war being waged along the river Vahs is the most obvious front of a larger conflict that has been brewing since the moment the occupation began," Meinherd said.

"You can cut to the chase, Brother Meinherd," Johann said, "or I will, for the sake of brevity."

"Tell me what you've read about the conquest according to Roth," Meinherd said. "Concisely, so our dear Markgraf doesn't have a stroke."

"Seventeen years ago, the Empire and its satellites invaded the Gaerschland with the help of the lords of the Rosenhohen," Faust said, "Their stated goal was to end our embargo, but when they took the capital, they executed the entire royal family and declared themselves our suzerain."

"I'm glad to see you retain history as well as you do teratology," Meinherd said. "Since then, numerous groups of nobles and peasants alike have fought to liberate our country, and only recently have all the disparate factions collected under the banner of the Volksheer."

"Nationalists, then," Faust said.

"You certainly have a way of taking the wind out of my sails, lad," Meinherd said. "I was actually excited for once."

"Good for you," said Ingrid, "just don't drag us into your war, and I'll be happy too."

"It isn't just my war."

"Enough!" Johann said. "I know what the imperials did to you at Wolfsstadt, Brother Meinherd. Believe me when I say I want nothing more than to expel every imperial wretch from our fatherland, but we will never win if we keep killing each other while they sit back and watch us do it. Faust, the late queen was the eldest daughter of the Herzog zu Kranzdorf, and to him, no amount of imperial gold will ever be enough wergild to ease his grief. He started this war to get revenge, but half his vassals are open imperial loyalists, and now the Vahs runs red with Gaersche blood."

"So, we should do something about it, just like my father wants," Faust said. Meinherd let out a bellowing laugh, keeling over and turning away. "What?"

"I hope it will be as simple as you make it sound, godson," Johann said, a shaky laugh escaping his own lips. "I pray it is that simple, and heaven help us all if you are wrong."

CHAPTER THREE

PETRA

What good can man do in this life that he cannot undo by acts of sin and depravity? Look within and see the shadow of the abyss that lingers there at the edges of our souls, merely waiting for a moment of weakness to lead us astray. Look within, my brothers and my sisters, and know that of all monsters let loose upon this earth, none are so dangerous as the ones born of man.

Alaric the Confessor, Sentinels 31:22-24

Petra ran with all the graveness one should have when a massive bahkauv is trailing behind by only a few paces at the very most. She jumped over a gnarled tree root that rose up like a fence, carefully minding her steps as she dodged bushes, rocks, and other ground clutter on the untamed forest floor. The beast let out a hungry roar, and she tried to double her pace again as she approached the rendezvous.

The subtle gleam of sunlight on wire caught her eye, and she dropped to the ground, sliding hard against a carpet of green and orange debris beneath the metal string, uncovering segments of thick hidden ropes. She turned to face the creature as it pounced from the darkness of the woodland and then dived off to the side as it sailed down toward her. It collided first with the wire and then with the half-exposed net, letting out a yowl when the ropes came up and around it, yanking it high off the ground where it swung helplessly among the trees.

The bushes to her left rustled as her master stood up from where he'd been hiding. He held his rifle loosely; the true silver bayonet was almost white against the dull greens and browns of the woods around them. A satisfied smile was plastered across his fuzzy face as he looked up at their prey. "How'd I do?" Petra asked after standing up and dusting herself off.

"Almost perfect," Heinrich said. "I think you could have done a bit better at the finish line."

"Shove off," Petra said with a laugh. "Let's see you pull that off with your creaky old knees."

"Ha! I could still show you a few things, girl. Now grab your gun and let's get this beauty down."

"I don't understand why we can't just kill it," Petra said, grabbing her rifle from where it hung on a nearby tree branch. The contract they had gotten from Laupen had only hired them to remove the bahkauv, not kill it, but Petra still wasn't sure why they'd go through so much trouble to keep the creature alive after it had killed someone. She watched as Heinrich began to disassemble his trap, spooling up the metal wire and collecting the pullies they'd hastily made and affixed to the trees.

He wrapped his fingers tightly around the rope, and Petra wordlessly came over to undo the last of the pullies so they wouldn't have to cut through it. The sudden slack pulled Heinrich's arms up, but he managed to get his balance and began slowly lowering the creature down. It thrashed about in the netting, but its stocky bovine frame and horns kept it firmly tangled in place.

One of the bahkauv's catlike limbs lashed out clumsily with its three sharp claws as it hit the ground, causing it to roll over onto its back. Heinrich pushed it back onto its side with a steel-toed boot as he pulled a small wooden box from his satchel. Opening the box, he took out a long syringe and a vial of dull yellow liquid, slotting the needle into the vial. He knelt down, putting a knee on the beast's shoulder to keep it from rolling over again, and carefully stuck the needle into its neck, slowly injecting the tranquilizing agent.

After a few minutes, the bahkauv's struggling stopped, and it fell into a deep sleep. "There we are, nice and sleepy now, and easy to deal with. Shouldn't be too hard to carry back to town now," Heinrich said, putting away his tranquilizer. "The real question is, why would we kill something as wonderful as this creature?"

"Wonderful creatures don't attack people just because they smell like boiled hops," Petra said.

"Most animals don't think twice about that particular scent." Heinrich pointed out. He began stringing up the rope to a large tree branch he had cut and cleaned earlier in the day. "Come on, now."

Petra groaned but complied, grabbing the opposite end of the pole and lifting it up onto her shoulder. The walk back to the open landscape of the farms and streams that surrounded Laupen took twice as long as it should have due to the sleeping beast dangled between the two Jäger. Finally, after an hour and a half of meandering and backtracking through dense woodlands, the two emerged to the sunlit expanse of grains and vegetables almost ready for the harvest.

A few spiked barricades were arranged around the short, cobbled walls that ringed the fields, a measure meant to discourage animals from hiding in the grains but that served little practical purpose. Farmers and children alike looked up from work or play to stare at the stirring beast that Petra and her master carried back into town. It had only mauled one person within this last moon, but it still caused quite a stir for such a quiet little village.

They passed through the east gate of the town's high palisade walls and its two militiamen, who stood on either side of the timber breach armed with old flintlocks. Each log that rose up from the base of piled stones was shorn sharp, forming a crown of jagged teeth around the top edge. Thin spears of equally sharp branches and waste lumber were plunged between the rocks. The defenses did their job well enough, but they did little for the people brave or foolhardy enough to live and work outside their comfort.

"I can't believe they actually brought it in alive," one of the guards said. The other responded with a snort. "Crazy bastards." Kaspar, the local militia captain, came jogging over to them, master, apprentice, and prey, with a hand raised and a fearful look. Petra couldn't see Heinrich's face, but she knew the expression he wore based solely on the deepening discomfort lining the captain's face.

"Herr Taube," the captain said. "You can't bring that thing into the square. What if it's still alive?"

"Well, I had already thought about that since I didn't really want to kill the thing. That's why I asked you to use some of the reward money to fasten a cage to a wagon. You have fastened a cage onto the dead merchant's wagon like I asked, right?"

"I have, but I would have refused if I had thought you would actually find a bahkauv."

"I think I would have preferred that," Petra said. "Then we could have taken the full price for this thing." Heinrich stifled a deep laugh, snorting and blowing air.

"Bring the wagon here so we can finally get this beauty situated. No killing it while it's caged, either," Heinrich said. "That goes double for you, Petra."

"Understood," said Petra and the captain, not quite in unison. The captain had the wagon wheeled around; a thick iron cage had been somewhat hastily warped and fastened to its top. Heinrich lowered his end of the pole and Petra followed suit, rolling her end from her shoulder and easing it to the ground. Her master tested the cage, frowning slightly at the width between the bars by the driver's bench. Shaking his head, he motioned for the militiamen to help him lift the sleeping bahkauv up and into the cage, climbed in after it, and carefully untied the net.

Master Heinrich pulled the top half of the net from the creature, untangling its horns and maneuvering its free limb while watching its head. After he had freed the creature from the net, he slowly backed out of the wagon and violently pulled the rest of the mesh out from under the beast. Petra shut and latched the gate as fast as she could, jumping back as the bahkauv woke up and began rocking the wagon back and forth with its attempts to break free. "Master, are we sure the latch will hold?"

"Not really."

"Then why did you wake it up like that?"

"I would also like to know that, Herr Taube," said the captain.

"You all worry too much," Heinrich said. "Just keep the drunks away from the cage and it won't bother anyone. But maybe you should go get us another two latches, captain, and a large, flat piece of wood to wedge between the front of the wagon and the cage." The militiaman shook his head and wandered off, shouting an order that he wanted someone to watch the creature at all times.

"Bahkauv don't attack drunks though," Petra said.

"No, but Kaspar doesn't know that."

"You really didn't think this through, did you?"

"I suppose I could have been a bit more specific. In any case, it might not attack a drunk for being drunk, but the alcohol could make someone dumb enough to get too close."

"So you *are* worried it'll break out and attack someone."

"Break out? No. Attack someone? Well, maybe just a little, but if I'd told the captain that, he'd have ordered his men to shoot it, and I don't want to see this poor thing dead unless absolutely necessary."

"Poor thing?" Petra said with an overly exaggerated scoff. "This poor thing already ate someone."

"Bahkauv don't eat people, Petra. We aren't its natural prey. I don't see any reason for us to kill it when we can just relocate it to a new habitat to make sure it doesn't kill anyone else," Heinrich said. All traces of his jovial nature were gone, worn down by Petra's continued defiance. That part didn't bother her any; she understood his naturalist stance. Even if she disagreed, she would try to follow his wishes as best she could. She at least owed him that much.

The rest of the day went on without incident. They negotiated for their payment, minus the fees for the cage and wagon, and secured their catch further before the sunset. With nothing else to do, the two returned to the church run by Brother Traugott, who had warmed to them over the last few days as they prepared for their hunt. The priest had told them of the condition of the young merchant's body in between complaints of having to give the kid last rites alone.

All his novices had left years ago, long before the civil war had started, and it didn't take much to tell the old man was lonely.

Candles burned low in the cupped hands of the statues of the Confessors, dripping melted wax down onto the stone floors. Farther in, the last lights of day cast sidelong beams through stained glass windows. The most striking of them was that of Alaric, father of the church. Angels with emerald green armor ministered to him in the wilderness, while down at the foot of the hill, a group of tribesmen cowered in fear and reverence at the presence of the divine messengers. That tribe would go on to help Alaric build the holy city of the Heraldic faith centered on that hill, and their warriors would become his sentinels, whose mantle the modern Jäger were to uphold according to the more devout members of the guild.

Brother Traugott sat with his hands laced and his head bent in prayer near the altar. A younger man sat beside him, dressed too well to be a villager but nonetheless praying with the old, aptly named priest. It wasn't too surprising, because Traugott kept his doors open for any passing traveler who hadn't enough coin to pay for more conventional lodgings, and for those who didn't want to sleep in unwashed beddings like Petra and her master.

Hearing the two approach, the priest ended his prayers and rose slowly onto shaking legs. Heinrich slung his rifle off his shoulder and knelt before the priest, holding the blade-tipped firearm up as he bowed his head. Out of habit more than piety, Petra mimicked the action, waiting until Traugott came and laid a wrinkled hand upon her weapon. Sometimes she thought that Heinrich's devotion to old ceremonies was tiresome, and she was sure he would have made a better imperial paladin than a Jäger. Yet his piety was matched by his love for the natural world, and she doubted he'd ever really fit in anywhere else. Not that that was a bad thing.

She waited until her master stood before doing the same, unwilling to upset him by breaking the procedures he tried so hard to keep. The stranger had finished his prayer and then lazily sprawled across the pew, halfway facing them. Heinrich spoke a few soft words of thanks to the priest, and their fellow guest caught his eye with a wave. "Erik!" Heinrich called out. "You're a welcome sight."

"Happy to oblige," Erik said, smiling as he stood. He was clean-shaven, with platinum blond hair that fell over either side of his face. "It's good to see you, my friend. Ottokar sends his regards."

"And an apology, I hope. How is the old man doing these days?"

"Angry at everyone and everything. Even more so than usual owing to some business I need to take care of."

"What sort of business could bring you all the way here from Lornern?"

"The kind I would appreciate help with," Erik said. "Orders straight from the mouth of the Großmeister himself."

"Here in the Vahsland?" Heinrich said.

"I am not at liberty to say more until you agree. Though I will say that you are the only person in the Vahsland who I trust to help me with it. Imagine my surprise, then, when I arrived in Kranzdorf only to be told by the guild staff that I had missed you and your apprentice by a scant few days. It was fun, though, tracking you two out here in the middle of nowhere. No offense, Brother Traugott."

"I would have been arrested years ago if Laupen were in the middle of somewhere people cared about," the priest said. He let out a short laugh that ended in a wheeze, and when he caught his breath, he let out a muffled curse. Grimacing, the old priest made his exit, ambling off toward the living quarters.

"Right. Well, I think I'm going to go help Traugott prepare dinner." Petra's declaration prompted no response from her master. She shrugged her shoulders as she left, her first few steps long and quick as she caught up with the old priest. "How can I help?"

"Same as the last two nights," Traugott said weakly. "Do not touch the seasonings."

"I said I was sorry." Petra tried to put on a penitent face but couldn't help cracking a smile at the minister's unflinchingly grumpy expression. "Fine, fine, I'll stick to chopping up ingredients. What are you going to make?"

"Stew," The two entered the small kitchen, ducking under the pots and ladles strung on hooks overhead. A cast-iron skillet sat on the bricks beside the small wood stove; Petra had scrubbed both clean the night before. She wasn't much good at cooking, at least, that was what everyone else told her. Her help might ruin dinner, but that wasn't going to stop her from trying. Besides, right now, nothing seemed more boring than listening to Heinrich and that Erik person talk circles around each other.

Petra double-checked her rifle's breach, then, satisfied there wasn't a round chambered, left it slumped against the door frame. She unburdened herself of her thick coat, throwing it over a chair in the corner, and rolled up her shirtsleeves. Traugott had busied himself with proportioning out ingredients, but he came over as Petra's eyes turned to her bayonet. He handed her a kitchen knife handle first, giving her a stern look of disapproval for even considering using her true silver as cutlery.

She couldn't fully understand why the priest took exception to her using a blade of angelic silver to cut beets when she normally used it to slice and stab monsters. The blade would get a lot dirtier plunged into a werewolf's flank, but she didn't think he would ever budge on his position. She stared at the iron utensil for a moment before taking it from Traugott, hoping to avoid getting any more lectures, and went to work dicing her half of the ingredients for dinner.

Traugott took care of the rest while Petra watched, trying to figure out what about his process made food edible. She wouldn't always have her master to cook more complex meals for her, and she couldn't always count on having a tavern to buy from or even the coin to buy it. Yet, as she watched the old man work, she just didn't get it. He was way too slow, or maybe that was the point? No, Heinrich moved a lot quicker when he prepared their meals on the road. Groaning, she marched over to the chair with her coat on it and plopped down, sinking in until her rear was barely clinging to the edge of the seat.

"Practice," said the priest.

"What?"

"When Herr Taube took you on as his apprentice, did you know how to shoot a gun?" he asked.

"Not very well," Petra said. She sat up, then, after a moment of staring blankly into space, she slapped herself. "I was a piss-poor shot when he took me on, almost as bad as my cooking."

"Language."

"Does that mean you'll let me help?" Petra said, choosing not to bring up his own poor choice of language earlier in the sanctuary.

"No."

Petra glowered at Traugott, who paid her no mind as he continued his watch over the pot. She got bored watching him and wandered off through the back door, letting her sleeves down as the cool breeze of the autumn eve rolled over the village. Sitting down on a small stone bench in the side garden, Petra let her attention play across each house, a different scene inside each one illuminated by the flickering light of candles and hearths. It gave her a nostalgic feeling.

A low yowl from the bahkauv in the distance cut through the peaceful scene. Petra cocked her head to the side and listened to how the noise changed the natural rhythms of Laupen. Footsteps hastened ever so slightly, doors closed with a little more force than usual, and shutters slammed down as people hurried to close them.

Not everyone was scared of the caged beast, though perhaps they should be. The bahkauv was detained now, but Petra had seen what its kind was capable of: a young man whose throat had been ripped out like a deer made prey to a wolf, an old woman given to the flame in a broken and bloody heap, the broken and stained bones of a girl no more than five. Heinrich might have been right when he said that they didn't attack people for food, but that level of dignity was little comfort to the dead. Maybe Linus had provoked it in some way, but they had found the creature's lair; it was far enough afield for Petra to know better.

From even farther away came another call echoing through the blooming night, much deeper and full of evident malice. Others' voices joined its chorus from hungry maws, which would never be slaked even after a thousand meals. Petra's eyes narrowed, unable to gauge their origin or even their direction, her body tensing out of reflex. Sometimes, a wild beast just went crazy and that's all there was to it. But in others, that madness was driven by fear of something worse.

Above her, the pure and melodious tone of the church bell rang out again and again as a warning. One for man and monster both. Heinrich came rushing out of the side door, holding his rifle and Petra's, which he handed to her without a single word. Her master didn't bother gloating about how he'd been right to spare the bahkauv, nor would he, but the voice Petra heard nagging her about it in her mind did so in his voice.

How many times was it now that she had misjudged situations like this one? How many frightened animals had she killed, or at least advocated to kill, for what amounted to being forced from their homes by something truly monstrous? Too many maybe, but either way, she needed to learn, needed to practice how to tell the difference between a monster and a hurt animal lashing out.

CHAPTER FOUR

FAUST

Know ye that I have seen the work of the pagans and I have known fear of them, but no longer. They may work their foul magics upon us, they may try to twist our flesh as they do their own, to corrupt our spirits as theirs have been tainted, but never shall their corruption find purchase in us, for we are saved. In time, all such fiends will find an end to their days, by one means or another, and as all men, they shall stand before judgment; may God have mercy on them all.

Clovis the Confessor, Confessions of Clovis 15:3-5

It had been four days since Faust and his godfather had left Tholst and crossed into the last familiar stretch of land that marked the boundary between the Dornwald and the Vahsland. Their intermediate goal was Naakt, where Johann's distant cousin, Marcel, ruled over the small stretch of borderland. Faust had only met the Burggraf zu Naakt a few times, during a scant few vacations north with Johann's family, and it was clear that the gruff man was naturally suited to his station. He was three years Johann's senior, but there was a closeness among the von Tollkirsches that never quite stopped feeling odd to Faust, though in a pleasant sort of way.

Rivalries were fairly common among the nobility, but no rivalries were deeper than those that festered between the branches of the old clans. The von Schwarzdorns had the distinct honor of housing one of the most bitter streaks of familial infighting, and they were far closer to the norm than Johann's kin. At least, as far as Faust had experienced in the Dornwald. Faust's current mission was the result of one such feud, and though his father had not elaborated in his letter, Faust had a few ideas as to what rebellion his father was marching off to face.

Chief among them was Faust's third cousin, the Graf zu Südwasr, who continued his house's longstanding tradition of regularly threatening to cut off access to the sea as leverage for whatever new policy he wanted passed or discarded in the assembly of lords. With any luck, his daughter Viktoria would survive long enough to succeed him, though that was never a guarantee. A prime case for that grim reality lay with the von Enns sisters, who by strange chance had all come to inherit one of their clan's major seats. Their favorite pastime in recent years was threatening each other with war on a biannual basis.

There were, of course, rumors that the odd series of events that led to the three von Enns sisters' current situation was not coincidental, but rather the result of their own calculated scheming. Their current hostilities would then be the result of a deserved strain of paranoia, turning each against the others in fear they would do to one another what they had supposedly done to their more distant kin. Faust was unsure just how much truth existed in those tales, or if they were merely the fancies of bored minds starved for entertainment, but it would hardly surprise him either way.

Regardless, thinking of such feuds was almost enough to make him sick to his stomach, even more so than riding in a carriage hell-bent on hitting every stone, branch, and dip in the road. He knew his hope that the politics of the Vahsland would be different was perhaps in vain, but he hoped nevertheless. From what he had heard of the Vahslanders, though, he imagined some of them would be far more concerned that Amalia von Enns had chosen to marry a lowborn imperial officer than they would be at the notion that she and her sisters had committed acts of kin slaying.

Faust pulled aside the lilac-colored curtain from the carriage window beside him and looked out into the dingy, but comfortable landscape. He passed by deep greens, golden grains, and wisps of smoke curling into the air above distant homesteads. This was why Johann, despite his own personal feelings, had chosen the path of neutrality. If they followed Meinherd's pleas and pushed too hard for capitulation instead of compromise, this region would be the first to burn.

Clearly, the priest would not be losing any sleep over that reality though. Meinherd sat with his head resting against the pillowed siding of the carriage wall at an angle that made Faust wince. Each jerk of the carriage only deepened the unnerving sensation that crawled over his skin, yet none of it seemed to affect Meinherd, who simply continued to snore peacefully in spite of all good sense and reason.

Johann was beside Meinherd in the corner opposite Faust, busying himself rereading the reports he had ordered to be compiled on the current state of the civil war. Ingrid had started the task, but in the end, it was the priest who had provided most of the material, only some of which was biased.

Faust had read them once himself, and that had been more than enough for him. He could scarcely tell what new information his godfather hoped to glean from pages of death tolls and logistical records.

"How long are we planning on staying with the Burggraf?" Faust asked.

"A day, at the least, hopefully no more than two," Johann said absently.

"Good. I want to get this all over with," Faust said.

"Agreed," Johann said. "But that isn't what you actually want to talk about."

"I have no intention of drawing you from your papers, so I am trying to avoid the subject."

"You are failing miserably though," Johann said. With a sigh, he shuffled the reports into their original order and returned them to their long envelope. "Every time I look over these pages, I feel as if something is off about the numbers."

"The casualties are immense," Faust said. "It seems unreal."

"Compared to the conquest, perhaps," Johann said. "Faust, did you ever read about the First Brothers War?"

"I read of it, why?"

"Comparing this war to its predecessor is like comparing a mule to a prize stallion. They are similar in nature and setting, but the last time the Vahslanders had a civil war, it was a far bloodier affair," said Johann.

"Muskets had only just barely come into regular use by that point, no? No one is foolish enough to charge lancer cavalry into an entrenched line of riflemen now, knowing the destructive capabilities of gunpowder weapons as intimately as we do now. Could that not explain the caution from both sides in their deployments?" Faust asked.

"It might be too soon to say." Johann turned to look at the sleeping priest and motioned with his chin. "But we need every piece of information we can get. I have some contacts among our peers in the region. Marcel will have some as well. We can also parse the opinions of those whose hospitality we end up relying on to obtain a better sense of the situation. So long as there is any hospitality left to be had."

"Would that really be a problem?" Faust asked. "I thought all the fighting was happening along the Vahs."

"Both sides have been sending parties of partisans to harass supply lines," Johann said, "Many of whom are likely unaware of the ceasefire."

"Which is why Ingrid was so worried about our escort?" Faust asked.

"Aye, at least in part, alongside the normal concerns of bandits and monsters, but those are ever-present worries," Johann said.

Faust gave a simple nod in reply. It was only natural to worry about the creatures that lurked in the wilderness. Even a common animal entirely unattuned to the more esoteric energies of the world could be deadly and should be accounted for. Not to mention the potential for upset that the war could be having on natural habitats. Creatures that were normally innocuous and placid could be driven toward man-made pathways and even whole settlements.

It seemed to Faust that his assertion in mediating between Johann and Ingrid had been the right one to make, though for reasons he had not immediately considered. Looking up, his eyes met those of his godfather's.

"Meinherd told me you have been favoring old teratology books. I thought you were going to give that up?" Johann said.

"You want to talk about this now?" Faust replied. He turned a glare toward the priest, whose sleeping visage was unfazed by the stare.

"Faust, I'm worried about all this, and I need to be sure that you understand the weight of what your father has dumped into our laps."

"What? Do you think I'll run off to go play at being a Jäger in the woods somewhere? Or that I won't be able to get the results we want and get us all killed in some fiery conflagration?"

"Both," Johann said. The cold surety in that single word struck Faust with more force than a blow from his combat instructor. He opened his mouth to respond, but no words formed on his tongue. His eyes wandered about the cabin of the carriage, flitting from one corner to the next before finally settling on the window. He watched the gentle light give way to shadows as the carriage entered into a cusp of woodlands.

"Faust, you said you would focus on your studies properly this time, but I keep hearing the opposite."

"I have done my part. What I read in my free time is none of your concern. You have nothing to worry about." His right hand clung to his left arm, feeling for the faint lines of scar tissue beneath his sleeve.

"I have everything to worry about," Johann said.

"What happened that day was no one's fault but mine. It was not my father's fault or that of any of the guards, and it was certainly not yours. I made my decision, and I learned from it. I keep learning from it."

"I can at least understand some of what you feel," Johann said. He let out a soft sigh. "I know you can handle a rifle now and I know that you have passed every test Meinherd has given you. I want to trust you, Faust, as if you were my own blood."

"Yet you still think me incapable of doing this."

"Incapable of what? Of singlehandedly getting two powerful men to put aside their egos and stop throwing peasants to their deaths to prove whose political opinion is more correct?" Johann let out a shaky laugh. "Not for a second do I think any of us could do that alone. We would need a miracle, and these days, I scarcely expect we will see one in our lifetime." He turned to look at Meinherd, whose whiskered head slumped down toward his chest as they hit a bump in the road, and laughed with Faust at the sleeping priest.

A shout from outside the carriage broke their laughter, and they quieted down to listen. They sat for a few moments until the driver called out and their vehicle slowed and came to a stop. Johann pulled back the curtain on his window and leaned close to it in a vain attempt to see what was going on. Grunting, the Markgraf opened the door and stood, half hanging from the portal, his head peering over the wooden frame.

"What's going on?"

"Milord, the main road was blocked, so we took a detour, but now there are carcasses on the road," said the driver. "Two hind and a buck."

Johann swung himself the rest of the way out of the carriage, leaving the door ajar. Faust followed, standing just outside the carriage, one hand clinging to the copper rail pinned to the outer panel.

Just as the driver had said, three red deer were strewn in bloody fashion across the dirt road, though Faust couldn't make out any other details from where he stood. Johann strode over to the corpses, taking a rifle from Ingrid.

"Why wasn't I informed about the previous roadblock?" he asked as he knelt down to examine the bodies.

"It would have taken too long to move it with our numbers," Ingrid said. "I supposed it would be easier to go around."

"That was hardly your call to make alone," Johann said. The Markgraf knelt down to examine the animals, but whatever he said to Ingrid was too quiet for Faust to hear. Letting go of the railing, Faust took a single step forward before Johann stood up and said something to one of the other guards. Faust heard a rustling from the trees above. As he looked up, he caught a fleeting glimpse of light and thought for a moment that he heard the faintest whisper of an expletive.

In a split second, it registered in his mind what the light was. He turned back to his godfather and shouted, "Get down!" The guard closest to Johann grabbed him and pushed him forward to the ground. Ingrid raised her rifle and started sweeping for a target.

The small stretch of wooded road exploded in a flurry of pandemonium. Werewolves leaped from the tree line, claws and fangs tearing into man and horse alike. Shots sang out in a deafening chorus, and Faust stumbled as he tried to run to his godfather, falling hard onto the ground. One of the foul creatures ran past him, a bullet flying clear over his head into the wolfman's shoulder. It crashed into a guardswoman, and her horse collapsed on top of her. Faust crawled over to her, pulling himself up into a crouch and placing his full weight on the creature's left arm. Yanking his dagger free from its sheath, he stabbed into the side of the werewolf's throat, a sick gurgle escaping its ruptured windpipe.

Faust twisted the knife and pulled the blade free, falling back as it came loose from the young lycanthrope thrashing and clawing at its throat. Tears clouded its eyes, but Faust ignored the creature's death throes and moved around the fallen horse, trying to lift it even slightly to free its rider. He couldn't get the poor animal to budge, so he instead turned to the rider herself. She was unconscious, her head laying in a small forming puddle of blood atop a stone on the roadside.

He lifted her head, ripping a section of his sleeve off to wrap around the cut to try and stem the bleeding before laying her back down gently onto the rock. His ears rang and his whole body ached, but he was far better off than the guardswoman. He looked around the chaotic scene for Johann, watching as a guardsman collapsed under the weight of a lycanthrope, the beast sinking its fangs into his shoulder and ripping off strips of cloth and flesh alike.

Yet that gruesome affair gave way to a glimmer of hope as Johann charged the beast, ramming his rifle bayonet into its side and toppling it over. The gunshot that followed almost completely dislodged the bayonet from between its ribs. Faust stood to try and rally to the Markgraf, but when his godfather saw him, he mouthed, or rather, spoke an unheard order. "Get Meinherd!" Faust nodded and doubled back toward the carriage, cursing himself for not thinking of the priest sooner. Miracle or no, his bell would still ring true.

The carriage had been left unharmed, though not for lack of effort on the werewolves' part. Those closest to the carriage had rallied to it, the driver clinging to one of the horses, desperate to keep them in check. Meinherd was already awake, at least partly, stumbling out from the open door as he clutched his head. The herald got his senses back and seeing the horror going on around him, his face turned to an image of fury. Faust ran up to the circle of guards, one grabbing him by the arm and throwing him toward the carriage as she and two of her fellows fired off a salvo into a charging wolfman.

Meinherd pulled his bell free from the loop on his belt and stepped out toward the havoc. He lifted the instrument high into the air and brought it down hard, repeating the motion again and again. With each chime, the sound became clearer and the ringing in Faust's ears grew quiet. Bestial roars rose from the throats of the remaining werewolves, and Faust watched as two of them slouched away in visible pain.

A beast larger than the rest stood tall and let out a raspy bellow that reinvigorated the remainder of the faltering pack. The assault seemed to intensify as Faust stood next to the dumbstruck Meinherd, neither of them knowing just what to do next. The guards in front of them let out a fusillade of shots, coordinating the best they could as the creatures tore through the caravan. Some of the werewolves ducked back into the thicket and then reemerged to attack from new directions, slowly bleeding the resistance dry.

The guard who had pulled Faust to safety disappeared in a blur of fur, her rifle clattering to the ground. Meinherd tolled his bell again, but it had little effect on the monsters. Faust chose then to rejoin the fray. He ran forward, dropping into a slide that tore at his knees as he neared the place where the spare rifle now lay. Shouldering the weapon, he pulled the bolt halfway back and, satisfied there was a round chambered, sighted down the weapon and began tracking a wolfman through the brush.

His shot hit a tree behind where the thing had been and drew its attention. As it charged from the brush at him, Faust cycled another round in and fired at its head, only to rip a hole in its ear. Faust prepared himself to dodge, unsure if he had the reflexes to do so, but uncertainty turned into amazement as the beast's head exploded into bloody chunks. A split-second reaction, purely instinctual, was all that spared him from infection as rivulets of the thing's accursed blood splattered onto him.

Faust looked up and watched as an unknown man ran past him and jumped over the freshly dead lycanthrope so he could tackle another. Four quick streaks of silver cut through the air as the man stabbed another monster's abdomen. He pulled a pistol from his waist and put two shots into its heart, another toll from Meinherd's bell ringing out across the battle a second after. The carriage driver screamed as a werewolf leaped onto the roof and sent the horses into a panic. They carried the cart away and Faust fired off a shot at the furred mass atop the ornate wagon, hitting his mark.

Elation warmed him even as he realized nothing he did or could do would save their carriage, though perhaps the driver might escape with his life. Without the gilded mass of wood between them, the remaining guards tightened their circle to protect Meinherd, but Faust ran forward, realizing too late for his own liking that Johann could have been trampled by the escaped horses.

Something edged across his vision and he ducked down just in time to avoid the sweeping arm of a werewolf. Faust fired a bullet into its right knee, obliterating it and nearly losing his grip on the rifle in the process. Somehow, he managed to right his grip enough to swing the rifle as a cudgel against the opposite joint, bringing it down face-to-face with him.

Pushing himself forward, he rammed the weapon barrel-first into the gaping maw before him, wet with crimson streaks of slobber. One hand went for his dagger while the other struggled to keep the jaws pinned open. A single stab brought forth a ragged whimper as holy silver sliced into the profaned flesh of the mutant's shoulder. He used the beast's tremors of pain as an opening to force it back, finishing the exercise with a swift kick to its remaining and likely cracked kneecap. As the beast folded backward, Faust fumbled to cycle the rifle's bolt, then turned his head and body so he was looking away from the beast before squeezing the trigger.

A clarion toll droned out behind the splatter of blood, bone, and brains. The road was quiet but for the labored breathing of men and women. Faust looked back at his work: a viscous mess of a corpse streaked along the blood-stained muck. He was half-soaked in it himself. His once-white shirt was dyed a deep carmine, and his brown pants were at least three shades darker. As he ran his hands along his limbs, feeling his skin, he confirmed that he was bruised and worn, but otherwise fine.

Johann limped over to him, all but collapsing into his arms as his leg gave way beneath him. Deep slits of crimson and pink were cut into his right thigh, and his nose was bleeding, but he was alive and otherwise well. The Markgraf looked over at the slumping corpse and then back to Faust.

"Clearly you can do a bit more than just handle a rifle," he said.

Screams drew both their eyes to the gathering of guards where a stranger had his pistol in the face of one of the survivors.

"What is the meaning of this, Herr Jäger?" Johann shouted. Then in a softer tone, he said, "Faust, help me over there, quickly."

"I promise, I wasn't bitten!" the guards shouted as Faust and Johann trudged over to them slowly. The Jäger was unimpressed, taking his free hand and jangling the lapel of his coat as an order. The guard looked away, backing up as his hands pulled his own coat tighter around himself. He was bloodstained and tired, not very unique traits at that moment, but even Faust could tell the man was protesting too much. "No, I-I would know if I was bitten, wouldn't I?"

"Do as the Jäger said; that's an order," Ingrid said, pushing her weathered frame through the circle of her subordinates to join Faust and Johann.

"Remove your coat, Karl," Johann said, "I need a tourniquet for my leg, I think."

"Milord," the guard, Karl, pleaded in a shaking voice. He took a step back, then turned and started running toward the trees. A gunshot coming from above them ripped through Karl's ankle, and the guardsman went tumbling into the muck. Faust helped Johann sit down and followed after the Jäger, turning back to watch Ingrid rip the sleeve from her coat and tie it around Johann's leg.

Faust caught up to the Jäger just as he violently grabbed Karl's collar and dragged him up to his knees. A swift and practiced motion stripped the man of his outerwear, letting him fall back to the dirt. He lifted the fabric up and examined the left sleeve, then turned back to the trembling guardsman. Faust knelt down beside him and grabbed his bloody arm, twisting his wrist so he and the Jäger could get a better look at the array of incisions that wrapped around his ragged flesh.

"Ask and I shall receive you, as you have received me," the Jäger said as Karl's screams for mercy began to turn into agonized grunts. The guard began to spasm; his limbs twisted unnaturally, and the bones within cracked as the Jäger continued his prayer, "That you may forevermore join in our great endeavor. Peace shall come at our hands, at the tips of our spears, and the bolts of our bows. Our path has but one end. Rest now, brother, for you will need your strength in the war to come. May the Harbinger and his Wild Hunt receive you."

Heavenly silver split flesh as the Jäger plunged his dagger between the man's ribs and into his heart. Karl's body thrashed against the blade, ripples flowing just beneath his skin as his limbs started growing. Then, almost more quickly than it had started, he went still with death.

"What's your name, boy?" the Jäger asked as he stood and wiped the blood from his blade.

"Faust von Schwarzdorn."

"Yorick auf Arensfeld, a pleasure. You were sloppy, little prince, but I think we could fix that."

"How about a bath for him first, Yorick? And you and everyone else, for that matter," Meinherd said, his hand hovering over Faust's shoulder. "I'll go prepare the holy water. Cecilia, I haven't seen you in an age! Get down from that tree and come say hello, will you?"

CHAPTER FIVE

PETRA

In those days, there was conflict between our forefathers and the tribes of the Ershaen who had dwelled in the land from the time of dawning. The land was drowned with the blood of generations 'til the Ershaen and their gods were driven to the deepest places of the wilds. There, they practiced their pagan magics 'til the seeds of the stigmata bore beasts from the hearts of man. Both Gaersche and Ershaen alike were cursed. None could escape the wrath of sin, and all were afeared in those days.

Ercanbald Bright-Eye, Second Antiquities 9:4-7

For three days, they waited for an attack that never came. The howling of wolves, or perhaps wolfmen or maybe something worse, lingered ever-present in the distance. Each night, they took watches with the town militia, and come sunrise, they did rounds about the wall, checking the posts for claw marks and the spikes below for traces of fresh blood. They found nothing of the sort, even as three days stretched into a full week. Whatever was out there, it was content with staying where it was for the time being, and that was a blessing all its own.

Petra trudged into the church, pulling off her mud-caked boots at the door, and stretched out onto an empty pew with her rifle cradled in her arms. Hers had been the last watch for that night, which was thankfully over now, the sun rising over the horizon and sending the worst of the beasts back to ground. One of the first things Heinrich had taught her that wasn't useful in combat was the difference between natural monsters and the accursed ones.

Despite what the superstitious always claimed, not every monster was nocturnal, and not every creature in the teratology books was born of some curse or foul act of magic. Heinrich had told her a few times that animals were just like people: while most were incapable of performing magic, there were plenty of exceptions that could. Not that she really understood any of that magic stuff either, something to do with the breath of creation that priests always talked about in sermons. Regardless of her mentor's lectures, she was simply happy to know that whatever was spending all night howling had slunk off somewhere else.

She felt the first kiss of the sun's warmth on her face as she lay there, listening to the sounds of Heinrich and Erik stirring from their pews, the gentle sighs of waking hunters, the shift of leather and fabric against flesh, and the familiar clicks of guns being loaded. A few tapping footfalls prefaced the shadow that fell over her, and she opened her eyes to see her master looming over her.

"Nothing," she said as a report of the night's watch. She got a curt nod from Heinrich in return before he left.

Silence returned to the church for a brief time. Erik sat somewhere up front performing his morning prayers and

Traugott was still sequestered in his personal quarters. She drifted into a half sleep, the vague shapes of almost-dreams flitting at the edge of her mind: her brother running through the field, a shadow in the rye, and a thin line of blood running down a jagged stake onto two tiny, innocent hands.

At some point, she must have fallen fully asleep, but the booming clang of the church bell reverberating through the building dragged her back into wakefulness with a start. She sat up, instincts kicking in, quickly scanning the room for threats only to find a few startled parishioners staring at her. She smiled, giving them a nervous laugh before picking herself up and hurrying outside.

Normalcy had gradually returned to Laupen since they caught the bahkauv, save for the presence of the creature itself, which remained caged in one of the public squares. Kaspar had kept true to his word not to kill it, and Heinrich had spent most of their money keeping the thing fed. Petra had passed more time than she liked to admit just watching it from a distance, trying to see what made it worth so much money and effort to keep alive. She still couldn't tell, but so long as Heinrich wanted it cared for, her hands were tied.

She resisted the urge to go there now, instead turning down the road that led her to the Greifenflügel. The barkeep, whose name she learned was Wendel after Traugott mentioned him one night at dinner, was busy cleaning tables with a wet rag.

"Herr Taube isn't here, little lady," he said, "Or do you want a drink?"

"Was hoping for a drink," she said.

"Coming right up." Wendel returned to his bar and prepared her a mug of something from the middle shelf.

"How much?"

"Free."

"What's the occasion?"

"Today would have been Linus' eighteenth birthday. At least I think so," Wendel said. He tilted his head for a moment before going back to the shelf where he poured himself a drink as well. Returning to where Petra sat, he said, "Only seems right to share a pint of his favorite beer with one of his avengers. To Linus."

"To Linus," Petra said, raising her mug and tapping it against the side of Wendel's. She took a sip, almost gagging, then said, "I wish he had lived so I could tell him how bad his taste in beer was."

"A damn shame you know the difference. Then again, I'm the one serving you, not that anyone here is going to care. How old are you?"

"Sixteen, but you grow up faster on the road."

"I bet. Why'd you join up with Herr Taube? Dream of adventure or just a bad home life?"

"Both, kind of," Petra answered. She took another sip of her drink before continuing. "Wasn't all bad at home, I just had nothing to keep me there."

"I know how that goes," Wendel said, "I'm from out east, a small town like this in the Herzland. Left when I was fifteen after I realized my older sister inheriting everything would leave me as menial labor." He pointed to the burns on his head, "Got these fighting as a partisan a few years later, but I got out before all that mess with the silent revolt."

"That where you got the name for your place here?"

"Nah," Wendel said, "Just a spur-of-the-moment sort of thing."

"Wendel, there's trouble!" One of Kaspar's militiamen came into the bar, his eyes flicking between Petra and the barkeep.

"What trouble?"

"Did the bahkauv get loose?" Petra said.

"What? No, a bunch of imperials just rode into town," the man said.

"Petra, you need to hide," Wendel said. "Simon, did you see if they had an inquisitor with them?"

"I think so, a guy wearing mostly white right? A few paladins too."

"Damn," Wendel said.

"What about Traugott?" Petra asked, "We can't just let them arrest him."

"You need to worry about yourself, girl," Wendel said. "Let us worry about our own. Where are the other two Jäger?"

"Gone to ground," Simon said, "I don't know where Erik is, but Heinrich is with Kaspar."

"Let him know his apprentice is safe," Wendel said.

"Like hell," Petra retorted.

"What's one priest to you?" Wendel asked. "You barely know the man and you want to risk a fight with the imperials over him."

"I didn't know Linus either, but I risked my life playing bait to capture the beast that did him in," Petra said. "I won't hide away in some dark room while a man who sheltered and fed me gets dragged through the streets like a criminal."

"Fine," Wendel said, "you can come with us. That way I can at least keep you from doing something stupid."

"Really?" Petra said. "I've fought and killed monsters twice the size of this bahkauv alongside master Heinrich."

"And I've killed men who thought war was just like the stories their mothers read to them before they ran off to play hero," Wendel said. The barkeep pinched the bridge of his nose and let out a sigh. "I don't doubt your ability, Petra, I doubt your judgment. If you kill one of them here, more will come, and none of us will be safe."

"Uh, I'll go tell Kaspar what's going on then," Simon said, leaving as hastily as he'd arrived.

"He didn't tell us which gate they came in from," Petra said.

"Of course he didn't, because idiots don't think about things like that. Come on, let's go."

Petra followed the barkeep out through the back door of the tavern and down a series of tight alleyways beneath fluttering clothes on drying lines. They made their way up toward the church, the sounds of hoofbeats and metal armor mixing with the discussions of the gathering crowds.

"You asked Simon about an inquisitor," Petra said, "what's so dangerous about them?"

"Can't lie to them."

"Seriously?"

"Seriously. Completely impossible," he said, turning himself to shimmy sideways through a particularly tight space. "Seen it happen more times than I'm comfortable with."

"Spooky."

They came to the end of the alley, Wendel holding out his arm as he peeked onto the street. Satisfied they were clear, he waved Petra along as he sprinted across the street to the next alleyway. Petra followed, catching a fleeting glimpse of a redheaded boy on horseback before she stopped in the dim light. This alley wasn't as cramped as the last, but it was more winding, the homes around it built less to plan than the shops nearer the market.

"Never saw a miracle before my time in the partisans," Wendel said. "Traugott's certainly never performed one, but the imperials do it all the time."

"I could never lie to my mother, doesn't make her a miracle worker," Petra said.

"Funny. Doesn't matter if you believe it or not, since I don't plan on tussling with them unless we absolutely have to." By the time they got to the church, it was too late. The procession of imperials on horseback was arrayed outside the church. Six of the eight were paladins wearing chainmail armor and red tabards, including the redheaded youth she'd seen earlier. A priest in a clean grey cassock with a purple sash sat beside the boy at the back, and at their head was the inquisitor wearing a white coat over white traveling clothes.

"What now?" Petra asked.

"We wait and see if they plan to take Traugott somewhere else or if they're going to hold him in his church for now. We only intervene if they bring him out and take him down a road where their swords and spears are a disadvantage."

"Or out of town, right?"

"They won't do that," Wendel said. "At least not tonight." They waited and watched as the imperials dismounted and entered the church, but never saw them bring the old Pfarrer out.

"Right, they'll set up shop there just like you guys did. They won't kill him, but he won't be comfortable either."

"Think we could sneak in and spirit him away?" Petra asked.

"Not without a distraction to keep the paladins busy."

"I can think of a pretty big distraction. How fast can you run?"

"Why do I think I'm going to regret answering that?"

"Well, you're around a lot of drinks that smell of hops, and I wouldn't want you to get eaten is all," Petra said.

"Like hell," Wendel said. "You are not going to release that damned thing in the middle of town."

"It fixates on things that smell of hops, so either we provoke it and lead it to the church to where the imperials will attack it..."

"Or it makes for my tavern and kills any innocent person unlucky enough to be between it and the Greifenflügel," Wendel interrupted.

"Or, option three, I run out to where we've caged the bahkauv, and you can go out there and cause a fuss about it being on the loose. Lead the paladins there, and I'll uncage it when I see them come out, then double back here and sneak in to get Traugott."

"All of those are terrible."

"Do you have a better idea or do you plan on waiting for them to bring him out in chains? By then, it might be too late, and you said it yourself: if we attack them, more imperials will show up, and if what you've said about the inquisitors is true, then the game is up."

"But if their men die fighting a monster and Traugott gets away in the confusion... That's only if we're lucky, though, and I don't like the odds."

"Fair enough. What do you think, Master?" Petra asked, peering over her shoulder at Heinrich as he came up behind them with Kaspar at his side. They were both brandishing their rifles, though Kaspar's was just about an antique.

"About what?" Heinrich asked. "I only just caught up to you."

"Your apprentice wants to let the bahkauv loose as a distraction to draw away the paladins so we can sneak into the church and spirit away good Brother Traugott," Wendel said.

"I suppose it could work," Heinrich said.

"You *what?*" Wendel said, a tad louder than he perhaps intended; he clasped a hand to his mouth.

"They'll kill the thing either way," Heinrich said, "And as much as I would like to relocate it, I'll prioritize Traugott's life."

"A shame, since we've spent so much keeping it fed," Petra said, "But at least we'll get some worth out of it."

"Hush," Heinrich said. "Herr Kaspar, you'd be best suited for alerting the imperials of the 'threat' caged in your town. Can you do that?"

"So long as the inquisitor stays inside, it'll be no problem," Kaspar replied.

"Go now. Petra, snake around to the church's side entrance and wait. Barkeep, I need you to stay here until the paladins leave. After they do, go to the front of the church and knock on the door."

"I have a name, Herr Taube. And what if not all the paladins leave?"

"Then keep them busy somehow, as well as whoever answers the door if they do. Be loud about it too. Petra, listen for Wendel, and sneak in while he distracts whoever they leave inside. Any questions?"

"Yeah, one," Petra said. "Where's Erik?"

"Gone," Kaspar confirmed.

"He left town after marking a rendezvous point for us on my map," Heinrich said.

"He really just left?" Petra said.

"We were going to too until I heard this plan of yours," Heinrich said. "Don't hate him for this, Petra. His mission is important. We leave by the south gate with or without our carriage."

"Whatever," she said. "Let's get on with this."

Heinrich hurried off through the shaded alley toward the caged beast with Petra at his heels, but she turned when she thought she was far enough from the chapel square. Peeking out from behind the cover of the small house and seeing that no one was looking her way, she darted across the street in a diagonal line into the nearest alley on the opposite street.

It took her a few minutes to circle back to the side of the church where she kneeled behind the stone fence that surrounded an enclosed garden. She watched Kaspar and four of the red-clothed imperials run down the road, their chainmail clinking as they went. She wasn't sure if the added protection against claws and teeth was worth all that noise, but that was their problem to deal with. She vaulted over the fencing and ran low to the worn wooden door that led into the personal quarters, pressing her back to the wall and shrugging her rifle's strap from her shoulder.

Petra propped her long gun against the stone wall, securing its muzzle in the groove between two stones so it wouldn't fall. With a practiced motion, she unbuttoned the holster on her hip and pulled her pistol free, chambering a round. "Excuse me, sirs!" she heard Wendel all but shout from around the corner of the building. "Is our priest available? I need to speak with him."

Still, she waited. Then after a pause, she heard Wendel say, "Well, I need advice and not the kind I can find at a bar. No, I won't calm down! She left me three moons ago and still hasn't come back!"

With that, Petra pushed open the door and slowly slid into Traugott's kitchen. Dead embers lay in a cold, grey heap on the hearth, and all the cookware hung properly from its hooks. She stayed low, careful not to disturb the pots and pans, or anything else as she circled around the room toward the hall that led to Traugott's bedroom.

Peeking into the sparse and solemn room proved fruitless, and he wasn't in the larder either. Petra fought the urge to sigh as she backtracked toward the kitchen and stood beside the door leading into the worship hall, left slightly ajar. Traugott sat on the steps of the altar's dais, his hands bound in old rope. "I should be out there with Herr Timaeus and the others," said a voice from out of her sightline. "I can help."

"You are helping, young squire," said another voice she couldn't place.

"How?" the young man asked. "One old man with his hands tied is hardly a threat, especially with Herr Varnham here."

"This old man can hear you," Traugott said, "And I won't be sassed by the child of an apostate."

"Pay the heretic no mind, Michael," came the second voice. "His words are as hollow as his church's unanswered prayers. Nothing worth lowering yourself to, I assure you."

"I-I will try, Brother Jeremias," Michael said.

"Good," Jeremias said. "Now through that door over there should be his quarters. It will be far easier to hold him there until the others return." Petra silently spun around on her heel, looking for a place to hide. It seemed luck favored her today, but she'd have to be the one to make something of this upturn. She entered Traugott's room and positioned herself so she would be hidden behind his door when it was opened, shutting it as softly as she could.

A moment passed, and the sound of footsteps and squeaking hinges marked their entry into the kitchen. The sound of boots on stone grew until finally, a hand came upon the door and swung it open. The priest was the first to enter, Michael following suit with a hand firmly on Traugott's shoulder. The young man was handsome, with sharp features beneath his curly red hair and green eyes that turned in shock at Petra's figure in his peripheral view.

Before he had time to think, she pushed herself against him, grabbing his mouth so he couldn't shout for help and nuzzling her pistol's barrel beneath his chin. "Hi there," Petra said in a low whisper. "I'm here for your prisoner, not you. Try something, and I won't hesitate to paint this wall with your insides."

"Petra," Traugott seethed.

"Oh, I won't have to, will I?" Petra smiled at the boy as he slowly shook his head to answer a clear "no" to her question. "Good, now I'm going to let go of your mouth, but you already know the rest, don't you?" Michael nodded a yes, but as she let go, the idiot boy took a deep breath and opened his mouth to call for help. He only managed a pained yelp before Petra punched him in his throat.

He fell to his knees, grasping at his throat and coughing as he slumped to one side. He steadied himself with his free hand, but Petra kicked him in his side, sending him sprawling to the floor. She reached for her bayonet, unsheathed the blade, and sliced the ropes that bound Traugott's wrists together. The old man rubbed his sore joints and then ripped two strips from the blanket on his bed. He made the first into a wad that he stuffed into Michael's mouth then tied the young man's hands with the other.

"Listen to the young lady next time, Herr squire," Traugott said. "You'll come out with fewer bruises. Their priest will come looking for him soon, we need to go."

"Wasn't planning on staying," Petra said. Michael thrashed against his bindings, looking up at Petra with frustration and anger. Their eyes met, and Petra gave him a wink before exiting, closing the door, and leaving the church behind.

CHAPTER SIX

FAUST

Glory be to the chorus of Heaven, who sing with every word
the power of our creator,
Glory be to the chorus of men, who join feeble voice ere to their
crystal song,
Glory be to Him who made Heaven and Earth and breathed
life into all that dwells therein,
Glory be to Him that smote the false gods and cast them anon
into the deep,
Let none deny His glory, writ in flames across the stars,
And with each breath, His breath, freely given, and now re-
turned in exaltation,
Glory be, Glory be, Glory be.
Sigilind Thrice-Widowed, Exaltations 41

What was left of the caravan managed to limp its way from the woods to Naakt in what seemed to be a reasonable amount of time considering the loss of half their horses and their only carriage. Faust and Ingrid took turns as Johann's crutch, though the Markgraf was faring better than some in their entourage. The woman who Faust had tried and failed to free from beneath her horse had bled out, though whether it had been from her head wound alone or some internal wound, they couldn't say.

They had gathered the bodies of the dead and burned them, Meinherd giving them their last rites as the pyres bore their spirits to the heavens. It was a shame they had no means of carrying the ashes, but with their situation as it was, doing so would have been untenable even if they had the urns. Weapons and ammo had been collected and a small sled had been made, strapped together with strands of clothing stripped from the dead and purified in holy water. The dead would be remembered and honored, but only so long as the rest of them made it out of the woods alive.

The walk was long but not unbearable, not impossible, even as one man's arm went wretched with an infection and with Johann's leg almost there. In the end, the presence of the two Jäger who had inadvertently caused the whole mess to begin with made things easier. Yorick was, in many ways, the very real incarnation of the ideal that Faust had read so many stories of but utterly disappointing in everything else.

"You get used to it," Cecilia had told him as they walked slowly down the open road. Her dark blonde hair had been let down from the tail she'd kept it in while they were in the woods. Faust remembered nodding, too lost in thought to respond until he looked up to see the haggard-looking herald, his hand resting on his little bell.

"You can place a mantle on the shoulders of a pig, but it will remain a pig," Faust said. She'd laughed at that.

That moment, though, was not the time for jokes. The group stood before the gate of Naakt, a pair of portcullises of iron lattices overlapping one another within a large archway of stone. Banners fluttered in the wind atop the parapets above where the von Tollkirsche seal flew, displayed on a Burggraf's shield with a field distinct from that of Tholst. Wooden slats were closed over the machicolations and only a few guards still stood on the walls above them, having rushed to get their lord and open the gate for his cousin and liege.

A low rumble of rudimentary machinery groaning to life sounded as someone within the castle started to raise the twin portcullises for them to enter. A rush of guards came out, dressed not too dissimilarly from Johann's men, lending their shoulders to the wounded and offering water skins freely. As they entered the castle's walls, the atmosphere changed, like entering a beehive. Distant conversations gave way to calls for supplies as Marcel's staff began assessing their status.

Faust shrugged off one of the men as politely as he could, assuring him he was simply tired and nothing more. He caught a glimpse of Marcel, dark hair shorn low to his head and an impeccable uniform moving through the crowd toward Johann. The two kinsmen spoke a few words to one another before Marcel's face went white with anger. Johann tried to catch his arm but missed, and Faust immediately knew where, or rather, who the target was for his ire.

Scanning the crowd, he found the two Jäger and began making his own way toward them, doing so a moment too late to stop the Burggraf zu Naakt from pulling his sword and holding it to the huntsman's neck. The Jäger barely reacted to the blade at his throat, and even Cecilia seemed unmoved by the threat to her mentor's life. It was as if they were used to this sort of thing happening.

"I hired you to clear the Larswald of its lycanthrope infestation, Herr Jäger," Marcel said. "Explain yourself."

"We needed to draw the accursed things from their lair, milord," Yorick said. "Thin their numbers out enough that we could clear the nest without burning down the whole forest."

"By baiting the road?"

"By baiting a road that no one took, owing to it being fairly well known to be infested with werewolves."

"You nearly got my cousin killed," Marcel said.

"Not my intention, though I suppose that hardly matters."

"No, it does not."

"We are alive, though, Uncle Marcel," Faust said. The Burggraf turned to him, and as their eyes met, the lines on his face eased slightly. He looked between Faust and Yorick before sighing and returning his sword to its sheath.

"You have my apologies, Yorick," Marcel said. "Can I assume that you took all the necessary precautions?"

"We did, your lordship," Cecilia said.

"How many casualties, Faust?"

"Three guards killed during the attack itself, one died of her wounds shortly after we drove off the beasts, another was found to be bitten and was granted mercy before he could fully turn," Faust said. "It is likely that our carriage driver is dead as well, as we never found him."

"The horses too, by the looks of you all," Marcel said. "A damned shame, all of this."

"How long has the Larswald had werewolves in it?" Faust asked. Marcel looked away. "My lord Burggraf, how long has your territory been beset by these accursed gluttons?"

"Four months," he said. "They overran the village of Halsmat seven weeks ago."

"You scourged it?"

"Yes. Then I sent for a Jäger."

"I would like to know why you waited so long, but I doubt you will be forthright with me," Faust said. He shook his head and then turned toward the keep. "We will need more men and supplies from your household than we originally asked of you, but it seems as if that would be difficult to furnish in your situation."

"Of course, my Prinz," Marcel said. With that, Faust turned to walk off, but then the world began to spin. His head was throbbing and he needed a quiet place to lie down and collect himself. He took a few steps before he started to teeter, collapsing to his knees and falling forward into the arms of one of Marcel's men. Curiosity, more than fear, defined his thoughts as he drifted on the edge of consciousness. Was he somehow infected, or was it simply exhaustion come for him at last? Probably the latter.

He awoke after several hours. How many, he was not entirely sure, but the night sky outside his window spoke clearly that he had been out for some time. Looking around, he recognized the plain accommodations of the guest quarters in Naakt, unadorned by finery and more comfortable for it. He pushed himself out of bed, folding the thick white sheets over and swinging his legs out onto the cold rug. Someone had undressed him, bathed him, and furnished him with new clothes. Heat rose to his face as he processed the information.

Shaking his head in a failed attempt to clear his mind through physical means, he walked over to the window and charted the stars. It was hardly his best skill, but trying to place constellations helped keep him from thinking about which of Marcel's maids had helped clean the stench of the road off him. On a hunch, he pulled at the collar of his shirt and sniffed the fabric, getting a hint of homemade perfume that sent him further down the mental spiral.

Faust rushed out of the room, his bare feet thankfully discomforted by the equally bare stone in the halls. He needed something to read, even if it were just a collection of bad poetry or mathematical notes. Anything that could keep him from thinking about her. There was only one place in the keep that Faust knew had books and luckily it would be abandoned at this indeterminate, but clearly late, hour. Marcel's study was empty and unguarded, so Faust let himself in, unconcerned with the impropriety of it.

The fur rug was different from the stone, but not unpleasant. Bookshelves lined one wall comprising the nearly full library of the castle; the rest spread amongst the dozens of bedrooms and the chapel built against the side of the keep. He walked past a plain oak table, two thinly cushioned chairs, and the cold hearth full of lifeless embers, but paused at the sight of what was spread out across Marcel's desk. A map of the region, its corners weighed down by an inkwell, two chess pieces, and a rock.

The map had notes scrawled on it, but the ink was too dark for him to make out in the dimly lit room. Circling around the desk, Faust pulled open the curtains, letting the light from the moon and stars illuminate the desk in pale blue. Dates were jotted down beside locations marked with dots and open circles with arrows connecting them and creating a timeline leading to and from the Larswald that tracked the infestation. It was hard to keep accurate records of werewolf outbreaks, owing in no small part to their habit of eating or turning most of the people they attacked. Yet this had a strange precision to it. It was like a battle plan.

Faust found the points marked for four months prior, when Marcel said the outbreak began, then followed the connecting lines to the first point of contact. In all the texts he'd read on the subject he had only rarely seen something like this. The dates led his finger deeper into the web rather than outward, deep within the Larswald. "Could it be possible?" he asked himself. "Maybe, but no."

He stood there, cupping his mouth with his hand. It was an outright certainty that the den was at that point or close to it, but first contact with an outbreak was almost never at the den; the beasts were far too active for that. They were also far too territorial to let anyone get that close and live. Every sighting and battle radiated outward in some direction from that spot. Halsmat only survived as long as it did because it was on the far side of the forest.

But even then, they should have known to evacuate the village as a precaution. Why wait more than two months to send a request for aid to the Jäger Guild when you know the outbreak is spreading?

The whole situation felt wrong, but he couldn't put his finger on exactly why. He needed to talk to Johann about it immediately, but then he winced as he remembered how late it was. His godfather would be asleep, keeping off his leg, an injury that would keep them here at Naakt for a span of time that would at least give him the opportunity to investigate this matter.

Faust committed the map to memory as best he was able and started for the door, but he came to a halt when he stepped into the shadows and into a realization. He spun around and started for the curtains, stopping again as he heard the unmistakable sound of footsteps on the hallway stones. Having nowhere to hide, he took three long strides toward the bookshelves, pulling a random volume and opening it to a random page before situating himself on the windowsill.

He had barely enough time to read the first three sentences when the door swung open, and the one person he had hoped to avoid stepped into the room. Nina was a comely girl, well aware of it, in fact, who worked as a maid for Marcel as a favor to her father, the physician employed by the von Tollkirsches. She was also a talented botanist in her own right, though she lacked her father's interest in medicine, favoring perfumery.

His eyes flitted between the text and the girl, her chestnut hair hanging almost limply against a face that lacked the vibrancy it usually held. Nina went about cleaning the ashes from the fireplace, unaware of his presence, and as much as he would have liked for her to be oblivious of him, he felt the need to make himself known. He let out a low yawn, fake as could possibly be but just unassuming enough to not give her too much of a fright. She jumped at the sound just slightly, letting out a squeak before turning to the window.

"Oh, Prinz Faust, why are you here at this hour?"

"I, I awoke not an hour ago and felt restless. A good book always eases my nerves, though this volume is rather failing at the task."

"The Burggraf will be upset if he knew you were in his study without his permission," she said.

"Yes, I think he might, but only if he is made aware of the fact," Faust said. Nina returned a nod, looking away, eyes downcast. The maid went back about her business, not once glancing toward Faust as she finished the task about the fireplace. "Is my being here troubling you, Frau Holland?"

"What? No, your grace, it's nothing," she said.

"Far be it from me to question you, but even I can tell something is amiss."

"It's my father. He hasn't written me once since this outbreak began."

"You are afraid he might have been made a victim?"

Nina gave a meek nod to Faust's question. It had been months since he had seen Doktor Holland at Tholst, longer even than the outbreak, but what Nina feared wasn't entirely impossible.

"Was your father called to Pellt?"

"No," Nina said. "His last letter mentioned only that he would be working in the villages."

"I shall keep his safety in my prayers, then," Faust said.

"Thank you, my Prinz. You had an encounter with them, how terrible are they?"

"Werewolves are hideous in their nature as much as in their appearance. I narrowly avoided death by their kind in my youth, and now I have narrowly avoided death by lycanthrope yet again. Believe me when I say that if a fool like me can survive them twice, then a man as brilliant as Coen Holland can as well," Faust said.

"I think he would be honored to hear you say that of him," Nina said.

"Then I look forward to the day I can give him such praise directly. What time is it, by chance?"

"It is some time after one in the morning," Nina said.

"Then I think it would serve us both to return to our beds. Loathe as I am to divest myself of this tome on," Faust turned the book over to peer at its cover, "the importance of bookkeeping in wartime." He returned the unread volume to its place upon the shelving and drew the curtains closed, leaving him alone save his racing thoughts. Only a passing thought was spared to the poor maid herself, but many were showered upon her present misfortune.

A physician made scarce before a major outbreak of lycanthropy? It was too timely to be a mere coincidence, and now Faust was growing ill at ease with the number of so-named coincidences that had come to present themselves. He stalked the halls, surprised at how few guards there were within the keep, but glad for it as he made his way not to his room, but to that of Nina's father. He pushed open the door and peeked inside before stepping into the unattended quarters.

The room was sparser still than even the rooms of the guest quarters, only holding simple furnishings and a plain brown rug. Most of the doktor's equipment would be housed in the infirmary for his aids and the other staff to make use of in his absences. But Faust was not interested in the herbs, chemical extracts, and beakers, but in the possibility of some correspondence that would point to why Coen had left to "the villages" and on whose authority. He turned over every stray piece of paper on the man's desk but found nothing that would aid him.

Likewise, the contents of his drawers held no evidence either. Maybe he was simply being paranoid after his encounter in the Larswald, but still, the feeling remained. Faust went to leave, but a childish notion crossed his mind, and he, in turn, crossed the room to the well-worn bed. He dug beneath the pillow, then hoisted up the mattress. Nothing was laid beneath it, but as he shimmied around the bedframe, shifting the weight of the mattress, his fingers pushed through a long, thin hole like an incision. He pried it open and found a singular stack of three peculiar letters. Each was marked with an ink stamp bearing the image of a six-pronged gear and the signature of one Alwin Dahl, physician, teratologist, and founder of the Erfinder Guild.

Faust hid the letters in the folds of his thin evening coat, making sure to return the room's effects to their original places on the off-chance his meddling might be noticed. Just as when he entered, he made doubly sure there was no one in the hall before stepping through the door and closing it behind him. Once safely within his room in the guest chambers, he read over the letters, hoping that something in the pages would reveal if his imagination was running wild like a hyperactive child or if there truly was something amiss in Marcel's burgravate.

CHAPTER SEVEN

PETRA

"I cannot promise you that this road shall be easy, but I can promise that you will not walk it alone. I regret that I will not be here to walk it with you." Those are the words that my dear friend Alaric gave to me the last time I saw him, and these selfsame words I give to you, my faithful companions. Though I leave you for the realm of the divine, know that I will always be with you in spirit just as Alaric and Clovis have been with me. Silence shall fall, but it shall never be the ruin of our immortal souls.

Gerlind the Confessor, Book of Silence 12:18-21

"Wait," Traugott said through ragged breaths. "I, wait. Petra, I can't keep your pace, child."

"Sorry," Petra said, slowing to a stop. The sounds of battle tore into the air, a cacophony of roars and screams and steel being rent by claws and teeth. The noise was the clearest sign that they still had time to escape unnoticed, yet, even Petra had to admit she was going too fast for the robed old man to follow. She stood there, weapon low, head constantly moving, watching for any sign of pursuit as she waited for Traugott to catch his breath.

Her heart was racing, adrenaline raging through her, telling her they needed to move, but she knew he needed to rest. Heinrich and Erik would be waiting for them, and if they were able to secure horses or mules for the carriage, they might be able to carry the priest all the way back to Kranzdorf. But they weren't going to go to Kranzdorf. Were they? That was why Erik had sought them or rather, Heinrich, all the way out here, wasn't it? She had never heard where he wanted them to go, but it certainly wasn't Kranzdorf. If it was, he could have just waited for them there.

"Are you able?" she said, barely even looking at the priest.

"Just a moment more," he said. "I'm afraid to say this is why I gave up my position as a herald."

"It shouldn't be very much farther," she said.

"All well and good, but that doesn't provide much comfort for my lungs. Or my bones."

"If you can sass me, you can walk. Now come on," Petra said. She continued on, dodging through alleyways and hurrying across roads, turning to cover Traugott as he struggled to make any sort of haste across Laupen. They needed to get to the south gate as soon as possible.

Their luck held as they made their way across town, the din of battle never fading but never increasing. They were skirting the fight, but that wasn't as good a position as it could be. The paladins were driving the bahkauv back to the square and back to the wagon they needed to spirit Traugott away to safety.

As they neared the square, Petra turned to her elder and said, "Stay here, I'll be back in a moment."

In a few turns, she found a place that gave an open view of the paladins and the beast as they returned to the plaza. Three paladins remained, battered and bruised but in far better shape than the bahkauv. The creature was cut to ribbons, but its wounds were black and charred, scorched shut by the holy flames that burned along the blades of its attackers. Petra knelt behind a pile of firewood and watched as the three armored warriors circled out to limit the creature's escape.

They were too few to do so, yet the presence of the cage-topped wagon provided an obstacle that the weary animal could not overcome. It would die by their hands, just like Heinrich predicted, and it would be a slow and agonizing death. Half of her wanted to shoot the poor thing, do it a single mercy, but the rest of her screamed against the suggestion. What mercy had it given Linus? What mercy would it have given her that day in the woods had she been just a hair slower? It didn't know mercy, not because it was some curse-born abomination, but because it was a stupid, lumbering, predatory animal that only understood prey and competition.

She turned, leaving it to its fate, listening to its cries of pain as flame-wreathed steel sliced at it from its attackers' probing weapons. Shooting it, she knew, would only alert the imperials to her location and to Traugott's. She wished she could be the one to burn it in her own swelling feeling of righteous indignation.

Traugott remained exactly where she'd left him, though he had found a small crate to use for a bench. The hems of his robes were dark with the muck of the alleys they had been crossing and his wrinkled skin was flushed. He wouldn't make it far on foot.

She beckoned him to join her again and he acquiesced, bracing himself against the nearest wall as he stood. The two took the rest of the walk slowly, circling the square until they got to the road that led south out of Laupen. Petra took the post of sentry again, and when she was assured that the paladins had returned toward Traugott's church, she gave the signal for him to move. The two left the village side-by-side and found Heinrich not too far into the brush.

"You're late," he said.

"I had a run-in with their squire," Petra said, "He wouldn't listen when I said not to try anything."

"You kill him?"

"No," she said.

"She did give him a good blow to the throat," Traugott said, the hint of humor causing him to choke on his own laughter.

"Did you get any animals to pull our carriage?" Petra said.

"No, and I'm sure you saw that we don't have a carriage anymore," Heinrich said.

"The imperials left the square," Petra said. "We can go back for our carriage."

"Which is useless without something to pull it."

"I know that, Master, but," Petra said, looking at Traugott, who glowered at her through his continuing fit.

"Don't patronize me," Traugott wheezed out. "I won't make it like this. As much as I hate to say it, I was better off confined to my quarters."

"I'm sorry," Heinrich said. "We should have put more thought into this."

"You're giving up?" Petra said.

"How could any of us have predicted a procession of imperial church members would ride into town?" Traugott said, his coughing subsiding.

"You're both acting like this is a lost cause," Petra said.

"Because it is one, you daft girl," Traugott said. "Please,

forgive me. I appreciate how much you care, but I am too old and too weary to travel on foot. Confessors help me, I'm too old to even walk across a small village."

"No, we can get a carriage."

"Petra Ebner," Traugott said, placing his hands on her shoulders. "You impious wastrel, you have a good heart, but that alone cannot solve every problem. This old man sees a great deal of potential in you and would hate to see it wasted on his behalf. Live, travel, pester your mentor as you learn from him, and please, for the love of God, learn to love God."

"Now you're patronizing me," she said. "Are you really okay with this? They may kill you after what I did."

"You aren't responsible for what they do to me," Traugott said. "I chose to follow, and it showed me I no longer can. If the imperial bastards choose to kill me because I ran, or if they simply throw me in some dungeon to die for ignoring their edict of compliance, well, I am old, and death was just around the corner anyway."

"If you have any final words, a message for a loved one, or for the rest of the church," Heinrich said, "we can deliver it. It's the least we can offer after all you've done for us."

"For all I've put up with from you, you mean," Traugott said. "I've no more family that I know of, but if you run into any of my peers, herald, or minsters, recite to them the thirteenth chapter of the Book of Silence."

"You wouldn't rather us recite the verses about Clovis' martyrdom?" Petra said. "It would make your death sound far more interesting." Petra's suggestion prompted surprised stares from her companions. "What? My family was, is, very pious."

"We will deliver your message, Brother Traugott," Heinrich said. "I look forward to seeing you when my own time comes to ride with the Wild Hunt."

"Bah, pagan syncretism," Traugott said. "But know that the sentiment is appreciated. May your watch endure, dear sentinels, till the stars fall and the Harbinger returns."

"I hate to be the one to ruin a touching moment like this, but no one is getting martyred today, not in this town anyway," Wendel said as he walked out from the southern gate.

"You have some way of smuggling me out of town?" Traugott said.

"Aye. That inquisitor did a number on my head, but I managed to avoid giving him anything concrete, well, aside from the fact that we had three Jäger in town looking to make themselves scarce."

"For what it's worth, I punched one of the paladins in the throat, so I think they'd have figured it out on their own," Petra offered in consolation.

"You could have said something about that before," Heinrich said.

"The inquisitor said they were going to be here a while and that I shouldn't worry about any monsters for the foreseeable future. But the thing is, I fought with a resistance group a few years back and I don't care to be around when he comes asking harder questions," Wendel continued.

"I saw the paladins cast fire from their swords," Petra said. "You weren't lying about the imperials."

"Of course, I wasn't. I'll get a carriage prepped and ready to go to Aschfeld in the morning. You can take my bedroom for the night, Brother Traugott, and hide in the back when we leave."

"You'll need an airtight excuse," Heinrich said.

"I have one, thanks to you and, technically, the paladins," Wendel said. "With the bahkauv dead, I might finally be able to convince those louts at the brewery to start sending me fresh supply again."

"I like it," Heinrich said. "I'd have gone with the old, 'I need to go to my third cousin's funeral,' trick, but with an inquisitor around, I wouldn't get two words in before that benediction spun the truth out of me."

"You probably do have a third cousin somewhere," Petra said.

"A simple 'probably' doesn't cut it with these guys. Besides, it's the intent they sniff out," Heinrich said.

"Best of luck to both of you with whatever business you need to help Herr Erik with, but Traugott and I should hurry along," Wendel interrupted. "Will you be okay going back through the alleyways, Brother?"

"No, but I used to walk miles upon miles of dangerous road with nothing but a tiny true silver bell," said the priest. "I will manage now as I did then. Maybe a bit slower. Petra, Heinrich, goodbye."

With that, the priest and the barkeep returned to their village, entering the unguarded gate and slinking off between the houses. Wordlessly, master and apprentice made their own departure, leaving Laupen behind and trekking their way into the woods. They walked for little more than an hour when they saw the faint glow of a campfire and made their way toward its light.

They found Erik tending to the flame and two rabbits roasting on a makeshift spit. Heinrich whistled as they got close and Erik returned the call, hand falling from his holstered pistol.

"What happened?" Erik asked.

"Had to get Traugott away from the imperials," Heinrich replied. Erik gave a slight nod in understanding. They sat down around the fire, the savory scent of roasting meat mingling with the acridity of the smoke.

"So," Petra said, "what is it that you need our help with? I missed that conversation, remember?"

"Oh, right," Erik said, "I guess you did walk out that night. There are going to be peace talks in the town of Elem, between the Herzog zu Kranzdorf and the Markgraf zu Althafen. Or their representatives, at least. Our guild needs a representative at the table and the Großmeister in Vorbotenruhe doesn't think that your Jagdmeister here in the Vahsland can be trusted to deal with this."

"I don't know her very well," Petra said, "but I can understand why."

Petra didn't care too much about politics but they were unavoidable, even in the Jäger Guild. No, especially within the guild. The imperials' Edict of Compliance didn't just outlaw the Heraldic Church; it also outlawed the Jäger and the Freikorps. They were all criminals in the eyes of the empire and their supporters within the realm.

"It's a bit more complicated than what you're thinking," Heinrich said. "Do you remember the Jagdmeister's full name?"

"No... wait... no... oh," said Petra as she slowly remembered that Jagdmeister Rika was a von Reinherz.

"Indeed," said Erik. "The Prinzessin zu Reinschlau was disowned by her family when she refused to disband the Vahsland branch of the guild. Needless to say, if we let her pick a representative for us at the negotiations, she might damn well go herself and ruin things by antagonizing her extended family."

"Might?" Heinrich said with a laugh. "The she-wolf would march straight into Althafen and shoot the Markgraf herself if she thought she could get away with it."

"Which is why Uncle Bertram thought it best that I represent us," Erik said. "But I needed someone with more knowledge of the local happenings."

"You sure Master is the best choice for that?" Petra said.

"Hush," Heinrich said, smiling.

"Wait, did you just say that your uncle is the Großmeister?" Petra asked. "The head of the whole guild?"

"All that's left of it," Erik said.

"Cool. So, Elem," Petra said. "That's a little way south of where all the fighting is, right? Why not hold the talks closer to the front line?"

"Oh, sure," Heinrich said, "let's hold our negotiations within firing range of all the cannons."

"It would keep people honest," Petra retorted.

"It would keep them scared," Erik said.

"Yes, better if we're the only ones feeling scared, surrounded by people who want us in chains," Petra retorted.

"When did you get so diplomatically minded?" Heinrich said.

"About the time I saw a man who sheltered and fed us bound by his wrists in his own church," Petra said.

"Both sides will be bringing forces to Elem, and the Herzog zu Dorneswik has agreed to oversee the negotiations. No doubt he will be sending a force of his own not beholden to either side of the civil war," Erik said. "I do understand where you are coming from, though."

"So will three opposing armies surrounding Elem make you feel better, Petra?" asked Heinrich. He took his knife and cut a slice from one of the roasted rabbits, popping the morsel of meat into his mouth.

"Not like it matters one way or another," Petra said. "I'm stuck with you, and I know you already agreed."

"What, you don't want to follow Traugott's example and attempt to martyr yourself before the imperials?" Heinrich said.

"Wouldn't be my first choice of how I go," Petra said, slicing a chunk of the cooked meat for herself.

"We have several dead drops and safehouses hidden around. You can stay at one close to Elem while Erik and I try to see some of old Bertram's demands met."

"It is a very long list, is it not?" Erik asked. "I don't know what my uncle was thinking."

"He's thinking we need to be allowed back into the Herzland and Rosenhohen," Heinrich said, "and I can promise you that having to skulk around the southern Vahsland is more than a bit tedious. I bet the Dornwalder branch didn't even notice."

"Hard to say, they have always been... different in how they approach things," Erik said.

"Well, let's hope that von Schwarzdorn's way is different enough to slap some sense into everyone's heads, then."

Their conversation veered off into old stories, old hunts, things they'd talked about days before, and then some. Petra didn't pay any more attention to the two men at that moment than she had the first few times they'd delved into the past. The night dragged on, and Heinrich volunteered to take the first watch. Petra wrapped herself up in her cloak and lay beside the dying fire.

An old prayer hung quietly on her lips, one her mother liked to recite to her and her brothers back home. She wasn't sure if anyone up in the stars was listening, but it didn't matter; the memory was all the comfort she needed.

CHAPTER EIGHT

FAUST

There I beheld our great teacher and knew the terrible fate the pagans had prepared for him. I wished to stop it, but I was not a sentinel. What hope was there for a scribe against a horde of warriors made frenzied like lycans at the scent of blood? As they set honored Clovis aflame, as the timbers sparked and fire spread from his feet up to his head, he looked at me, but his eyes were not his alone. He did not scream. He smiled. He smiled at me, a silver halo gleaming in each eye. He smiled at the one too cowardly to save him. He forgave me, and I wept.

Uhtric the Pardoned, Confessions of Clovis 17:23-27

Faust was only slightly tired by the time morning came, having spent nearly two hours reading and rereading the letters he had found in Doktor Holland's room before going back to bed. He had expected to eat breakfast with Marcel's wife, Elizabeth, and their family, but when he asked about it, it seemed they had gone on an extended vacation sometime the year before. While he wanted to tie this news to his suspicions, the reality was that the Burggräfin was afraid the war in the Vahsland would spill over the border and put her and her children in danger.

That was hardly an unreasonable line of thinking, and in any event, her family in the Herzland would be far more well-supplied with the luxuries she had grown up with, which Naakt lacked. For his own part, Faust almost found himself preferring the near-spartan furnishings. Simple but comfortable was more than enough for him. Yet, as Faust walked the halls of the now-awake castle, he couldn't help but think that it would be some time yet before Marcel's dear Elizabeth came home.

The day had not made more guards visible inside the keep than he had seen patrolling it the night before. There were plenty of men and women patrolling the walls, but only a handful was tasked with maintaining internal security. It was tempting to say this was because he was assured of the quality of his forces on the outer walls, but Faust knew better than to fall for that tired idea. Naakt was missing more than half its garrison because the majority of Marcel's personal forces were busy trying to keep the werewolves pinned within the Larswald.

Faust wasn't sure about the exact numbers, but even if Marcel sent his entire force, the Larswald was simply too large a tract of woodland to fully encircle with the forces he had at his disposal, let alone with a mere half of them. It was a fool's errand to even try, which is how Faust and Johann's convoy was able to slip into the woods, to begin with. Tradition and good sense both made it clear that he should have sent for aid as soon as possible.

One of the few guards in the castle stood watch outside Johann's room, guarding the injured Markgraf against any potential threat. The guard let Faust in without a word. Johann's quarters were decorated in the same fashion as the room Marcel had loaned to him and every other guest who graced his halls. Faust's godfather was, however, afforded a wider, or perhaps deeper store of pillows, which he was all but buried within. His frown was deeper still than his body as one of Nina's compatriots tried to feed him his morning soup, spoonful by spoonful.

"My arms are more than capable of holding my own silverware," he grumbled, trying desperately not to simply snatch the spoon from the woman's hand. She let out a well-practiced giggle but continued to hold the full vessel in front of him until he leaned forward and accepted the bite.

"Faust, good, maybe you can save me from my caretaker," he said as he saw Faust enter the room.

"I can take care of him through breakfast," Faust said. The maid frowned as she let the spoon fall into the bowl and made egress from the room.

"Marvelous," Johann said as he took hold of the spoon and began shoveling the broth into his mouth. "I have been told that I need to stay off my leg for the time being, but Marcel has agreed to furnish us with another carriage. I plan for us to leave tomorrow at the earliest, but no later than the day after."

"What about replacements for our guards?"

"He has none to spare us, but I plan on writing letters to our peers across the border explaining our predicament. With any luck, they will spare us a few men for each leg of the journey, and we can gather their opinions along the way."

"Helping us dilute the bias you and Meinherd have against their position by exposing us to their hospitality and generosity," Faust elaborated, "is a fine arrangement if we may obtain it, but I worry about Marcel and his people."

"Marcel is a fine lord, and his people are tough," Johann said. "A shame what befell Halsmat, but what else could he have done?"

"Did Marcel ever make mention of these events to you before yesterday?"

"Would that he had, you would have been one of the first to hear about it, I assure you," Johann said.

"Yet you still trust him to handle the situation?"

"He is blood," Johann said, "so I trust his judgment."

"I see." Faust had expected this, but it still stung to be proven right. The von Tollkirsches were far too trusting of one another for Johann to even start to question why Marcel would keep the outbreak secret. Would revealing the contents of Dahl's letters to Doktor Holland change that? Probably not.

"I was surprised, though. I think he is a tad embarrassed, not that he would ever admit to it. Thick-headedness, I tell you." Johann continued. "I'm also sending word back home and to Pellt to send aid immediately."

"Good, good," Faust said, "I would hate to think we would leave this issue unattended, botched as its handling has been already."

"Don't insult my kin, Faust," Johann said, the light tone of his voice gone in an instant. "Marcel has done everything he could to solve this problem."

"Everything except ask for help," Faust retorted, just as coldly. He and Johann stared at each other for a minute in stilted silence, until finally, Faust walked back toward the door. As his hand lay on the cold metal doorknob he stopped, sighing, and said in a hushed tone, "Are we really so willfully blind?"

He left Johann to his throne of cushions, unsure of his next step. He had hoped to have more time to parse the truth of the outbreak from the front Marcel presented, but that no longer seemed possible. They would be leaving much too soon for him to do anything. Confronting Marcel now would only lead to a schism with Johann, as Faust had almost sown just moments before. Walking through the near-empty halls, he passed by the open door to the inner kitchen, where Nina was working to prepare for lunch.

Her father was a central figure in this tragedy, though he had little of the courage needed to give her opinion such grave import without more solid proof. Leaving before she could see him, Faust wandered through the castle, his mind running down the list of people he could share his suspicions with. Ingrid was in no position to do anything, though she would jump at the opportunity to free herself from the feeling of shame brought on by her ill-timed choice. Likewise, Meinherd, while perhaps pliable, was too embroiled in their political envoy to be useful.

That left only Yorick and Cecilia, the very people who Burggraf Marcel had hired to deal with the accursed kin that made the Larswald their home. He was loath to trust the master, but Faust would gladly swallow his revulsion of the man if it meant ending the threat. Sunbeams kissed his skin as he exited the keep onto the high walkway of the castle parapets, his face turning to scan the yard below. Yorick auf Arensfeld stood before a group of young men and women, all draped in plain clothes and armed with training weapons.

He drilled commands to them: hold, strike, hold, guard, hold, fire. Their responses to his calls were poorly timed and uncoordinated, and Faust could not help but feel thankful that none of them had actual firearms, lest they shoot the man in whom he would need to place his trust. What a tragedy that would be. Faust let out a short, dry laugh as he circled the wall to the stairs built into the stone nestled between the curtain wall and the side of the barracks.

Cecilia was sitting on the edge of the lower landing, perfectly still as she watched the drills.

"Do you plan to pounce on one of the recruits?" he asked. She didn't even jump.

"No, but I need practice just as much as they do," she said, smiling ever so slightly. "I heard your footsteps."

"I would hope so. You would have a hard time hunting monsters if you had issue hearing perfectly obvious footsteps on stone."

"I also saw you snooping about the castle last night."

"Ah." Faust took a moment to collect himself, fidgeting slightly where he stood. "Then I suppose this makes things easier, actually."

"I have no intention of telling Marcel that you had a tryst with one of his maids," she said. "I would half expect him to be more surprised if you..."

"I am not sleeping with Nina," Faust said.

"Then why did you both slip into his study?"

"The one coincidence in this entire castle, and that is what you picked up as suspicious?"

"Well," Cecilia said, "I suppose it is odd that the Burggraf would send for the Vahsland Guild to deal with this outbreak."

"My first question answered before I even asked it," Faust said. "Would it interest you to know that the von Tollkirsches' primary physician, Nina's father, went missing shortly before the outbreak began?"

"Physicians get caught up in outbreaks all the time," Cecilia said. "Diseases or curses. If they can help, they try, then they die, especially if the patients turn into virulent, bloodthirsty monsters."

"How about if said physician had been in contact with the head of the Erfinder Guild?"

"Alwin Dahl?"

"You know him?" Faust said.

"My brother works for him," Cecilia said. "Sebastian introduced me to him when Yorick and I had to go to their guild to sign off on a shipment of rifles."

"How well do you know him?"

"Well enough to know he unsettles me, but Sebastian trusts him. I assume you think he has something to do with this outbreak, along with the Burggraf's missing doctor?"

Faust knelt down, reached into the folds of his new vest, and pulled out the three letters he'd found in Doktor Holland's room. He held them out to Cecilia, who looked at them for a moment, somewhat confused, before taking them.

"The first two are rather mundane at first, mostly just medical jargon that I found nigh impossible to understand," Faust said. "I suppose that's the problem with only having half a conversation. But it explains why our good doctor was unwilling to discard or destroy them. The third, you will find, contains the key to this particular cipher."

Cecilia checked the dates on each of the first two letters, moving them to the back of the stack until the third was on the top. She opened it, eyes traveling back and forth across each sentence until she got to the bottom. "This cannot be right," she said. "I mean, I understand the purpose, but these methods... No, there must be a mistake."

"I agree," Faust said. "Having had the pleasure of Coen Holland's acquaintance, I find it hard to fathom that he would stomach such methodology. That said, I need to ask you another question."

"What?"

"Do you know how often we have outbreaks of lycanthropy in the Dornwald? Per year, per month, use whatever metric you think best."

"Five," she said.

"Per what, Cecilia?"

"Five per year"

"If only we were so lucky," Faust said. He paused, gaze drifting to his scarred arm. He undid the cuffs and rolled the sleeve up, holding his arm up to her so she could see the pale streaks of tissue. "We have around five outbreaks per season," Faust said, "an average of twenty outbreaks a year. Most are stamped out quickly since the Dornwald branch of your guild spends most of its time within our dukedom's eponymous forests, but sometimes they aren't."

"So that day in the woods was not your first time seeing them up close," Cecilia said.

"When I was nine, my family attended a banquet held by one of our vassals, alongside every noble not too sick to travel. I wandered out of the feast hall and then out of the castle and into the woods. I barely made it out with my life. Other people lack such luck as to have an entire castle up in arms when you go missing," Faust said. "When faced with that, is it any wonder why someone would compromise their own morals in a vain hope that he could help the man who found the cure for the Nachzehrer curse also find one for lycanthropy?"

"Sure, but how do I fit into this?" Cecilia said.

"Take these letters and keep them safe. If you trust your master, then let him see them, but if you think for a second that he would cover this up, then keep him in the dark. When the time comes to clear the werewolves from their den in the Larswald, look for any evidence that corroborates the letters and keep Marcel from getting his hands on it. Send whatever it is you find to my father in Dorneswik."

"Okay," she said.

"I can give you a letter with my signature and seal on it," Faust said.

"I can use my own," Cecilia said.

"Should have realized it sooner from the way you speak," Faust said. "My apologies, Prinzessin."

"None needed," she said. "I am a von Willensstark."

"Herzlander," Faust said. "I take it your parents sent you to the Vahsland to escape the fighting in the heart of the country?"

"Only for the fighting to follow us into the western lowlands," Cecilia said with a laugh. "I joined the Jäger Guild before that happened though. Mother was furious, but father understood."

"Did you want adventure, or are you a kindred spirit in worrying for the plight of the lower classes?"

"I joined because I wanted to prove I was just as capable as my older sister, but then I started seeing this in the same way you do." Cecilia pointed over her shoulder at her back and then down to her right leg. "I have had a few close calls of my own, and I know now just how dangerous it is to live without high walls to keep you safe."

"We are in a unique position to help people."

"I am sure Dahl sees himself in the same light," Cecilia said.

"No doubt, but if the path that takes us there is worse than the road we are already on, well, it is hard to imagine a road much worse than this one," Faust said.

"I trust Yorick," Cecilia said. "His attitude on the way here is a result of stress."

"Because Marcel hired two of you to do a job that needs ten, likely in order to cover up his involvement with whatever experiments Doktor Holland was performing."

"It will be better if I tell him now than for him to find out on his own," she said. "Otherwise, he will do something stupid."

"Thank you," Faust said.

"I should be thanking you. Without you, we would still be thinking we were risking our lives to placate the Burggraf's thrift. Well, Yorick still thinks that, for the time being."

"I am not entirely sure that this is better," Faust said.

"Maybe not," Cecilia said, "but it contextualizes things."

The rhythmic shouts from Yorick came to an end, and the trainees broke formation as they ambled back toward the barracks. Faust took that as his cue to leave, but as he started to rise, Cecilia grabbed his wrist.

"Be careful in the Vahsland."

"I will be far safer, I think, than you will," Faust said.

"I mean it," she said. "Monsters are predictable, people aren't."

"Do you know something worth sharing?"

"There has been a rumor around Kranzdorf that the leader of the Freikorps is planning something big," she said. "He and the Herzog zu Kranzdorf have had a tense relationship since the day they joined forces at the siege of Mastrok."

"Are there any rumors as to why the Herzog is even willing to come to the table?" Faust asked. "From what I was told, he has every reason to want the war to continue."

"His health is in decline," Cecilia said, pushing a lock of hair off her face. "No one is sure what is causing it or if he is even truly sick, but his nephew has been acting as his regent for weeks. Officially, at least."

"That would change things," Faust said, resting a hand

against his lips. This call for peace could be the decision of a more level-headed figurehead in Kranzdorf, or maybe it was simply a ploy to lure out the Herzog's enemies. Yet, even if this new regent was honestly pursuing an end to the conflict, they would still need to be wary of malfeasance on the Frei-korps' part. Did they have anyone they could trust going into this negotiation beside themselves? "Oh, thank you for the information."

"I hope it helps; you might just have the harder job, after all."

"Yes, I think I would rather be risking life and limb hunting down wolfmen than playing diplomat between a bunch of angry aristocrats and jaded militants."

"I do not envy you, just like I don't envy my sister Adelaide anymore. Being the firstborn seems quite nice until you start to think about all the responsibilities that come with inheriting a family title. I, at least, get to shoot the things that make me frustrated," Cecilia said, looking back at her mentor. "Most of them, anyway, which is far more than you get to."

"If only the rest of us were so lucky," Faust said.

CHAPTER NINE

CECILIA

And the archangel spoke to me of the only war, the one war, that had raged from the time before the dawning of the world when our creator forged mountains and dug the trenches of the sea. He told me of the dark tides that had swelled thrice now, by their reckoning, to swallow man and all the works of his hands. "We are the Harbinger," he spoke to me, "but fear ye not the message of our lips, for we stand with you from this day until the last day."

Alaric the Confessor, Second Harbingers 2:4-7

It had been a week and a half since Prinz Faust and the Markgraf zu Tholst had left with their priest and what remained of their guards in a plain carriage, adorned only with the standards of their families. It had been a few days more since Cecilia had informed Master Yorick about the letters Faust had given her that day on the stairs. He had taken it as well as could be expected, which is why she had waited to give them to him until they were out in the wilderness, far from the prying ears of any of the Burggraf's men.

But at that moment, with tempers moderated to a more manageable level, their group stood prepared to root out the accursed from their den and grant mercy to them all. Allied soldiers from the other von Tollkirsche houses had arrived over the past few days, and now they had a far better cordon around the Larswald. They had not been idle while they waited, of course; they had spent the intervening days continuing their procedures of baiting and slaying.

The task was slowed by the necessity of its sparing use to avoid creating a pattern that even the diminished minds of the accursed could recognize. Nachzehrer were far easier to fool, but if she were being honest with herself, Cecilia preferred hunting lycanthropes. It was easier to kill them without hesitation for any number of reasons. They were more bestial, if not more grotesque, acting and looking less like a sick person in pain and more like the monsters they really were.

Yorick had taken to organizing what the Burggraf zu Naakt had so kindly referred to as "the final offensive," choosing the most skilled and the least vainglorious to join them: three squads pushing in from as many directions, tightening the proverbial noose around the werewolves' den. It was tempting to simply march into the woods with their full force, drive them from their home, and crush them against the waiting wall of men on the other side, but such notions were idiotic. At best, it would lead to the depopulation of the natural predators and throw the ecosystem out of balance. The worst case would see these soldiers, most unprepared to fight unnatural predators in their own environment, fall or be turned until the armies of the three territories were depleted and the ranks of the accursed grew swollen with new packmates.

It was well after dawn when Yorick gave the signal and their small force entered the Larswald. Cecilia had become intimately familiar with the terrain since she and her master had first entered it, and she felt comfortable beneath its boughs. Gentle light streamed down through the canopy of leaves and branches swaying in the overhead wind that kissed her cheeks with the telling chill of fall. It tempted her to bring her scarf up over her face, but she knew that doing so might worry the soldiers with them. A Jäger with their face covered was one prepared and ready to fight the accursed, at least as they saw it.

Their march was slow and deliberate. Most of the werewolves would be sleeping peaceably in their den, which, if Faust was correct, would be a laboratory hidden deep within the forest. Putting that part aside, the undeniable fact remained that not every one of the creatures was asleep. There were always sentinels, and all it took was one to rouse the rest.

Despite all the grim implications it would carry, Cecilia hoped Faust would be proven right. If they had to fight what remained of the pack at once, it would be far easier to do so if they could enter and hold a building with few points of entry. Even better would be an underground lab, whose buried halls would funnel the beasts to a singular point where their enlarged forms would hinder them.

They still had no idea how many werewolves were in the heart of the Larswald, but they had killed dozens of the creatures already, and they could hardly risk waiting any longer. Even with all their precautions, the werewolves would eventually come to realize they were being hunted, that those gunshots cracking in the distance were not just random encounters but targeted assaults on their number. This would be their best chance to put an end to the threat.

They walked for hours, disguising their movements whenever Yorick got one of his weird feelings, then continuing toward the point the Burggraf had given them. Cecilia kept a firm grip on her pistol, letting her rifle hang across her back. If anything came at them, Yorick would be the first to realize it, long before they showed up. She needed to be able to free her hands to climb if he gave the signal.

She wasn't terrible in a fight, but she was admittedly weaker than some of the other apprentices. Dietmar was built like a lumberjack, and Petra, well, she was Petra. Both of them were a special type of crazy. Sure, Master Yorick would get up close when he needed to, but if he could end something from afar, he would do it in a heartbeat. But those two, it was like they needed to be up close to a monster, needed to feel the thing's breath on their necks, or its blood on their hands as they killed it. It was like they took pleasure in it.

Confessors help her, how she wished either of them were here, preferably with their own mentors. Anyone from the guild, really, from Kranzdorf or from wherever the Dornwald branch was from. Just anyone but soldiers dressed like purple minks armed with single-shot rifles. The soldiers were probably really good at standing atop walls and taking potshots at whatever got too close that wasn't supposed to. But shooting a werewolf in a nice open space was far from the same as shooting one weaving between trees.

Even someone like Faust, who had very likely been trained by a professional marksmanship instructor, had made the mistake of not considering the effects of the terrain on the flow of battle. Just like the day of the attack on Faust's caravan, it would be up to her to save the idiots on the ground from the discomfort of a sturdy tree branch.

Yorick held up a hand to stop them at one point, and within a few seconds, Cecilia was perched high atop one of the nearest trees with her rifle cradled in her arms. He wandered off after giving a silent command to stay put and came back a few minutes later, wiping his bayonet clean on his pants. She let out a soft groan, knowing what would come next. She dropped down from the tree, joined the front of the parade to approach the dead sentry, and rubbed her legs against the side of the dead werewolf.

The others looked between her and Yorick until he pointed at the dead monster. Slowly, they followed suit. Consuming curse-ridden blood or saliva would turn you, as would getting any in your eyes, up your nose, or in an open wound regardless of whether you had been bitten. Rubbing yourself against their dirty, matted fur, however, would not, but it would help disguise your scent beneath the particular musk of theirs.

Cecilia felt filthy, even through her clothes. She knew it would take her exactly three baths to wash the feeling of griminess out of her mind. And a fourth, special kind of bath if she ended up dripping with werewolf blood just to make sure she did not contract the curse by accident. They kept vials of holy water just for that purpose. From what Sebastian had told her, holy water neutralized the foul magic in the blood. For that reason, it was also the base for the medicine that could cure a person of the dormant strain of the Nachzehrer curse, which they also carried vials of in their traveling bags.

Now, though, she was almost hesitant to call it a cure at all. She had seen someone try to administer a dose to a person who had already turned, a task done with great difficulty and which yielded no result besides a broken nose to the man giving the dose. It couldn't do anything to save someone who was already a monster; it could only stop the affliction before it started to act upon the body. Werewolves, though, turned within hours, sometimes even minutes, and almost always without warning. The afflicted would show no symptoms one moment, then burst into violent, bone-breaking spasms the next.

The priests called it the Curse of Gluttony, an apt name because werewolves spread their curse through bites and would eat almost anything made of flesh. The guild always said they were the easiest breed of the accursed kin to root out because even if they were harder to kill than most, they were easier to track. One werewolf could start a pack by turning game hunters, woodsmen, and lovers looking for a romantic hideaway. If they had a male and a female, they could start procreating. Even still, no matter how fast they spread, they could never hide among unafflicted humans.

Vampires and Nachzehrer, on the other hand, could hide for years without anyone noticing. Luckily, vampires didn't make more vampires very often, and with Dahl's medicine, they stopped a lot of Nachzehrer outbreaks before they even started. But even a single scourged farmstead was one too many. They would end this outbreak, purge every last lycanthrope they could from the woods, and avenge the injustice done to the people of Halsmat and every other victim. Not that vengeance would be much of a comfort to the dead.

Finally, they neared what should have been the area Burggraf Marcel thought, or perhaps knew, was the home of the werewolves' den. They fanned out, approaching slowly. What most of their group expected was just a collection of holes in the ground, or maybe some nest-like lean-tos built over a fairly circular area, but that wasn't what they found. No, what they found was what Cecilia and Yorick had expected to find after reading the letters sent to the Burggraf's physician.

They stood on the edge of a fairly shallow dell, through which a thin creek flowed. The trees hung overhead, some at odd angles, reaching their limbs out as if to cover the low vale. A large hill on the opposite side of the dell overshadowed everything. Into it was carved the opening of what had once been a mineshaft. Or something that was, at the very least, meant to look like one.

Yorick ordered them to wait. Nearly half an hour later, one of the other squads finally came up from around one side of the hill behind them, slowly descending into the dip in the earth. Cecilia let her master go first, trailing behind as he followed the others down toward the creek. The third squad joined them shortly after, traveling alongside the stream. Yorick spoke softly to the other squad leaders, explaining the potential layout of the den and what dangers to keep watch for inside and out. Cecilia had already envisioned several possible iterations of passageways in her mind earlier in the day, but Yorick put the proof to his experience with a plan that far outstripped her own.

Their squad would enter the den while the other two stayed outside guarding the exit with one looking inward and the other watching their flank. Cecilia slid her rifle from her shoulder, laying the firearm on the slope; it was too long to use inside a tunnel. She pulled the slide of her pistol to chamber a round, sending out a short prayer for her twin brother to whatever angels might be listening. Most of the guild was either using older models, while a brave few were armed with unrefined development models. Cecilia's weapon was special, a custom build handcrafted for her by her ever-brilliant brother, Sebastian.

She and Yorick were the first inside. They entered the dark, damp hole with deliberate steps, letting their eyes adjust to the darkness before going deeper into the earth. The tunnel went on for a few paces before it began to slope downward. At the top of the slope, a minecart sat on rails flanked by a loading dock of wooden planks. They approached the drop and found a simple winch system set up to lower the cart down and a staircase running to one side of it.

Without warning, Yorick cut the rope that held the cart in place and kicked it toward the edge. Metal screeched as it rode the line and crashed against whatever stop was set for it, likely breaking it in the process. Cecilia let her arms fall slack at her sides, her shoulder slumping low as she looked up to the dirt ceiling. She resisted the urge to groan and took a deep breath before she went over to the edge and knelt down, pistol at the ready. The others did the same, their shorter carbines aimed down into the mine.

A tide of angry fur and flesh came at them from the hole, howling and snarling with hunger and rage. The beasts were met with the first volley of fire from ten guns, then a second, a third, and a fourth. The werewolves tried to climb up the slope over the bodies of their kindred. Those that succeeded were shot, tumbling backward and toppling more of their number. It was a bloodbath, a slaughter, even, and the beasts were too stupid to comprehend the irony of it.

Cecilia had unloaded four magazines of pistol ammunition into the slavering creatures at the base of the mine by the time they made enough headway to be worried. She only had two more magazines.

"Fall back! To the entrance of the mineshaft," Yorick ordered. The group was more than happy to acquiesce, turning back and running for the light of day outside. Cecilia turned to fire a shot at one of the first werewolves that made it far enough to clamber onto the wooden landing, her master doing the exact same.

Cecilia and Yorick fell in line behind the soldiers, ducking out of the way of the second squad. "They're coming!" Yorick yelled as Cecilia wrapped her fingers around her rifle. She started climbing the hill using her bayonet blade as a climbing pick. Gunshots rang out, though not as loudly as when they were in the tunnel, but that might have just been due to the ringing in her ears. She found a spot with good footing and anchored herself there as best she could, turning with her rifle to the battle unfolding below.

A pile of dead and injured werewolves was already beginning to form within the semi-circle of soldiers. The people who had gone down into the mine with Cecilia and Yorick had taken a place in front of the second team, their empty but bayoneted rifles held like pikes to brunt the charge of any beast that managed to make it to the line. Some of the third line had also joined the second, abandoning their posts to help stem the flow of lycanthropes.

That the beasts kept coming was simply absurd. Cecilia watched over the third line, who was oblivious to the two werewolves coming up behind its group. She fired two shots, claiming two pelts, so to speak, but those kills seemed to be the werewolves' only sentries.

The slaughter ended after only about seven minutes from what Cecilia could tell, but it had felt a good deal longer. So, too, had the number of werewolves seemed far greater than what it likely was.

She let herself slide down the hillside, joining her master as he stood beside the pile of corpses. "How many do you think were in there?" she asked.

"Well, we seem to have about thirteen here, maybe more inside," Yorick said as he kicked one of the corpses. "We'll need to burn them all. Who wants to volunteer to haul up the bodies from the mine?" None of the soldiers were so eager this time. "Didn't think so. Four of you need to go inform the cordon around the forest, the rest of you stay here while we go make sure all of the ones down in the pit are dead."

Cecilia sighed as she followed her master back into the mine. They masked up with scarves and goggles to protect themselves on the off chance there were any drippings. When they got to the landing they peered over the edge, and Yorick fired a shot down into the pile of furry corpses. Getting no response, he struck his flint and tinder to light a torch that had been left hanging on the wall, then used the torch to light a second one and handed it to Cecilia.

They slowly made their way down the stairs, watching carefully for any sign of movement. Cecilia held both torches while Yorick took her rifle and affixed her bayonet, using it to probe the dead werewolves closest to them at the bottom of the slope. Slowly, they made their way over the bodies and into the deepest recess of what no longer looked like any mine Cecilia had ever been in. It resembled a prison.

Dozens of rooms with busted-open wrought iron doors lined the walls leading to the end of the corridor. She stopped before reaching one of the doors, hearing the faint sound of whimpering, just barely, through her earplugs. There was only one thing that could mean, and she would let her master deal with it. She pressed on while he dealt mercy to the malformed things that looked half-toddler and half-jackal.

The door at the end of the hallway was wooden, or its splintered remains were, and she stepped through the jagged edges into what looked like a laboratory with smashed beakers and vials, a bloodstained operating table, and shreds of research notes strewn about the floor. Faust had said to look for any evidence she could collect, but from what she could see, there wasn't anything she could take with her that could corroborate the letters he had entrusted to her care.

She took a deep breath to calm herself and regretted it instantly; the stench of death and rot hung thick in the air. She gagged but managed not to puke. They would have to spend a few more days combing the woods for any signs of stragglers, but when that was done, they would go back to Kranzdorf to give the guild its share of their reward. Cecilia would also need to speak with her twin and somehow convince him to spy on the teacher he idolized. That twisted her stomach almost as much as the smell in the air around her.

As they left, Yorick threw both torches down into the darkness, the bodies catching slowly. They wouldn't burn completely, but with any luck, the fire would spread to the supports and collapse this monstrous place down on top of itself.

CHAPTER TEN

PETRA

*And when the dusts of war had settled over the dead, it was
the sons of Stenwarl who stood the victors. Around that ancient fortress they had carved high walls, and upon them stood
sentries armed with bows who slung death upon all who came
to break them. Thousands came and were ground against
those walls like grain against the millstone, and not even the
lord of Vaon, schooled in the old ways, stood a match for them.*
Odoacer the Timid, Third Antiquities 9:14-17

"This is all a load of horse..." Petra stopped as
Heinrich's hand all but slapped her in the face
when he swiftly raised the signal for them to
hold. She and Erik readied their rifles, listening for the faintest sound of whatever had spooked Heinrich. Underbrush
rustled, the boughs above swayed, and birds sang exactly as
they had for the entirety of history when things were normal.
Then a twig snapped, and so did Heinrich.

Before Petra could even blink, he was running, bayonet
freed in one hand, pistol in the other, charging forward toward

the sound. They followed as well as they could, but the dense ground cover made it difficult. "Son of a...!" a voice cut off, and as they approached, they found its source: a man in a patchwork uniform with frizzy black hair and Heinrich's blade at his throat.

"Let him go, Heinrich," Erik said. "He's with the Freikorps."

"I've been around enough of them to know that," Heinrich called back. "Just giving him a good scare." He removed his blade from the man's throat and wrapped his arm around the mercenary's shoulder, smiling at Petra and Erik.

"Like hell that's all it was," the man said, rubbing his throat and checking his fingers for blood. "I take it you guys are the ones Oberst Kalb is waiting for? Jäger Guild representatives, right?"

"We are," Erik said. "Though I was not informed which of Herr Falkenrath's people we would be meeting."

"Tilo Abeln," the man said with a quick salute. Tilo lowered his fist from his heart and continued. "I'm a Feldwebel with the Tenth Korps. The Oberst has had a lot of us out looking for spies, monsters, and you. Glad we can scratch that last one off the list."

Petra snorted a laugh.

"You that eager to shoot something?" Heinrich asked.

"Just a little jumpy out here, you all know how it is. Especially you, Herr..." Tilo trailed off inquisitively.

"Taube, but you can call me Heinrich. And yeah, the last few days have put me a bit on edge. Sorry about before."

"We can share stories on the way to camp," Erik interrupted. "How far out are we?"

"Not far from camp, at least, but it'll be a day's walk to the talks," Tilo responded.

"What's one more?" Petra said. She'd lost track of how

many days they had spent traveling from Laupen to there. Each day blended into the next between bouts of walking and their shifting watches at night. They'd spent four days on the road from Laupen to the next dead drop, where they restocked their rations and left some coin in compensation. Erik's purse, of course, because theirs were spent after the business with the bahkauv.

"We could have made better time, but we ran into some imperials," Erik told Tilo, who was now leading them off deeper into the woods.

"From the holy orders or the Auxilia?" Tilo asked. "We've caught a few enemy scouts from the Auxilia, but orders are to escort them back to their side of neutral ground."

"The former," Erik said. "A few paladins, one inquisitor, and a priest."

"Tried to save one of our priests from them, but it didn't go as planned," Heinrich said.

"Damn shame," Tilo said. "I met a herald once who'd been imprisoned at Wolfsstadt. Poor lady has some nasty scars."

"Is that why you joined the Freikorps?" Erik asked.

"Joined for the coin," Tilo said, scratching his nose. "Not that it matters at this point."

"You could quit," Petra said.

"I may have joined for the money, but I've stuck around for the cause."

"The cause of not letting the Viceroy and his lapdogs put you out of work," Petra said.

"Ah, the camaraderie of the Aushansa," Heinrich said, laughing. "I wonder if the imperials have realized that half this mess could have been avoided if they weren't such uptight pricks?"

"I hardly think they care, Heinrich," Erik said. "Will this Oberst Kalb be joining us at the talks?"

"Not that I know, better to ask him yourself," Tilo said. The conversation carried on in brief, meaningless trickles of questions and answers until they finally neared the camp. The trees and underbrush thinned out and gave way to open grass where a myriad of tents was set up behind an array of hastily made picket barriers.

"Home away from home," Tilo said as he led them through the camp where men and women in the same grey and blue uniforms as Tilo, some more well-kept than others, milled about.

Two men carried a crate in front of them; Petra followed them with her eyes and saw a line of cannons down the way they were going. The scout took them to one of the larger tents, which flew a blue and white flag from its central pole. Inside, a group of officers went over papers and maps.

"I don't think I like our odds," Petra said, leaning over to Heinrich. "They don't seem to be planning for peace."

"We're knee-deep in enemy territory," Heinrich said. "I'd be planning for a fight too."

"Thank you both for the ringing endorsement," Erik said.

"Welcome back, Feldwebel Abeln," said a gruff man with greying brown hair. "Are these our Jäger representatives?"

"Aye, Oberst," Tilo confirmed. "Nothing else to report, sir."

"Good work," Kalb said. "Now, report to the mess, and take the rest of the day off. I'll have someone else cover your sector."

"Thank you, sir." Tilo left through the tent flap.

"I expect you have a letter to confirm your identities, or do I have to put you in chains?" Kalb asked. Erik stepped forward, pulling a ring from his finger and handing it over to the officer. He then pulled out a letter and passed that to the man as well.

"I would appreciate if you could avoid breaking the seal on that," Erik said. "My uncle only sent me with one copy, and it might damage my case if you tamper with it."

"Noted," Kalb said. Petra watched with an eyebrow raised as the man broke the seal anyway, reading the letter and then returning it to its envelope. He gave it and the ring back to Erik. "Did my scout tell you how many spies we've had try to infiltrate our camp?"

"He made mention of a few," Heinrich said.

"More than a few," Kalb said. "I'd have them shot if not for the fact I am keenly aware their masters have us surrounded. Leutnant Horn, arrange for lodging for our guests, even if it's just a tarp over open sod. And find von Morgenkranz."

"Luxurious," Petra said. "Master, do we need to be here?" Heinrich looked to her, shrugged, and then turned away as the officer walked between them and out of the tent.

"The Burggraf zu Ritterbach will be glad to know you've arrived," Kalb said, his attention divided between Erik and his war map. He pointed between several red and blue flags. "These are all the enemy positions that we know of; most of ours, too. We've all agreed to keep to ourselves and play nice, at least until someone fires first. Which the imperials seem to be upholding."

"Do they know about this position here?" Erik pointed to a blue flag off of the main camp on the map.

"No, luckily, they don't," Kalb said.

"I find that hard to believe with all the spies around," Heinrich said. "Not that we met any on our way here."

"They're there, and honestly, I'd be concerned if there weren't any," Kalb said. "We may have let slip that we lost a patrol to werewolves in that area. The fools haven't even bothered checking."

"I take it your men cleared the area with no effort, then?" Erik said.

"We can handle a few strays."

Petra turned toward the tent's entrance as the sounds of some minor commotion edged closer and closer. A man burst in through the canvas flaps in an overly dramatic fashion that matched his bright yellow and white attire. She was a bit disappointed at his appearance, but she didn't know why. Maybe she had hoped that the lord of a castle would dress a bit more sensibly, but he was a von Morgenkranz, after all.

The blond-headed dandy hurried toward Erik, who met his eagerness with a look of confusion. The Burggraf took Erik's hands in his and said, "I am so pleased that you made it safely, Erik. How is your mother faring these days?"

"She has regained much of her strength," Erik said. "Alban, what are you wearing?"

"This?" Alban said, looking down at himself. "Dear cousin, this is the latest fashion, or at least, it will be in a few months."

"Please tell me you have something more somber to wear for the negotiations," Erik said.

"They're related?" Petra whispered in Heinrich's ear.

"Oh, Father will be the one dealing with all that mess," Alban said. "I came because he told me you would be here. You look terrible, by the way."

"My clothing is functional," Erik said.

"Your clothing is absolutely filthy," Alban retorted. He looked Erik over and clicked his tongue in disappointment. "I will have our staff prepare baths for you and your fellows."

"Prinz Alban, where is your father, the Burggraf?" Kalb asked.

"My son could hardly place his ass from his elbow on a picture of himself, let alone tell you where I am and am not," interjected the Burggraf zu Ritterbach as he entered the tent. He was more of what Petra had expected, in plain black clothes and a gambeson vest not unlike those worn by the soldiers in the camp. His face was more weathered than his son's, but they had the same taut jaw and warm brown eyes.

"Did I forget to mention that Erik is a prinz?" Heinrich said.

"Must have gotten lost somewhere in the woods," Petra said.

"Well, now you know."

"Father, spare me your barbed words," Alban said, rolling his eyes. "Erik, I can take your friends with me to our tent to wash up while you, Father, and the Oberst discuss your important matters."

"We're fine right here," Heinrich said.

"Speak for yourself," Petra said.

"Lovely," Alban said. "I'll take the young lady with me, maybe even find her something nice to wear. We have plenty of functional clothing to match that fierce face of yours. You will look majestic."

"No take-backs," Heinrich joked, pushing Petra toward the posh noble. "I'll let you know our part in this mess, my majestic apprentice." She opened her mouth to fire back a retort, but only let out a yelp as Alban grabbed her by the wrist and all but dragged her from the tent. He was stronger than she had anticipated, but if she really wanted to, she could have gotten free of him. She likely would escape once the wardrobes were brought out, but a bath sounded amazing.

"You don't get along well with your father, do you?" Petra asked.

"I get along well with everyone," Alban said. "Some people just have a hard time getting along with me. My father happens to be one of those people."

The prinz led her to a yellow and white tent deep within the camp but well away from the command tent and the bulk of the military preparations. Entering the tent, Petra picked up the scent of perfumes and liquor. Alban clapped and said, "Someone needs to prepare the bath; we have a guest in dire need of a good scrubbing! Our staff will take good care of you."

"Uh, thank you," Petra said.

"Think nothing of it. You are a friend of Erik's, after all."

"He's your cousin, right?"

"Third cousin," Alban said, taking her by the elbow and leading her into a side room of the massive tent where a wooden tub was being filled by a trio of maids. He stepped back behind the curtain-like door, closing it behind him, but staying close enough to talk through it. "I doubt you care much for the tangles which comprise our family trees in the nobility; truth be told, I know far too many of us who care far too much. That said, I think you know, at least, that Erik is from Lornern, yes?"

"Master Taube said he operated out of the guild in Lornern, but there are a lot of Jäger from the Herzland and the Rosenhohen who fled to our guild here, so I didn't assume," Petra said as she undressed. One maid took her coat and scarf, another took her boots and pants, and the last took her shirt and underwear. She stepped into the cool water, reaching out in hopes one of the women would hand her a brush, but instead, the nearest maid grabbed her wrist and began scrubbing her arm.

"I suppose that would make sense," Alban said. "His mother, Auntie Lisbeth, was born a von Morgenkranz, you see, and our grandfathers are first cousins."

"Okay, I thought you said some people cared way too much about all this stuff?"

"They do, which is why I am actually somewhat scared," Alban confessed.

"What do you think I can do about any of this?" Petra asked.

"You are one of his friends."

"Look, I appreciate the bath and the hospitality, but I barely know your cousin."

"Third cousin."

"Whatever," Petra said, yanking an arm free from the clutches of the overly zealous maids. "My master is friends with Erik, and I'm along for the ride. If you have a monster for me to shoot, then I'm your girl, but I don't want anything to do with all this nonsense."

"I imagined as much," Alban said, "though I suppose I already expected that I would have to make my impassioned speech to your mentor."

"You aren't going to win me over with that sad tone," Petra said.

"That was not my intention. You are right, my worries over my cousin's safety are none of your concern."

"Third cousin, remember?"

Alban's laughter filled the air like a wheezing pig's squeal.

Petra continued, "Between my master, you, and your father, I'm sure Erik will have all the information he needs to navigate this political manure patch and come out okay."

"I truly hope so," Alban said. "We have lost too many family members to these stupid wars, and Confessors know that we are not the only ones who have been left grieving. You have my apologies and my thanks."

"For what?"

"For listening to me go on about my problems when I have yet to even ask you your name," Alban said.

"Petra," she said.

"Well, Petra, how about I go and prepare a few outfits for you while you finish with your bath?"

"That sounds good," Petra said, "though please don't pick anything too showy. I'll never hear the end of it."

"I make no promises," Alban said, his voice ever so slightly more distant than before. The sound of trunks being opened and rummaged through came through the curtain interspersed with commentary from the prinz that made her more worried with each interjection.

CHAPTER ELEVEN

FAUST

We came to this land because a messenger from above called us to these hills and high vales, yet you would send us back from whence we came? Perish such thoughts, and spare us your words of empty kindness. Our home is gone; we have nothing to return to, and here is where we were promised refuge.
Vulferam the Blessed, First Habringers 3:7-9

The rest of their journey to Elem had so far been a quiet and peaceful one since leaving Naakt some weeks ago. Their few stops were full of banal pleasantries in small townships and villages where headmen or minor lords offered them supplies and sometimes a few soldiers to help escort them to the next settlement. The shadow that hung over Marcel's territory was gone, replaced by the longer, more ominous one cast by the civil war.

The nobility may have been well-versed in putting on airs to dissuade the lowborn populace that anything was amiss, but for all their efforts, they were failing spectacularly now. Faust had spoken to many of the men and women who helped escort them along each leg of the road from Naakt to Elem, and every one of them had a story to tell. Everyone either knew, or at least knew of, someone who had been close to the fighting.

How much of their reports were accurate in detail and how much were imaginings born from misremembrance and misinterpretation, he could hardly tell. One detail they all shared was that the war had gotten far more brutal after the intervention of the Freikorps. The scope changed with each telling, but Faust was able to piece together an idea of the situation that fit, if a bit unevenly, in the place of the truth.

The early days of the war had supposedly been more traditional: armies marched across the Vahsland and fought in open fields before retreating, a few sieges were set and broken, and only a few thousand had died across those first four months of fighting. Then the siege of Mastrok happened. It had been a fairly lengthy affair, with some rumors saying that the Herzog himself had nearly starved with his men inside the town. And then a single company of the mercenary guild broke the encirclement in a single decisive offensive action. Things had been escalating ever since that day. Many said the mercenaries had long since seized control of the war effort from the Herzog; what else would explain their supposed brutality on the battlefield?

Just as important was the tone with which these stories were told. The people were terrified, to be sure, and knowing that one of the Freikorps' companies was encamped just north of Elem made them even more so. They were deep in the lands loyal to the Markgraf zu Althafen, deeper than any of the fighting had reached so far. Yet many of their escorts, in spite of their fear and anger, saw the Herzog zu Kranzdorf as nothing more than a sad, senile old man driven mad by grief. They pitied him even as they cursed him for driving their home into war. Faust did not need to ask them to elaborate.

Until these conversations, Faust had viewed the war from the perspective of an outsider. All of the death and destruction was a tragedy that pulled at his sympathy and made him sick to his core, but it was a distant thing in which he held no personal investment. He knew he needed to be objective at the negotiating table; he had to hear the positions of all parties without granting excessive favor to either. The knowledge of what horrors would continue to befall the people of the Vahsland should the talks fail weighed heavy on him, but it also encouraged him to press on toward the goal.

Yet the shell of purpose he had mustered as a bulwark against his own doubts began to feel terribly small as they approached their ultimate destination. As they closed the distance of that final stretch of road, the walls of Elem loomed higher and higher over them like an angry giant. Looking up at the town's fortifications filled Faust with a surge of anxiety. Beneath him, his mount responded to the sudden stiffening of his muscles with a whinny. Faust tried to relax himself as he leaned forward just far enough to put a hand on the chestnut-colored horse's neck. The animal had been a gift given to him by the lord of a small town called Valte, and he was thankful for it for more reasons than he could count. The horse had a cheery and affable demeanor, more so than some people Faust had met, and riding it was an almost calming experience. It had also made speaking to their escorts far easier and provided him a means by which to keep his distance from his godfather.

The business in Naakt had left a sour taste in Faust's mouth as they rode off, and it came surging back up his throat each time he looked at Johann across the small, cramped carriage. It was, perhaps, petty of him to blame Johann for Marcel's actions, but the way he had shut down Faust's concerns so quickly made him almost as culpable. It would be weeks, if not months, before he would know if he was right about the outbreak in the Larswald. But if it turned out he was, well, he didn't like dwelling on the implications of that any more than he liked thinking of what failure at the talks would lead to.

As such, Faust had chosen the simplest solution, one that kept him busy so that his absence from the carriage was justified beyond doubt. Now, however, his position outside the carriage presented him with the steady reminder of just how little time he had before he would need to face the great political dragon. He almost wished it were a real dragon. Like Cecilia had so plainly stated; at least he'd have been able to shoot at it for what good it would do him in the end.

That dread came to a head as he saw the waving banners of the lord of Elem, its fields quartered with teal and grey and bearing a Freiherr's shield upon which a brown eagle perched on a wreath of wheat stalks. Faust had been informed of the taciturn nature of the Freiherr, but such a fact did little to assuage his unease; he may find an ally in this lesser von Arensfeld lord, or the man would prove an enemy with the resolve of a brick wall.

They reined in their horses as they approached a band of bannermen with two mounted figures between them.

"Greetings, my friends," the horsewoman said. "Which one among you speaks on behalf of the Herzog zu Dorneswik?"

"I speak with my father's authority," Faust said, trying to steady his breathing in the same way he would during shooting practice. The horseman's eyebrows raised as his lithe face twisted in a look of surprise. "My name is Faust von Schwarzdorn, Prinz zu Dorneswik, heir to the ducal seat of the Dornwald," Faust continued.

"Well met, my Prinz," the man said. "I am Norbert von Arensfeld, Freiherr of this once tranquil township. Forgive my astonishment, but we were expecting your father."

For his own part, Faust was surprised as well. From Norbert's thin frame hung a subdued teal suit that lacked the frills Faust had expected of a Vahsland lord.

"No need to proffer any apologies, your lordship," Faust said, cursing himself silently for the shakiness in his voice. "My father had a matter arise, which I am not at liberty to disclose, and sent me in his stead. I am accompanied by Johann von Tollkirsche, the Markgraf zu Tholst." He made a motion toward the carriage, which was bare of the heraldry their first was furnished with. "Our original carriage was lost in a lycanthrope attack, but I retain my letter of introduction should you require it."

"In due time," Norbert said. "We received word ahead of your troubles, you see, and I would be remiss if my first concern was not the wellbeing of you and the Markgraf. The other delegates have all arrived, but they will wait as long as you need to recover, I assure you."

"Most gracious of you," Faust said. "May I presume to ask what accommodations will be afforded our escorts?"

"My barracks shall be open to your men," Norbert said.

"I will make the necessary arrangements," the horsewoman said.

"Thank you, Rachel," Norbert said.

"Ingrid can provide assistance on that front," Faust said. "She is head of the Markgraf's personal guard."

"That won't be necessary," Rachel said.

"Good," Ingrid said, irritation buried ever so slightly beneath her voice. "I need to stay by his grace's side. After all, he is still recovering."

"If you both insist," Faust said. Both women responded with firm affirmations, in unison. Norbert snickered at the exchange before turning his horse. He and his guards led their caravan into the walls of Elem, the thick, cold stone giving way to vibrant colors. Houses and shops, some built atop one another, lined the streets. Stalls were set up beneath the shade of overhanging second and third floors. A crowd had gathered, undoubtedly having seen their lord leave and eager to see what he returned with.

Apparently, Faust did not disappoint. The people of Elem gave him a hero's welcome, which he felt far from deserving of. Maybe when the talks were over, if he managed to get the two sides to come to some compromise, he might think such adoration fitting. He could hardly tell if the pomp was merely the way of the often-eccentric Vahslanders or if this was some manufactured event, the work of the Freiherr to ease his people's worries. Faust smiled and waved; his cheeks tinged with heat all the while. He had never received such a warm welcome on any of the rare occasions when his father allowed him to return home to Dorneswik.

"I think I would have preferred staying in the carriage for this," he said to Ingrid, whose short laugh told him he would have to get used to this sort of thing. That she was right did nothing but deepen the blush on his pale cheeks. Thankfully, the unexpected parade did not last too long, as the castle lay only a small distance from the southernmost gate through which they had entered Elem.

Elem's castle was unlike that of Tholst and Naakt, built

neither upon a hill nor at distance from the township proper. Its walls were slightly taller than those that ringed the town, though shorter than the highest peaks of the rooftops in the surrounding boroughs. To compensate for the danger, the buildings nearest the castle had been kept to a single story and placed some distance from the walls, though there were tell-tale signs of previous construction closer to the fortress.

Norbert silently led them from the outer gate to the inner one, dismounting his black mare and handing off the reins to a waiting attendant. Faust followed suit, leaving his weary steed in the care of Norbert's stable hands. He stretched his tired muscles and walked across the sparsely grassed field to his latest host.

"Call on Brother Basilius," Norbert said to one of his many courtiers, a man dressed in an outlandishly vibrant shade of green. "The Markgraf is injured and will need to be attended to."

"Your lordship," Faust said with a small bow.

"My Prinz, I will have a report of our current situation sent to your quarters," Norbert said.

"Thank you," Faust said. "I was just about to ask."

"It might also profit you to know that the other delegates are not here."

"Forgive me, but I thought you said they had already arrived?"

"Oh," Norbert said, scratching his chin. "A miscommunication, then. They are at Elem, but not within my walls." Faust nodded his understanding. "Mayhap you should climb to the top of the keep after nightfall. The view is... daunting."

With that, the Freiherr took his leave. Another of his courtiers, a woman wearing a red dress that matched her fiery hair, led him into the keep through winding corridors and into the guest wing.

The décor reminded Faust of Tholst, though thankfully he did not have a placard of his family's heraldry to deal with here. The colors were warm and inviting, deep and earthy. They were Dornwald colors. Meant to make him feel comfortable, no doubt, or to make his father feel comfortable. What rooms Johann and Meinherd would be given was anyone's guess, probably something garish and with knitted doilies. He took off his dark brown riding coat and hung it in the armoire. A knock came at the door, and he crossed the room to open it.

Meinherd entered, hastily slinking to the small table and its two matching chairs that sat beneath the room's window.

"What can I help you with?" Faust said to him from across the room.

"You can provide me sanctuary," Meinherd said as he massaged his temples. "They sent an imperial priest to attend his grace. Ingrid is furious."

"Are you not?"

"Oh, I am, but I prefer to stay away from the hauptmann's teeth-gnashing," Meinherd said. He took one of the crystalline cups from the table and poured himself some water from the matching jug. "I would go treat with the nationalists, but I feel that doing so might endanger you."

"Endanger us," Faust said. "Whatever position you may hold on the subject at hand, you are here as my advisor. So, advise me."

"I don't know who will represent the opposition... the collaborators, if you would prefer," Meinherd said.

"Call them what you will, save for 'traitor.' I would hate to accidentally call them such at the negotiating table," Faust said.

"That would be suitably horrible," Meinherd said with a clipped laugh. "But I have no doubt that both sides will fling around that vicious accusation with more fury than any soldier on the front."

"How do we deal with it?"

"How do you think?"

"Remind them both of the immensity of the tragedy, remind them that we are all countrymen," Faust said.

"Naïve, but your youth may just let such an argument slide," the priest said.

"What would you suggest, then?" Faust said.

"Remind them that if they don't make nice, this war will escalate," Meinherd said. "Lornern is one step away from rebellion itself and more unified in that cause than the Vahsland. If they continue, then they risk the widowed Herzogin zu Vortbotenruhe coming to her father's aid, and the Herzlander lords still loyal to the late royal family will soon follow behind, emboldened to pursue their resistance more openly. Ohrnen will do as it always has and join whichever side it feels most threatened by, which will be the nationalists if Lornern mobilizes for war."

"Which would split the realm in two overnight," Faust said. Faust knew it would be even more brutal if the whole north rose up in rebellion against the Viceroy with no real guarantee that their cause would succeed. Perhaps that was what kept the other nationalist-leaning lords from intervening thus far. "I want your honest opinion. Who do you think is winning?"

"The nationalists," Meinherd said bluntly. "When the war started, the Herzog made several blunders that nearly cost him the war, that much anyone will admit. But then the Freikorps intervened, and they have ground this conflict to a standstill. As far as I know, the Viceroy has yet to commit any of his legions to the war effort, so for now, the stalemate remains."

"Wait," Faust said, "could that be the reason for these talks?"

"Do you think that the Viceroy has tipped his hand?" Meinherd said.

"Would it not explain the sudden change in policy in Kranzdorf? You said that the mercenary companies had drawn the war to a standstill, but if an imperial legion were to take the field, they may not be able to sustain the current status quo of the war." The two men sat in silent thought. Faust half expected Meinherd to drift off to sleep, but he remained alert and furrow-browed.

Night fell not long after their conversation died. As he looked out the window, Faust remembered what Norbert had told him.

"We need to go to the roof of the keep," he said plainly, walking out of the room and asking the teal-garbed guard to lead them there. Meinherd followed, getting several wary looks from the lightly armed woman. She took them to the roof and left them alone atop her master's castle, slack-jawed and worried. To the north were hundreds of lights from the Freikorps' camp. They had expected as much, but they hadn't expected the similar number of lights to the east and west. Elem was surrounded on three sides by armies, two of which would gladly kill the third if given the chance. That the talks would be a battle of sorts had been obvious, but this, this was absurd.

"Well," Meinherd said, "I take it back, you don't need to remind them of how this can escalate."

"Yes, I-I think they are all well aware of that fact without me stating it," Faust said.

CHAPTER TWELVE

PETRA

The blessings of hard work are in more than the fruits of the harvest alone. Just as your fruits taste that much sweeter having grown them of your own hands, so too do rest and leisure more please the soul when they are rewards to yourself for a long day's labor. Rest well and work well, my friends. This is how we shall raise up a nation from this fallow soil.
Gerlind the Confessor, Ruminations 2:1-5

The entire tenth company was abuzz like a hive of riled bees, rushing around their camp, nearly trampling Petra any time she decided to take a walk. She found it somewhat annoying, but since they otherwise left her alone, she tried to let the near-collisions slide. Heinrich had avoided the problem of the crowded camp altogether by volunteering himself to the cause of the army's game hunters. She knew him well enough to know he was also doing it to keep them from overhunting.

Nature, though, often did a fair enough job of maintaining itself without her master's intervention. What nature couldn't manage was the sheer personality of Alban von Morgenkranz. The man's natural state was to be overbearing like a needy mother who fulfilled herself by dressing up her children. Petra had never worn such nice clothes before now, and the softness of her new plain black pants and white shirt almost made her feel vulnerable.

If more nobles were like Alban, there would be fewer wars and far more frilly clothiers' shops, and honestly, she wasn't sure which would be more terrifying. As she approached the von Morgenkranz's tent, the sounds of an argument brought out another fear: if Alban was in charge of the country, he might damn well start a war over a diplomat's poor fashion sense. He may seem benign and friendly now, but maybe that was only because she was Erik's guest.

"I am not wearing that to the negotiating table!" she heard Erik say through the canvas.

"And what will you wear?" Alban replied, his voice sharp like a scolding mother. "That ragged coat is in no condition to be seen by higher society, and neither, might I add, is any piece of your traveling gear."

"That thing looks like the sky sneezed on it," Erik said. Petra had made her way into Alban's section of the tent as the two kinsmen argued, and found them standing at odds across a table draped in a bright blue coatee with white accents across the chest, shoulders, and cuffs.

"It is periwinkle," Alban insisted.

"If I wear it, I will look like a peacock," Erik said, his eyes glancing over to where Petra stood. She gave him a small wave, only realizing then that she'd been staring at his bare chest. His eye twitched, but as if spotting an opportunity, he grabbed the coat and held it up to her, saying, "What do you think?"

"Petra, hello, dear," Alban said. "Please tell Erik he's over-reacting."

"Could you two please keep me out of this?" she pleaded. Erik's eye twitched again, and Alban pouted. She sighed, looking away as she said, "I think something in green would suit him better, Prinz Alban. The banner of the Jäger Guild is green, and..."

"And?" Alban said, his tone making it clear he saw the faint blush rising to her cheeks.

"And it would complement his eyes," she blurted out. Alban squealed and she didn't know why she had expected any other reaction from him. "Is it getting warm in here?"

"I certainly hope not," Alban said. "You seem to have an admirer, Erik."

"It's not like that," Petra said.

"Quit torturing the poor girl, Alban," Erik said, clearly glad to no longer be the focus of Alban's attention.

"You have a type," Alban said to Petra. "Almost everyone does. Tell me, is it older men, or is it the muscles?"

"The muscles, okay, Confessors help me," she said. "Can't you go back to pestering him about what shirt to wear? Please, Erik, put on a shirt."

"No, this is much more interesting," Alban said. He grabbed a plain white shirt and threw it to Erik before stepping in front of Petra to block her view. "Erik is off-limits and much too old for you."

"Please, shut up," Petra begged.

"Do you have anyone back in Kranzdorf, or maybe back home where you came from?" Alban said.

"I would rather walk unarmed into a werewolf's den than answer," Petra said.

"I second that," Erik said. "Alban, must you pry into everyone's love lives?"

"Only the pretty ones," Alban said. "You really would rather be butchered than talk about this, dear?"

"Absolutely," she said. Alban grabbed her shoulders and hung his head low, taking a deep breath.

"Fine, fine," he conceded. "My apologies, I seem to have gotten carried away. Just give me one name!"

"Alban! Would you care to explain to me why it was that I could hear your vapid squawking from halfway across the camp?" Alban's father pushed open the thin divider and stepped into the room. The prinz shrunk back, his pale skin a shade closer to death than before.

"My apologies, Father."

"Spare me. Why is this peasant still sharing space with us?"

"This peasant has a name," Petra said.

"We went over this before," Erik said. "She and her master are my guests."

"Her master makes himself useful. What do you offer us, girl?" the Burggraf said.

"What do you have to offer to me?" Petra replied. She caught a glimpse of Alban looking on aghast, jaw hung low, while Erik buried his face in one hand. "I kill monsters for coin, what do you do, besides sitting in your gilded tent blowing hot air out your ears as you order people like me to die on your behalf?"

"Get out of my tent," he ordered in reply, his face cold and stony.

"Treat your son better, you cock," she said as she walked out, making sure to come as close as possible to bumping into him without actually doing it. Neither Alban nor Erik tried to come after her, but it was better that way. She needed to cool her head, and it would be easier to do that the more distance she put between herself and the problem. Heaving the stress from her body with a long, deep breath, she wound her way around the camp, hoping it would cool her head before she said anything else that might lead to her losing it.

Why was she even here? Sure, Heinrich had brought her along to the camp, but she could have gone with him out into the woods. She could have used the practice when it came to tracking, but she had stayed here, playing dress-up with a pair of princes. Alban's father had a point. She knew he was right, and it shouldn't have hurt her so much to hear it said.

Before she realized it, she found that she had walked to the edge of the camp. A few sentries lined the fence at intervals in either direction, watching the distant walls of Elem across the open plain. She stared at the walls too, not out of any sort of expectation, but just to look at something. They were something. Nothing good or bad, really, they just existed. They were different from the spiked logs surrounding Laupen.

Petra punched herself in the face without any hesitation, leaving a throbbing pain in her teeth. The nearest soldiers turned toward her, confused, worried, it didn't matter. She felt like she was on stable footing again. "What are you looking at?" she said, head swiveling between the sentries on her left and right. They murmured something before turning away; the one on the right even puffed out his cheeks as he blew air from his pursed lips.

She kept staring off toward Elem, her thoughts easing out bad memories until she caught a glimpse of movement. The figure was indistinct, but whoever it was, they were on foot. Petra almost punched herself again as the figure got closer, their indistinct silhouette the product of a heraldic priest's robes. What stopped her was the reaction from the camp sentries. They saw the person too.

The priest began ringing his herald's bell as he got closer, the soothing toll his plea of peaceful intentions. Luckily for the mutton-chopped man, his message was received, and the guards let him come to the edge of the camp unmolested. "Name and purpose?" one of them asked.

"Brother Meinherd," said the priest, scratching his bare chin. "I represent the Prinz zu Dorneswik."

"Don't know him," said the first guard.

"You idiot, weren't you paying any attention to Franziska yesterday?" said the second guard.

"I never listen to Franziska," he replied.

"You're an ass," the second said. "We're sorry about this, Brother. Aren't we, Gert?"

"I make no apologies," Gert said.

"I take it that this Franziska turned you down, Herr Gert?" Meinherd said with a dry laugh.

"She did not," Gert said.

"Did so," the second guard said.

"Shut your mouth, Gil," Gert said. Now it was Petra's turn to laugh. Gert and Gil.

"I don't want any lip from you, girl," Gert said, "not after we watched you slug yourself in the jaw."

"And who might you be?" Meinherd asked, turning his full attention to Petra.

"Petra Ebner, apprentice Jäger," she said.

"Is your master the representative for your guild?"

"No, Brother, but we did come with him."

"Can you lead me to where he is?" Meinherd said.

"I'd rather not. At least, not right now," Petra said.

"And you likely won't tell me the story as to why you won't lead me to him, will you?" Meinherd said, rubbing the bare stretch of chin between his whiskers and rolling his eyes. He turned to one of the guards, Petra couldn't remember which one was Gert and which one was Gil and wasn't sure he could either. "Can one of you gentlemen tell me where I can find any of the representatives?"

"Look for the bigger tents," replied the guard who Petra presumed was Gert.

"You're an ass," said Gil, definitely Gil.

"You don't know where they are either," Gert retorted.

"I don't care who knows, just point me toward someone who does," Meinherd said. Both Gert and Gil immediately turned and pointed at Petra. The priest let out a long sigh. "The champions of a free Gaerschland; Confessors help us all."

"Fine," Petra said.

"What was that?" Meinherd said.

"I'll take you to Erik, at least where I last saw him. He should be in the von Morgenkranz tent still," Petra said. She turned and started walking. Going back to that tent was the last thing she wanted to do, but standing there listening to Gil and Gert and the priest go back and forth ranked a fairly close second. "The Burggraf is kind of an ass," she said. The little tingle of the herald's bell looped to his belt told her he was following close behind. "Erik is nice, though a little distant at times."

"I'll keep that in mind," Meinherd said. As they made their way through the camp, Petra had to stop once to wait on Meinherd as a trio of soldiers carrying crates of munitions separated them across what passed for a street.

"Is it always this busy here?" Meinherd asked.

"We've only been here a few days, but from what I've seen, yeah." Petra ducked down to avoid a swinging gun barrel as some idiot thrust it up to check the sights. "Half of it is probably just to give them all something to do besides wait," she continued. "Keeps their minds occupied."

"Moving crates usually does work better than punching yourself in that regard, I've found."

"Well, I'd rather not haul boxes of bullets from one end of the camp to the other and back every day," she said. The rest of the walk toward the Morgenkranz tent was silent, aside from the jingling of Meinherd's bell and the general clamor of everyone else. After a few minutes, Petra stopped, pointing to the large, multi-sectioned tent, and said, "That one."

"I don't imagine they'll be particularly inclined to see me if I just waltz in."

"Trust me, the Burggraf might be less inclined if I walk in with you."

"Did you have an 'I spilled something on his nice rug' sort of disagreement, or the 'I'm lucky to still have my head after that' flavor?" asked the priest. Petra replied with a simple gesture, dragging her thumb across her throat. "Those are always fun," he said.

"You have an odd idea of fun, Brother Meinherd."

"This coming from a girl who thought it would be a marvelous idea to hunt monsters for a living," he replied. "You'd be in good company with Prinz Faust."

"I really doubt it," she said.

"I do too, speaking realistically. I don't know you well enough to make such judgments," he said. "All I need is a brief introduction; you'll be done in a flash."

"A herald needing someone to herald their arrival? That's a first."

"I'm starting to see why the Burggraf might not like you."

"Whatever, let's get this over with." They entered the giant tent. The Burggraf zu Ritterbach was taking a light meal of fruit at the table in the middle of the room. He looked up, cold hate on his face until he glanced at Meinherd. "I present to your lordship the heraldic priest, Brother Meinherd, helper for the prinz, Faust von something."

"Faust von Schwarzdorn. The Prinz zu Dorneswik, your lordship," Meinherd said.

"Yeah, that," Petra said. "I'm leaving now."

"Stay," the Burggraf said as if she were a dog. She opened her mouth to respond, but held her tongue as Meinherd stepped between her and the nobleman.

"As was so inelegantly said, I have come to speak with your lordship and your fellow representatives to obtain a list of your demands for my Prinz," Meinherd said.

"You will have them," the Burggraf said before biting into a pear. "To which side does your Prinz lean?"

"Prinz Faust errs on the side of peace, as unhelpful as that may sound to you. I have made sure he understands our cause as best I can, but he has insisted on remaining objective."

"Typical. I expect nothing else from the Dornwald. Tell me, priest, were you at Wolfsstadt during the revolt?"

"I was, your lordship," Meinherd said.

"Rodolf," the Burggraf corrected. "Come sit. You too, girl. I have met many heralds who faced the imperial brand. How long were you imprisoned?" he asked Meinherd. Meinherd took a seat, signaling for Petra to sit in a chair further from the Burggraf with a tap as he walked around the table. Reluctantly, Petra walked over and sat down, feeling out of place.

"I have the illustrious honor of being one of the first dragged off in chains," the priest answered dryly. "I was there when the capital fell, and I stayed when the dust and ash had settled. I made no attempt to hide from the inquisitors."

"How I would prefer it if you were the church's diplomat

instead of Brother Falvard," Rodolf said. He downed an entire glass of wine in long draft. "He is a good man, but naïve, like your prinz, I imagine."

"I know of him," Meinherd said. The herald drummed his fingers on the table, and his lips tightened in thought. "Many spoke well of him when last I was in Vorbotenruhe, but I have never met the man myself."

"He speaks well, but not much else," Rodolf said. Petra hadn't met this priest, likely because she didn't make a habit of sitting in on little talks like these.

"Girl, no, Petra," he said, pausing to roll her name through his mind. "You have fire for a tongue. I respect that more than any long diatribe of fanciful words. Eloquence without substance, that's how you see us all." The noble raised his cup to take another sip of wine, grunting in frustration as he remembered a moment too late that he had already emptied it. "As one warrior to another, I begrudgingly admit that you are not entirely wrong."

"Is that supposed to be an apology?" she said.

"Let neither of us kid the other," Burggraf Rodolf said, "I am here because I have been ordered to be here. Your circumstances are similar, as are yours if I were to guess, Brother Meinherd."

"More so, having seen the lights of three war camps from atop Elem's keep," Meinherd said.

"Our enemies and their masters have brought two armies to bear against our one company," Rodolf said. "I promise you, however, that we will not be threatened into submission. Tell that to our negotiator, and that he should prepare a route of escape for when those traitorous dogs show their colors."

"An optimistic person would have used the word 'if' in place of 'when,'" said Meinherd, "but I agree that 'when' is more apt."

"It has never been a question of 'if' they would," Rodolf said, pouring and downing another glass of wine. "Their table is full of traitors to their liege lord, to their country, and to their faith. Rest assured, they will not hesitate to betray the Dornwald's trust too."

"Of that, I have no illusions, your lordship," Meinherd said.

"I told you to call me Rodolf." The Burggraf slurred the last part of his own name. "As for you, Petra. My idiot son has taken a liking to you."

"Do you have to call him an idiot?" she said.

"Yes, because he is one. He came out here on the fool notion he might bring out even the faintest spark of the boy Erik was in the past and now he refuses to leave, even as the noose tightens around our collective neck."

"If you are really so concerned about his wellbeing, then just tell him that," Petra said, but the brief hint of emotion that flashed across his face told her he already had. "Where are Alban and Erik?"

"Hell if I know," Rodolf said. "They left sometime after you did."

"Lovely," Meinherd complained, "more walking."

"Walking is half of your job, Brother Meinherd," Rodolf said. "So, I suggest you get to it."

"I'll go with you," Petra said. She expected the priest to point out how much she had fought against him earlier when he'd asked the very same thing of her, but he didn't. His eyes, she saw, were fixated on the Burggraf, who was pouring his third glass of wine. They left him there to drink himself into a stupor.

CHAPTER THIRTEEN

FAUST

On the second day, the maker plucked metal from the heavens and forged the great dragons in the flames of stars, that they might have dominion over the skies. On the third day, the maker dredged bedrock from the ocean depths and sculpted the mighty leviathans to hold dominion amongst the seas. Finally, on the fourth day, the maker made man from the dust of the land, and to us, he gave dominion of the continents and all that dwelled therein.
Alodia Storm-Mother, Book of Dawning 1:11-13

Faust woke slowly and comfortably in the large bed he had been afforded in Elem's castle. He lay still, watching the sunlight pry its way through the edges of his curtains. The sheets were, in a word, divine. For this moment, he could almost forget the terrors that surrounded him, that surrounded Elem. Three armies were ready to kill each other at a moment's notice, and whether that notice would come rested almost solely on his shoulders.

Deep down, he knew that notion was false; however, his heart cared little for that fact. It was his job to keep the two sides from killing each other. It was his job to lead them to some form of compromise that would keep the rest of their factions from surging one way or the other across the dukedom, leaving naught but a trail of ruin in their wake.

Monsters were far simpler. A monster wasn't human; it wasn't a person with hopes and aspirations. Killing an overgrown, misshapen beast was simply survival. And when that beast was a mutant, cursed and twisted, trapped within a cage of madness, well, death was a mercy. But death would offer no such mercy here.

With great hesitation, Faust got out of bed, exchanging his evening wear with something more formal. His host had arranged for new wardrobes to be prepared for his guests, though Meinherd had refused outright. His closet would be forever filled with identical matching robes. Throwing aside that thought, and the singular moment of levity that came with it, he pulled an earthy green waistcoat over his black shirt, securing his cuffs with brass bracelets made to look like briar wreaths.

He pulled the curtains aside, sat down at his table, and read over the short letters that Meinherd had procured from the nationalist camp. Their demands were not so far off from what he had expected. The traitors should put down their arms or use them to join in expelling the imperial menace. The heraldic church clergymen and all guild Jäger should have protection when traveling through collaborator lands. Reparations should be made to the families of the soldiers who died fighting in the armies of the nobility and the Freikorps.

The list was as unreasonable as it was short, though perhaps "unreasonable" wasn't the most precise word for all of their demands. The heraldic clergy was afforded some protection in the Dornwald, Meinherd's position in Johann's court was proof enough of that, and Lornern all but ignored the Viceroy's edicts with impunity. As it was, the occupational government relied almost entirely on noble collaborators to enforce its laws, so it was up to each lord whether inquisitors from the imperial church could hunt down and arrest heraldics. The same, of course, could be said in regard to the Jäger.

That left demands one and three as the main points of contention in Faust's mind. He sat there for a moment, gazing out the window at the town below. He chided himself. For the imperial collaborators, any of these concessions would risk putting them at odds with the very same agents who they let romp around their lands. Granting free passage to the Jäger would anger the imperial paladins. Doing so for a herald would mean upsetting the inquisitors and the imperial clergymen who had happily replaced their Gaersche counterparts.

Faust tossed the pages to the table one by one until only the Burggraf zu Ritterbach's warning stared up at him in full. The tension permeated everything. He'd seen the armies encamped in the distance some nights ago. He knew exactly how they felt. Johann still had yet to return from the von Reinherz camp, but there was no doubt he would receive a similar message from them. We will not be threatened? Well, the other side had the same thought, so they also decided to bring hundreds of soldiers armed to the teeth to prove it, and now look where they were.

He gazed longingly toward the bed as he got up and made his way to the door. Norbert had opened the castle to him with few restrictions, and Faust had no intent on violating the fragile trust between them. A gentle rapping against the door startled him, and he composed himself before opening it for one of the castle manservants. Faust still did not know the man's name, owing in no small part to the fact that Faust had only heard the man speak when he extended his master's invitations.

Those invitations had themselves been quite rare, owing perhaps to the Freiherr's reputed aversion to small talk. Though it behooved Faust to think anyone would be capable of cheerful discussions over breakfast when the stress of their situation was souring his mood and ruining his appetite. Faust politely accepted Norbert's invitation and followed the well-trimmed butler to a small dining room attached to the Freiherr's personal apartment. Norbert sat at the table, a napkin tucked into the collar of his shirt and a frown creasing his face.

"Your lordship," Faust said as he crossed the room and sat across from Norbert. With a gesture of his hand, Norbert signaled for their breakfast to be brought out. The elder manservant and a younger apprentice brought out an assortment of fruits and pastries. Faust hesitated, neither particularly hungry nor desiring to eat before his host, which Norbert didn't notice. He had the subtle start of bags beneath his eyes, and he stared off blankly at the wall just above Faust's head.

Finally, the lord of Elem began to eat, sampling the grapes and nothing else. Faust begrudgingly took a small, flaky bread roll for himself, watching the Freiherr and his concerned butler. He raised an eyebrow, then sighed, his face returning to neutrality. "My lord," Faust said, finally breaking the silence. Norbert jolted a bit as if he had been half asleep, and Faust continued. "I presumed you desired to speak with me?"

"Yes, of course, I-," Norbert stammered. "Pray, forgive me, Prinz Faust. I was finalizing some paperwork until late into the night."

"For my part, I believe I will be ready within the next day or so," Faust said. "I should be prepared to officiate the talks as soon as the Markgraf zu Tholst returns with the talking points of the Reinherz camp."

"I could have furnished you with the talking points of both camps," Norbert said. He took a small cake and bit off a minuscule portion.

"Now, I must ask you for forgiveness," Faust said.

"Yes, well, I do suppose it is understandable," Norbert said. He let out a stifled sigh, rubbing a hand down his face. "I had tried to foster a neutral ground for these talks, but my attempts have been a resounding failure."

"Not necessarily. No one has shot anyone yet," Faust said.

"Yet," Norbert replied.

"And that armistice shall continue if I have any say over it," Faust said.

"Confessors," Norbert said. "I truly hope you can. Each day seems to prove more and more that this was a terrible idea."

"Confessors?" Faust leaned back in his chair, meeting Norbert's cross look with curiosity.

"Yes, I swear by the Confessors still. Sometimes, by the imperial saints when I have to deal with one of the Viceroy's men."

"I was just intrigued, your lordship," Faust said.

"Intrigue is a fair word for it, I admit. I have walked a very fine line these last few years, as my mother did before me. Not that my miserable efforts match her skill at court," Norbert said.

"Confessors, you are depressing," Faust said. Norbert jolted awake all over again, his eyes wide. Faust likely shared the look, his words bewildering himself too. But even more surprising was the little bit of relief he felt in his heart. "I feel like I am drowning. My father is the one who should be here, but he is not, and I am, so what am I to do? If I run away, I stain myself forever, brand myself a coward before the whole of our nation.

"But staying means risking an escalation. One wrong word, and the sparks of war will spread and light the rest of our tinder pile of a country aflame. I know how you feel, and I know you feel it more keenly than I do. You have offered the lives of everyone in Elem as hostages in the hope that your goodwill would bring your opposition to the table," Faust said.

"And now both sides see fit to spit on my goodwill," Norbert said.

"What of it?" Faust said, "You did not call for this armistice, but you have made it possible. If you want to blame anyone, then blame me. I arrived later than expected, and now I insist on relying on my own subordinates to canvas the field on the off chance you would try and mislead me."

"I do find it offensive that you would expect treachery from me," Norbert said.

"As is your right, just as it is mine to expect intrigue and deceit."

"How can you be so calm about this? You are barely more than a child."

"That is, well, it is a simple thing, really," Faust said. He rubbed his scars through his shirt sleeve. "Though I find it hard to put into words."

"A warrior's clarity in battle," the manservant offered. "Begging your pardon, sirs."

"Nothing so heroic as that, I imagine," Faust said. He felt heat rise to his cheeks and he looked down, seeking escape in a plate of scones.

"When you are ready to begin the talks, Prinz Faust, you need only say the word," Norbert said, "but I want you to know that none of my fears are abated."

"It would be foolish if they were," Faust said as he recomposed himself. "I should return to my preparations. Try and get some rest in the meantime, your lordship." He got up and took his leave of Norbert's company, hoping beyond hope that Johann had arrived in the interim. His stomach rumbled with dissatisfaction, but he had more important things to deal with. Though he did not doubt the sincerity of the Freiherr's words and worries, he still felt it best to proceed with him held at arm's length.

Would that he could keep them all at arm's length. Faust stopped where he stood in the middle of a narrow corridor half-lit by candles. He slumped against the cold stone, pushing off of it before sitting down to avoid damaging his clothes. The chill nipped his back, but he appreciated the discomfort. What did he really know about any of this? He had certainly spoken with the eloquence and grace expected of a ducal prince, but where did the script end and his own thoughts begin?

He felt his stomach churl and fought to keep his meager breakfast. Who was he to speak to Norbert of cowardice and courage? Why did he think to lecture a man working himself ragged for the sake of peace, not just for his own holdings, but for his dukedom as if he were the coward? Faust the brave warrior, never shirking in the face of beast and man; so brave that he offered no comfort to a girl mourning her lost father.

Faust shook where he sat, but not from the cold of the stones at his back. Minutes passed in silence marred only by ragged breaths. The waves of emotion ebbed low at some point, then the shaking stopped. His breathing steadied and he stood up on uneven legs and offered a short prayer to the angels in thanks that no one had seen him like that. Confessors, he needed a book to read, or a target to shoot. The Freiherr would likely suffer a stroke or some other episode were he to take to the silent range.

He wandered the halls for an hour before returning to his chambers. Walking was hardly productive, and it did little for his nerves, but it would have to suffice in lieu of more preferable pastimes. He greeted the guards and staff along the way, and aside from returning the gesture, they kept to themselves. It was almost unsettling, but nothing compared to the emptiness that had fallen over Naakt. Nearing the guest wing, he caught a glimpse of Johann, cane flashing as he limped into his quarters.

Faust strode down the hall, stopping for a beat in front of his own door before continuing to that of the Markgraf. He knocked once before entering. Johann met his appearance with a raised eyebrow and silence.

"When did you return?" Faust asked.

"Not too long ago," Johann said. "I knocked. Was your nose buried in a book?"

"I had a meeting with the Freiherr this morning," Faust said.

"Ah, then my timing was only just off," Johann said as he sat down. His room was nearly identical to the one Faust was staying in, but its layout was reversed, and it was decorated in teals, whites, and greys. Johann propped his bad leg up onto the other chair, then, realizing Faust had no place to sit, went to remove it from the seat.

"I can stand," Faust said. "How fared your business?"

"Poorly and painfully. I feel like a fool hobbling around like this."

"I was sure it would win you sympathy."

"Hardly. I had to refuse seeing their healers more than a dozen times."

"Most people would call that sympathy," Faust said.

"Sympathy does not usually entail a meeting with an inquisitor," Johann said, leaning back in his chair. "They always talk about how marvelous their miracles are, but Norbert's priest barely did a thing for my leg."

"Hobbling about, as you put it, is far better than not walking at all," Faust said.

"They want complete surrender from the Herzog zu Kranzdorf," Johann said. "They also want free passage for all their church members and for the guilds of the Aushansa to be disbanded. Also, the Graf zu Cemich wanted me to tell you that we..."

"Need to have a plan for a swift escape for when the nationalists turn on us," Faust finished.

"They told you the same thing?"

"The Burggraf zu Ritterbach, apparently," Faust said.

"Was he drunk?"

"Meinherd said he was," said Faust.

"If Meinherd thought he was drunk, then he must have been terribly drunk," Johann said. "Can I assume that the list of demands was one-for-one as well?"

"Close enough to make me wonder why any of us even came here, to begin with."

"Further war does seem inevitable. You may need to leave before these sham talks even begin."

"No," Faust said. "As little hope as I have for what I can do here, I think that at the very least, my presence might keep Elem safe."

"They can take Elem without killing you," Johann said

bluntly. "Whoever holds you hostage could also blackmail your father into fighting on their behalf."

"And if they kill me, they risk his enmity," Faust said.

"Are you certain you want to do this?" Johann asked.

"No, but what other choice do we have?"

"Well, there is certainly running away," Meinherd said as he came into the room.

CHAPTER FOURTEEN

PETRA

Long have we feared that which lurks within the darkness. But I tell you, though the eventide falls and all is dark, it is for but a time like the blink of an eye to our maker and his holy hosts. For every age of eventide, a new dawn has come by his providence. Fear not the dark for it is fleeting. Fear not that which lurks within, for it shrinks before the eternal light. If your heart is set to fear, take arms of truest silver and set your sentinels to watch.

Alaric the Confessor, Sentinels 2:1-6

When it seemed that he had finally sobered up, the Burggraf zu Ritterbach offered Petra the closest thing to a real apology she expected the man could stomach. Said apology had apparently been preceded by several hours emptying his stomach and several more sleeping the night before, according to Alban. Now he was bright-eyed and ready on the backwoods trail, a rifle in hand and a blade strapped to his hip. Joining him on this hunt was Petra's version of an almost apology. The two had an unspoken understanding:

they had both made asses of themselves, but they had both said things that were entirely correct.

So they walked side by side on a recently revitalized forest trail, cut clean by the camp's foragers and game trackers. Alban had elected not to join them, preferring the isolated bubble of civilization he had created for himself in the camp. His avoidance of their company also kept him away from his father's barbed tongue. Their only companions were a few of Rodolf's guards. Their traditional dress uniforms were replaced with more muted travel clothes, though with the rich tailoring of the outfits it would hardly have made a difference if they had worn their golden-hued sashes and armbands.

Around them, trees rose high into the sky, their leaves turning dull shades of yellow and orange in the autumn chill. Birdsong and the subtle sounds of the forest mingled with their footsteps. The distant sounds of the Tenth's camp were clear at their back, and all their worries were left behind. For today, they were simply hunting.

Petra secretly hoped they would find something big, some monster to kill that could give a face to her feelings. Heinrich had told her a word for that once, and she tried to remember it as she scanned the forest floor for any sign of wildlife. The Burggraf, on the other hand, wanted a boar or a buck crowned with high, jagged antlers. Putting a bullet into either wouldn't bring her any sense of catharsis. *Catharsis.* That was it.

She toyed with the word for a moment before letting it slip away. There were more important things to remember right now, first among them was the dried pile of dung on the side of the trail. This was always the part Petra had trouble with. Her master could glance at a turd and tell you what creature shit it out, when it did so, and what it ate the night before. Give him two pieces of feces, and he could tell what direction its owner was walking based on which one was fresher.

Heinrich was sort of like the traveling palm readers they sometimes came across in towns, though his readings were actually accurate, and the shit was a lot more literal. Petra was almost glad to be devoid of that talent, but for the evident usefulness it had in doing her job. She knelt down to examine it, but her mind came back blank. Still, she diverted off the trail and pressed deeper into the forest.

If anyone doubted her decision, they didn't think strongly enough about it to say so. It certainly worked for her. About half an hour later, she found tracks, which she could, in fact, read. It was the only thing she could comfortably say she could do while on the trail. The Burggraf would have his boar, it would seem. Wordlessly, she followed the pattern of depressions in the soil, kneeling occasionally to clear fallen leaves from the animal's worn prints.

The path led them deeper still into the thickest part of the forest, the dark of its boughs broken by the nip of the autumn foliage. Dead leaves crunched beneath their boots, a surefire way of alerting any prey to their presence.

Petra had a friend back in the guild who lived for this sort of hunt. She would just climb a tree and wait, for hours even, until a target presented itself. Cecilia's method wouldn't do much good right now, though. Even if Petra had wanted to try it, the noble and his men hadn't followed her all the way out there to sit in a tree and twiddle their thumbs until some animal or another wandered by.

Petra knew their type because, in a way, her views on hunting weren't so dissimilar. The struggle before the kill was what made it satisfying. Game hunting didn't carry the same feelings as hunting monsters. Sure, she couldn't eat a werewolf like she could a deer, but a deer couldn't eat her like a werewolf could. There was no moment of triumph, no catharsis in watching the life fade from the eyes of a helpless animal, no rush to hit her blood as in a hunt turned to a dance of claws, teeth, lead, and true silver.

Men and women in the upper crust like Rodolf, and those who clung to their coattails, wanted to dominate nature and feel powerful. Their noble blood afforded them food in any castle, or at least it had before the war. They didn't need to forage for their own food, but they still wanted hunts like these. Petra didn't question it. It was as it was and had been, and likely what it would be for a long time regardless of her thoughts on the subject.

She kept her head down, eyes on the hog's tracks, and tried to avoid getting pulled into all the commotion that most people made their lives around. The trail ended abruptly in another carpet of brown and orange. Petra cleared the leaves ahead but found nary a hint of the hog's trotters in the dirt. A tingle went up her spine. It was a normal thing that happened, but its significance was about when and even more about what.

Careful not to act out of the ordinary, Petra checked the rest of the leaves around the final prints. Dried blood stained some of the bottom layers, not even a day old by her reckoning. She took a deep breath as she cleared that final layer, finding a very different set of prints. "Oberst Kalb is a damned good liar," she muttered to herself.

"What was that?" Rodolf said.

"I said that Kalb lied to us, and we need to head back immediately."

"But we haven't found the boar," one of the guards protested. "Which way do the tracks lead?" Petra pointed in a direction almost perfectly askew from their previous course. "So we go that way then?"

"Only if you want to join your precious boar in a were-wolf's stomach," she said.

"What did Kalb lie to you about?"

"He said his men had the werewolves under control," she said. A low growl came from the thickest rise of bushes some paces away, and Petra slowly rose to her feet. For a moment, her knuckles went white as she gripped her rifle, but she forced herself to loosen up. This was no big deal; one were-wolf bereft of its pack was hardly a threat. Then a branch snapped from the opposite direction. Two werewolves wouldn't be a problem either.

Petra let out an annoyed moan as the third werewolf made itself known behind their group, her shoulders drop-ping as she let her head fall back. In an instant, she leveled her rifle and, turning quickly, put a shot into the brush. Her ears rang painfully, but it didn't matter. The accursed beasts weren't going to give her the opportunity to put in earplugs, though that did mean she couldn't tell if she had hit her mark or not.

Pulling up her scarf to cover her mouth, she fell to a knee and fired a second shot into the bush she was sure the first one was in. It wasn't. The mangy thing came running on all fours from the brush to the left and she adjusted, firing again. It had barely hit the ground before she swung her rifle to the second. One of Rodolf's guards had his bayonet stuck into its left hand; its right had skewered the man's side. The Burg-graf put a bullet through its head, the back of which blew open like a splattered fruit.

The rest of Rodolf's men had made quick work of the third, but Petra still kept her rifle ready. She was done speculating how many of the bastards were in the woods; all that mattered was getting out. She watched as Rodolf examined their one casualty and administered mercy to the man. He had five holes in his side, short and jagged, woven between his ribs. If Rodolf gave him last rites, she didn't hear it over the ringing. He got up and cleaned the blood from his sword, so she signaled the retreat.

As much as she wanted to stay and deal with the mongrels, she knew doing so would be a bad idea. At best, she'd be wasting her time, and at worst, she'd be out there alone as the Burggraf's men spirited him to safety. She and Heinrich could always come back out there and finish the job later, and by ensuring that Rodolf made it out alive, they might even be able to leverage a nice fee out of him for it.

Pushing her way to the front of the group, she kept an eye on the hog tracks. She didn't trust any of Rodolf's men to not get them all lost in a panic. They were about halfway back to the first print she'd found when something hit her full force from her left, carrying her off into the trees and trampling her underfoot. She rolled in the leaves and brush, gasping for air as she settled on her back. Each breath that followed sent waves of pain radiating through her chest.

It was bad, probably tied for the worst pain she'd ever experienced. She was still alive though. With a wince, she pushed herself upright and flexed her arms and legs to see if there were any broken bones. Satisfied, she hobbled to her feet, looking for her rifle as she stumbled a few steps forward. Her head was swimming like she'd drunk too strong an ale, but the feeling was half as pleasant.

The creature that hit her was big and gone for the moment. Whatever it was, she was going to kill it. She retrieved her scarf from a bush and dusted it off before wrapping it

tightly around her face again. A dull and repetitive thudding presaged the thing's return. Petra turned almost in a full circle looking for her gun and found its stock sticking out from a pile of leaves. She ran for it, ducking low to grab the weapon and spinning around to face the coming creature. The werewolf was larger than the others, but it was too small to be an alpha. It would be dead soon.

Taking a deep, painful breath, Petra shouldered the rifle and squeezed the trigger. Nothing happened. Her eyes went wide as she realized the gun was jammed. Sebastian was going to kill her if she survived this. She sidestepped the lupine fiend at the last moment, hitting the beast across its shoulder with her rifle as a cudgel. Sebastian was definitely going to kill her. The blow had no immediate effect. The creature slowed to a halt and turned around to face her.

It rose up on its hind legs, angry huffs escaping its dank maw. Petra stared it down, pulling her bayonet from its sheath on her torso. She flicked the blade and sent a flash of light into the fiend's eyes through a reflection. A mad snarl masked the sound of leaves crunching beneath her boots as she rushed forward and jammed the blade deep into its side, twisting it between two ribs before yanking it out and twirling away.

She danced between its swipes, ducking down as it went for her head and parting its skin with swift strokes of true silver. Another flash of fur and claws barely missed her side, tearing into her coat as she flung herself back. Her foot slipped from under her as she put her weight down wrong, the leaves beneath her sliding forward and sending her backward. The werewolf gained the advantage and towered over her, putting a pawed foot down upon her chest.

The pressure of its foot pushing against her ribs forced

the air from her lungs, and she stabbed it in the ankle. Petra rolled out from under it as it lifted its leg to grip its wounded joint and fell to its side in a briar patch. She stood up, stalking over to the wounded beast. It had rolled onto its belly, trying to untangle itself from the thorny bush, and Petra kicked it in its bleeding ankle. With a single stroke, she plunged her blade into the lycanthrope's back and turned it to sever its spine. She unholstered her pistol and pointed it at the back of the thing's head. Standing up, she turned her head and pulled the trigger.

It took her an hour to find her way back to the trail, and another two to limp back to the clearing. Rodolf and his men were nowhere to be seen, not that she blamed them for leaving her. She was looking forward to seeing the looks on their faces when she showed back up, though. Trudging into camp, she caught a few sidelong looks and not much else. She managed to make it a few paces more before she tipped forward and collapsed onto the ground.

That, at least, got people's attention. An older man in a well-tended uniform rushed over and knelt down to check on her. His shadow over her seemed a tad darker than it should have been, and his words sounded like distant mumbling. Someone else helped him roll her over, and she saw four blurry faces and a blue sky beyond them right before blacking out.

CHAPTER FIFTEEN

ERIK

Then a great multitude flocked to me, calling out with trembling voices, "Tell us, tell us what the angels spoke." And unto them did I speak of those many things. Of all that was told to me I confessed, but the multitude was afeared and many fled from my presence. Yet did there remain a small number, and they made of this hallowed place a home. They chose two of their number, Wulfrid and Sighild, a man and woman bound by marriage, to be their leaders. I anointed them, dripping oils upon their heads and binding their arms with silver bands.
Alaric the Confessor, Second Harbingers 2:15-19

Erik was lost in thought as he walked along one of the worn dirt paths of the war camp until a soldier barreled into him. His whole body swiveled to the left and reached out to grab the man's wrist. "Careful now," he said, waiting until the soldier steadied himself before letting go. "Are you okay?"

"I'm fine," the soldier said, "but the Oberst just put out a search order for the Burggraf zu Ritterbach."

"Explain."

"The little Jäger girl led the Burggraf and some of his men out on a hunt this morning," the soldier said.

"Not that part, I know that part," Erik said. "Where are they now?"

"The girl came back just a bit ago, alone and beat to hell and back. She's still out cold in the infirmary and no one knows where the Burggraf is right now."

"We need to go then," Erik said, sprinting off toward the woods. The soldier was right behind him the entire way, at least until they neared the camp's border. Erik heard his footsteps veer to the right and he slowed to a stop to look after him. He was heading for a tent, and it took Erik a moment to realize neither of them was armed. Hissing out a curse beneath his breath, he doubled back the way he came.

He entered the Morgenkranz tent with enough force to shake the poles and riggings, and he heard Alban squeak in shock from behind the thin cloth divider barring his space. Ignoring that, Erik hurried to gather his hunting gear. He strapped on his pistol holster and bayonet sheath, checking both weapons to make sure their bindings were secured. A quick and practiced motion confirmed his rifle was also in good condition. All that was left was his proper scarf.

He unwound the pale blue cloth Alban had dressed him in from around his neck, folding it as neatly as he could before replacing it with the ragged, mottled green one allotted to him by the guild. Alban might complain about his sense of fashion, but he would doubly complain if he got dirt and monster gore all over his imported Alzorani silks. Turning to leave, he found his third cousin standing in the middle of the exit. He was dressed in black and white garb lined with golden lacework.

"Alban, I need to go," Erik said.

"Petra is injured," Alban said.

"And your father is missing. I intend to go aid the search."

"Father can take care of himself, and he has his guards besides," Alban said. "I know I cannot stop you, but please come with me to see her."

"Do I look like a physician to you?" Erik said.

"You have that look in your eyes again, Erik," Alban said. He brought it up damn near every time they met, though Erik had no inkling of what he meant. "What can you do that all of Kalb's men cannot?"

"What can I do for Petra by crowding her bedside? At least out there, I can do something."

"And how, pray tell, do you intend to find father's trail? You had scant thought of that, had you? As I see it, Petra is the only one who knows whereabout they had wandered off to this morning. Kalb's scouts have mapped these woods incessantly since they arrived, Erik, fearing as is their wont that our enemies will slash at our outstretched hand. If they cannot find him by the time Petra regains consciousness, then she will have answers that will help lead him home."

"I'm afraid we don't have time for that," Heinrich said as he stepped through the tent flap behind Alban. He laid a hand on Alban's shoulder and said, "Word just arrived from Elem castle. The young prinz has called for both parties to assemble."

"We can hardly go along with that while Father is missing," said Alban. "Can't Kalb ask for a postponement?"

"I second that," Erik said. "The Prinz zu Dorneswik has already delayed these talks for several days; we have right to request a delay of our own."

"Preaching to the converted here, friend," Heinrich

agreed, "but the Oberst has it in his fool head to carry on like nothing's happened."

"One damned thing after another," Erik said.

"I suppose that means I am to take father's place then?" Alban asked.

"Unless you have any closer kin than Erik here," Heinrich said. "Hey, at least you'll be in good company with our mediator."

"Heinrich, keep us apprised of Petra's condition," Erik said.

"She'll pull through in no time," Heinrich said.

"Does this happen often?" Alban said, his voice wavering.

"Specifics aside? Yes. I don't know what the hell happened out there today, but this isn't the first time she's come out barely breathing. Won't be the last either," Heinrich said. "Harbinger help us all."

"Alban, we need to go," Erik said. "Thanks, Heinrich."

"All right," Alban said, taking his leave of the tent. Erik followed close behind, but Heinrich caught him by the shoulder as he tried to pass him.

"Don't blame yourself for this," Heinrich said, letting him go. Erik knew he meant well, but it didn't matter. Neither of them would be out here if he hadn't gone out of his way to track them down and ask. They would still be risking life and limb, but for their own sakes, not for his, or his family of fools. Rodolf would be here drinking himself to death, and there wouldn't have been any argument for Erik to try and fix by suggesting a damned hunt.

He caught up to Alban easily, not that it was much of a contest to begin with. They walked in silence through the near-empty camp, only a few guards left to patrol for spies. A full retinue, however, remained stationed around Kalb's tent, and a woman armed with a short carbine led them inside. A stone tankard pelted the inside wall of the tent, splattering its contents on the fabric and the floor on impact.

"Calm yourself, Oberst," said Brother Falvard. "Diplomacy is not an enemy to be surrounded and outmarched."

"Like hell," Kalb said, turning to the young priest. Falvard didn't flinch, nor did he sigh, he simply stood his ground like a stone against a breeze. His amber eyes flicked over to the two new arrivals, and Kalb's own gaze soon followed.

"We are here as requested," Alban said.

"Well met, Prinz Alban," Falvard said. "I pray your father returns to us unharmed."

"Were that he would do so now," Kalb said.

"Why did you not ask for another day, Oberst?" Erik said.

"We can't risk any more delays," Kalb said, rubbing his hand down his face. "If the Burggraf is dead, then delaying avails us nothing. Prinz Alban will sit in his father's stead one way or another."

"You said 'if,' yet you act as if my father is already dead," Alban said.

"No, I simply believe his death is the most likely situation."

"What the Oberst has yet to mention is that he harbors suspicions that the lord Burggraf has been captured by imperial spies," Falvard said. "So, in either case, we cannot afford to delay the talks another day."

"Captured?" Alban said.

"I thought you had a tight lid on the spy situation?" Erik asked, meeting the Oberst's glare with one of his own.

"We capture them and escort them back to their side of the line, but if we can't find Burggraf Rodolf, then we can't be certain what happened to him, and I won't write off the possibility," Kalb said.

"Fine, fine," Erik said. "We are talking in circles now. When do we leave?"

"Within the hour. I've sent for two wagons and some supplies," Kalb said.

"Rations to prevent a possible poisoning," Falvard said with a smirk.

"Two wagons?" Erik said.

"We're taking half my guard with us," Kalb said.

"Rest assured that the collaborators will do the same," Falvard said, "under the guise of representatives from the imperial church."

"I will ask Heinrich to come with us as well," Erik said.

"What about Petra?" Alban asked. "You would have us leave her here amongst strangers?"

"Of course not, Alban. We have two wagons; we can bring her with us."

"Absolutely not!" Kalb said. "I won't allow it."

"I do not recall ever having joined your army, Oberst Kalb, remind me if I have," Erik retorted. "What? No harsh rebuke? Nothing? I thought so. Alban, go look for your father's notes. And prepare the new formal wear we worked out for me."

"Right," Alban said, quickly leaving the Oberst's tent.

"Brother Falvard, may I have a word in private?" Erik asked, watching as the priest stepped around the table, his robed figure flowing toward the exit. A step behind him, Erik came out of the tent and walked with him until they were out of earshot from Kalb's men. Falvard was a bit too clean for a herald, even more so for one who traveled halfway across a dukedom with an army clothed in barely more than rags. His curly hair and youthful, freckled face contrasted with an expression of near serenity that unnerved Erik every time he looked at him.

"What did you wish to discuss, Prinz Erik?"

"I want your honest opinion," he said.

"I always give it."

"Do you think we have any chance of pulling this off?"

Falvard appeared to think the question over, his hands raising up to his waist. He twisted a ring around his finger, one inscribed with a crescent moon. It didn't look like von Abendberg heraldry.

"No," Falvard said, breaking Erik's train of thought. "And I think we both know the reason why."

"Right. The Oberst is looking for a reason to start shooting and Rodolf, well, we both saw how he was handling this."

"Perhaps it is wrong of me to say this, but I fear that the Burggraf's disappearance might turn out to be a blessing for us yet," Falvard said. "Now, I really should return to Kalb, lest he make some rash decision without me there to temper him."

"Pray, bless me if you would," Erik said, kneeling.

"Blessed is he who follows the path of angels, who walks the road less traveled, and speaks the word of truth. Blessed is he who watches over the helpless, who toils e'er toward the goal and raises high his brother and his sister. Go now, heir of the sentinels, and may the Harbinger keep you on your hunt."

"Thank you, Brother," Erik said, rising to his feet. He watched Falvard until he was out of sight, then made his way to the infirmary tent. Something about the herald made him uneasy. Then again, Kalb, Rodolf, Petra, the whole damned situation they all found themselves in, all of it was making him uneasy. He shrugged through the flap of the off-white canvas field hospital, a handful of physicians moving about the cramped spaces the tent was divided into.

"I'm looking for the other Jäger," he said to one of the medics who stopped as she noticed him. The woman pointed him down the right wing and motioned for him to follow.

She led him to the third "room" on the back side of the tent. Petra was asleep on a small bed that took up most of the space, her face bruised and swollen. One of them, he knew, was self-inflicted, but the rest were new additions. No doubt, the rest of her was just as bad.

Heinrich sat on the roughshod rug, leaning back against the side of Petra's bed. "I told you, she'll be fine," he said, but he sounded more like he was trying to convince himself.

"Heinrich, we have less than an hour before Kalb wants us outbound for Elem," Erik said. "I want you to come too, and bring Petra."

"You have some plan to fix this, I take it?"

"The Freiherr has a healer from the imperial church in his staff. If we take her with us..." Erik stopped as Heinrich hoisted himself off the ground.

"You'd trust her to the same people who've spent the last two decades throwing ours into dungeons? The same people who killed your..." Heinrich clenched his mouth shut, looking away.

"I doubt they had anything to do with what happened in Stenwarl that day, but you are right. Trust is hard to come by."

"Then leave us here," Heinrich argued.

"That is not an option."

"You know damn well it is."

"So what, we just leave her here to sleep off her injuries?" Erik fired back. Heinrich looked at him for a long while, not saying anything. "This one is my fault, and you know it. Let me make it right," he continued.

"If the imperial whoreson tries to do anything, and I mean anything, that isn't absolutely necessary to heal her, I will shoot him," Heinrich said.

"Noted. And I will endeavor to make that point clear to the healer as well."

"Ottokar is going to have your head for this, you know."

"We can tell him we held the healer at gunpoint if you think it would make the old man happy," Erik said. His shoulders loosened the tension he didn't even realize they were holding.

"It just might," Heinrich said. "Go, do what you need to prepare for this mess you've dragged us into. I'll take care of her." Erik gave him a brief nod, one Heinrich didn't even see as he went about extracting his apprentice from the bedsheets. Soon, the infirmary was behind him, its medics drawn to a rancor as Heinrich carried Petra out of their care.

Erik hurried into his kinsmen's tent and began stripping. He shed his wardrobe and swiftly replaced it with the slick outfit he and Alban had spent a few hours deciding on dark grey pants with high black boots, a plain white shirt that lacked the lace and frills Alban favored, and a deep green damask vest with a repeating floral pattern in silver. Alban came out of Rodolf's section of the tent with a stack of papers and a satchel, trying and failing to fit them into the leather compartments while walking.

They made eye contact, and Alban cleared his throat at a manservant who went rushing off to fetch their coats. Erik took the satchel from his third cousin and held it open so he could get the rest of his father's notes into it, saying, "That is quite more than I was expecting."

"Yes, well, Father might be a drunkard, but he is a well-organized one," Alban said. "If he was not, he would likely never get any work done at all."

"Are you okay?"

"Not particularly," Alban said. "We do not always see eye-to-eye, but he is still my father, and his absence hurts more than his disapproval. I am also horribly ill-suited to play the role of a Burggraf."

"You still mean to forfeit your inheritance?" Erik said.

"Viktoria has been working feverishly to secure her father's permission," Alban said. "But if mine has gone off and died, then all her hard work will be as dust in the breeze."

"Viktoria von Schwarzdorn? I thought you two stopped speaking."

"Yes, that Viktoria, and no, it was only for a season."

"You came to meet one of your future in-laws then?" Erik asked, pulling on the long black coat the butler brought him.

"Hardly," Alban said. "Different branch of the family and all that."

"Right, and the two branches hate each other if I recall correctly. I hope our mediator is not a party to his kinfolk's petty feuding."

"Enough of that," Alban said. "We have our own feud to deal with here and now, no?"

"Yes, I suppose we do," Erik said.

Before Kalb's hour was up, they had gathered back at his tent, joining his procession toward the edge of camp closest to Elem. Heinrich was already in one of the two ramshackle wagons, sitting with Petra's head in his lap as she lay sprawled across the rest of the bench.

Erik jumped in with them, offering his hand to Alban to steady him as he climbed up. Kalb, Falvard, and most of the guard took the other wagon, and a few carbineers mounted their own horses. The Oberst whistled, and the two cart drivers coaxed their mules into motion. Elem stood placid in the distance, yet something told Erik she was anything but unaware of the dangers that lurked outside her walls. It seemed a superstitious thought but, Harbinger help him, the muted evening sky looked to be a portent of danger.

CHAPTER SIXTEEN

FAUST

Leaving the comforts of my master's table, I resolved myself to head east, out into the lands our forefathers had once called home in ages long since passed. There did I find many whose own forebears had known ours by the names of kith and kin, and I confessed to them the truths master Alaric had taught me. From village to village I roamed, loathed by the pagans who spat curses upon my head with the same tongues that first greeted me as a friend. Yet, never did I think to falter, even though often I was afraid, for to falter was to consign them to damnation.

Clovis the Confessor, Confessions of Clovis 5:1-6

Faust stood in the courtyard of Norbert's castle near the entrance of its great keep as the first in the long procession of representatives rolled in through the castle gates. The Freiherr's guards stood at attention lining the road and the walls above, displaying arms as welcome and warning both. Norbert was a few steps ahead of him and to his left, ready, if only barely, to be the first to welcome his new guests. That these guests had spent the better part of the month rattling sabers at one another was enough to warrant the steely reception.

The first of them to arrive was an ornate carriage upon which hung two banners. Both bore the sea-griffin standard of the von Reinherz clan, one on the shield of a Markgraf in a quartered field of crimson and white, the other a Graf's shield on a checkered pattern of white and green. A contingent of soldiers rode with the carriage, each wearing sashes bearing the Graf's colors.

Behind them were the delegates of the imperial church and their escort of paladins, a wash of red tabards around two specks of white and purple. Norbert had explained that each of the three holy orders would send representatives, though Johann had only spoken with one of them during his visit.

Two of the warrior priests each bore the imperial banner, a tricolor field of red, white and purple with a golden sun outlined in black at its center. Inside the sunburst was a small black halo, surrounded by what appeared to be a ring whose arc was broken at the cardinal and intercardinal points to allow the rays radiating from the halo to shine through. The three bands shared their hues with the colors of the imperial church's orders, while the sunburst represented the anointed crown of the imperator.

It was as clear a message as any that church and state were entangled within Palidria, though Faust was less schooled on the particulars than he would have liked for this occasion. How closely did their actions and rituals match with those of the heraldic priests that he knew? What was their relationship to the collaborator lords, and how much sway did their teachings and ideologies have on them?

He watched as the imperials dismounted, trying to parse how the members of the orders interacted with one another and with Norbert's men. He almost jumped from his skin when Johann cleared his throat behind him. Resisting the urge to turn and glare at his godfather, Faust readjusted his attention to the man he presumed to be the Graf zu Cemich. He was a tall man with a large gut that his well-tailored outfit was designed to draw the eye away from. His warm, light-brown hair hung down to his neck and curled up at every end. Even his beard was full of tangled coils, and above them sat a pince-nez, golden-framed and fastened to his coat with a golden chain.

"Norbert, my boy," he said, clasping the Freiherr's hands in his own. "I must thank you again for your infinite patience, were it that we could have dined with you more often these last few weeks."

"Such is always a pleasure, as is this, of course," Norbert said as he turned to Faust and Johann. "May I introduce to you Faust von Schwarzdorn, the Prinz zu Dorneswik."

"It is an honor, your lordship," Faust said. "I do apologize for the delays I have caused."

"Think nothing of it. I have often heard tales of the dangers that lurk within the Dornwald's more untamed quarters. Lamprecht von Reinherz, Graf zu Cemich, and the honor is all mine, I assure you. A pleasure to see you again as well, dear Markgraf," the Graf said, turning to greet Johann.

"I have a sitting room prepared for your party, my lord," Norbert said. "My staff shall show you the way." The Graf smiled and gave a few more platitudes before following a manservant into the keep. "Do not underestimate Graf Lamprecht. He is an affable man at leisure, but a fierce foe in negotiations."

"That was my impression of the man as well," Johann said. "Be wary, lest you fall entrapped in his word games." Faust nodded in understanding, filing the warning away as the imperials approached. The inquisitor in white took the lead. He was clean-shaven with black hair cut close to his head, and he wore a stern look that matched the hard, square lines of his face.

"Ave, your lordship," said the inquisitor. "And ave to you, young princeps. I am Evander, executor of the holy order of the scales."

"Well met, executor. I am Faust von Schwarzdorn, Prinz zu Dorneswik." The inquisitor bowed his head slightly. "Pray forgive me, but I know little about your order besides its function as the legal arm of your church."

"It would be well-pleasing to enlighten you," Evander said. "Perhaps when these talks are concluded, we could make arrangements to extend our reach into your father's diocese. Prelate Timaeus, Brother Aelius, and I shall represent our respective orders."

"The Graf zu Cemich has gone ahead to the sitting room I have prepared for you, executor," Norbert said. "I hope that such an arrangement is not to your displeasure?"

"I would rather a room apart from that glutton, but I see the wisdom in your course. I shall tell the others." The executor, some rank of inquisitor as it were, left to speak with his fellows. He singled out two men, one in a black cassock with a purple sash around his waist and the other in a chainmail suit with a crimson tabard over top of it. A young man about Faust's age lingered close by the elder paladin, perhaps an apprentice of some kind.

Evander soon returned up the stairway with his compatriots close behind. "Lead the way," he said. Norbert signaled for another of his men to take them to join the Graf. Norbert let out a heavy exhalation when the three had disappeared.

"Certainly a charming bunch," Johann said. "You played that marvelously, Faust."

"Their zeal is at times a bit unnerving," Norbert said.

"I meant what I said. I would like to know more about their faith, if only to understand how ours and theirs could coexist," Faust said.

"Unlikely," said Johann, "and try not to say anything to that effect around Meinherd."

"Where is the good herald?" Faust said.

"Drinking or sleeping, or sleeping because of drinking. Never have I been so glad of that man's vices." Faust was hard-pressed to disagree.

Not long after the imperials came the nationalists. Theirs was a far less opulent entrance: two plain wagons and a handful of mounted carbineers. Faust had expected to see the equivalent of the von Morgenkranz clan's golden sunburst, the Heraldic Church's silver bell strown beneath a winged halo, or even the newly coined colors of the reorganized Freikorps. Yet here they were without a single banner. No heraldry, no colors, save the ones dyed and dulled on their clothing. He couldn't help but appreciate their lack of pomp. Still, it was worrying in its own way.

Their introductions were just as plain as their choice of vehicle. "Egon Kalb. A pleasure and what have you," said the Oberst and representative of the mercenary guild, before walking straight into the keep. Faust was afraid for Norbert's wellbeing, but the Freiherr kept up a placid front like a good noble. Kalb matched Meinherd's description to a letter: impatient in the face of courtesy and taut as a bowstring at full draw. He could hardly tell whether the man or his pristine uniform was more tightly pressed.

"It is a great pleasure," said a blond man in a black coat with yellow cuffs and filigree. "I am Alban von Morgenkranz, Prinz zu Ritterbach."

"Apologies, my Prinz, but we expected your father, the Burggraf," Norbert said. Alban tensed up for a moment, but quickly regained composure.

"My father has taken ill, I am afraid, a passing sickness brought on by poor-quality game. But he would not have us delay ourselves on his account."

"The prinz is more than prepared to fill his father, the Burggraf's space on the table," said another man in a similar outfit in green, lined with silvery threads. His eyes were a striking grey and a similar color streaked through his blond hair. "Erik," he said in introduction. "I represent the Jäger Guild."

"A pleasure to meet you both," Faust said.

"Delighted," Norbert added. "As I was going to inform the Oberst, I have a sitting room prepared for your party. Gregor shall be happy to lead you there and see to your needs before the talks proceed."

"If we could make a small request of you," Alban interjected. "One of our friends was injured at camp recently, and we would be most grateful if you could lend us the aid of your healer."

"Why, of course. Gregor, have Brother Caleb called to the unused pantry on the east wing. I hope that does not offend either of you, but I fear what sending an imperial priest into your sitting room will do to the already sour mood of the Oberst."

"Yes, I do believe that will be most sufficient," Alban said.

"I'll tell Heinrich," Erik said, turning back down the stairs and into the courtyard. He spoke a word to another man,

Heinrich, Faust assumed and the two lifted a young woman from the wagon. A flash of orange hair drew Faust's eye as the apprentice paladin who had lingered out in the courtyard hurried off into the barracks, but his attention quickly returned to the Jäger.

Another man, a herald by his dress, passed by the Jäger at an odd sort of pace in spite of the half-dead girl being hefted along beside him. "Your lordships, Brother Falvard. Will Brother Meinherd be joining us, my Prinz?"

Erik and Heinrich shuffled by as Falvard spoke, the girl draped across Heinrich's back.

"He will not," Johann said.

"A pity. I found him to be quite an engaging partner of discussion, not much like the picture painted of him by the apostles."

"I believe you would find him most unusual in many ways," Faust said, "for good and ill both." Falvard laughed like a ripple on a still lake.

"He seems a man of many passions, yet none at all," Falvard said. "A truly mercurial fellow and one whose hardships should have earned him a place of honor. Meaning no offense to your household, Markgraf."

"Some taken," Johann said.

"Gentlemen," Norbert interrupted. "We should head inside now that everyone is here. Prinz Faust, Markgraf Johann, we will go directly to my great hall. Brother Falvard, follow my man, Achim." The herald bowed his head, then moved toward the older butler. The Freiherr turned on his heel, a worried look on his face. "Heavens help me, they have not even seen each other, and I am already starting to perspire."

"Rest your mother's soul," Johann said.

"What?" Norbert said.

"I confess I did not know her well, yet her reputation pro-ceeded her," Johann continued. "She would die all over again if she were here to see you melt like a snowman in spring over a few greetings."

"Spare him your crude attempts at encouragement. You have no room to lecture anyone on familial reputation after our time in Naakt," Faust said.

"I thought you had let that go," Johann said.

"Excuse me, what are we talking about now?" Norbert said.

"No," Faust answered, ignoring Norbert's confusion. "But we have more important matters to deal with than your will-ful ignorance. Apologies, your lordship, and please, lead on." Inside his mind, he was screaming at himself, even as he fol-lowed Norbert into the keep and its great hall. He chided his own childishness, for one; for another, his ever-growing alignment with the same vapid farce of polite politics he so disdained.

Drapery hung from the ceiling of the great hall in golds and reds, teal and green. It added life to the drab grey room lit by candles hung from the walls and an imported chande-lier made of enchanted crystals. Two long tables were set apart from one another along either length of the room, with small standards laid out before each seat with the colors of the factions present. A third, shorter table was set to connect the other two, placed to oppose the dais with only a single chair. Faust's chair.

Norbert hurried across the room and sat on his ancestral seat, raised high on the dais to remind everyone present that they were here on his accommodation. Faust took his own seat, preparing himself as best one could, imagining the Markgrafin in Tholst when she would set aside her children as they bickered. He sent an unspoken prayer for the health of his godmother Alena, for Olivia and her awful new dress, and even one for Ludwig, who was no doubt marching back to Dorneswik with Faust's father.

"Are we prepared, Prinz Faust?" Norbert asked, a slight shake in his voice.

"Not as much as I would have hoped, but as prepared as we can be. Call for them."

Norbert rang a tiny golden bell, and the guards in attendance left the room through doors on either side. Faust closed his eyes, trying simultaneously to both think of the lives he had never met but was now responsible for, and to ignore the soul-crushing weight of it. The men of note filed in slowly. Graf Lamprecht and Evander and his companions came from one side, Oberst Kalb, Prinz Alban, Falvard, and Erik from the other.

Thanks in no small part to Norbert's decorations, the men found their seats swiftly, and Norbert raised a hand to signal to end the murmuring that came in with them.

"Lords, holy brothers, and gentlemen of the guilds, I thank you for being here and for the patience you have all shown along the way. As host, I will take no part in this discussion. Heed, then, our mediator, the honorable Faust von Schwarzdorn, Prinz zu Dorneswik, heir to the ducal seat of the Dornwald."

"Thank you, Freiherr Norbert," Faust said, standing, "for opening your home for this moment that begins the end of this terrible conflict that has plagued the Vahsland. Though both parties are aware, for the sake of posterity, I remind you all that I have had men in my trust collect each of your talking points for this day. I will help guide us upon each discussion and will intervene only for the sake of bringing order and to suggest means of compromise when I feel it necessary.

"Owing to the fact that it was the household of the Herzog zu Kranzdorf who initiated this push for peace, I am inclined to give the floor first to the Prinz zu Ritterbach," Faust said, watching as Alban jolted a bit in his chair before standing up.

"Th-thank you," Alban said, jumping slightly in his seat. "The time for peace has come, my friends. The Herzog, through his regent and heir, Prinz Mathis, has extended this invitation that he might make restitution with his rebelling vassals. He is willing to accept terms of peace that will grant the Markgraf zu Althafen and all aligned with him a new, temporary contract of scutage in lieu of providing men and arms for the liberation of the realm."

"I now give the floor to the Graf zu Cemich," Faust said. Alban sat back down, fidgeting with imagined wrinkles in the edges of his waistcoat. Lamprecht was already standing when Faust's attention turned to him.

"My dearest cousin, the Markgraf zu Althafen, is willing to accept terms of peace should I find them to be agreeable. We hold to our stance that we utterly refuse to raise arms against the Viceroy when no heir to the royal throne remains. Nor, then, shall we accept terms which levy taxes on us for the purpose of plunging the rest of the realm into upheaval."

They were certainly off to a marvelous start.

"If I may?" Falvard said, but Faust raised a hand to silence him.

"We shall come to the matter of religion in a moment, Brother Falvard. As it stands, my lords, I believe that there is room for negotiation. Prinz Alban, what manner of increase in taxation would this new contract entail?"

"Oh, um, an increase of five percent of the southern lords' next two harvests, or a twelve percent raise in the monthly due of coinage."

"Unacceptable," Lamprecht muttered.

"Please keep hold of your tongue, my lord," Faust said to the Graf. "Now, would the household of the Herzog be willing to make exceptions for the lords whose territories have been ravaged by the war?"

"I believe his grace would find that acceptable," Alban said. Faust nodded and waved a hand toward the Graf.

"This is merely war reparations under a different name, and we all know it," said Lamprecht. "We also know that his grace is ill and that your armies have not gained any ground in months. Why, then, should we agree to pay even a single denarius into the coffers of Kranzdorf?"

"A fair question, if bluntly put," Faust said.

"The answer is simple," Alban said. "Your side broke faith with their rightful liege and have grown *fat* on the spoils of your betrayal."

"I would caution the Prinz zu Ritterbach on his choice of words," said Faust.

"My apologies, Graf Lamprecht," Alban said. "A poor choice of diction on my part. Allow me to rephrase. The lords of the southern Vahsland have clearly not paid a single thaler to their rightful lord since the outbreak of this horrendous war, and I would wager that not a single thaler more has made it into the purse of the Viceroy in that time either. We believe, then, that your coffers would be full enough to reimburse our lost tax revenue. In smaller increments than you owe us, of course."

Faust felt his teeth clench tight as he tried hard not to glance frantically between the two nobles as Norbert was. He had misjudged Alban, and so had everyone in the room, with the peculiar exception of the Jäger, Erik, who sat with his lips curled inward. It was entertaining, certainly, but it struck him with a frightful sensation.

CHAPTER SEVENTEEN

PETRA

*I dreamt of those who went before me and knew that soon it would
be time to join them, though it saddens me to leave when so much
work remains yet unfinished. I trust in you all to carry on our great
work and to carry on the confessions, you who have ever been our
faithful heralds. Do not mourn me when I am gone. Do not mark
my grave with pillars of stone. Spread my ashes among the flowers
that my empty vessel might feed the earth.*
        Gerlind the Confessor, Book of Silence 12:12-17

Petra hadn't realized she was dreaming until the dream
turned happy. The warmth of blood and sunlight was
replaced by the sensation of a thick blanket as she
willed herself awake. Maybe a nice dream was better, but it
wasn't hers. Those memories didn't feel right, and she
wouldn't linger in them. Her ribs hurt, and her chest too, but
not as much as she recalled. It was dark, so night must have
already fallen while she was asleep.

What greeted her was not the sight of a dark canvas ceiling, but a wooden floor hung upon thick wooden beams

laced with spider's silk. The pain in her chest spiked when she sat up, and she slumped back into the surprisingly comfortable blankets. Maybe the dream wasn't so bad after all.

"Welcome back, kid. How're you feeling?" Heinrich asked from his seat on a barrel in the corner of the otherwise empty room.

"Like I had a fistfight with a werewolf and almost lost," Petra said, turning herself over despite her ribs' protest. "Where are we?"

"An old pantry in Elem castle."

"Only the best for us, right?"

"Yeah, did you see the Burggraf fall? Did he die, or was he turned?" Heinrich asked.

"What? No, not that I saw, but we got separated on the way back to camp. I thought he left me behind. Wait, why are we in the castle?"

"The peace talks have finally started. Alban has taken his father's seat, and Erik, well, Erik thinks it's going to go south and didn't want us sticking around the camp."

"Sorry about that. We could have gotten a head start back to Kranzdorf if I hadn't been sloppy."

"You're never sloppy." Heinrich hesitated and continued, "Okay, well, maybe every so often. How many?"

"Four that I know of," she said.

"Did the Burggraf leave you behind as bait, or did you really get separated?"

"The fourth furry shit blindsided me, dragged me off into the woods. I would have kept going if I were in the Burggraf's position too."

Heinrich clearly believed her. It wasn't quite what he had taught her, but it was understandable.

"How's Alban doing?" Petra asked.

"Don't know, they haven't called it quits yet, so he must be doing well enough."

"No, I meant…"

Heinrich held a hand up to stop her and said, "I know. He was a little shaken up, but I don't know him as well as Erik does, so what do I know?"

"You know shit, like, actual shit," she said. Heinrich stared at her for a few seconds, then started laughing. She started laughing too when he almost fell off the barrel.

"Fair point," he said, wiping tears from his eyes. "Maybe if you listened when I talked, you wouldn't have been blindsided by werewolves."

"It was only the one," she said, wincing a bit as her sides settled into a more standard pulse of pain. "Kalb told us his men had it under control."

"I know," Heinrich said softly.

"He lied to us."

"I know."

"Master."

"Petra, I know, and I plan on doing something about it, but right now, you need to rest," Heinrich said.

"But…"

"Enough, please. One problem at a time."

"Fine," she said, rolling onto her back again. A spider plied its way across one of the webs above, away from the wrapped carcass of its last meal. "Does this room come with free food, or do we have to pay for that?"

"It came with free medical, though I'm not sure what rates the holy order of the scroll charges. Best to leave it on Erik's tab, let him deal with it."

"I'm sorry, what?" Petra said as she sat up, this time ready and prepared to power through the ache. "You let one of them heal me?"

"I stayed in the room if that helps?"

"Somewhat, but after what they were going to do to Traugott?"

"He wasn't the first, and he won't be the last," Heinrich said. "I thought you didn't care about all this. What changed?"

"I don't, it's just, I knew Brother Traugott," she said.

"Don't worry about it. Freiherr Norbert's healer wasn't at Laupen, and since he was willing to wave his hands around and do his hoopla to heal you, I'd say he isn't as stuck up as most of his ilk."

"He did a piss poor job though. Did I mention I feel like I lost a wrestling match with a bear?"

"No, but I'd stick with the 'fistfight with a werewolf' thing, it sounds more impressive," Heinrich said.

"Oh, shut up," Petra said, swinging herself out of the makeshift bed and looking around the room to find her boots off to her side. As she pulled them on, she said, "He didn't do anything weird?"

"He did a lot of weird things, but they were all the clothes-stay-on sorts. He came in, said some prayers in his mother tongue, and waved his hands about like a witch. And they call *us* the pagans."

"Point taken. I'll admit though, I think I remember hurting a lot more when I got to camp," Petra confessed.

"Considering you went face-first in the mud, I'd say you're a lot better off now. You really don't plan on listening, do you?"

"Listening to what? Going back to sleep won't do me any more good right now. Where's the food?"

"Gah, fine, fine, let's go pester the maids and butlers like beggars," Heinrich said.

"We're going for food. If I find you hitting on the man's maids, I will slap you," Petra said.

"Should I have you checked for stigmata?"

"I'd have turned already and you know it."

"Not if you have black blood in your veins," Heinrich said.

"That's an old wives' tale. You're old, but you aren't an old wife."

"Like hell, I'm old," he said, making his way to the door. "I'm middle-aged, at worst. You can talk about old when you finally meet my old master."

"The guy who trained Erik too?" she asked, exiting the dreary pantry and entering a well-lit hallway. They started walking down in one direction, technically lost, but they would get somewhere eventually.

"The same," Heinrich answered. A manservant came around the corner up ahead, and he shouted, "Hey friend, can you point us toward the kitchen?!"

"Who are you, exactly?" the man asked.

"Is that any way to talk to guests?" Heinrich quipped.

"Oh?" the butler said.

"'Oh' what?" Petra said. "I don't think our host told all his people we were here."

"Clearly a misstep on his lordship's part," Heinrich said. "We're here with the representatives. Your friend, Brother Caleb, patched up my apprentice here with his hand-waving."

"Kitchen, please, or do you have any of those fancy finger snacks the nobles like with you?" Petra asked, watching the confused butler as he just stood there scratching his head.

"I was, indeed, not informed about more guests, but I suppose I could show you to your side's sitting room if it pleases you," the man said.

"Sure," Heinrich said.

"Is there food there? Does the imperial hand waving thing always make people this hungry?" Petra asked.

"I think that has more to do with the fact you slept through lunch," Heinrich said.

"There are refreshments prepared in the sitting rooms," the butler answered. "Which delegation are you both attached to?"

"The von Morgenkranz," Heinrich said.

"That makes sense. This way, please."

Petra and Heinrich shared a look and an unspoken question, but they followed the manservant nonetheless. He led them through a maze of inner pathways and passed at least a dozen and four doors, finally entering into the seventeenth one by Petra's count. The room within was much more spacious and more actually decorated and lived-in than the pantry. Well, if you didn't count the spiders, of course.

Leather chairs with golden studs sat around a medium-sized table of dark wood with frilly placemats before them. A pair of couches with green-blue fabric cushions were set opposite each other on either side of a long, low table topped with stacked plates of bite-sized foods. Petra made a beeline there, taking a whole plate of small sandwiches from the top of the framed stack.

She popped one of the little jam sandwiches into her mouth, barely chewing it before swallowing. Heinrich sat opposite her, taking a glass of sparkling wine and sipping it with a look of disappointment. Shouting shook through the only other door into the room, and Petra pointed toward it while she chewed her fourth little morsel. Her master shrugged and mouthed one dreadful word: politics.

"Enough!" was the last word before the room dipped back to quiet. Petra didn't recognize the voice, but it sounded like a younger guy, probably the prinz that Meinherd had mentioned. Another two sandwiches later, the door swung open with enough force that it crashed loudly against the wall. Kalb was the first to enter, to no surprise whatsoever. The slamming door had given him away even before she turned to look at him.

Falvard was close behind him, a welcome alternative to the fuming officer. She watched as Kalb threw himself into one of the leather chairs, pulled a flask from inside his uniform, and took a drink. A familiar sound of excitement brought Petra's eyes to Alban, who looked like he was dressed for a funeral, or as close to dressing that way as he could stand to come.

"Petra, darling, I am so glad you are okay," he said, then interrupted himself, "No, no, I must keep my serious face. Oh, I was so worried about you."

"Thanks," she mumbled through wet clumps of bread and jam.

"You two should have seen him," Erik said, closing the door behind him. "He held his own quite well. Glad to see you came out okay, Petra."

"You flatter me," Alban said.

"What happened to the Burggraf?" Kalb said.

"We were ambushed by werewolves," Petra said. "His lordship was still alive with most of his guard when one of the wolves dragged me off away from the group. I don't know where he is now. I thought you said your men had dealt with the local werewolves?"

"We had," Kalb said, letting out a frustrated sigh, "but apparently they weren't as thorough as they claimed."

"Such a terrible shame to let even a single one of them go without mercy," Falvard said. "Though I daresay that you likely dealt their numbers quite the blow, young Jäger."

"With any luck, Father will come out unscathed," Alban said. "I wish the same could have been said of you, though."

"Not the first time I've taken a beating like that," Petra said. "I take it your fight's going well too?"

"Oh, well, no, not entirely. My father's notes were quite comprehensive, however, and I have given no ground, as the Oberst might say."

"Not for this, I wouldn't," Kalb interjected. "Half of your success has come from our little mediator. If not for him, I think von Reinherz would have toppled you thrice already."

"We are certainly blessed in that regard," Falvard said. "I worried for you, my Prinz."

"I am simply grateful that the Graf zu Cemich is such a slovenly boar," Alban said. "It makes me angry the way he stretches those fine garments."

"Alban," Erik said, "we have talked about this."

"I cannot help it, cousin. Those clothes were made to make a person beautiful, not to be spread fit to burst over the belly of a self-important pig."

"The one time your judgmental streak has worked in our favor," Erik said, as he let his head fall into his hand. "It was a good play to bring up their contributions to the Viceroy."

"Good, because I was mostly guessing on that."

"We're all doomed," Heinrich said. "Spare me a drink, Kalb. This wine is much too sweet." The Oberst tightened the cap of his flask and tossed it across the room to Heinrich, who undid the stop and took a draw, shaking with delight. "Much obliged."

"Well, Father's notes outlined how the Viceroy has simply co-opted the old royal tax structure. Since that meant all taxes paid to the crown were collected and shipped directly by the estates of the Herzöge, I simply surmised that they would have neglected to create an alternative," Alban said.

"Like guild members trying to avoid paying their dues by isolating themselves off in some countryside village," Heinrich said.

"That's the one joy of getting kicked out of the Hansa," said Kalb. "Jäger, give me back my flask." The flask flew across the room again, back into the hands of the Oberst.

"So Alban clearly struck a nerve. Now we just need to drive the wedge deeper in between the Graf and his imperial allies," Erik said.

"I agree," said the priest. "We must do what we can to remind the imperial clergy that they side with those who would betray their own country. Sow distrust and discontent among them."

"If they lose support from the Viceroy's agents here, then we'll have gained the upper hand. That said, it's an obvious tactic, and they might close ranks simply to present the illusion of unity," Kalb said.

"Does anyone want any of these?" Petra asked, holding up the near-empty plate. "I can move on to something else if you do."

"Confessors," Alban said, "you really ate the whole plate's worth? Think of your figure."

"Think of your head on a pike if you let yourself get distracted, Prinz Alban," Kalb said.

"Were you not just lecturing us on how our opponents would present a united front, Oberst?" Erik said. "Or do you believe that we can win without employing such a strategy ourselves?"

"This isn't about winning," Heinrich said. "It's about all the lives you people have wasted."

"Their deaths will only be in vain if we don't come out ahead in these talks," Kalb countered.

"I am afraid that you cannot see the forest for the trees, Herr Heinrich," Falvard added.

"Keep pushing war reparations," Kalb said, turning to Alban. "Call them whatever you like, but keep pushing that until the topic shifts."

"We will get to the needs of the Aushansa soon enough," Alban said.

"I can take point on that if you want, Oberst," Erik said.

"Agreed," said Kalb. "But I imagine that they will split us beyond that."

"Noble against noble, monster hunter against monster hunter," Falvard said. "The young Prinz Faust seems to be poetic if nothing else."

Petra finished the last bite from the small plate and set it back at the top of the stack. She could deal with feeling left out of this particular discussion easily, but the food could be better.

CHAPTER EIGHTEEN

FAUST

Arnfried von Steinmetz personally led the assault, and with sword in hand, his army broke the hosts of Vaon and set Radobod von Gerhardt fleeing behind his gates. With great engines of war, Arnfried threw asunder those gates and marched to Radobod's high hall. There, he threw down his sword and broke bread with his enemy, taking Radobod's daughter for a wife and binding their realms together with libations poured for the honored dead.

Odoacer the Timid, Third Antiquities 10:28-31

"Harbinger, help me, I think I am going to go insane before this is all done," Faust said. He leaned back in his chair, twisting himself so he could just barely see Johann. "Do you need to trade places?"

"My leg is fine, and this is hardly the worst negotiation I have been at. Oddly enough."

"Then there is hope for us yet. Let me guess, it was a marriage interview?"

"My own, actually," Johann confirmed. "Alena's father was a terrifying man, and her mother looked at me like I was some small rodent."

"I do not envy it. How am I doing?"

"They have yet to shoot each other, so at this point, I believe we are still well off," Johann said.

"It is quite hard to shoot someone without a gun."

"True, I suppose I am just used to people having arms at these sorts of things."

"No one ever thought of disarming the parties before?" Faust asked, sitting up.

"Who would openly defy hospitality?" Johann said with a chuckle. "It has happened, of course, though I only know of one time within recent memory. Damned if I cannot remember all the details, but it was around the time of the Merudain Fury."

"I vaguely recall reading about that," Faust said.

"That was back when I was about your age, I think. Messy business, but to the point: the Burggraf zu Wolkehorst cut off an idiot's hand, pistol and all sent clattering against the floor because he had dared to draw it at the negotiating table. That idiot was his own cousin, by the way."

"Well," Faust said, "that is certainly one way of dealing with familial indiscretion. Not the route I would take."

"Really?"

"All I wanted was some acknowledgment from you that Marcel was acting out of turn," Faust said. "You keep acting like it was a silly little mistake, but people died because of him. An entire village scourged because he did not ask you, or anyone else for help until it was too late."

"What difference would it make if I had? Would those people rise from their graves and pat us on the back for caring so much that they had died? It is a tragedy and one we will ensure does not repeat itself, but the sort of confrontation you want will only drive him to further isolate himself from us." Johann sighed, and his cane tapped against the stone floor as he shifted his weight.

"Handle it as you will, then. It is your domain, after all, and he is your vassal and kinsman," Faust said. A long silence hung between them until Norbert returned, all too happy not to reopen the issue. "Should we continue letting the lords argue, or should we move on to another topic?"

"That solely depends on them," Johann said. "They have precedent."

"And the other representatives have positions of their own," Faust said.

"Which they will gladly argue in circles about as well," Johann said.

"Should I call everyone back in?" asked Norbert.

"Yes," Faust said. "Yes, but maybe walk very slowly. Are you all right?"

"I will be fine," Norbert said, pausing for a moment before admitting, "when they all leave, that is."

"I will toast you to that," Faust said, "when they have all left, of course. 'Let us be done with this anon.'"

"A quote from Nacht ober Zauberstein? I was unaware you had any interest in theater," Johann said.

"Father and Mother took me to a production once, it was certainly memorable."

"'Lo the rise of the scarlet moon bathed in blood, that foul omen of ruination.'" Johann said. "It is frightfully close to a blood moon."

"A few days yet," Faust said. Hopefully, they could conclude these talks before then. Superstitions aside, the blood moon marked the hour of the vampire, and they had enough problems to deal with already. He watched with apprehension as Norbert went to fetch his staff. Two maids entered the room as he returned, each taking a door, knocking on it, and entering the thresholds.

Shortly thereafter, the tables were once again filled, and it fell to Faust to lead them off. "Welcome again. I believe that it is time to move on to the topic of the assembled clergy unless, of course, your lordships wish to continue your earlier discussion." Men from both sides leaned over to speak in hushed tones.

"We accept your generous offer, Prinz Faust," said Brother Falvard, "if our imperial counterparts would have it so."

"We would," said Evander.

"Then as I gave the first remarks to the Prinz zu Ritterbach, I shall now start the floor with your side of the aisle, Executor," Faust said. He had expected the priest to stand, but it was Evander himself who took the initiative.

"It is by the decree of the honorable Viceroy Severus, with full authority bequeathed him by our most radiant Imperator, that the dissolution of the Heraldic faith be made absolute across the viceroyalty," he said. "That many of the local patricians, yourself included, honorable mediator, should still retain the service of and offer sanctuary to such criminals does nothing to endear you to the rest of the empire. It is the Viceroy's position, then, that all patricians within his dominion shall abide by his edict posthaste under threat of suppression by the legions and auxiliaries under his command. That is all."

"Brother Falvard," Faust said.

"Thank you, Prinz Faust," the herald said. "This decree is unsurprising, as is the vain and hollow threat by which the

Viceroy has sought to avail himself at this negotiation. You have tried, Executor, and you have failed on more occasions than I can recall, to round up and imprison all of our number who have served the faithful of the Gaerschland. Our faith predates your own, even unto the beliefs of your own Saint Drakon, with whom we share a common patron archangel.

"That you would silence us who have remained faithful to our angelic patron does your entire church a disservice. You who abandoned the faith of your forefathers when the first host did not swoop down to heed your every beck and call. You who already bow before three of the high council of heaven.

"You would deny us, decry us as faithless pagans when it was our most holy Confessors who first brought the word of angels to these western reaches. We do not need be enemies, though you have tried at every turn to make us so. All we ask is coexistence; let our churches share the common forum, and let the will of each man and each woman decide which virtues and which angels they best align with."

"We refuse," Evander said.

"Care you to negotiate?" Faust asked, feeling his stomach begin to tense. This was turning awful.

"On what grounds? The first host abandoned us, and they abandoned you, yet you still give them faith and fealty. What miracles are left to you? What precious gifts do the heavens shower upon you but hunks of metal that lay waste to lands better left to the farmer? I will simply reiterate, comply, or face the consequences."

"I suppose that is that then," Falvard said. "I do apologize to you, Prinz Faust, and to you as well, Freiherr Norbert. Were it that humanity was one of their virtues. Nevertheless, we heralds will not abide the edict of a tyrant even if it means we shall all burn like the innocents of Stenwarl."

"That settles that issue then," Faust said, willing his voice not to shake. "May we then move on to the issue of the Jäger Guild? Herr Erik, the floor is yours."

"Our position is simple. We too will not abide the Viceroy's edict. The creatures which terrorize our lands are simply too numerous, and we shall not entrust the protection of our people against those threats to the arms of uncaring foreign occupiers and their sorcery."

"Herr Timaeus," Faust said, gesturing toward the lone paladin at the table. He was not quite as stern of face as Evander, but his mouth was drawn tight.

"There is no need for your militants in the Viceroy's dominion," said the paladin. "The holy order of the sword is more than enough to root out the corruption in your woodlands."

"A fair notion," said Erik, "but may I ask when your order intends to begin such an endeavor? In my experience, including one recently, in fact, your holy knights seem far more concerned with threatening old men in heraldic churches than culling monsters from our countryside."

"We will keep things civil, gentlemen!" Faust said. This was getting out of hand, and he had to try something to get them back in order. Why were they even here if they intended to just proclaim their lack of desire to cooperate or compromise? "Would it not be possible for Jäger and paladin to work together in this for the safety of the people?"

Both men opened their mouths to speak when a soldier burst in through the door to the nationalists' sitting room. He wore a ragged blue and grey uniform and was panting heavily. An older man in traveling attire was a pace behind him, throwing his hands up in the air and turning around to reenter the room. The soldier came to Kalb's side and took a deep gulp of air before whispering something in the Oberst's ear.

"What is going on?" Faust asked, turning quickly between an equally stunned Johann and the nationalists' table. Kalb shook his head a few times, eyes closing as he listened. The others around him struggled to hear what the messenger was saying, but one word clearly caught Prinz Alban by surprise. Faust went to say something, but the Oberst stood up, slamming a hand down on the table.

"We're done here," Kalb proclaimed, grabbing Alban by his arm and dragging him from his seat violently. "I can't believe I even once trusted that any of you meant to speak in good faith. Traitorous shits, the lot of you."

"Unhand me, you brute," was the prinz's reply. Erik, who had never returned to his own chair, bolted after the others, leaving the great hall through the sitting room. Faust looked at Falvard, the only remaining representative on that side of the room, the same satisfied look plastered on his face even as the other side came alive with clamor. The herald calmly pushed himself back and stood, taking his leave of the negotiations as well.

"What the hell just happened?" Faust said. "What could have possibly made them think of leaving now?"

"We need to leave, now!" Johann said. Faust didn't argue. He followed Johann around the empty table toward Norbert, who was breathing rapidly on his dais. "Send a warning out to your guards."

"Right," Norbert said, almost tripping down the steps as he hurried out the back door of his own hall. They took the same door but veered right and around.

"We need to get Meinherd," Faust said.

"We need to stop the Oberst before he does something stupid," Johann replied.

"I think it is a tad late for that. You hobble back to the

guest wing and get our herald; I will go see if I cannot catch up with them." Johann nodded and turned around, leaving Faust to sprint down the hallway in search of answers. Two turns later, he caught sight of them.

"Erik, what's going on?" asked a young woman with brown hair, the same one Erik and his companion had carried into the castle earlier that afternoon.

"I wish I knew. Kalb, slow down, you whoreson."

"They've pulled one over on us, Jäger!" Kalb said.

"The hell does that mean?"

"They have the Burggraf," Kalb hissed.

"How?" Alban said.

"Shit," the girl said. "I'm so sorry, Alban."

"Enough talk," Kalb said. "We're leaving, and I will be getting your idiot father back."

"I'll help," the girl said.

"Just shut up," Kalb said. "Where has that rat priest gone off to?"

The collaborators had kidnapped the Burggraf zu Ritterbach? Faust stopped in his tracks as their conversation veered off the topic he wanted to know more about. What the hell was going on? He felt a biting chill as a hand wrapped around the back of his neck. Brother Falvard's hand. The herald put a finger to his lips and smiled. Were those fangs in his mouth?

Wordlessly, Falvard let go of his neck, moving the hand to his chest and staring intently into Faust's eyes. Their amber hue flickered bright red for an instant and the next thing he knew, he was up against a wooden door with pain radiating from the back of his head. He pushed himself forward and looked down the hall. There was no one. Who had he been looking for? Dammit, he had been trying to catch up with the nationalists to try and bring them back to the table. What had happened? Wait, the priest, Brother Falvard, had been there beside him, and then he was gone.

Was Falvard a vampire? Was he really a bloodsucker, or was Faust's mind playing tricks on him? He slumped backward and slid down the door, heartbeat pulsing in his throat. He had to tell Johann what he'd heard, Norbert too, before... A gunshot in the distance rang out, and then more and more followed it. Elem was going to be a battlefield. He'd failed.

CHAPTER NINETEEN

PETRA

From the moment I set foot upon these shores, I knew that this would be where I would die. I have no fear of it, nor of the pyre which shall carry me home. Uhtric, my dearest friend, I commend you, for you alone have braved this land of madness with me when all others would not. For your conscience, know that I grant thee pardon from your grief. You have not betrayed me as you so think, but shall carry my glory in your heart for all your days. Be well, my friend, for when next we meet, it shall be on ever more distant shores than these.

Clovis the Confessor, Confessions of Clovis 14:24-31

Petra stood glowering at the paladin holding a sword to her throat. Given the chance, she would gladly wipe that smug look off the woman's face, maybe even rip out a few strands of her pale blonde hair for good measure. To her left, she heard the Oberst grunt in pain as he grabbed the blade of the man in front of him and punched him in the face, then the distinct crunch of breaking bones as the man fell backward.

While the woman was distracted, Petra reached for her sword, moving just out of the way in case she came to her senses. Then came a gunshot to do her work for her. The woman's face contorted in pain and she fell to the ground, clutching at her side, flames curling around her fingertips. Petra caught her sword before it hit the ground, wincing as its edges bit into her hands.

She quickly flipped the weapon around, careful not to let it slip and cut her again. It was a far cry from what she was used to, but it would do. A clash of metal scraping against metal came as the old officer crossed swords with another of the "holy" warriors. Petra twirled on one foot to engage one herself, swinging the blade a bit too wide. Her new opponent easily dodged the blade and thrust in before she could bring the hefty hunk of metal in her hands back around.

The sword was a bad idea, after all, so she dropped it and sidestepped the jab at her chest, grabbing the paladin's wrist with one hand and smashing his throat with the other. She twisted his wrist as he collapsed to his knees, plucking the blade from his hand when it started to slip from his grasp. Another gunshot, much closer, put one more of the self-righteous pricks down for the count. She looked over and saw Heinrich, a grim look on his face as he brought his pistol up to point at the sky.

Alban looked beside himself, his cheeks puffing in and out and his throat contorting as he tried not to puke while hyperventilating. It was almost always hard to see your first death. Petra had been just about the same, although hers had been a lot more gruesome. More gunshots rang out, and now her head was starting to hurt. Kalb gestured toward something, and her eyes followed his outstretched arm to the barracks.

Freikorps soldiers had formed a half-circle in front of the doorway, rifles ready and a number of dead around them. Rather than telling them to stay at the barracks, Kalb waved for his troops to push toward the stables. He'd get no complaints from her. Things weren't exactly turning out as she had expected, but it wasn't really a surprise either. Erik would have some explaining to do later as to why he thought any of this was a good idea, but that could wait until they'd escaped.

Seriously, though, why the hell was she here? She was happy to be able to protect Alban, he'd been nothing but good to her, but wait, why was he there too? Why were any of them there if this was how things were going to turn out? She let out a growl that she couldn't hear as she ran with the others toward the stables. Most of the animals inside were freaking out, thrashing around in their pens, while a few warhorses and army mules stood there like they just wanted to get on with it. Petra could certainly relate to the sentiment.

Kalb's troops hurried to prep their horses while Heinrich and Erik stood watch outside. Poor Alban was huddled low against one of the interior walls, clutching his head and panting hard. She took a step toward him but then turned around, going up to Brother Falvard and tapping him on the shoulder. He'd be better at helping Alban than she would. He was a priest, after all, it was what they were supposed to do. His gaze turned to her, and she stepped aside to point at Alban.

The priest frowned, the side of his mouth curling just a bit as he thought it over. Why wasn't he doing anything? She made a little motion like ringing a bell, yet he still didn't move. Looking down at his belt, she intended to just yank his bell off and ring it herself, but he didn't have one. What sort of a herald didn't have a bell?

Biting back the urge to scream, Petra went back toward

Alban, kneeling down and grabbing his shoulders. He looked up at her, his face white with fear. He mouthed her name, no, he'd said it, and she just couldn't hear him. If a certain someone hadn't lost his bell, she wouldn't have this problem right now, but it didn't matter. She didn't really know how to comfort anyone, but she still had to try.

"It's going to be all right," she said, not sure if he was able to read her lips.

Alban swallowed hard, jolting beneath her grip as another gunshot ripped through the air. "Look at me," she ordered. "Just look at me, and ignore everything else. We are going to be fine." He looked away, his eyes drifting all over the stable until his gaze finally came back to hers. He gave her a weak nod, and after a few minutes he stopped shaking, and his breathing steadied. She helped him up to his feet, keeping a tight grip on his arm as they walked to the back of the stable.

The soldiers led their mounts through the now clear corridor into the courtyard. The gunshots seemed to have stopped for the time being, so at the very least, the local guards weren't going to do anything just yet. Hopefully, that would mean they could get a carriage or a wagon to put Alban in. The prinz sat back down, this time on a small, overturned bucket. Luckily, he didn't seem to be lapsing back into panic. Petra gave him a gentle squeeze on his shoulder before turning to go check on the others.

She had only taken four steps when an intense wave of heat hit her, and she covered her face with both arms. Hot air kissed her cheeks as she moved one arm to look out at the billowing flame outside. She looked back at Alban but chose to continue outside. One last paladin now stood between them and their escape, bright red flames lapping across his blade, sparks dripping to the ground like raindrops.

"That is far enough," he said. "Submit yourself to our custody and I can assure you a fair trial under imperial law. Refuse and you shall burn in flames divine by the grace of Saint Helvius."

"Don't look down on me!" Kalb responded defiantly. "I know your kind, and I know your imperial law is worth piss." The Oberst stood like a statue against the flames, with Erik and Heinrich behind him. Falvard, the worthless herald, was nearby, doing nothing, of course.

The paladin looked unimpressed, his head tilting slightly to the side. "Are you quite finished?" he asked.

Kalb roared like an animal, but before he could charge forward with his stolen sword, Erik stepped in and knocked the Oberst out with a blow to the back of the head. "Finally, someone here with a little sense," remarked the paladin.

"You will be true to your word and ensure that we receive a fair trial?" Erik said.

"Always." He let out a tired sigh and sheathed his weapon. The flames dissipated into nothing, leaving not even a single burnt blade of grass on the lawn beneath him. He walked forward, but when Erik reached out a hand to shake on the agreement, the paladin punched him hard in the stomach. Erik doubled over as he said, "That was for my men, you rabid mutt."

"Bastard!" Heinrich leveled his pistol at the paladin's head, but it was clear he didn't see the man in white racing toward him.

"Master! Right!" Petra called out, but it was too late. The inquisitor brought down his blade in a clean stroke and cut Heinrich's hand off just below the wrist. He screamed as his hand and pistol both clattered against the ground, the impact causing the gun to misfire, hitting the paladin in the leg.

The paladin's face twisted into a scowl as the leg buckled beneath his weight.

"Evander!" he said, "Are you a fool?"

"Healing a gunshot to the leg is far easier than trying to put your brains back into your skull, Timaeus, you know that," said Evander, the man in white. "Or were you just hoping to earn your martyrdom that much sooner?"

"Help me up then," Timaeus said, then turning to the guards on the walls. "What are you dogs waiting for? Come down here and arrest these criminals. Damned provincials."

"Hold your tongue, Prelate," Evander said, his comrade's title punctuated with a scathing lilt. "Or have you forgotten that by law I am also one of those 'damned' provincials you so look down upon?"

"Mayhap you are, Executor, but at least you revere the right angels," Timaeus said.

"You, girl," Evander said as he turned to look at Petra. "Grab your master's hand, we should be able to reattach it."

"You cut his hand off, and now you want to put it back on?" she asked.

"Well, yes. I have found that it is harder to tie restraints onto people with one hand."

"You're a monster," she said. He laughed at her.

"I suppose you think you would know, then. Typical. Grab the man's hand, or I slit his throat right here." Begrudgingly, she followed his orders, walking over to Heinrich slowly, like she would if faced with a large predator. She picked his hand up from the ground and started prying his fingers from the pistol. She tossed the bloody extremity at the inquisitor, but kept the gun. She knew better than to try and use it right now, so she ejected the magazine and cleared the chamber before tossing it aside.

"I'll take the hand back now," she said. Evander obliged her, chuckling as he tossed her Heinrich's hand as if he found it funny that he had thrown a hand underhanded.

"Could you two stop playing catch with my good hand? Dammit," Heinrich said, as he pushed himself up off the ground with his left hand. He was still bleeding badly from the stump that was his right arm and Petra had to catch him when he stumbled.

"You are so melodramatic," Erik said, having rolled onto his back. "You would still have your good hand if you had just kept it to yourself."

"I think the phrase you're looking for is 'thanks for losing a hand trying to protect my hapless ass,' but maybe I'm just old school," Heinrich said.

"Both of you just shut up," Petra said. "Get your healer then, imperial, before he bleeds out."

"Right, come along. Timaeus, I will be inside whenever you get done playing in the dirt."

"Michael!" Timaeus called. "Get out here and help me." Michael? Wasn't that the name of the boy she'd confronted back in Laupen? Then it hit her: none of the paladins that had tried to encircle them had looked familiar, but she recognized Timaeus and Evander. It took a great deal of will to keep her fury from reaching her face. She'd deal with them if she got the chance, but right now, getting Heinrich's hand stitched back on was more important. That and protecting Alban. Alban? Was he still in the stable?

Petra didn't look back, she couldn't. If Alban was still hiding then maybe, just maybe, he could escape without them. It was a long shot, but it was better than giving away his position. She hauled Heinrich back toward the castle, his arm draped around her shoulder. Erik was probably carrying

Kalb, or one of his men was. They'd been just as dumbfounded as she'd been, in all likelihood. Better that than doing something stupid like her master had done.

"There had been more of you? It seems your little princeps and one of his guards managed to escape," Evander said coldly. Petra felt herself tense up, nearly losing her footing as Heinrich shifted his weight wrong. "So this place will become a battlefield, after all. A pity."

They weaved their way back through the castle, but instead of the sitting room, Evander led them to the dungeon. Petra and Heinrich were put in a separate cell, and she steadied him as he sat down on the rickety cot. Shortly afterward, an imperial healer entered. Heinrich lifted his handless arm to wave at him, then frowned as he stared at the stump. "Mind putting me back together?"

"First her and now you?" the priest said. "I'm starting to think you people enjoy getting hurt. Give me the hand." She realized as she handed him the hand that he must have been the guy who did his hand-waving thing to her. He grabbed Heinrich's injured arm and placed the severed hand back in place. Frowning, he twisted it slightly and Heinrich let out a curse. He twisted again and then nodded with satisfaction.

Petra watched as the imperial priest closed his eyes and began to pray in the imperial tongue. At first, nothing happened, but then a faint purple light began to radiate from his hands and Heinrich said, "What the hell?" The light seemed to travel from the priest's hand down into Heinrich's arm, spinning around like a firefly inside it and illuminating it from the inside. As it spun out from the bone, Heinrich's fingers twitched and he jerked around, but the priest kept a firm grasp on him. The flesh seemed to stitch itself back together as the light reached the skin and faded into nothing.

Heinrich flexed his fingers, then yanked his arm away and rubbed the healed wound. There wasn't even a scar; it was simply like it didn't happen. "You're okay for an imperial," Heinrich said.

"My calling is to heal. It matters not to me if I heal a pagan or one of the faithful."

"We aren't pagans, but whatever," Heinrich said. The priest shrugged and then left; the door of their cell was closed behind him by a guard. "Thanks, Brother Caleb," Heinrich called out, but he got no response.

"So, what now?" Petra asked.

"We wait and hope Kalb's men can win this battle without him."

"Well, shit, that sure makes me feel better."

"Just don't start pacing, I feel dizzy enough as it is," Heinrich said. "Actually, you know what?" He didn't finish his sentence. Petra tried and failed to catch him as he fell over onto his side. Her shoulders slumped as he started snoring. She took the other cot for herself, lying down and staring up at the ceiling. Now that she thought about it, she preferred the old pantry. The spiders made better housemates.

CHAPTER TWENTY

FAUST

*Long did they watch in fear as the hosts of heaven flew like
stars across the sky, winged warriors crowned in light that tore
the darkness from the night and set the profaned to ruin. In
those days, longer ago to the Confessors than their days are to
mine, our ancestors called the host by a different name: The
Wild Hunt. For when they rode, the whole of the earth was
set to upheaval, and none could stand before them. They bore
the wrath of the Harbinger, and now his righteous fury is ours
to bear by the grace and will of the maker.*

Odoacer the Timid, First Antiquities 10:3-8

Nine days had already gone by since the peace talk
ended and Norbert placed Faust and Johann under
house arrest. Faust knew he wasn't doing it out of mal-
ice, but it still felt like a betrayal, all the same. Then again, it had
been Faust's intention to use himself as a bargaining chip to try
and keep the two armies from directly assaulting Elem, so it was
hardly surprising that Norbert would co-opt the strategy for
himself. The efficacy of the plan, however, was rather limited.

From his room, he could see nothing of what was going on outside. His window faced away from any of the mess he was responsible for causing in some small way. No, he had already been over this again and again: he hadn't been the one to cause any of this. There was never any hope of compromise. This so-called peace talk was nothing more than a reaffirmation of their declaration of war. He should have listened to Johann.

Several times over these last few days, he had tried to listen through his door, but what little he could hear was inconsequential. The distant sounds of guns and cannons and a faraway but constant tolling of church bells were his only signs that the fighting was still going on. From what he had seen, Oberst Kalb's army should have been easily enveloped and crushed by now. They were surrounded deep within enemy-held territory and lacked their commander.

Faust stopped pacing, his head turning toward the door. Admittedly, he did hold some biases of his own for the nationalists' cause, but if he was objective? Neither side had come looking for anything other than total surrender, even as the civil war had drawn to a prolonged stalemate. Why were both sides so sure of victory? Better yet, why would the nationalists offer to come to the table and then agree to risk coming so far beyond the front in the first place if they knew they would ultimately be betrayed?

His stomach turned as he finally started to put the pieces together in his head. Maybe this had been their plan all along. They offered peace with one hand while pretending to hold a dagger behind their back with the other. It was all a farce meant to goad the collaborators into doing something that made them look like the aggressor. Worse still, thanks to their allies in the imperial clergy, it was working.

The game was clear to Faust, but anyone looking at this situation from the rest of the realm would only see the lord of Elem imprisoning his own guests at the behest of his Palidrian overlords. Unless they all got out of here, the Dornwald, no, the whole damned country would be dragged into the flames sparked by the Herzog zu Kranzdorf. He hurried over to his window, threw open the panes, and peered down to the walls below.

Climbing down was not an option; it was simply too high. Climbing over to Johann's room was also out. Maybe if he screamed, letting his voice trail off, it would trick the guards into opening the door. What good would that do, though? They made sure to reclaim his utensils after every meal, and besides, killing them would only make the situation worse. Faust ran a dozen possibilities through his mind, each more absurd than the last, until a knock on the door brought him back to reality.

Norbert entered the room unaccompanied, the guards shutting the door behind him. The Freiherr looked at the open window, then at Faust, and said, "Close that. I need to be sure that what I say here remains private." Faust obliged, reluctantly closing the window and discarding the notion that he might reverse his role as the hostage here. "Thank you. I am going to get you and the Markgraf zu Tholst out of here, my Prinz."

"Oh. Forgive me, I really was not expecting that."

"We have to be quick about it," Norbert said. "A few of my most trusted are already preparing horses for your group."

"I feel that the executor and prelate would not take too kindly to this plan," Faust said.

"Aye, which is why we need to do it tonight." Norbert's

gaze drifted to the side as he spoke. "Brother Falvard and Oberst Kalb escaped their holding cells."

"How and when?"

"No one knows for sure. The woman on duty said she remembered the herald calling her over for something," Norbert said.

"And then the next thing she knew, the cell was empty and the two were nowhere to be found," Faust finished. Norbert's eyes darted back to meet his, a question forming on his lips. "I had a similar encounter with Falvard the day of the talks. I think he is a vampire."

"A vampire? In my castle? Are you certain?"

"I thought so at the time, but afterward, I thought I was just going crazy in the moment. Now, though, I think it is the only explanation that fits."

"Herr Timaeus may have come to the same conclusion then," Norbert said, his hand wrapping around his mouth. "The prelate led most of his remaining paladins out into the township proper to hunt down Falvard and Kalb. Herr Evander went with them as well."

"Are Prinz Alban and the Jäger still in the dungeons?"

"Actually, we never found Prinz Alban. But yes, the Jäger are still in their cells."

"Did anyone speak to them about the escape?"

"Evander did," Norbert said. "I do not know what they told him though."

"We need to speak with them," Faust said.

"We what? No, we cannot delay, the war has already begun spreading out of the Vahsland."

"I feared as much. You are really going to hate what I say next then," Faust said.

"You cannot design to take them with you?"

"Only if they act genuinely surprised when I ask them about Falvard," Faust said.

"No. No, it is too much of a risk."

"Not taking them is the riskier endeavor. You saw how few men we had left when we arrived. Norbert, we will need all the manpower we can get if we are to make it back to the Dornwald safely."

"What if they're in league with the others? Faust, the Freikorps has already broken through the western front, and Kalb will be reinforced within the next few days. Word from Urzburg has been less than favorable as well."

"I understand your concern, but why would they be left behind? I think something big is going on, and I think we will need the Jäger, not just to get home, but to find out what is really happening behind closed doors in Kranzdorf."

"I hate this, but I think I see your point," Norbert said. "I want you to know that I am not a gambling man. Do you know how hard it is to trick an inquisitor?"

"No, but something tells me you have become an old hand at it."

"Half-truths and misdirection," Norbert said with a sad, lifeless grin. "I'll take my men with me when I leave. In thirty minutes, one of the maids will come and bring you and Johann to the kitchens."

"One more question. Where is Meinherd?"

"Pretending to work as my new stable hand," Norbert said.

"A half-truth."

"Technically not a lie, and that has made all the difference. Half an hour from the moment I leave, remember that." Norbert left, and Faust quickly changed into his travel gear. He wouldn't need the formal wear anymore, but he still took the time to fold the clothes into a neat stack on the bed. Another knock came at the door. One of Norbert's maids pushed it ajar and ushered him to follow quietly.

The guest hall was empty as Norbert had promised. Johann was ready and waiting for them just inside his room. He was still favoring one leg and leaning slightly onto his cane, which he held in front of him with both hands. They snaked through the castle, down toward the ground floor, and into the kitchen where half-prepared dough lay lumpy on finely powdered stone counters. As the maid left, Johann took a seat by the exit and said, "You know this is not your fault?"

"I processed that, yes." Faust let out a frustrated sigh. "You were right, we should have left."

"True," Johann said, "but I respect why you did not want to. While we are at it, I suppose I owe Ingrid an apology."

"Telling me that does absolutely nothing," Faust said.

"I know."

"Besides," Faust said, "I went along with your idea to not bring more men."

"I wanted to bring even fewer," Johann said. "She has been avoiding me."

"Well, we have been under house arrest."

"No, before that, not that it surprises me you had not noticed."

"Since I was avoiding you too," Faust continued.

"Olivia avoids me all the time when she gets the mood for it," Johann said. "Children."

"People," Faust said.

"Yes, people." Their conversation died off, and not long afterward, Norbert came into the kitchen with a candle burning on a brass holder. He looked between the two Dornwalders and motioned to a smaller side door that opened to a cramped, winding staircase. Following him deeper into the earth, they entered the common area of the dungeon. A wooden desk sat at one end of the room near an iron gate with a cabinet of keys hanging on the wall behind it. Norbert set his candle down, retrieving a keyring from one of the hooks.

"You can likely see now why this escape was so unexpected," Norbert said as he opened the first gate and led them down the cell-lined hallway. They stopped in front of a cell where two of the Jäger sat. The older one, Heinrich, if Faust was remembering correctly, leaned back against the stone wall, humming a quiet tune. The other occupant was the young lady whose name Faust didn't know. She stared at them intently, her hazel eyes hawkish in intent beneath her slightly messy brown hair.

"What do you want?" she asked.

"To talk," Faust said.

"Your inquisitor friend already got everything out of us," she said.

"He was no friend of mine," Faust said.

"You're from down south," Heinrich said. "Dornwalder, right?"

"Yes," Faust said.

"Stop staring daggers into him, Petra. They don't like inquisitors where he's from."

"My father does keep sending them away whenever they come to petition him about arresting our heralds and Jäger. From what I am told, at least," Faust said.

"Prinz Faust," said a familiar voice from the next cell over. "You want to know what happened when Falvard and Kalb escaped, yes?"

"That was my hope," Faust said. "Herr Erik, right? You represented the Jäger Guild."

"Correct. Could you come over here, please?"

"Go, princeling," Petra said. "We were asleep when it happened." Faust nodded at her, then turned to walk to the next cell over where Erik stood behind the bars with his arms crossed.

"First, I need to ask," Erik said, "why do you care how they escaped?"

"I think Brother Falvard is a vampire," Faust said, seeing no reason to lie. He had hoped for and expected shock, but instead, Erik just nodded.

"That makes sense. He just asked the guard to let him out, and the woman did it. Then she pretended like the cell was occupied until the next guard replaced her."

"Really, Erik?" Petra said. "You're just going to go along with that?"

"Hush," Heinrich said.

"Petra, Heinrich, did either of you notice whether Falvard had a bell with him?" Erik asked.

"Sorry, I wasn't really paying attention to his belt," Heinrich said.

"I wasn't either," said Petra. Faust heard a quick intake of breath from her cell. "Wait, actually I did. Notice, I mean. When we tried to get out of here. I wanted him to ring his bell to help calm Alban down, but he wouldn't, and when I went to grab for it, there wasn't one."

"That's hardly proof," Johann argued.

"No, I think it is," Erik said, his expression darkening as he seemed to ponder the revelation. "There might be one other thing. Prinz Faust, where is Brother Meinherd?"

"He is hiding in my stables," Norbert answered. "Why?"

"I noticed that Brother Falvard wore a ring with an insignia on it," Erik said.

"You want to ask Meinherd if Brother Falvard is from a noble family?" Faust said.

"Exactly," Erik said.

"I fail to see what that will tell us," Norbert said.

"I agree with the Freiherr," Johann said. "Nobility joining the church is not uncommon. Meinherd himself is of noble birth."

"I'm lost," Petra said.

"Give them a minute," Heinrich said.

"But what if Falvard is of common birth? The sigil on his ring could give us some clue as to who sent him," Faust said.

"The church sent him, right?" Petra said. "Or am I going crazy over here?"

"Johann, if I am not mistaken, Meinherd told us that this was the first time he had met Falvard, correct?" Faust asked.

"I believe so, but he did know him by reputation."

"You mean this Falvard could be an imposter?" Erik asked. "That is a possibility. If he has some means of changing the color of his eyes, then it stands to reason he could change other parts of his appearance as well. Perhaps well enough to even fool the people who might have known the real Falvard."

"Norbert, release them," Faust said.

"You really want to take them with you?" Norbert said.

"Please, say yes," Petra said. "I will hunt you down if you don't."

"Do it," Faust said. "Erik, regardless of whether this Falvard is the real one or a fake, I need you to promise me that you will find him."

"On my life," Erik said. Norbert singled out the correct key for the cell and opened the door. Erik stepped out and extended a hand toward Faust. They clasped arms while Norbert moved on to the other cell, Heinrich and Petra leaving the small room behind.

"Follow me," Norbert said, turning back the way they came. He passed the desk and the nearer door, which likely led somewhere else in the castle, and headed back toward the staircase. Yet, instead of ascending the stairs, he knelt down at their base. It was only as he undid a lock and lifted the bottom few steps that Faust realized they were wooden. The upper stairs were carved from stone all the way up to the kitchen, and it was painfully obvious now that this was the door to a hidden escape path.

"Go through here, and take a right when you come to the fork," Norbert said. "Follow that path to its conclusion, and it will deposit you in a secret room in the walls just behind the stables. Take my candle, but snuff it out before you leave the wall, and leave what's left in one of the empty stalls."

"Thank you, your lordship," Johann said.

"You can thank me by making it home safely," the Freiherr said.

"Gladly," Petra said, grabbing the candle from the desk and pushing her way to the front of the group. The girl plunged full forward into the darkness without any hesitation. Heinrich shrugged at Erik before the two followed her into the tunnel. As the light dimmed with the slowly growing distance, Johann and Faust joined the others, the sloped door closing behind them.

CHAPTER TWENTY-ONE

MICHAEL

Having scoured accursed Stygia from the face of the earth, the Emperor of Blood and Iron set about to rebuild his dominion. Four years of plenty followed those dark three of war and desolation. Yet, even as the lands of his forebears healed, he himself fell ill with Pride, and its stigmata pierce his heart and turned him from righteousness. When Saint Drakon came to him and spoke, hoping succor could be spared for holy Valnorath, yet was he denied by him who he had called brother in days of woe.

Saint Petrus Antonius, Annalium Ruinosus LIII

Michael stood behind the stables with his hand outstretched, prayer beads coiling between his fingers. He imagined flames forming in his upturned palm. He imagined flames appearing in the open air. He imagined a pillar of flames falling from the sky into his hand.

What he got was a headache. His arm fell down to his side, the beaded rosary nearly slipping completely out of his hand.

He sat down beside his pack, almost collapsing in on himself as he let out the air in his lungs in something that was halfway between a sigh and a wheeze. Why was this taking so long? Herr Timaeus could manifest holy fire as if he was heaven-sent, and the others were almost as good at it as he was. A quick prayer, and flames burst from their fingers, arced across steel. That was what was supposed to happen, anyway.

How long had it been since Timaeus took him under his wing? More than a year, less than two, but the days sort of bled together, and he couldn't put his finger on an exact timeframe. In all that time, he had failed to manifest a miracle even once. It was frustrating. Was he doing something wrong? Did the angels just not like him? Why wouldn't they ever answer his prayers as they did for everyone else in the church?

Timaeus was always so dismissive; maybe it was his fault for being a bad teacher. Maybe if Herr Evander were to teach him, then he would finally make progress. Would he though? Probably not. He had broached the topic with the priest they were escorting to that backwoods village, Jeremias, when they were alone in the old church. Evander and Timaeus had equivalent ranks, but the Sword and the Scales had different methods of recruitment and, bluntly, Michael did not qualify to be an inquisitor.

The thought that he would never be a member of Evander's order was hardly a disappointment though. He liked the idea of being a paladin, of killing monsters like the heroes in the old tales. Alexis liked to say that heroes were just idiots who died young and never accomplished anything, but the empire was full of heroes. Herr Timaeus might be a bad example, but a single blemish was not enough to spoil a bouquet. That, too, was something Michael's sister liked to say, more often than not in reference to him.

He reached into his bag and fished out his prayer book, opening it to the dogeared page that marked the first prayer of courage. Reciting the lines of High Palidrian script, he held out his free hand again and tried to open himself to the angels. Not a single spark. Damn. On a whim, he flipped back to the prayers of justice, picking one at random and reading it aloud. He was getting good at High Palidrian at least, even if his skill at thaumaturgy was lacking.

Feeling defeated, he closed his prayer book, returned it to his pack, pulled out his canteen, and took a swig of water. Casually, he recited the prayer of Saint Helvius from memory, and the briefest spark flickered across the leather beneath his thumb. He jumped up to his feet, staring at the canteen intently. Did he really just get a spark? Blessed saints, he did.

Holding out his hand again, he recited the prayer one more time, but nothing happened. What? No, he just had it. His face contorted and he threw his canteen at the stone wall, water splattering out of it and leaving wet splotches that slowly trickled down. This was not how it should be going. He was a von Rosenberg; they did not fail like this. He wouldn't be the blemish to mar the bouquet.

Throwing fire should have been simple. Every other squire he had met could invoke angelic fire, and every student of magic attending the new athenaeum in Rosenstadt could conjure aetheric flames with ease. So why was he failing at something so simple? Minutes ticked by as he stood there, boiling in his own emotions. The thumping of gunfire and the dull drone of those damned bells kept on softly in the distance. He was about to let out a scream of frustration, but he stopped, took a deep breath, and then slowly let it out through his mouth.

As calmly as he could, he strode over to the wall and knelt down to retrieve his canteen. Then he noticed something odd. The streams of water running down the wall seemed as if they stopped almost an inch off the ground. He ran his finger along its edge and found a barely visible line in the wall where the water was pooling. His own family's castle had secret tunnels that ran throughout the whole compound and even down into the city itself, so he found it more intriguing than strange.

Pressing an ear against the stone wall, he could just barely make out a faint scratching noise from the other side, interspersed with little taps. There was definitely a tunnel hidden in the curtain wall, and Michael was sure that there were people inside trying to open this secret door. Sliding his hand over the rough stone, he tried to find any switch on his side of the wall that might open the hatch. He was about to give up when he felt a stone give ever so slightly beneath his fingers.

He depressed the stone, and the door in the wall pushed out with a ragged groan. Surprised, he backed away, almost tripping over his pack as the section of wall swung outward. A girl who he recognized almost instantly stepped out, and she quickly tackled him to the ground. His head bounced in the dirt before being pushed back into it, a familiar hand clamping down on his mouth for the second time in the last month. Damn it all, she was starting to make a habit of this.

"Wait, I remember you," she said, her eyes lighting up with sick glee. "Oh, this must be all kinds of embarrassing for you." Michael stared up at her, eyes narrowed, and let out a bothered grunt. She smiled, almost looking halfway pretty as she gloated in his face. "How about you listen this time when I tell you to be quiet?" He nodded as best he could with his head pinned to the ground. "Good boy. Wouldn't want to have to punch you again."

"Friend of yours?" said a scruffy-looking man with a tattered sleeve.

"Met him in Laupen when I tried to rescue Traugott," she said as she let go of his mouth and got up off of him. He sat up, rubbing the back of his head and checking it for blood.

"Seriously?" the man said.

"He's Timaeus' squire, I think," said a boy about his age, maybe a year or two older. "Or am I mistaken?" Michael just stared at him. He had short black hair parted to one side and pulled slightly back. He seemed to be of noble stock, but that did not necessarily mean anything at that point. Several other men came out from the tunnel, one older and walking with a cane and the other middle-aged and hawkish in appearance.

"'Quiet' doesn't mean you can't speak at all, smart ass," the girl said.

"Herr Timaeus is my mentor," Michael said with a huff. He shot her a cautious glance, but she seemed disinclined to hit him again.

"Well, guess that means you're coming with us. Can't have you reporting to your master that we came through here," said the scruffy man.

"You what?" Michael said, heat rising to his face. Him, a hostage? What absolute nonsense were these people spewing?

"Tie his hands, and keep an eye on him," the hawkish man said. "I'm going to go see if our horses are prepped."

"I'll come with you," Scruffy said. "Petra, be a dear and play nice."

"Bite me," Petra said as the two middle-aged men walked off. She undid a ribbon wrapped tightly around her sleeve. "Give me your hands," she ordered.

"You have got to be joking," he said, but as she balled her fist around the ribbon, he held his hands up and then moved them out in front of him. Petra tied his wrists together with the black ribbon and finished it with a cutesy little bow. The look in her eye told him she knew exactly what she was doing and was loving every second of it. This was ridiculous. What had he ever done to her to deserve this?

"This is an odd turn of events," the man with the cane chimed in, "but turnabout is fair play, as has oft been said."

"Her, I know, but who are the rest of you people?" Michael said.

"You don't know me," Petra said.

"If we are going to bring him with us, I think we should gag him," said the young man. *What?*

"I only had the one ribbon unless you have one squirreled away somewhere, Faust."

"Faust?" Michael said in a low tone.

"I do not," Faust replied before addressing Michael. "And yes, Faust as in von Schwarzdorn, the Prinz zu Dorneswik, if that was what you were thinking. So you can stop gawking. Johann, do you have anything we can gag him with?"

"I left my spare socks in Norbert's guest quarters, I am afraid," Johann said.

"I have a used sock," Petra said. "Two, actually."

"Please, for the love of the saints, I beg you, do not put your filthy socks near my mouth," Michael said.

"I don't love your saints," Petra said.

"He does have a point, though. A dirty gag might poison him," Faust pointed out.

"And he could always choke himself on a clean one," Petra retorted.

"Fair point," Faust said.

"I think it best we drop this topic before he screams for help," Johann interrupted.

"Our fathers are peers of the same station, yet you talk to me like this? I had heard Dornwalders were rude and uncultured, but this is absolutely unimaginable," Michael said. He watchted as Faust and Johann shared a conspiratorial look.

"On second thought, I say we go with the young lady's dirty sock idea," said Johann, the lines on his face growing tight.

"W-wait, that was uncouth of me. I spend too much time with Timaeus, and his negativity seems to have infected me like a bad rash. Can we start over?" His eyes darted down to Petra's boots, and he shuddered as a chill went down his back. "Prinz Michael von Rosenberg. My father is the Herzog zu Rosenstadt. A pleasure to meet you all."

"Von Rosenberg, huh?" Petra said. "Never heard of them."

"His father rules the Rosenhohen out east on the imperial border," Faust said. "I think it was his grandfather that turned traitor when the empire invaded." Michael felt his eye twitch as Faust slandered his family name.

"And I should care about that why?" Petra said.

"No idea." Faust turned his attention back to Michael. "I think I met your sister once. Alexis, was it?"

"Pompous, rabid she-wolf?" Michael asked.

"With flowing red hair like hellfire around her head?"

"That was her," Michael confirmed.

"She insulted the Dornwald too, so I guess I can see the resemblance."

"Ah, good, Meinherd is here," Johann said, drawing Michael's attention to one of the new stable hands, the one with the mutton chops.

"Just talked with Erik. He, Heinrich, and Ingrid are preparing the horses. Should be ready any moment now."

"And you came out here to avoid the heavy labor?" Faust
said.

"I've been shoveling horse shit for the last few days,
thanks to you. I've felt cleaner mucked up with lycan blood
than, well, all this." He motioned down at his brown clothes,
which were a few shades darker around the lower portions
of his legs.

"Hello, again, Brother Meinherd," Petra said, giving the
man a small wave. Wait, did that mean he was a priest?

"Oh, Petra. Punching others instead of yourself today?"

"That was one time, and I haven't punched him yet, either."

"Let us keep it that way, thank you," Michael said. In a
hushed tone, he added, "You violent ape." Clearly, it wasn't
hushed enough, as a moment later, Petra hit him in his gut,
and he collapsed onto his knees and fell to his side, clutching
his stomach. This girl was a damned she-beast, hardly better
than his elder sister. He couldn't breathe, and tears welled in
his eyes as he struggled to fill his lungs against the pain. He
was sure he would be coughing up blood before long.

"Should have kept your mouth shut," Petra said.

"I thought I told you to play nice?" Heinrich said as he
rejoined the group.

"He had it coming," Faust said. And he had the nerve of
calling the von Rosenbergs traitors? Michael opened his
mouth to try to speak, but he could only hack and wheeze as
he lay there in the dirt. Faust came over, grabbed hold of him,
and hauled him back to his feet, saying, "Come on, now. I
take it the horses are ready, Heinrich?"

"Most of them are. Hell, they even prepared a carriage
for us."

"Wonderful," said Meinherd.

"They also found our missing prinz," Heinrich said. Michael watched as Petra beamed at the mention of Prinz Alban, one of the fugitives Timaeus and Evander were out searching for. Now he knew how the man had evaded capture for so long; they never did think to look for duplicity from Freiherr Norbert. That was their mistake. He would go along with this for now, but the very instant he saw an opportunity to turn this hostage situation around, he would take it.

Faust helped him hobble around the stables and into the plain carriage before leaving him there with the crippled Markgraf and the shit-stained dandy, Prinz Alban. His golden hair was now messy, matted, and light brown, and he sat uncomfortably in his rugged plain clothes. The equally filthy Meinherd took the last seat in the carriage, and not long after that, they began their journey.

CHAPTER TWENTY-TWO

FAUST

Soon, I found myself weary of the solitude of Vorbotenruhe and so set out from her gates to travel the lands as I had done in my youth. I left before dawn, sparing no words for my sentinels and apostles. Faithful though they were, I desired to once more walk as the common man and not as the honored teacher. Of my plans, only Sighild was made keen, for she had long mourned her departed Wulfrid, and I could not bear to bring more sorrow to her heart.

Alaric the Confessor, Confessions of Alaric 23:1-5

Faust was glad to be riding again, even more so now that he was reunited with the chestnut pony Norbert's kin in Arensfeld had gifted him. Whatever happened with this war, he hoped their family, every branch, came out of this mess okay. They were good people, even if he was not quite on the same page as them on everything.

Ingrid and Heinrich had been the first out of the gate. Faust and Petra followed close behind, with Erik and the rest of their retinue from Tholst tailing behind the carriage. They hastened along eastbound, passing numerous streets that would carry them back to the southern gate, but so far, each of them was too small for the carriage to enter. They were more or less following the same route Norbert had paraded them through when they had first arrived at Elem, though the circumstances were far less frivolous and hopeful this time around.

People went about their daily business, milling about between colorfully painted buildings as if to convince themselves nothing was amiss. There was some commotion as people in the street quickly dove out of the way of the passing Dornwalder caravan, shouting obscenities at them as they rushed to escape the township. Clearly, Norbert had decided against instituting a lockdown. He seemed to think the fighting would remain outside the town for at least a few more days, but the gunshots sounded louder from here than they had from the courtyard.

A series of deeper reports called out from cannons outside, their payloads cracking against the northern walls a moment later. Norbert's prediction, or maybe "hope" described it better, was quickly proven unfounded. Not long after that, the city bells began to ring, and screams rose from the northern side of town. Faust could see nothing from his saddle, but that didn't stop him from glancing to his left at every intersection.

"Eyes on the road," Petra said in a raised voice.

"I know, but..." Faust said, looking north again as they went through another t-shaped crossing. There was a crowd of people running south and a flash of something dark leaping down from a nearby rooftop. "Werewolves!"

"What?" shouted Ingrid and Heinrich in unison.

"Damn it all!" Petra said. "Master, I think this was what Kalb meant when he said he had the werewolf problem under control!"

"Doesn't matter!" Heinrich said. "We keep going."

"The next crossing looks wider going south!" Ingrid said, raising a hand and waving it right to signal to the carriage driver. They hit the intersection and pulled to drive their horses to the south, a screeching of metal coming from the carriage behind them as it evened out.

"Petra, what was that about Oberst Kalb?" Faust shouted. She looked at him out of the corner of her eye, then back to the road, and finally back to him.

"Later!" she said, refocusing on the road. The screaming and gunfire were getting louder with each moment, almost matching the beating of hooves against cobblestone as they sped toward some sort of freedom. A group of guards rounded a corner ahead of them and Faust opened his mouth to shout a warning, but a death glare from Petra stilled him in his saddle. The armed footmen narrowly avoided being trampled, pressing themselves tight to walls that rose up on either side of the street.

Petra was a Jäger, even if she was technically only an apprentice. She should have known how dangerous this situation was. "We need to warn someone," Faust urged, but the others either didn't hear him or just didn't care. Were they really willing to sacrifice Elem and her entire population to escape? Was he willing to?

He ran the thought experiment in his head, weighing the lives in Elem against the lives of everyone in the realm. That was the math of it, the ruthless calculus that justified scourging entire towns off the map; it was the reason cartographers had long since stopped marking the newer and smaller towns entirely. Who would care when some small village disappeared overnight if they had never known it existed in the first place?

Everyone remembered the false scourging of Stenwarl, though, when the empire burned half the capital to the ground. This entire damned war was started for the sake of avenging a measly handful of lives lost in those flames, and now the Herzog's mercenaries seemed keen on sharing the misery. How many lives would it take before all these idiots were satisfied that they had earned justice? How much bloodshed and suffering enacted on the innocent would it take before retribution was earned?

What, then, for all those lives? Where would their justice be? How would the common man avenge his son or his daughter? What Petra had said about Kalb was still bothering him too. Even if she would not divulge the details, he had a sick feeling that told him he knew what she was thinking. His instinct was corroborated by the werewolves flooding into Elem the moment after Kalb's men breached the walls, and the way she immediately mentioned that he'd reported having that situation handled.

It fit too well with what he knew from Naakt, however little that may be, in truth. The Freikorps and the Jäger Guild were part of the Aushansa, alongside the guild founded by Alwin Dahl. That man, made famous for his medical breakthroughs, had been involved, if tangentially, in the outbreak in the Larswald. If the Erfinder Guild was having werewolves captured for experimentation, it stood to reason that their only source of subjects would have to come from the mercenaries, because the Jäger were oathbound to eradicate them.

Vampires and werewolves though? What the hell was going on? He had no love for the occupational government, but if the nationalists were willing to weaponize the accursed, were they any better? Faust wanted to scream, but instead, he just hurried his horse along to move even faster. He was left with one simple question: was he willing to do nothing while Elem was scourged, even knowing this outbreak was manufactured? No, he would have no part of this mummer's farce.

He steeled himself for death and started to lift the reins to steer his mount left when he heard the crash of wood and metal against stone behind him. The carriage was overturned in the street, its horses mangled atop each other and the driver sprawled lifelessly beside them. A lycanthrope stood atop the carriage, eyeing their group for its next target. Faust realized the irony of the situation and almost laughed in shock.

Beside him, Petra fumbled with the empty air, instinctively searching for weapons she no longer had. One of the Tholst guards trailing them fired at the beast, and it decided then to pounce from its perch onto the man. His bravery was more praiseworthy than his aim; he screamed as the werewolf made a meal of him.

Faust leaped from his horse, tossing the reins to Petra before hurrying over to the carriage. Climbing up the side of the driver's bench, he began prying open the bent, splintered, and skyward door. Through the window, he could see Alban and Meinherd collapsed atop Johann and Michael on either side of the interior. The door finally gave way, and Faust nearly fell backward off the side before catching himself just barely and offering a hand to the men inside.

Alban was the first to recover from the collision. He took Faust's hand, and Faust hefted the blond prinz out with ease. "Get to the horses," Faust ordered, reaching in and grasping one of Michael's bound hands. The grip was awkward, but Faust got the squire out too. "Are you both okay?"

"My damned leg," Johann said through gritted teeth.

"I'll help lift the Markgraf up," Meinherd said, clearly winded. "You pull him, then help him off. I can get out on my own." The herald rolled onto the other door and stood up, pulling Johann off the wall and helping him stay on his good leg while Faust grabbed his hand. Faust pulled Johann up while Meinherd pushed him from below until he was sitting on the edge of the door. Johann slid over to the side where Ingrid stood ready, rifle aimed toward the werewolf now tearing through their rear guard.

Faust helped his godfather lower himself into the arms of his guard captain while Meinherd, true to his word, pulled himself out of the carriage with ease. Faust jumped down from the side of the carriage and grabbed Ingrid's rifle, backing away slowly to cover the others in case the beast turned their way. Meinherd jumped down too, pulling his shirt off to reveal a torso covered in splotchy burn scars.

"Hand me the gun," the herald said. Faust complied, then ran to his horse and climbed back into the saddle. He had half expected the others to leave without them, but as Petra helped Alban up onto her horse, he chided himself for the thought. They may have been willing to leave Elem to its fate, but that decision had not been made out of spite.

Erik was the only one of the rear guards to join them, though he looked significantly worse for wear and was without his horse. He passed Ingrid and Johann, shaking his head as he counted their remaining horses. They had four mounts and nine people. "Someone is going to have to stay behind," Erik said.

"I vote we leave the redhead," Petra said.

"What?" Michael said. "Do you know who my father is?"

"Some big noble, if I recall. Don't care; you aren't one of ours."

"His father is the Viceroy's most vocal supporter amongst the nobility. We can use him for leverage," Erik said. "I vote for myself. I have the best chances of surviving this nightmare on foot."

"Not a chance, Herr Erik. I know who your mother is, who you are, and between knowing that and how bad my leg feels..." Johann said. Faust watched as he fought himself out of Ingrid's grip and then tumbled to the ground in visible pain. "I cannot ride a horse like this." He started crawling back toward the carriage, batting Ingrid's hand away when she tried to pick him up.

"I can't let you do this, my lord," she said.

"We can tie you to a horse," Faust said.

"We barely have time for this conversation. Go now, and get my godson home safely. Damn it, Ingrid, my mind is made up, stop trying to help me."

"But... it is my duty. To protect you and your family," Ingrid said.

"Tell Alena and the children that I am sorry beyond words... that I died well for kin and country. That is your duty now," Johann said. "See them to safety Prinz Erik."

"Understood, my lord Markgraf," Erik said. He ran quickly back the way he came and returned to the carriage with another rifle. The Jäger knelt down beside Johann and Ingrid, handing the Markgraf the rifle and some spare ammo. Meinherd climbed up behind Faust and held him back as he struggled to get off the horse. Ingrid exchanged a few hushed words with her liege before she stood up and got back on her mount. Faust watched as she reached down and hauled Michael up into the saddle in front of her with Erik's help. Erik got onto Heinrich's horse, and they left Johann behind.

Faust struggled with the reins as they rode away, but Meinherd positioned his hands to ensure Faust's efforts were futile. A gunshot rang out loudly behind them, and Faust turned as far as he could from atop his mount. He couldn't see his godfather at all, only the sudden billowing plumes of ruby-red flames spilling out into the intersection. Spinning around to peer back from the other side of Meinherd, he got a better view of the flames and a single shadow of a figure in their bright hues.

"Master Timaeus!" Michael shouted, drawing Faust's attention toward him just in time to see Ingrid jerk him back close to her and whisper something into his ear. Whatever she threatened to do to him was enough to shut his mouth. Horrific cries and the roar of flames soon overtook the soundscape of Elem, punctuated by the percussion of guns and cannon.

"Turn us around, Meinherd!" Faust said, still struggling against the herald's control over his horse. "Meinherd! Meinherd!" His protests went unanswered, but still, he continued begging, tears streaking down his face as a blaze of scarlet light consumed the streets behind them.

CHAPTER TWENTY-THREE

PETRA

It was deep in the midst of that terrible winter when the stranger came to me who called himself by the name of Uhtric. A farmer had found him half-dead from the frost and brought him to my asylum that he might be saved before his death. How little it was that we had known then, but soon he recovered himself and spoke to me of Clovis. I grieved for a time, knowing that he was lost to us. But as I spoke with Uhtric, I came to realize that Clovis was not truly gone, for his passion and his will lived on in the hearts of all those he had touched.
Gerlind the Confessor, Confessions of Gerlind 30:21-26

Faust had barely spoken since they made their escape from Elem, that is after he stopped shouting at Meinherd. Petra tried to understand, but she had basically run away from home and never looked back, so the thought of caring for someone like that was difficult. Then again, she had gone back for Traugott, and she would have gone back if it had been Alban. She knew them, but it wasn't the same as how he knew his godfather.

They had traveled a good deal south, enough to clear the fighting and get a head start on the imperials. "Herr Timaeus will come for me," Michael said often. Too often. If she could get him and Faust to split the difference on talking, she would. Michael almost never shut up unless she threatened him. Or if Ingrid did. Maybe he was into that sort of thing.

Regardless, they had stopped and made camp in the dead of night on the side of the open road. Erik wouldn't let them make a fire, but it wasn't like they had anything to cook anyway. Dinner was a few strips of jerky and hardtack, which was a commodity now that their wagon was gone and most of their supplies with it. Erik and Ingrid took the first watch, shooting down Heinrich's offer by pointing out he still needed to rest.

Erik did too, but Petra wasn't going to be the one arguing with him, or anyone else, over who got which watch. First watch also meant keeping tabs on the loudmouthed redhead to make sure he didn't try to sneak off in the night. She pulled her coat off and lay down in the grass; it was actually more comfortable than the cot in Elem's dungeon. Turning her head, she watched as Alban tried to figure out how best to comfort Faust.

Alban was a hugger, but he was keenly aware that he was filthy and didn't want to subject anyone else to his muck. Faust's reaction to his attempts sent a wave of embarrassed unease through the older prinz, and he slunk off without a word. That was the last thing she saw before she drifted off.

She was having the dream again, hers, not that other one with the kind warmth. She felt the cruel heat of blood on her small hands, the pinch of a splinter pressing deeper into her finger as she clutched the short stake tighter. There was screaming from the thing and from her little brother, Ben.

Father and Luger, the eldest of them, came running with a few of the field hands. They spoke gibberish she couldn't understand, then father ripped the stake from her hands. The splinter caught painfully and ripped some of her skin.

Petra woke up at the same place as always, right as her father slapped her hard. She sat up, her coat falling into her lap in a heap. Heinrich looked over to her and gave a small nod. He was used to seeing her do that by now. Alban, however, had not had the distinct pleasure. He shuffled over to her, hands reaching out to hover a few inches away from her. "Did you have a bad dream?" he asked quietly.

"Yeah," she said. "It's nothing to worry about though." She leaned over and hugged him, feeling him stiffen under her touch. "I'm dirty too, so it doesn't matter."

"I am so sorry. I should be the one comforting you kids, but I..."

"Just shut up and take in the moment. I don't do this often," Petra interrupted. Heinrich snorted as he tried and failed to laugh as quietly as possible. She let Alban go and stood up, going over to sit beside her master. "How much longer till my watch?"

"A few minutes," Heinrich said, then turned to Alban. "You can go ahead and get some sleep, my lord. Petra will finish off for you."

"Okay," Alban said quietly before scooting away to find a soft spot of sod to lie down on. They sat in silence for a few minutes, neither saying a word as they listened for the same two things. The first was danger, and the second was for Alban to fall asleep. When Heinrich was satisfied the prinz had settled into sleep, he let out a ragged groan.

"He isn't doing well either."

"No shit," Petra said.

"Actually, a lot of it." Heinrich paused briefly and said, "Sorry. This isn't the time or place for jokes."

"What's the plan?"

"We'll go south, help escort the princes to the Dornwald, then double back once we reach a castle called Naakt. Apparently, Yorick and Cecilia were there when Prinz Faust and the Markgraf were heading up this way, so we can grab them if they're still there," Heinrich said.

"What about Erik?" Petra asked.

"What about him?"

"Don't give me that. Is he coming with us, or is he going to go on a one-man mission to hunt down Falvard?" Heinrich's uncharacteristic silence answered her question just as well as words would have. "That's just the way he is, isn't it? Why?"

"Not my story to tell, kiddo. Erik's always been like that, as long as I've known him, at least."

"So he'll just go running off alone into danger while we run to safety with our tails between our legs?" Petra said.

"We're going to come back, and we're going to bring help," Heinrich said.

"He'll be dead by then," she said.

"Have a little faith."

"That's not good enough."

"Too bad," Heinrich said. "Time's up. I'm going to sleep. Have fun with the statue." He got up and went over to Faust, shaking him awake and telling him it was his watch now. Heinrich took Faust's spot in the grass as the black-haired prince stood up and sat beside Petra. He faced the other direction and said nothing as he stared out into the night.

"You feeling all right?" she asked. He didn't respond, letting a long silence draw out between them. She glanced at him a few times, his face a mask of indifference.

"No," Faust said suddenly. "No, I am not."

"Uh, sorry," she said.

"Why?"

"I don't know, isn't that what people are supposed to say when they hear someone isn't feeling well?" Petra said.

"Maybe. You stayed. Back when the carriage first overturned."

"Well, yeah, I needed to make sure Alban was safe."

"I am sorry too," he said.

"For thinking I'd run off?" Petra said. Faust nodded. "Don't worry about it. I, uh, I would have if things were different, so you don't need to apologize." They eased into another long silence. Faust had apparently exhausted his willingness to talk. She couldn't help but wonder why he opened up to her, though. She could understand why he wouldn't talk to Meinherd and that woman, Ingrid, but why with her? Would it be weird to ask? Probably.

"I heard your conversation with Herr Heinrich. I have not slept."

"I take it you don't like the idea of leaving either, then?" Petra asked.

"Johann might not be dead. There was a paladin in the flames. Maybe they took him prisoner. Even if he is dead... No, I refuse to accept it without proof. I need proof. I cannot go back home until I know for certain."

"The others won't agree to that. But I guess that's why you're talking to me then, isn't it?"

"You do not want to run away either," he said.

"This isn't our fight, or it wasn't," Petra said.

Faust let out a morbid laugh. "No, it was not, but these people seem hellbent on dragging us all down with them."

"You seem dead set on this, so I take it you have a plan of

your own?" Petra asked. He motioned with his chin, and she twisted her torso and neck to see what he had gestured toward. She followed his eyes; their icy stare was fixated on Michael. "We co-opt the hostage situation?"

"We could wait and trade him to his father for some nebulous political gain in the long run," Faust explained, "or we could trade him back to his paladin master for my godfather."

"You think that crazy bastard would go for it?" she said.

"He has to," Faust said. He must have caught the look she gave him out of the corner of his eye because he elaborated. "They need the support of his father to keep the rest of the nobility in check. The ones not already inclined to side with Prinz Alban's family, at least."

"That's only half a plan, though. I know a few dead drop locations we can get supplies at, weapons, ammo, and food. No telling which ones are stocked, but that'll take care of some of the how."

"We can use my life and his as leverage," Faust said.

"But that leaves me high and dry if we get captured. Nobodies like me don't get political immunity."

"I can always threaten to kill myself if they try and hurt you," Faust said. Petra sat there quietly for a moment, unsure if she had heard him right. He wasn't serious, was he? "They can always just call my bluff, but I can try and be as convincing as possible." There it was.

"Right, so, we take prince asshat in the dead of night, leave all our friends here without any guards at watch, and hope they don't get eaten or killed. We also bank on them not just turning around and dragging us back south. Not to mention, we'd be walking into a town currently stuck between two fighting armies and a pack of rabid beast-men," Petra said. She looked up at the stars, leaning back onto her hands.

His plan was stupid, beyond stupid if she was being completely honest. Going along with it meant almost certain death for both of them. And for Michael, but he didn't really count. They could probably use him as bait if they ran into any werewolves, and that would buy them a few minutes. If she went along with it.

She turned to look at Faust, but instead of that dead, fish-eyed look he had earlier that evening, she saw a boy deep in thought. Was she really willing to risk her life on a scheme cooked up by some quick-witted princeling? "You said your father was a Herzog, yeah?"

"I did, though I do not see why that is relevant. Oh."

Yeah, if they made it out of this alive, she was going to be rich. "Sure, why the hell not? I've risked my life for a whole lot less anyway."

"We can discuss your price on the road," Faust said. He stood up, dusted himself off, held up an arm, and bit the fabric, using his other hand to rip the sleeve off below the elbow. Faust wadded his sleeve up into a ball as he walked over to Michael, gently opened the sleeping boy's mouth, and jammed the gag into it.

Michael woke up wide-eyed as Faust yanked him up by his collar and held him at eye level. "You listen to me. I am going to take you back to Elem, and I am going to trade your sorry, pompous ass to your equally pompous master in exchange for my godfather's life. Do not resist me, or I will hurt you. Do as I say, and you can be back home in Rosenstadt feeling sorry for yourself in no time. Understand?"

He must have because Faust hoisted him to his feet and pushed him toward Petra. She grabbed Michael's wrist when he came close and held him there as Faust rifled through their few remaining packs. He finally grabbed Meinherd's, and it jingled slightly as he slung the strap over his shoulder. Michael motioned toward his pack and made a muffled grumbling noise until Faust picked it up and brought it with him.

Petra almost pulled Michael off balance as she leaned down to scoop her own bag up off the ground. She followed Faust as he started toward the horses lying a few paces away from the group. He knelt down and put a hand on the head of the one he'd been riding, then stood up and carried on north.

Petra caught up to him and pointed off slightly to the west. "We should head that way until we hit the river. That way, we'll have a reliable source of drinking water." He changed course without a word, and she tugged Michael along behind them. She didn't want to mention the supply drop with him in earshot. With luck, they'd find replacement weapons and enough ammo to last them to Elem. If nothing else, they could restock on travel rations.

CHAPTER TWENTY-FOUR

FAUST

I spent half my life as a listless wanderer, but now I have found purpose for my feet. Never am I truly tired, even as my body gives way to aches and pains, because my soul burns brighter now than in all the days when my flesh was hale and full of life. I am still a wanderer, but I am no longer listless, for I know my destination.
Alaric the Confessor, Confessions of Alaric 25:24-27

The three kept walking until the sun came up, and they sat down for a short break to eat something. Their rations were still meager fare, but it wasn't the taste that kept Faust from eating. His stomach felt like it was in knots, and even though he knew such a thing was physically impossible, it was still an apt metaphor for how he felt. His head hurt, his stomach churned, and his heart felt like it was being boiled.

"Faust?" Petra said, looking at him with a slight expression of concern.

"Could you repeat that?"

"You need to sleep."

"I am fine," he said.

"I asked if you needed sleep, and you just stared off down the field. You aren't fine. There's a thicket not too far from here, I'll go scope it out and see if it's safe. If it is, we can stay there until nightfall."

"We should be sleeping at night like normal people," Michael said. They'd ungagged him so he could eat, and Faust really, earnestly wanted to strike him. Doing so would be counterproductive, though, at least for now.

"We're more likely to get spotted during the day," Petra said. "At least out here. We could always try to play ourselves off as a couple of weary orphans looking for shelter, but unless you two can stop speaking all proper all the time, I don't think they'll buy it."

"If the locals had any sense, they would have fled when the mercenaries attacked us," Michael said, then added, "'Us' being exclusionary to the two of you, of course."

"The idiot has a point," Petra said, "but I still think the thicket is our best bet for today."

"I do not need to rest," Faust said, but as he stood up, he lost his balance and staggered a few steps before sitting back down. He took a deep breath. "I will begrudgingly concede to you that point. I'll make sure he doesn't slink off while you are gone."

"Thank you," Petra said, finishing off her last biscuit with a swig of water. Faust watched her leave and walk across the open plain toward the pointed thrust of woodlands in the distance. Michael squirmed against his bindings as he tried to reach for a bit of jerky in his bag. He had the meat stick halfway to his mouth when he dropped it into the dirt.

"For the love of... Faust can you please untie me, for Saints' sake?"

"No," Faust said.

"What am I going to do? You two are taking me exactly where I want to be going. Running off on my own would get me killed, as will starting a fight with you with that wild woman around," Michael said. Faust didn't bother responding to him. He was correct, but being correct was not going to win him the argument.

"I would expect you, of all people, to understand the importance of treating your fellow with respect," Michael said. Faust felt himself shoot up from his spot in the dirt in a motion more like an out-of-body experience than a voluntary action. He had Michael by his collar again. Anger pulsed through him, then subsided like a swell of water flooding over him and thinning out. He dropped the other noble, falling backward when he stepped away and tripped on Michael's pack.

Faust started laughing as he looked at Michael. "Fellows? What, because our fathers share the title of Herzog? Because we both share the title of Prinz? I am heir to my house and all the responsibilities that come with it. What the hell will you inherit?"

"I..." Michael said, his face flitting through several emotions before settling on a twisted snarl.

"Struck a nerve then?" Faust said. "I know your type. You would have thrown us all to the wolves if it meant saving yourself. Nobility? What nobility? Has your blood made you any braver, any more competent? Or does it just hang over you like a blade on a string, demanding you pretend to be better than you are?"

"Shut your mouth!" Michael said.

"Both of you, shut up!" Petra said. When had she gotten back? "You two idiots are going to get us caught. Now, shut your mouths before I do it for you."

"You cannot speak to me like that," Michael said, his eyes wet and angry.

"Bunch of damned children," she said as she shoved the soggy wad of cloth back into Michael's mouth, forcing it open with a hand on his jaw. "You should know better," she said as she turned to Faust. "The hell is wrong with you?"

"Seems like a growing list," he said with a small smile. "Sorry."

"The tip of the thicket's clear. Can you make it on your own? I can't exactly carry you and drag him."

"I will crawl if I have to," Faust said. He dragged himself up from the dirt and grass and managed to lift the pack he had taken from Meinherd without falling again. Petra led Michael by the wrist, and Faust followed as they crossed the field to the edge of the trees. She plunged into the dense foliage, and he took great care to trace her steps to avoid anything that would trip him again. She took them farther in than he felt she could have gotten in the time she was gone, but he said nothing.

They ended up at a large tree that grew at the peak of a small mound of dirt too small to really call a hill. Thick bushes surrounded the mound, thorny and uninviting to anyone, even the sole Dornwalder prince. Petra rounded the tree to one side where the mound had collapsed, or rather, had been dug away between two large roots. "Get some sleep," Petra said. "I'll take watch."

Admittedly, Faust felt exhausted and sick. Some sleep would do him good, and she had made a valid point about traveling during the day. His little outburst with Michael had all but secured this detour and was likely why Petra had led them deeper into the woods than expected. There was still the possibility that the others would have continued south since Prinz Alban and Meinherd were not fighters and would need protection.

Erik might still come for them on his own, but even that was preferable to being ridden down by the whole lot of them. If he was the only one to come looking for them, Faust was sure he could be convinced of the plan so long as it left him free to hunt Falvard afterward. Faust would even join him in that if he could, and there was little doubt in his mind that Petra would volunteer as well.

He was thankful to her for coming along; it was the only reason he was willing to do this. Nestling himself into the hollow, he watched as Petra shoved Michael in beside him. It would be warmer with him there, and it would make it harder for him to make his unlikely escape. Faust closed his eyes, letting his head drift onto the dirt wall to his left. With a little bit of effort, they could easily thatch a roof together for the hollow. Not that they had the time. But maybe...

Faust woke up as swiftly as he had drifted off, feeling surprisingly well considering the odd angle he found his head. Maybe Meinherd had been onto something the entire time. He laughed, genuinely laughed, at the thought of that damnable, near-narcoleptic herald. It must have been fairly loud, too, because he heard the sudden rustling of leaves from outside the hollow.

Prying himself out from beside Michael, Faust stood up and stretched. Petra was nearby, fully composed and looking at him with a question on her face. "I remembered something humorous as I woke up," he said.

"Is it a joke I would get?" she said.

"Probably not, and explaining it will just detract from it," Faust said.

"Cool, love being left in the dark. Actually, I don't really care. You feeling better now?"

"Much, and I mean it this time," he said. "How long was I out?"

"About five and a half hours. We still have daylight to burn if you want to get some more sleep," she said. She brushed a strand of brown hair from her face, pushing it behind her ear and pulling away a leaf in a continuous motion.

"No, but I can take over for you here," he said. Looking back into the crook at Michael, he asked, "When did you take the gag out of his mouth?"

"Just after you passed out," she said, pointing to a low-hanging branch nearby where his sleeve was hanging out to dry. "Next time, you get to be the one to do that."

"Deal. But that cannot be the nastiest thing you have done for money, can it?"

"Not even close. I'll take you up on that offer, move over." Faust took a step to the side and Petra moved from her watch position into the crook between the dirt wall and Michael. "I haven't seen anything, but that doesn't mean much."

"I am more than well aware," Faust said. He held up his sleeveless arm and showed her his scars. It perhaps was not the best thing to insinuate his understanding by misleading her, but it was expedient. He knew the situation could deteriorate at any moment. He also knew that when it did, it could come in any form, not just that of a monster. One venomous snake, insect, or arachnid could end them just as quickly as anything else.

He took Petra's seat on a fallen log that was partly rotted underneath but still able to hold some weight. She had arranged their packs beside the hollow, and though his stomach grumbled, he stayed where he was. Her suggestion had played out well so far, and it raised his image of her a fair bit. Yorick had taught him to temper his idealization of the

Jäger, but they were still proving his best bet in this horrid race.

He made a mental note to ask her to teach him what she knew when she woke up. And to ask how long she had been an apprentice. Maybe he should ask that one first, though. No, on second thought, he would avoid that question and stick with asking for a beginner's course. Whatever skills she lacked, he could potentially fill in with his own training and general knowledge.

They might damn well be able to pull this off after all.

CHAPTER TWENTY-FIVE

PETRA

As I coughed up my life's blood, thinking that surely, I would soon die, he came to me. He had wings that shone with light, and he laid a hand upon my head, and I was made whole. Then he told me, "Vulferam, take the weak and the sickly, and spirit them away from this place cursed by war and blight." I objected at first, thinking it cowardly to flee when my strength had been renewed, but he showed me a sign and I knew that he was right. The others who were strong would survive the tyranny of the dread wyrms, but we who had been weak had no future in these lands.

Vulferam the Blessed, First Harbingers 1:10-15

Petra had almost forgotten how unnerving it was to travel at night without any weapons. She had a dagger she'd taken from the armory at Elem, but it was only made of steel. Technically, anything would die if you stabbed it in the right place regardless of what type of metal you poked into it, but she felt better when she had true silver on hand.

Another technicality was that they did have some true silver, but it was in the form of the little bell Faust had lifted when he took Brother Meinherd's traveling pack. Every so often, she would hear it jingle in the bag as they walked. She would also occasionally see Faust's hand move to the flap of the bag whenever some animal called out in the night. Maybe he'd also seen a few dead heralds somewhere, though, because he never quite went through with the motion.

They had set out at dusk toward the Arol River and carried on in a mostly straight path going north by northwest. The dense patch of woods they had first camped in gave way to farmlands as they got closer to the river. Following the winding path of a quiet brook, they eventually made it to the edge of the river a day or night later. It turned out Michael had been right about something.

"This house is empty too!" Petra said, poking her head into a small cottage. The one-room building sat unoccupied. Food sat half-eaten on the table, playing feast to flies. A pair of beds, one larger than the other, was on the other side of the cottage with a bedsheet hung between them. Her older brother had tried that once. It hadn't ended well for him. She entered and started poking around through the cabinets.

There weren't many supplies in there that they could use. There wasn't even a single jar of jam or honey anywhere. Maybe they had a smokehouse nearby with some preserved meats. The mill might have grain left in it too. At least she hoped so. It had been a few years since she'd tried her hand at fieldwork, and she wasn't looking to start again here. Picking fruits she could do, that was easy, but they didn't have time to deal with anything more labor-intensive.

She grabbed one of the chairs from the table and took it across the cottage, setting it at the end of the bedsheet divider. Using her not-silver dagger, she cut through the end of the rope holding the sheet up and watched as it fell to the plank floor in a heap. One more cut later, she started coiling the rope for later use. She eyed the sheet for a minute, mulling over whether they could use some of it later.

She cut a few squares and a couple of long strips, folded them, and placed all but one of them on the chair. Petra filled the one square she had with charcoal from the dead hearth and tied the ends together to make it into a little white pouch. She added the pouch to her pile of salvage and hefted the lot of it out of the cottage with ease. Michael gave her a confused look from where they had left him, the rope now tied around his wrists and fastened tight to a fencepost.

"You're too pretty to be a horse, so stop pretending you are one," she said as she dropped her stuff down beside their bags.

"I remind you that you are the one who tied me to a post like an animal," Michael said. She was really regretting unstuffing his mouth, but she was too busy right that instant to do something about it.

"And your master tossed me and mine into a cage like animals, so I think we're even."

"Only if you untie me," he said.

"I like you right where you are at the moment," she said, winking at him. The little gesture infuriated him, and that made it almost worth having to listen to him.

"I found an old spear," Faust said as he came out of the other cottage brandishing a rusty-headed weapon. "It should be better than nothing. If nothing else, we can give some bastard lockjaw. Can monsters even get lockjaw? Oh good, you found some rope."

"No idea," Petra said, answering his question as she stuffed the rope into her bag on top of the cloth. "I'd think that would be the sort of thing you would have already read about.”

“Untie me, damn it!” Michael said, thrashing uselessly against the fencepost.

“The only sicknesses related to monsters that made it into the books I read were the curse-borne ones that turn people into beasts,” Faust said.

“That shit throws me for a loop,” Petra said. Most of the guild just sort of hand-waved it away as something that didn’t matter. Track them and kill them, in that order, and grant mercy to anyone infected you meet on the way. Of course, it wasn’t really that simple, but Petra had fallen into that mindset herself on more than one occasion. She missed her pouch of medicines, but there was no replacing that unless one of the supply drops had a few vials to spare.

“Leave it to a simpleton like you to misunderstand something so obvious,” Michael said.

“Oh? Go on then, oh great scholar of the fencepost,” Petra jabbed back.

“The church, the true church, that is, teaches that the accursed kin are born from the seven stigmata,” Michael said.

“The heraldic church teaches the same thing,” Faust said, rolling his eyes.

“Does your failed church know that the stigmata originated from the Archons of old Stygia?” Michael said. A strand of his orange-red hair fell onto his forehead, and he tried and failed to blow it back up.

“Black blood,” Petra said. “It’s nothing more than an old story used to scare children.”

“They did exist though,” Michael said, “just not this far west. The forefathers of the empire fled here after the Stygians brought about the fifth Eventide.”

"We've been dealing with werewolves and nachzehrer for a damn long time longer than that," Petra said.

"Leave him," Faust interrupted. "We need to search the other buildings."

"Fine by me," Petra said. Faust was already heading toward the mill, and she moved toward a small shed behind the cottage she'd just left. She found a few more tools inside, mostly useless though. They could use a pitchfork in a pinch, but it wasn't ideal.

"Faust!" Michael called out. "I know you can still hear me! I also know you look to be rather studious! You know I am right!" If he could hear him, Faust didn't respond, which was fine. Michael was making way too big a deal out of an idle conversation. Abandoning any thought of finding something worth using in the toolshed, Petra left it, the door hanging open listlessly.

"I know that old bedtime story too, you know," Michael continued. "Black-eyed men with blacker blood would come and scoop up bad children who stayed up too late."

"Turn them into wolves, yeah, yeah, and you want me to believe it's not a load of..." Petra's words trailed off as she picked up an odd sound. She held up a finger to Michael and hoped he understood the universal sign for "shut your mouth." She listened. Her breathing, Michael's breathing, the rush of the river, and the squealing of the water wheel. Then there was a shout. Rushing over to Michael's side, she untied his rope from the fence post and started pulling him toward the mill.

Faust was just coming out of the mill when she and Michael approached it, a bag weighed down with grain in his hand. She grabbed his free hand and dragged both boys inside the house, sidling up between the corner and the doorway. "What?" Faust asked, voice low.

"People. Don't know what direction," Petra whispered. He nodded in response, then gave Michael a look before setting down his bag of grain. Who knew if any of it was actually usable? She didn't think Faust ever had to work a mill before. She stared at the bag for a minute and said, "Shit." Faust followed her gaze to his bag and his eyes went a bit wide in understanding.

"What?" Michael said.

"Our bags," Faust said. "By the fencepost?"

"The grass by the first house," Petra said. "I'll go get them." Faust grabbed her arm to get her attention. She expected he was going to try and stop her, but instead, he simply mouthed "be careful" before letting go. Leaving the mill, she ran back toward the cluster of cottages and pressed herself against the wall of the closest one when she made it. There hadn't been any sign of whoever it was she'd heard. Yet.

Slinking over to the far corner, Petra peered around the side to find no one. She slid slowly over to the other side of the wall, peeking just barely out from behind the wall when a man in a ragged red uniform walked into the yard. He had a rifle, one that looked to be an old muzzleloader. She didn't need an education in heraldry to know he was one of the collaborators' men.

Several more soldiers joined the first, all of them just as haggard as he was. There were about five in total: three men and two women, each one a deserter. Petra had seen how deserters acted once, and the memory sent a shiver down her spine. The people who had lived here were lucky they'd fled when they did.

"Check the houses," one of the women said. She must have been an officer, or at least the ringleader for their desertion.

The group split up and started searching through cottages, not that they'd find anything. Their leader stayed outside while the other four each took a cottage. She was of average height with a lean build, from what Petra could tell. When she turned, Petra saw she had a bolt-action rifle. That was a better find than anything they'd gotten from the homes.

Circling around the back of the cottage as quietly as she could, Petra checked the next corner and darted across the open space to the nearest cottage. She made just enough noise to draw suspicion, and she heard the leader start walking her way. Thumbing her dagger, she decided to leave the steel in its sheath. What came next would go better if both her hands were free.

As the barrel of the rifle poked around the edge of the wall, Petra started forward. She grabbed the barrel of the gun and yanked it and the woman toward her. Slamming her against the wall, she clamped her free hand over the woman's mouth to silence her. Her friend inside the cottage would come out any moment now. Petra pushed against the rifle and twisted, likely breaking the woman's trigger finger in the process, before pulling it free from her grasp.

In as quick a motion as she could muster, she let go of the deserter's mouth and stepped back, righting the rifle in her grip and aiming at the woman. Petra didn't necessarily want to shoot her, but she would if it came down to it, and the deserter knew that. Still, the woman lunged at her. Without hesitation, Petra swung the weapon around and bashed the woman across the head with the wooden stock, knocking her out cold.

Petra clicked her tongue as she opened the bolt. It was empty. She was still going to keep it, though. She ran out into the yard, quickly scooped up their bags, slinging their straps over the rifle like a washing pole, and sprinted off awkwardly toward the mill. Her escape hadn't been as clean as she'd hoped; a chorus of shouting came from the collection of homes behind her.

"We've been had!" Petra called out. Faust came out of the mill, tugging Michael behind him, and Petra veered off to the right. A gunshot rang out, but the shot went wide. Petra nearly lost hold of the rifle as the bags swung wildly on the end of it. One of the bags came loose, but as she turned to look back, she saw that Faust had caught its strap. The four deserters weren't following them anymore, but she kept going. The green sod gave way to a vegetable field, but she didn't stop.

"Petra!" Michael called, and she turned back to look at them. Michael was standing on his own, the rope around his wrists leading down into the dirt. She dropped everything as she stopped, almost tripping over her own feet in the process. Faust had collapsed in the dirt, still gripping the rope and bag tight in either hand. She checked him for injuries, anything, maybe he'd been hit by that gunshot earlier, but she didn't find any wounds.

"Give me my prayer book," Michael said. "Quickly."

"What will that solve?"

"Prayer of healing. Look, I know you do not trust me, but I can help him." Petra shook the bag Faust was holding, listening for the jingle. It wasn't the one with the bell in it, so there was a chance it was Michael's. She dug through the pack, the absence of rope telling her it was his. She found the little prayer book and handed it to him, pre-opened. He flipped through the pages as best he could until it appeared he found a prayer he thought would work.

"Oh, divine Father, blessed giver of life, be kind to this lost soul, grant mercy to his flesh, and make it whole by the power through which you first forged it."

Nothing happened. Michael repeated the prayer, but still, nothing happened. He said it a third time. Nothing.

"He isn't injured. Try a different prayer."

"There are three dozen prayers of healing," Michael said.

"Well one of them has got to work." She ran back to where she had left the other two bags, shaking them to find out which one had the herald's bell in it and pulling the silver instrument from its folds. Rushing back to Faust's side, she rang the bell but got the same results that Michael had. What the hell was wrong with him?

"Can you two please stop with that racket?" Faust said.

"Faust, what happened?" Petra said

"I think I tripped over a root," he said as he rolled onto his back. "Maybe a gourd, who the hell knows?"

"You got a little blood," she said, flicking a finger across her upper lip below her nose. He gave her a look and wiped the blood from his face but just smeared himself with mud.

"Great," he said, clearly tired. He sat up, then looked down at his own empty hand and back up at Michael. Michael raised his arms, taking a minute to register that no one was keeping hold of his leash. Petra was ready to race after him, but he just stood there, trying to close his prayer book. "Fine, cut him loose, Petra."

"If you say so," she said, taking care to untie the rope from around the redhead's wrists. He flexed his hands about, rubbed his wrists, and rolled his shoulders.

"Finally," Michael said, holding one hand out to Faust while the other slid his prayer book into his waistband. "You now owe me your life, by the way."

"Not a chance in hell," Faust said, taking Michael's hand.

Petra watched their brotherly moment with an exaggerated expression of disgust. "We are still going to keep a close eye on you."

"I am more than happy to oblige you both if you insist on me not taking any watches," Michael said.

"Pretty boy needs his beauty sleep," Petra said. "Okay, moment's over, let's keep moving before those guys realize we haven't gotten as much of a head start as they think. Are you okay?"

"My entire front is sore, but I will live," Faust said. "I feel like dead weight right now."

"How do you think I have felt?" Michael said.

"Oh, uh, here," Petra said as she handed Faust the bell. He took it and returned it to Meinherd's bag, shouldering the pack and tossing her hers. Okay then.

CHAPTER TWENTY-SIX

FAUST

From that day on, the sons of Fridwald von Schwarzdorn and Gautbert von Rosenberg would wage war upon each other. For ten generations, they have feuded and for ten generations have the southlands been devoured by the War of the Briars. So long has it been that even I cannot say whether there is truth in what I have told you of its origin.

Odoacer the Timid, Third Antiquities 27:19-21

Faust stepped over another body half-buried in the mud. A von Reinherz banner, one from Althafen, lay trampled and torn not far from the fallen soldier. The deserters they had encountered a few days ago should have been warning enough, but he never expected this. The Freikorps had utterly crushed the collaborator forces. He could think of so many words to describe the situation, to rationalize it, and reduce it to a single concept. "Horror" is what he settled on.

He tried to figure out how an army could be so badly defeated like this, but his answer was hardly comforting: rain.

Petra explained that only one of the deserters had been carrying a modern weapon, which made the solution obvious. It had rained at Elem and soaked the black powder most of the collaborators' levies needed to fight effectively.

Cannons, guns, it didn't matter what the weapon was, if it used black powder, it was useless in a heavy storm. The mercenaries had access to better weapons, and most all of them were career soldiers. Most of the dead here wore uniforms not quite fitted to them. They might as well have been fighting demons for all their lords had prepared them for. They probably thought they had been in their final moments, at least.

To Faust's left, Michael puked again. How the squire of a paladin could have no stomach for the dead was beyond him. The sight of so many dead was horrific, but he knew getting sick over it would only slow them down, and that was not something he could afford. Someone else would eventually come and give these men and women their last rites. Someone else would eventually come to put the bodies to the flame.

Petra let out a hitched breath from up ahead and kneeled down to go through another ammo pouch. She'd furnished a few dozen bullets for her rifle so far. Her Jäger supply drops had been a bust. They'd only found a few stale biscuits in one and a rotten piece of jerky in another. The detour had been the right call though, all things considered.

Had they made it here any sooner, they likely would have gotten caught up in the hell these poor people went through. Elem was in sight now as well, her walls weathered but standing. Howls from within told him all he needed to know about what was going on just over that stone horizon. Going in there would be dangerous, but he would do it if it meant finding Johann. He owed him too much to just run away now.

"Are you done?" he said, turning back to Michael. The other prinz wiped the bile from his lips and scowled at him.

"How can you two see this and not be ill?" Michael said.

"I've seen worse, usually people torn to gory ribbons by whatever my master and I were sent to kill," Petra said.

"This is fairly tame," Faust said. "Petra, you said Kalb was camped just north of the town, right?"

"Yeah, but who knows if he's still there?" she said before letting out a frustrated groan and complaining, "Who made this ammo bag?"

"Did you find another one full of mud?" Faust asked.

"If we find a source of water, I can try cleaning them, but I don't want to waste what we have now," she said.

"Saint Clarita, matron of the sword, intercede for these fallen warriors that they not be lost to the heavens."

"Michael," Faust said.

"Saint Valens, protector of the abandoned, watch over their families as they grieve and deliver them from poverty. Saint Drakon, unrelenting bulwark against the darkness, grant me strength to persevere through this great evil."

"Michael!" Faust said. "Leave them."

"Michael, Faust is right, we need to keep moving," Petra said.

"You two are really something else, you know that?" Michael said. "I thought you people would care about giving the dead this one last kindness. Or do they not deserve last rites because they converted to the imperial church?"

"That is rich coming from you," Faust said as he turned to face Michael. "How many times have you insulted the faith of our people since I met you? How many times have you done so, period? You call us pagans, call the heraldic church a failed organization, and stood with people who want our faith eradicated from the earth. I was there, in that castle," Faust pointed toward Elem as he spoke. "I watched your mentor and his comrade call for the dissolution of our church and for the mass arrests of our priests. Do you even know what your church did to the heralds they arrested?"

"I..." Michael stammered.

"No? But you have seen the results," Faust continued. "Where did you think Meinherd got his scars?" Michael had no quip for that, no retort. Good. Faust had given him a chance, and he was throwing it away by wasting time that could be better used finding Johann, all so he could play priest in the mud like a child. This place was a tragedy made real. He was not so cold as to deny that. These people did deserve something, just not the empty words of a brat who, on any other day, would have gladly stood by as those he called mentors ordered them to their deaths.

"If you can pray and walk, then be my guest. But right now, I am more concerned with the living," Faust finished. Thankfully, Michael could not pray and walk at the same time.

They crossed the battlefield in a little more than an hour. A dead horse lay atop the leg of its rider, her throat slit and face aghast. A few carts had been overturned for cover; two dozen or so bullet holes and a pile of bodies showed the futility of the act. Craters full of sludge dotted the plain, but the gentle rise of dirt around their edges made them easy enough to avoid. One corpse stared up at Faust as he stepped over it. The boy was only a year or two younger than he was. He had probably lied about his age to go fight, only to end up here with his legs gone and a scream plastered across his still face.

A flock of vultures crowded around a mound of dead a few paces to the west, and Michael threw a stone at them to scare them away. He lacked the will or means to do anything more and had given up the idea of praying for them. Another horse was draped across a row of wooden spikes, its body hanging almost as limp as the ropes tied to either end. A raven swooped down, landed on the horse's neck, and stared at them with its head cocked to the side.

There was an old Ershaen legend about corvids and battlefields, but Faust quickly turned his mind from it. The dead were a grim enough portent on their own without the help of old pagan ghost stories. Nearby, Petra knelt down next to another body and yanked a long knife, sheath and all, from a fallen soldier in blue and grey. He envied the totality of her indifference. He felt ill. How could he not with the stench of decay and gunpowder ever-present in his nose? The only thing holding him together was the overriding need to find and rescue Johann.

Faust was sure that some deep plane of Hell probably looked like this, but dwelling on it availed him nothing. Nor did it help him to realize that every story he had heard of the Freikorps' brutality in battle had been no exaggeration. These thoughts entered his mind as swiftly and unwanted as a thief, scurrying off as quickly as they came when he shooed them away. He glanced eastward to Elem, eyes scanning the parapets atop her walls and finding no one.

How many souls had survived the initial onslaught? How many had escaped as they had? And how many remained within the nightmare their home had become? He had no satisfactory answers, but he damn well intended to get them. They had abandoned his godfather in that cursed town, and he had no other place to look. But first, they would need better weapons.

Petra was like a carrion animal in her own right, flitting like a crow from one body to the next, rifling through their pockets and fiddling with their guns. She had yet to keep a single firearm though, discarding each one back into the mud after peering into their open chambers. The only thing she kept was the ammo, but whether she could actually use any of it in her own stolen weapon was beyond him.

A sudden bellowing of distant cannons shocked Faust to his knees. He crashed into the muck as projectiles whistled through the air toward Elem. Another salvo called out as he got back to his feet. The crash of artillery shook the earth; someone was taking to the deed of leveling the lycan-infested settlement. At least the Freikorps had stayed to clean up their own damn mess, though it far from absolved them of their sin.

He followed Petra as she picked up her pace through the filth, leaving her task of picking through bodies unfinished. A slopping sound from behind him drew his attention to Michael, who then stood half-submerged in an impact crater. "Petra!" he called out, turning around to dredge his bargaining chip from the hole. He took Michael's outstretched hand and pulled, slipping as the ground gave way beneath his feet.

"Careful!" Michael said as Faust's boot skimmed the side of his head. Petra had come around now and helped Faust up, the two each taking one of Michael's hands. They pulled him free from the mud, the space he left behind collapsing into itself with a wet plopping noise. Michael's white clothes were ruined, stained deep with the wet black of the place that crept up his legs and onto his chest.

The thumping beat of artillery kept on as they pushed toward its source. Hopefully, Petra had friends among the mercenaries who would lend them weapons and help them pierce into the heart of Elem. Finally, the blackened, murky terrain began to give way to weary fields of grass. The last of the dead lay at rest behind them and the booming song of war stood before them.

Rows of barricades like pikes plunged into the earth stood at the far end of the northern clearing. Behind the wooden rampart was a row of cannons, their long barrels angled high to lob more ruin onto that wretched town. Soldiers in the all-too-familiar blue and grey stood amongst the larger pieces. It was doubtless that the mercenaries saw them as they approached, but by some miracle, they kept their munitions firmly in their weapons.

"Stay here," Petra said, leaving them in the open as she started toward the camp. The mercenaries took unkindly to her advance and leveled small arms toward her. Almost without thinking, Faust ripped open his bag and pulled out Meinherd's bell, waving it above his head so it could be seen as it rang. The serene toll cut through the deafening roar of the cannons with otherworldly grace, and its message reached the Freikorps. Guns were lowered, and a woman pushed one of the men aside and started toward Petra.

Faust and Michael made up the distance about the same time as the woman, coming to stand on either side of their friend. The woman was barely taller than Faust, with dark blonde hair cut short in the back and a long braid tied into one side of her bangs. Her face seemed frozen in a permanent scowl, and a long scar cut a line from the middle of her forehead down to the right side of her chin. Cold blue eyes examined them each in turn before coming back to Faust.

"You don't look like a herald boy," she said, in a scratchy voice.

"Because I am not one," Faust said. "I was traveling with one until recently, though." He took his signet ring off and held it out to her. She took the ring and looked it over.

"How do I know you didn't take this from someone else too?" she asked with a raised eyebrow.

"I suppose you cannot, but does it really matter?"

"It does if you don't want to get shot."

"I don't recognize you," Petra interjected. "You aren't one of Kalb's, are you?"

"Thank the Confessors for that," the woman answered with a sneer. "I'd kill him myself for leaving me this shitshow if he wasn't so useful to the cause. Who are you?"

"Petra Ebner, apprentice Jäger. I was here with my master not too long ago when Oberst Kalb was in charge."

"Could have used you a few days ago, though I suppose you lot were right in the thick of it, weren't you?"

"Got thrown in a dungeon when everything went to hell," Petra said. She pointed her thumbs at Faust and Michael and continued, "These guys helped us escape with our heads. We got separated from everyone else, though."

"That's a damn shame, but that doesn't explain why you came back," said the woman.

"Someone I care about might still be in Elem," Faust said. "If he is, then he was likely taken to the castle. Do you know if anyone is still alive in there?"

"Son, I don't know, but I wouldn't keep my hopes up. I should introduce myself. Abigail Melsbach, Oberst of the Fifth Korps."

"Faust von Schwarzdorn. She's Petra and he's..."

"Michael, just Michael."

"Well, you all look like shit," Melsbach said. "Come on, we'll get you cleaned up, and then we can discuss your missing person." She tossed Faust his ring, and he slid it back onto his finger as she turned and walked away. Melsbach shouted to her men to keep firing when she walked by, leaving the artillery crews to their work as she led the three new guests into the camp.

"When did Kalb leave?" Petra asked, hurrying a few paces so she was walking directly beside Melsbach.

"Two days ago, shortly after I arrived. He took his Tenth along with Haas and her Eleventh Korps west to put pressure on Althafen. My men are here to hold the flank. Keep the bastards from regrouping and turning his siege on the city into their own Mastrok. He also left all of his wounded here, so I get to babysit them too."

"And the werewolves," Petra said.

"And the damned werewolves," Melsbach said.

CHAPTER TWENTY-SEVEN

PETRA

Just as you are to take a portion of their toils, so too should you give them a portion of your own, that all men and all women should be afforded the blessings of their fellows. For it is only by means of fair and mutual trade that a community is born and maintained. Give of yourself in trusting that your neighbor shall do the same, and you both shall be happy for it. But know that to break that trust is to sow discord through all society.

Gerlind the Confessor, Book of Tiers 2:25-29

Growing up the daughter of a poor farmer, Petra had sometimes wondered how the upper classes lived. Joining the guild let her take fleeting peeks into that world, but her days in the camp had been the first time she got to experience luxury for herself. As a basin of cold water was dumped over her head, she found herself missing Alban and his staff and their warm baths. Shivers shook through her body as she was handed a sponge and started scrubbing.

She heard the splashing of water through the thin cloth divider that separated the men's and women's bathing quarters. Michael yelped like a wounded animal as he too got the same treatment. A few days ago, she would have felt satisfied at that. Now she found herself worrying about his well-being. Heat touched her cheeks, and she shook the thoughts from her head. She scrubbed harder and faster, hoping the sensation would scour away more than just the grime on her skin.

Someone handed her a towel when she was done and then left as she dried off. The soldier came back with a change of clothes. She had expected a Freikorps uniform, but instead, the woman handed her an outfit leftover from Alban's frontline wardrobe consisting of a white button-up shirt, light grey pants and overcoat, and black leather boots that glistened in the light.

There was also a shoulder holster of black leather that had her old pistol tucked safely within, courtesy of Oberst Melsbach. She pulled on the clothes quickly, thankful for their warmth as she stepped out into the cool autumn evening with her hair still damp. The soldier led her through the camp toward what had been Kalb's command tent, now occupied by Melsbach. The table with the regional map was still there, though now a new host of markers were spread across the sheet.

Faust was escorted in shortly afterward, dressed in another of Alban's fashionable sets. He was wearing charcoal grey pants with a long, sleeveless, black gambeson coat pulled over a white shirt and strapped tightly shut around his torso. He had a dagger strapped around the lower portion of his left arm, the pommel ending just before his wrist. His black hair was glistening wet and pulled straight back.

He walked by her and leaned forward onto the table, his eyes staring blankly at the map. Melsbach came out of one of the back sections of the tent, looking between the two of them. She cleared her throat, but Faust didn't take his eyes off the marker for Elem. "Prinz Faust," she said. Petra came up to the table and jabbed an elbow into his ribs. He looked lazily at her, and she motioned toward the Oberst.

"How soon can you get me into the castle?" he asked. Petra let her shoulders sink.

"That depends on you both," Melsbach said.

"Wait, what?" said Petra.

"I don't trust either of you and your friend even less, which is why he isn't here. You tell me you stole that bell, but expect me to believe you didn't steal your ring. And you, girl, care to explain why there was a note with your name on it attached to the clothes you're now wearing in the von Morgenkranz's tent?"

"Our guild's representative was related to them," Petra answered. "And Prinz Alban is extremely kind."

"What was your representative's name?"

"Erik," Petra said.

"Erik what?" Melsbach asked, her eyes narrowing as she rasped out the last word.

"Erik von Silberstern," Faust clarified, "sole surviving son and heir of the late Gerulf von Silberstern, former Herzog of the dukedom of Lornern and sitting lord of the sacred city of Vorbotenruhe."

"What?" Petra said. She had known Erik was a nobleman, but neither he nor Alban had ever told her his full title. Maybe she shouldn't have been too surprised though.

"You didn't know?" Faust said.

"He never said."

"That still leaves my question for you," Melsbach said, glaring at Faust.

"As I already explained, I am the Prinz zu Dorneswik. I took that bell from the herald who acted as my advisor, a man by the name of Meinherd." A look of surprise flashed on Melsbach's face, hanging there for a second before she returned to stone.

"Meinherd as in, bald-headed with silly facial hair and burns across his torso?" she asked.

"You know him, then?"

"Aye," Melsbach said as she pointed to her scar. "An imperial soldier gave me this at Wolfsstadt while I was trying to set Meinherd and the other heralds free. Was he doing all right?"

"Aside from the part where he forced me to abandon my godfather to the mercy of the imperials, he was doing exceptionally well," Faust said, but Melsbach didn't react to his daggered tone.

"I'm sorry to hear that. But it does lead me to my next question. Your friend had an imperial rosary in his possession. Were you aware of this?"

"We are," Petra said.

"He is my bargaining chip," Faust said, raising a hand to his chin as he lips pursed in thought. "Michael is the squire to the man who likely has Johann, my godfather, held in captivity. I plan on trading him."

"That makes some sense, but I can't help you right now." Petra watched as Faust's face went stark white, his eyes wide. He opened his mouth to say something, but Melsbach raised a hand and said, "I can't get you into Elem because it's a hellscape rife with bloodthirsty beasts. Your godfather is as good as dead already if they took him back to the castle. But if he was taken by the imperial church, I might know where else he could be."

"Obviously, there is a catch," Faust said, "so spit it out already." Petra didn't like the look in his eyes, but she kept her mouth shut. This was his quest, and it was his decision on how to handle it, for better or for worse. Melsbach took a stone marker from the side of the table and tapped it onto the map.

"On top of everything, we also have a vampire problem, though, by the looks on your faces, you know that already."

"We had a run-in with him," Petra explained.

"You want us to kill him for you," Faust said.

"I want *her* to kill him, specifically, but you're more than welcome to help. The faster you deal with this, the sooner you get what you want."

"How did you find out?" Petra said.

"I have eyes," Melsbach said. "Half of Kalb's sick were suffering symptoms of anemia, and all but a handful have bite wounds. Egon is no genius, but even he should have been able to figure that out, yet he didn't. I suspected the bloodsucker had infiltrated his inner circle. I guess I was right."

"The vampire was the man we knew as Brother Falvard," Petra said, "I could pick him out in a crowd, but I need more to go on than that. Have there been any recent victims?"

"A few, but Brother Falvard is already on his way back to Kranzdorf, so it can't be him."

"Another vampire then?" Faust said. "How many of Kalb's men were preyed upon?"

"Nineteen, maybe more depending on how many recovered before I took over this camp."

"Then Falvard had help, or maybe he infected someone else with his curse before he left," Petra said. She knew how to kill a vampire, but finding them was sometimes tricky. "How many days until the blood moon?"

"What day is it?" Faust said.

"The twenty-first," Melsbach said. "It's going to be any night now."

"No time to waste, then," Petra said. "We're going to need more weapons."

"That can be arranged, though I don't have much true silver."

"We won't need it so long as I can put a bullet through its head," Petra said.

"We need to find the vampire first," Faust said. "Oberst, I need you to have Michael brought to the infirmary tent."

"What are you thinking?" Petra asked incredulously.

"Michael can use imperial prayers to heal wounds," Faust said, rubbing his nose.

"Let the victims tell us who attacked them? Surely, it can't be that easy," Melsbach said.

"With their hypnotic powers, no, it won't be," Petra said, "but we have Meinherd's bell too. If we use both together that should help us clear their heads enough to get something decent. If nothing else, we can just run around camp ringing it, waiting for someone to start acting strange."

"We tried that already," Melsbach said. "We still have the church bells Kalb used to keep the werewolves away from camp." Petra looked down at the map table. Most of the markers meant to be the collaborators had been removed, but there was something else missing. She slammed her hand down onto a point off to the east of the camp.

"I think I know where to look," she said, getting raised eyebrows from Melsbach and Faust both. She frowned at Faust and said, "I think Kalb had some men around here. I don't remember where exactly, but I do remember that Erik asked him about it, and that was when he mentioned the werewolves."

"I fail to see how that relates," Melsbach said.

"No, Petra's right," Faust said. "There was an outbreak in my homeland, which I believe was manufactured. Kalb could have easily done the same thing here, and if he did, he would have needed a safe place away from the prying eyes of anyone who might object. It would need to have some infrastructure, but such that could be concealed from enemy spies."

"You think Egon started this outbreak on purpose?" Melsbach said.

"Werewolves flooded into the streets of Elem the moment his cannons breached the walls," Petra said. "What other conclusion is there? We can't be sure if your vampire is at that camp, but this gives us a better idea of where to start looking farther afield."

"You should still have Michael heal your wounded and sick," Faust said. "Squeeze some use out of him, and maybe we can get some valuable information. Just don't hurt him. I still need him, after all."

"He'll be safe with us, so long as he doesn't try to set anyone on fire." Melsbach called in one of her men and told him to take them to the armory. They followed him out of the tent and into the camp. Behind them, the sinking sun cast evening rays down across the fields and over the tents, shadows playing in their wake. Petra looked to the large yellow tent that had been her home for a few days, its peak rising up above the sea of grey and blue.

The man led them to a larger tent, which had a fence of wooden planks fastened around its base. Inside, they found rows upon rows of rifles. Most were of Gaersche make, but a handful looked to be imports from distant Kessia. A hand extended to block her path as she stepped toward the exotic fare, and the gruff, bearded face of their guide motioned her back to the more basic weapons.

She tried the exaggerated pout that never worked, tallying another failure to her long list before giving up and picking out a standard-issue rifle. It was nothing spectacular, but it was sturdy and would get the job done. The bolt worked fine, but the release for the internal magazine needed to be oiled. She took a bayonet too, fastening the blade to the end of the rifle and giving it a swing through the air. The blade held perfectly.

"You do know how to use that, right?" she asked Faust as he picked up a pistol.

"Of course," he said as he pulled back the slide, checking the chamber and then clicking it back into place.

"Good," she said with a laugh. "I was worried you'd be more used to swinging a sword around."

"Johann made sure I knew how to use both, but I do prefer firearms."

"I'm sorry we have to do this," she said.

"Save it. You of all people have nothing to apologize for. Petra, regardless of what happens, I will repay you for everything you have done for me."

"Yeah. I mean, I expect as much. We just need to get through it in one piece."

"I suppose you are right," he said, walking out of the armory and leaving her with their escort. Petra let out a sigh as she slung her rifle over her shoulder. The idiot forgot to get any ammo. She took two small bags and filled them with eleven clips of rifle ammo and a pair of pistol magazines.

They would also need some other provisions, food and water, maybe some medicine if Melsbach could spare any. She left the armory and hurried to catch up to Faust. He was probably going to get himself killed. He might even get her killed if he kept up like this. "Faust!" He didn't respond to her; he just kept walking.

She followed him through the camp, dodging through mercenaries as they went about their business. "Watch it!" one of them said as she collided with him, spinning around to give an apologetic look before turning back toward her friend. Were they really friends, though? Did that even matter at this point? He was a client, but he was also willing to help her see the job to its completion. A lot of people wouldn't even think to do that.

Passing through another intersection of tents, she did a double-take as she caught a flash of black to her side. Faust was leaning forward onto a crate, his head hung low. He wretched and there was a sickening wet slosh as his vomit splashed onto the earth. She approached him slowly and put a hand on his shaking shoulders. He tensed up beneath her touch, head turning toward her. Each of his breaths was slow and shaky, and sweat was beginning to form beads on his brow.

"It's okay," she said, rubbing her hand across his shoulder.

"No, none of this is, I..." he said, swallowing hard before continuing. "I-I need to find Johann, I need to find him and apologize."

"Shush," Petra said. "Leaving him wasn't your choice."

"I am so sorry, you can have whatever you want, I promise, I just..." he said.

"You need to calm down," she said.

"Yes, I just, we need to leave, go kill Melsbach's monster, so I can focus and not think."

"We will," she said. "I'll lead us there, just focus on the hunt."

He nodded, licking his lips. His breathing steadied, and he stopped shaking.

"Better?"

"For now," he said. "Thank you."

"Don't mention it," she said. She let him stand up on his own, though she stayed close enough to catch him if he fell. Alban would kill her if she let anyone ruin the outfits he'd left behind. When Faust turned around, it was almost like she was seeing him for the first time again. His face and posture were more relaxed, and he gave her a weak smile.

"Lead the way," he said.

CHAPTER TWENTY-EIGHT

FAUST

When a man gives in to his vices with abandon, he destroys all within his path in their pursuit. Family is of little meaning to him and friends even less so. He twists his soul to satiate cruel hungers, and in feeding them, so too does his dark soul twist his flesh. This is the source of the stigmata. Beware them who are marked for damnation, lest, in their fury, they spread their curse to you.

Alaric the Confessor, Sentinels 14:1-5

Faust crouched down in the grass, his rifle shouldered and trained on the doorway of a wooden structure half-buried beneath a mound of earth. Petra was circling around the mound from the far side, making one final check for other entrances. It had taken them the better part of the night to find this compound, but they knew better than to be hasty.

He could not help wondering if Cecilia and Yorick found someplace similar in the Larswald. At the moment, it was an immaterial correlation, but maybe he could find them and follow up on the matter after he had rescued Johann. Petra came into view in the brush on the opposite end of the hidden camp. She gave him a signal and he advanced down toward the bunker. They took positions on opposite sides of the large doorway.

Petra pushed open the door slowly and quietly, peeking through the crack for any sign of habitation. When the door was wide enough to enter, she slid inside, keeping her pistol ready. Faust entered in on her heels. The inside of the room was spartan and plain; it contained a handful of beds and a single large, round table with chairs around it. The place had been abandoned, but in a more orderly fashion than they had seen in the small hamlet earlier in the week.

There was nothing of note and no signs that someone had been staying there since the Freikorps left it cold. Faust left the bunker and looked around for something, anything really. He felt off, like something or someone was staring at him from somewhere, but there was nothing else in the small ditch save the other handful of hills. Petra came out and put a hand on his back.

She was a much more caring person than he had expected. If he had to be out here chasing ghosts with anyone, he was glad it was her. The hairs on the back of his neck stood up and he cursed himself for acting like a superstitious child. There wasn't anything there.

"We should probably head back, see if Michael got any information," Petra said.

"That might be for the best," he said, rubbing his neck. Yes, he was a bit spooked, but it felt familiar in an odd way. He looked around the shallow vale again, giving each hill a few moments beneath his gaze, all but one, which his eyes drifted from much sooner than the rest. Faust licked his lips and turned away, but when he saw Petra's eyes move quickly from the same hill, something clicked.

He knew exactly what he was feeling now, and it wasn't some passing chill or the unease of his mind playing a trick on him. He almost laughed. Almost. Instead, he slipped his rifle over his shoulder, letting it fall taut on its strap as he pulled his pistol free from the holster beneath his coat. In a single, swift motion, he turned and fired back into the hill. Petra jumped, cursing, but she wasn't the only one. Faust unloaded two more rounds into the hill, pacing toward it even as he felt murderous intent emanating from it.

A figure stepped from the solid slope of earth, which shimmered as he passed through it. Glowing red eyes set like coals in a pallid face lined with light brown hair and a short beard burned with anger as the vampire charged at him. Faust dropped to one knee and put two more shots into the thing, hitting it in the shoulder. It hissed out a curse in some foreign tongue before another shot whizzed overhead and tore a hole through its jaw.

Petra rushed forward as it spun around and fell face-first into the sod. She looked it over and grimaced as it let out a deep gurgle. It was poetic for the bloodsucker to die choking on its own vital fluids. Faust stepped through the illusory hillside, leaving her to the task of extracting a trophy to prove their kill. Another wooden bunker lay beneath the real sections of the hill, but there was nothing in its face that could have created the illusion so far as Faust could tell.

He walked toward the doorway, kicking something solid and shiny out from a nest of dead leaves in the process. The magicked image of earth fell away, fizzling out along its edges like the sparkle sticks used at festivals. After a moment of searching, he found the object he had kicked, a signet-style ring, turning it over in his hand. It had a crescent moon insignia with a pattern around it that didn't match any heraldry he knew offhand.

Petra came over and joined him, her hands bereft of any bloody token. "I don't have anything to neutralize his blood," she said with a shrug as he looked at her. "But that should work. I think Falvard had a similar ring."

"I do remember Erik mentioning it, though I don't recall what Meinherd's opinion on it was," Faust said.

"There was a lot going on," Petra said. She tilted her head toward the newly revealed bunker, and he nodded. They entered it much the same way as they did the first, though this one had more space on the inside, and there were cages where the other had beds. There was sobbing from behind a desk at the back of the room, and Faust made his way toward it. "It's okay," Petra said. "We killed the monster, you can come out."

A young girl came out from behind the desk, dark red hair falling messily over her face. She had tears in her eyes, and Faust took a few steps more in her direction. She raised her balled hands up to her eyes to wipe the tears away, and he saw a ring on her finger that all but matched the one he had picked up outside.

He kept his pace steady as he approached her. When her eyes were covered, he pulled the dagger from his arm and jammed it into her gut. The girl let out an agonized roar, digging her fingernails into Faust's sleeve, but he freed himself from her grasp easily. As he pried her fingers from his arm, her ring came off of her finger, and the soft brown of her eyes gave way to a bright and bloody scarlet.

The little vampire bared her fangs and lunged toward him, but he stepped aside, and she tumbled to the ground beneath her own momentum. Petra put a bullet in her head, and she stopped moving, her blood pooling on the dirt floor. "Let me check your arm," she said, grabbing it and pulling back his sleeve. The monster had been kind enough to not bleed on him at least, but his blade was soaked red.

"You're not going to protest that you weren't bitten?" Petra asked.

"I know that vampirism is not spread through bites. If it were, then we would have a lot more of them to deal with back at camp." Older books on monsters liked to make that claim, but it had been disproven decades ago by more educated men and women. Vampires only sired new vampires by feeding humans their blood. Such was their curse; the heralds called it the stigmata of pride.

The discovery had saved a lot of lives, more than anyone could probably count. Alwin Dahl likely saw himself in the same light. He had done more even than the old great scientists in that regard. Maybe history would know him only for the ends he achieved, and maybe those older generations of discoveries had been made by the same crooked means.

There were no beakers or test tubes here, however, nor a single jar of medicinal herbs. This place was nothing more than a prison. Still, the discovery was enough to satisfy Faust's curiosity, and he left the bunker with Petra close behind. The hunt was over far sooner than he had anticipated, and the thought gladdened his heart. They had two tokens of their kills. Hopefully, that would be enough to satiate the Oberst. Whatever information she had needed to be worth the time they wasted on this trivial affair.

They took a more direct route back to camp than they had toward the compound, which saved quite a bit of time on their return. The bright morning sun also helped immensely. It took a little more than an hour before they crossed into the camp and nearly an hour more before the Oberst would see them. Faust was exhausted, almost more so than that first night after the siege. He sat on a small crate, elbows digging indents into his thighs.

Petra was sprawled out across a pair of larger crates, an arm draped over her eyes to block the light. The Oberst came to them directly from her forward post, casting shade over Faust as he looked up at her. "Well?" she asked. He pulled the two rings from his pockets and handed her the dirtier one. She looked it over and asked, "What's this?"

"What color are my eyes?" Faust said.

"Green," Melsbach said. He slid the other ring onto his finger, and she let out an unimpressed humph. "They turned brown. So this is how they managed to hide among normal people for so long?"

"Brother Falvard had one as well. You should start looking for people with these."

"How the hell do they even work?" Melsbach said.

"I don't know, but they do," Petra chimed in. "One of them even made a fake hill."

"It what?"

"Mages can put spells on an item, 'enchantment' I think it is called," Faust said. "Eastern magi are considered better at it than imperial magi, but I doubt these fiends have trade partners across the Sunburst Sea. Though I suppose it could not hurt to investigate at a later date."

"I'll look into it," Melsbach said, rolling the dirty ring around in her palm. "The deed is done then?"

"There were two of them," Petra said. "A man and a little girl."

"I stabbed the little girl," Faust said. "I'm going to keep her ring, by the way."

"And I shot her," Petra said. "She had a whole crying routine, awful stuff."

"Any normal person would have fallen for that sort of thing," Melsbach said, "but I guess you two aren't normal people."

"It's probably better that we aren't," Petra said.

"So this is the fake hillside ring, I take it?"

"It is," Faust said, answering both women in one phrase before reminding Melsbach why they were still there. "You had information."

"Right," Melsbach drew the word out for a bit, her tone tilting upward at the end. He was too tired to care how she said it though. "You have held up your end. Kalb's scouts reported that a group of imperial churchmen left Elem from the east and then turned northward."

"No shit?" Petra said.

"What towns are in that direction?" Faust asked.

"The von Bernstein lands, for one, and a major pass into the Herzland," Melsbach said.

"I think I know where they're going," Petra said. "Master Taube and I were in a small village called Laupen when Erik found us and asked us to come here with him. That was where I first met Michael, he was traveling with Timaeus, Evander, and a priest named Jeremias."

"Would they have already passed through by now?" Faust said.

"I don't think so, but we might need to ask Michael if they'd stop there."

"Are you two done with me?" Melsbach said.

"Yes, thank you, and goodbye," Faust said, standing up. "Wait, where is our friend?"

"He's still in the infirmary, I can show you," she said.

"I know where it is," Petra said, rolling off her makeshift bed. She grabbed Faust's wrist and led him away from Melsbach and through a winding path of tents and soldiers toward a longer tent. Through the fabric, the moans of the injured and the clinking of tools could be heard, and as they came closer, the gentle voice of Michael in prayer.

"Saint Isaura, have mercy on these souls, though their cause is not your own, yet is their life precious before our maker and divine Father. Heal their wounds by the power of He who works through you and grant them succor that their hearts may be turned from wickedness and torment unto glory."

They found Michael on his knees at an injured woman's bedside. His rosary was wrapped around his tightly clasped hands, which were level with his face. The woman's leg was gangrenous, rotting around a wound soaked in pus and blood. She had a cloth gag in her mouth to spare her from biting off her own tongue from the pain. A group of medics stood around her, some holding her down while another stood with a bone saw and another with a large needle.

All their preparations and precautions were meaningless in the end. A gentle, lilac-hued light entangled Michael's beaded necklace, sparks falling sideways toward her leg like raindrops to the earth. Each droplet of light sent radiant waves through the wound, and the rot began to recede. After a few minutes, the wound was fully closed, and the woman fell still on the bed. One of the medics wiped down her leg with a wet cloth through the tear in her pants, while his companions moved on to other patients.

"Petra, Faust!" Michael said, standing up. He walked over to them, his face flush and dripping with sweat. His arms flew open and he pulled them both into a hug. "A week ago, I struggled to even heal a minor scratch. Thank you, both, so much."

"For what?" Faust said, fighting to free himself from the other boy's grip.

"For this, and please, pray forgive me. You were right, Faust. I'll admit it. I was so busy feeling sorry for myself that I lost sight of everything and everyone else. I think maybe that was why my prayers went unanswered."

"Good for you?" Petra said, her cheeks gaining a slight blush. She could easily get out of his hug, but she waited until Michael let go.

"I will need to prove myself to you both, I feel, but right now I very much could use a meal." He smiled as he left the infirmary, and Petra shrugged at Faust as he cocked his head. When they got to the mess, Michael pointed them toward a table and came back with three bowls of beef stew. "So, how fared your hunt?"

"Killed two vampires," Faust said.

"It was a lot easier than I thought it would be," Petra said.

"Oh, good, I thought I was the only one who thought that," Faust said.

"Marvelous," Michael said, "though perhaps a shame we could do nothing for their souls."

"Are you..." Petra paused mid-thought, pursing her lips a bit as the redhead looked at her. "Are you sure you're... okay?"

"I have never been better. Timaeus is, was, a terrible teacher, and more than a bit of a bigot, but he was right when he said it would come naturally. It just turns out that I was looking in the wrong direction, for the wrong reasons."

"And you came to this conclusion after healing a handful of people who want your family dead?" Faust asked, barely masking the skepticism in his voice.

"Yes," Michael said, before turning his attention to his lunch. Fair enough.

"Right, well, remember when we first met?" Petra said.

"Oh, when you held me at gunpoint and then punched me in the throat? That hurt, by the way, but I understand why you did it."

"I am not okay with this," Faust said

"I am," Petra said.

Faust shut his mouth and raised a finger before putting his hand down. "Michael, why are you acting so different?"

"Faust, hear me out," Petra said. "Maybe shut up, and let him be nice."

"Thank you, Petra," Michael said. "Faust, between your angry ravings and seeing how death and disease care little for affiliation, I had a personal epiphany. Let us leave it at that."

"Sure, fine, whatever," Faust said. "So bringing things back, what were you doing in Laupen?"

"We were helping to establish a base there before heading to Elem," Michael said.

"For what purpose?"

"I was never told for what," Michael said. He tapped his cheek with a thumb as he thought. "I do not entirely believe it would serve as a base for anything more than the most basic functions typical of our Orders though. Conversions, ministrations, monster hunts..." his voice trailed off as the word "inquisitions" hung unspoken on his open lips.

"Do you think Timaeus would stop there for an extended period of time?" Faust said.

"That would be my guess," Michael said softly.

"I have friends there that can help us," Petra said. "They could help organize a hostage exchange."

"I could help as well. Our priest there, Jeremias, is trustworthy, as is Herr Evander, I think. That would defeat the purpose of the hostage exchange though, never mind," Michael said. Faust stared at him for a moment but said nothing.

"How long will it take us to get to Laupen from here?" Faust asked, ignoring Michael entirely.

"Not long," Petra answered. "We had to take the long way here because we thought some paladins would be looking for us after we let loose a bahkauv in the town square."

"That was you! The others were annoyed, but they had more important things to do than chase after you," Michael said. "It should only take three days, maybe four, to get there if we take the main road."

"Should we travel at night?"

"That didn't last us very long the last time we tried it," Petra said. "But it might be best if it's dark when we get there. Less chance of someone recognizing either of us." She motioned between herself and Michael a few times.

"I will go speak with Oberst Melsbach about supplies, and we can leave whenever we wake up," Faust said.

"I second that motion. Are you going to eat that? I will if you do not want it," Michael said. Faust looked at him blankly and spooned the stew into his mouth, staring. "Point taken."

CHAPTER TWENTY-NINE

PETRA

Where they fell, the abyss began to form, a pale reflection of the deep sea of primordial nothing which the maker had made full with creation. Often did I hear their fain whispers and knew them to be lies, for many were my brethren who heeded their call, and into a man did they turn loose foul things upon the earth, the breath of creation made putrid in their lungs and the words made profane upon their lips.
Alodia Storm-Mother, Book of Dawning 3:4-7

Petra jumped over the edge of an embankment and slid hard down the barren sod, her boots splashing into a cold stream. Bullets slammed into the ground above her and sent dirt flying down over her head. Next to her, Faust jumped from the stream, his pistol drawn and aimed up the slope as he backed away.

Michael was already running, having no means of fighting at range. They'd offered him a gun before leaving the Freikorps' camp, but he refused to carry anything more than a cavalry sword. He'd been all upbeat until a few minutes ago when his overly happy ass had drawn some unhappy people to attack them. She still had no idea who the hell these people were, but asking them was the last thing she cared to do at the moment. Second to last. Dying was pretty much rock bottom on that list.

Faust put a bullet over the top of the embankment, and a gravelly voice cursed from atop the slope. Petra shook her head as she jumped back onto dry land, and her boots squeaked as she ran after Michael. Spying a patch of dead leaves, she spun around on her heel, sliding backward a few paces before dropping to a knee and leveling her pistol. She fired two shots in the direction of their pursuers while Faust caught up.

"Piss off!" she said, but that only seemed to make the other guys angrier. Who would have guessed? She fired one more shot, hitting one of them in the leg and sending him tumbling headfirst down the embankment. One of his comrades slid down to help him, and she used the distraction to make off into the woods.

She could see Michael up ahead, a flash of white and bright red moving through the drab brown. Faust was like a shadow in his deep black clothes; had it been night, he would have been damn near imperceivable. Why they weren't traveling at night was a decent question that she couldn't answer. Maybe when these lunatics stopped shooting at them, she could get there.

"Saint Drakon!" Michael yelled. "Unrelenting bulwark against the...!" She watched as the tree to his right exploded into wooden shrapnel and he jumped sideways, his arms covering his head.

"Less praying, more running!" Faust called to him.

"Trust me!" Michael replied. Faust roared out his frustration as he turned and fired several more shots. Michael continued, "Saint Drakon, unrelenting bulwark against the darkness, grant me strength to persevere through this great evil!" The woods ahead lit up like a wildfire, and Petra stumbled and fell forward as she turned away from the light. Faust was there in a moment, helping her back to her feet as the light shot by them like an arrow and imbedded itself into the ground. A wall of light flooded out to either side of it and the men stopped on the other side, unwilling to cross it.

"What the hell was that?" Petra asked as she and Faust caught up to an almost giddy Michael.

"Saint Drakon was known for carrying a bow that shot arrows of light," Michael said. "He stood alone against the fall of..."

"Save it for later," Faust interrupted. "How long will it last?"

"I have no idea," Michael said.

"Then we need to get moving. Are you hurt, Petra?"

"Just sore," she said. Her knees hurt a bit and she was certainly winded, but nothing that would slow her down. Faust nodded and picked up his pace as they continued into the woods. After a few minutes, they slowed down and turned back in the direction they'd been going before being ambushed. "Think they were deserters?"

"Could have been," Faust said.

"They could also have been highwaymen," Michael said.

"Not likely with a war going on," Faust said. "Army outriders would flush them out. Maybe they were nationalist partisans. Your imperial prayers are all well and good, but there is a time and a place for them."

"My prayers just saved our lives," Michael said, a hint of his former indignance returning. Well, his affable attitude had been nice while it lasted.

"Yes, your Saint Drakon saved us from a situation that you and Saint Clarita got us into," Faust said.

"Guys, enough," Petra said.

"I seem to recall plenty of times in which you complained about how I belittled your faith, Faust," Michael retorted, ignoring Petra.

"Two days," Faust said. "It has been two days since you got your personal revelation, and while I am happy for you, I do not see why you need to bother your saints every five minutes trying to invoke their powers."

"I am not invoking anything," Michael said. "The saints were blessed as conduits of light and virtue, and so we pray to them now as angels because they, more than any of the heavenly host, are sympathetic to our plights."

"Seriously, do we not have anything better to discuss? Dinner maybe?" Petra asked, rolling her eyes as the two blatantly ignored her.

"Frame it however you like," Faust continued.

"I will, thank you very much. And besides, it is not as if you heraldics are much different."

"We do not pray to the Confessors," Faust said.

"Yes, well, it is hard to tell since you barely seem to pray at all," Michael said.

"I believe prayer is a personal affair. I pray in thought only and trust the Harbinger to hear me."

"But never answer," Michael said.

"I..." Faust said.

"I said, enough," Petra interjected, slapping both of them upside their heads. They turned to look at her, and she almost hit them again for the looks they gave her. "You two can argue about religion later, but we just barely escaped from a group of angry lunatics."

"Right," Faust said, "which had been my point before I lost the plot."

"I got a bit carried away myself," Michael said. "Quiet conversation then. What is our plan when we get to Laupen?"

"I know some people who can sneak us in," Petra said, though, in truth, she wasn't sure if any of them were still there. Wendel might have skipped town, but Evander hadn't stayed in Laupen long, so there was a possibility he'd still be at his bar. It was unlikely that Traugott had left, but whether he would be able to help them was another thing entirely. Their best bet would be the local militia.

"Then what?" Michael asked. "Petra, you already infiltrated the chapel once, do we go that route?"

"No. Remember, we had a big, angry animal to act as a distraction."

"This is a hostage exchange, Michael, and you are our hostage," Faust said.

"On paper," Michael replied with a smirk.

"Figurative hostage, yes, keep giving me that look," Faust said.

"I simply asked what we're going to do because we need some form of a plan," Michael said.

"We turn you over for Johann and then go home," said Faust.

"You can't think it'll be as simple as that, can you?" Petra said, rubbing her temples. "They already took your godfather prisoner, they could just surround us and imprison us regardless of whether it's before or after Michael strolls far enough away."

"I am more than well aware," Faust said, cringing beneath the look she gave him. "Sorry. Tone. I know. I am thinking on it."

"Faust, I know Herr Timaeus and how he approaches things. I can help you," Michael said.

"Your best means of helping is to act like a hostage. Now

that I know your imperial miracles work, I cannot trust you with any plan we make. The last thing I need right now is for you to go bumbling your way into revealing our plans the moment Evander uses an inquisitor's prayer."

"I suppose I see your point," Michael said.

"Can you counter his prayer with one of yours?" Petra asked.

"No, I am afraid to say it does not work that way," Michael said.

"Explain," Faust said.

"I thought we were done arguing over our religious views, seeing how Petra asked us so politely."

"This will not be an argument," Faust said. "You said you wanted to help me, so explain how the miracles work."

"Petra? May I?" Michael asked.

"Go for it, just keep from shouting at one another. Do you two need to sit down for this? I could go try and capture some game."

"We can set up camp," Faust said. "But you need to be here for this."

"Okay," she said as the three slowed their pace. They found a nice spot of open sod around a fallen, gnarled tree and set up for the evening. Faust leaned against the tree, and Michael sat with his legs crossed on the grass. Petra took a seat beside Faust, deliberately placing her back against a twisted knot.

"All right, to be concise," Michael began, pulling out his prayer book and holding it up alongside the rosary tied to his hand, "these are tools of study, given to all new members of the church, not too unlike the heralds' bells. We revere three archangels where you revere one, and while we are split between the three Orders by patron, the covenant bound by the first Triumvirs allows us to call upon all three in times of crisis. Using prayer, we call upon them to work miracles through us to affect creation, since unlike magi we cannot do so by our own will."

"You call this concise?" Petra mumbled, scratching her cheek. "I'd hate to hear the long version."

"Then why pray to so many different saints?" Faust said.

"Like I said before, we can pray to the angels, but we do not know many of their names. We certainly know the names of our patron archangels, but to call upon them as we are would be unworthy. Only the saints can call upon the archangels directly, so we make do with asking them for intercession. Each saint has some miracle or work they were most known for in life, so in most cases, we pray to the saint which has the strongest ties to whatever effect we desire. This is not entirely necessary, as all thaumaturgic power comes from the same source, but many believe it expedites the process."

"Is Timaeus a saint?" Petra asked. The whole conversation was a bit beyond the pale for what she normally cared for, but Faust was right; if what they were walking into was going to end in a fight, she needed to know what they were up against.

"Thank all good grace that he is not," Michael said. "Living saints are apparently quite rare and far between. That said, there are currently three of them, none of whom are in the Gaerschland."

"Good for us," Petra said, "or maybe just me. I'm not really too big on belief, so I guess that means that I'm at a disadvantage against your old master."

"Not necessarily," Michael said. "Miracles can affect the world around us, but only so far as it doesn't alter the state first willed by the Divine Father. Things which deviate from his will, from simple lies to the spells worked by magi and maleficar, those can be 'righted,' so to speak, by the miracles we invoke."

"Can your miracles stop a bullet?" Faust interrupted.

"I have seen it happen once," Michael said.

"Your buddies weren't exactly bulletproof," Petra said, regretting her poor choice of words as Michael's mood turned dour.

"And therein lies the difference between magic and miracles," he said. "A mage's power is of themselves, where we rely on our angelic patrons. We have more limits to our power. Chief among them being the need to live and act in accordance with the virtues of our patrons to be worthy of the rewards. If one cannot do that, then questions of scope and effectiveness are immaterial."

"Which is why you couldn't wave your hands and heal people before a few days ago?" Petra said.

"I think so, yes," Michael said.

"So frame of mind can affect how your abilities work. Interesting," Faust said. "The heralds wander for similar reasons, diligence being our faith's chief virtue."

"Maybe that is why your prayers go unanswered," Michael said. "How could anyone properly practice hard work if a higher being made your burden lighter every time you asked? I cannot see myself in that, but I believe that I can respect it."

"I..." Faust's words died in his throat as a deep, bestial bellow rumbled through the woods. Petra was up on her feet with her rifle shouldered in seconds, trying to place the call to the right monster. The sound was too deep for it to be a werewolf, but too monstrous and otherworldly to be another bahkauv. A sudden sickness came over her, like a bad hangover.

Faust screamed as he clutched his ears. He had the same terrified look in his eyes that he'd had during his episode back at the war camp. He kept muttering something that almost sounded like the word "sorry" over and over again. She was almost certain she knew what the thing was. The name of it was on the tip of her tongue, but she couldn't quite remember.

Petra felt something wet and warm on her hands, and she looked down, seeing streaks of blood. Then there was a stinging pain in her cheek. She thought she heard her father, and that was when she realized what this damned thing was. "Michael, get the bell!" she said. Michael was kneeling, rosary clutched between both hands. His lips moved in a prayer, but she couldn't fully hear him; her father's voice was screaming in her head.

Letting out a growl, she went for the herald's bell herself, rummaging through Faust's bag until she felt it, cold against her hands. She pulled it out and rang it over and over until the voices that weren't really there stopped, and the only warmth on her hands was what they produced themselves. Michael stopped praying, but Faust kept muttering apologies to himself.

"What is wrong with him?" Michael said.

"Panic, caused by a drude. They make you see nightmares. I think he's more susceptible to it than most."

"But I see no creature around us," said Michael, just as a chorus of faint screams sounded in the distance. "The men who were after us earlier?"

"Most likely. Help me get him up, we need to leave before that thing comes for us."

"You want to leave them to it?" Michael asked.

"With Faust like this, yeah," Petra said. "Besides, they already tried to kill us, why should we help them?"

"Because we are better than that," Michael said.

"No, we really aren't," Petra said

"But is it not our job to hunt monsters?" he said.

"Michael, we're both just apprentices. You can do your fancy light show now, but I'm underequipped to fight something like that, and I can't afford to try. This one isn't our responsibility."

"How can you say that?" he said.

"Easily, because in the time we've had this discussion, half those men have already been killed," Petra said. "Now shut up and help me get Faust to his feet." Michael's eyes looked everywhere except at her as he helped her pick Faust up off the ground. He was still shaking and muttering to himself, his breathing coming in ragged gulps between each unintelligible word.

Eventually, when they were farther into the woods, away from the drude, he regained himself. His final muttered words were a simple, "Thank you."

CHAPTER THIRTY

FAUST

With his mighty host, Reinhold von Steinmetz seized the fortress at Veltrae and proclaimed from her high walls that any who would dare could try and uproot him. For three and fifty days, the armies of the Dornwald and the Rosenhohen besieged the fortress, but more often did they clash with one another for the feud between their forebears. A great multitude died upon the fields, but of the dead, a mere few men numbering no more than four hundred fell to the blades and bolts of the Herzlanders in Veltrae.

Odoacer the Timid, Third Antiquities 28:11-14

Faust and Michael stood together in the shadow of the trees at the edge of the woods that surrounded the small village of Laupen. The walls were a pittance compared to those of Elem, barely tall enough to obscure the rooftops of single-storied homes. A few watchtowers rose up, manned by militiamen who answered to the person Petra had left to go find. When they approached, she told Michael and Faust to stay put, going out alone and waving to some of the guards.

True to her word, she had talked her way into the town on her own, and now they were left waiting for her to return. "I really think we need to talk about it," Michael said, trying what little remained of Faust's patience. He was referring to the drude attack, tangential as it had been to them. His attempts to play counselor were trite and unwelcome.

"I am perfectly fine now," Faust said. It was the truth, but he knew good and well that now was not what Michael was referring to. The damned creature had shown him visions of Johann, dead and mutilated in any number of ways, his voice whispering accusations. Illusory as the hallucinations may have been, it was all the more reason for them to hurry.

"Your mind is unwell, my friend. At least let me try and do something."

"When did we start being friends?" Faust said.

"I had imagined it was when we met, being peers and such, but that did not pan out as I thought since you wanted to tie and gag me," Michael answered. "Then I presumed it was when we were pulling one another up from the muck. That has happened several times to varying degrees."

"Look, just because you are not entirely wrong on the matter of my health does not mean it is yours to deal with. This is my burden, and I will shoulder it."

"Then I do hope Petra hurries," he said. Truly, it was the first thing to come out of his mouth all day that Faust could unequivocally agree with. Dusk began to fall, and with it came a certain kind of dread different from what the nightmare carried in its call. The moon hung low over the horizon, steeped in red like a hot coal. This was the vampire's moon come upon them at last.

He pressed his hand to his mouth, praying into his palm for the last hope he had to call on. *Please, oh Harbinger on high, by your power, please let Johann be safe.* Whether the prayer was heard, he did not know, but he knew there would be no answer. Saving Johann was also his burden to carry, and he hated leaning so heavily on Petra and Michael to see it done. As irritating as Michael was at any given time, he appreciated that he had stuck through until now.

"I think that's her," Michael said, pointing toward the nearest guard tower. Petra's head poked up above the wooden wall and let out a high whistle, almost birdlike but for being off-key. They had worked out a plan over stale biscuits and spit-roasted rabbit the night before, and now they would put it into action. Only the divine could guess whether it would be for better or for worse.

Michael held out his hands, and Faust bound them with a rope, not tight enough to hurt him, but tight enough to not seem too obvious. They walked out of the woods and toward the gate. Petra had already left her perch, leaving the guard alone in his tower staring down at them expectantly. He really hoped these people knew how to act.

"Who goes there?" the guard asked.

"I am Faust von Schwarzdorn, Prinz zu Dorneswik, heir to the dukedom of the Dornwald, and I request entry!" The guard nodded, calling down for the gate to be opened. More militia exerted themselves to open the thick plank doors for them. Faust and Michael strode through the opening in the wooden gate and the defenders of Laupen closed it behind them with the same restrained haste they had used to pry it open.

Petra met them inside alongside a man with burns on his face. "Is everything prepared?" she asked him.

"Aye, just about," the man responded. "We've had about enough of those imperial bastards making a mockery of our hospitality."

"Faust, Michael, meet Wendel, local barkeep and veteran partisan," Petra said. Wendel's face lit up in shock, and he turned to her. "Oh please, it isn't like they wouldn't have figured it out on their own," she responded.

"You still don't say shit like that out loud, girl," Wendel said.

"Did the paladin have a prisoner with him when he arrived?" Faust asked.

Wendel cleared his throat and said, "He did, a nobleman by the looks of him. Though that was just what some of the lads told me. I didn't see him for myself."

"Good, thank you," Faust said. "That is more than enough."

"Not quite," Wendel said. "The girl here's told me some of what your plan is, and I think it'll work, but it might take a bit more time to get the rest of the militia organized. The inquisitor has Kaspar under careful watch, so I'll need maybe an hour to get instructions out."

"Kaspar would be your captain, yes?" Michael asked.

"I remember you," Wendel said. "Petra, you do realize...?"

"Yeah, he's the squire that came through here a while ago; we know," Petra interrupted. "He's what we're banking on, actually."

"Those imperial 'bastards' were my traveling companions for a time," Michael said. "Though I will be the first to admit that some of them are not the kindest people. Less so now that they have been sent out into what many of them think to be a barbarous backwater. No offense meant, of course."

"Yeah, sure," Wendel said.

"No, I really did not mean offense," Michael stammered.

"He's one of us," Petra said. "Gaersche."

"I know a Rosenhohen accent when I hear one," Wendel said.

"In any case, Herr Wendel, I would like to start as soon as possible," Faust said.

"As would I. Petra, take your friends back to my bar. I'll let you know when we're ready. Have a lot of people around here who would be happy to see these imperials sent home, but not nearly enough of them with the right training for what we need."

"They will not go quietly, even those who do not desire to stay," Michael said. "Our orders came from the ranking clergymen in the viceroyalty. Signed off by Viceroy Severus as well." Wendel rolled his eyes and walked away, flipping Michael off before he turned the corner. "Was it something I said?"

"Most of it, probably," Faust said. "You have that effect on people."

"I do not," Michael said, laughing. "Okay, maybe I do, but you are hardly one to talk."

"True," Faust said.

"Completely," Petra said. "Now let's get moving, I need a drink before the shooting starts." She started off into the village, leading them through crowded alleyways and thin crossings between low homes of wood, stone, and basic plaster. It was an unremarkable place, far from the luxuries of his home, but a great deal cozier than the open road and vast stretches of woodlands. Still, as always, it was Petra leading the way, at least for this one final time.

On an open street, they arrived at the Greifenflugel, a lonely bar bereft of both its master and patrons. Petra was the first inside and was almost behind the bar before Faust had even gotten a seat. "Either of you want anything?"

"I do not partake," Michael said as Faust untied his wrists.

"Something cheap," said Faust as Petra pulled a bottle from the middle shelf. She got two mugs and filled them up, froth foaming around their rims. Faust took the cup offered him and drank, the alcohol burning his throat. He coughed a bit, but after a while, the feeling settled.

"First one's always something," Petra said.

"I would not know," Michael said, "unless you wish to speak of first kills?"

"That isn't a subject I like to talk about," she said. Faust had gotten the feeling that she was not entirely keen to discuss personal matters, but she had always seemed so open about her work.

"My first was a kobold," Michael said. "Runt of its litter I think, but it gave me a hell of a fight. That was the day I passed my initiation. So, who is next?"

"Werewolf," Faust responded. "On the road between Tholst and Naakt. It was fairly recently too."

"When you were traveling north for the peace talks?" Michael asked.

"If you can even call them that. One of the beasts raked Johann's leg fairly well. We should have never involved ourselves with any of these people."

"Master Taube and I were in the same boat," Petra said. "Erik roped us in because he wanted someone he trusted. Imagine that the one time I didn't run away from something it would turn into all this."

"Neither of you could have known," Michael said. "I, well, I think it prudent to confess that I had some inkling of how things would go." Faust's arm stopped halfway from his lips, the mug hanging heavy in the air.

"You knew?" he said.

"Not in any certain way. I was only told where we would be going, but I knew Timaeus' views, and I questioned why he of all people would be chosen to represent our order. Herr

Evander was the more even-handed of the two, so I hoped his presence would temper my..." Faust had his hands around the boy's collar before his drink clattered to the bar. His knuckles went white as he crumpled the fabric between his fingers.

"Faust," Petra scolded as she leaned over the bar to grab one of his wrists.

"What do you think I could have done?" Michael asked.

"You could have warned someone," Faust said.

"I was just Timaeus' sad little squire, incapable of doing basic miracles, let in because my father is a local patrician key to the Viceroy's regime. Oh, yes, I was indeed aware of how it looked. Between my family and my failures, I was obsessed and angry, exactly as you painted me to be. I did not know what was going to happen. I still do not know every detail, only the small pieces I have gleaned from you.

"Even had I known, what would have driven me to intervene? You two have shown me a view of our fatherland I never got before. Those whom I thought of as allies have tried to kill me, and those who I saw as enemies have called me a friend. Had I known all of this then, I would have said something, even if it cost me my head. But I did not, and no amount of regret will change that. I am sorry for what has happened, which is why I want to help you now, genuinely, with no regard for my own gain or well-being."

"You have the right of it, I suppose," Faust acquiesced, his arms falling to his sides as he collapsed back onto his barstool. He spun in his seat and let his arms and head rest on the wet countertop. Michael was no more responsible for this series of tragedies than he was. They had both been wrapped up in themselves, blind to the dangers that lurked before them.

"When I was a kid, I killed a feldgeist," Petra said. Faust looked up, beer dripping off his chin. She threw him a rag, and he cleaned himself up as she continued. "It attacked my little brother, and I ended up stabbing it. My father slapped the sense out of me when he saw what I did."

"We are a little past that now," Faust said, "but thanks for sharing I guess."

"Sorry, it's just this conversation was getting a bit too heavy for my liking," Petra said.

"No apologies required," Faust said. "If anything, I owe you one."

"No," she said, "I ran away from home a few years after I killed the feldgeist, then I ran off and joined Heinrich when I couldn't make it on my own the old-fashioned way. I even ran away from here when I realized I couldn't save one defenseless old man. Maybe none of those times were so cut-and-dry as that, but either way, I'm tired of running away and leaving things half-finished."

"Agreed," Faust said, lifting his arms out of the small puddle of beer. They were almost at the finish line, the end of this leg of the journey, but what next? He would see Johann back home, but afterward? Would he try to hunt down Falvard? What connection did the vampire have with Dahl and the captured werewolves? There were so many paths he had barely considered until this moment.

He almost lost his footing when he stood, but caught himself on the counter. The door to the bar opened and Wendel came in, his face panning between the three of them before it landed on Petra. She hid the bottle of booze behind her back, laughing at the barkeep's sour expression at seeing her behind his counter. "We're ready," was all he said before he turned around and left.

"Remember, Timaeus' flames are real enough, but do not let them distract you from his steel. I daresay his blade is more dangerous to either of you than holy fire," Michael said.

"Hopefully it won't come to that," Petra said, "but if it does, let's hope he can't deflect bullets." They walked out of the Greifenflugel onto a nearly empty street where a few militiamen stood waiting with Wendel, armed with outdated guns and a pitchfork. The scarred barkeep led the way down the street and toward the church. Toward Johann as well, hopefully, and the curtain call for this sick farce.

The church steeple rose like a spear, cutting a dark silhouette against a sky soaked in a deep crimson by the blood moon overhead. Faust stood some paces away from its doors, unarmed before the half-circle of paladins and their drawn steel. Petra stood to his right and Michael to his left, the ropes once again woven around his wrists.

Wendel and the militia were waiting just out of sight, in homes and on the far slopes of rooftops, watching for trouble. No, not trouble. They were waiting for an excuse. They wanted this to turn out poorly, and Faust was sure the paladins wanted much the same. Maybe this time he could do something to prevent bloodshed, to keep Laupen from becoming another Elem, but that really was not up to him.

The militia wanted the imperials out, and the imperials had no intention of leaving; they were at the very impasse that defined this entire civil war and the rebellion growing around it. He wanted easy solutions, but there were none; there was only survival. "Timaeus!" Faust yelled. The doors of the church began to part, and from the gap came the prelate.

"Prinz Faust," Timaeus greeted him. "And here I was,

wondering when I would get the chance to finish what we started in Elem. You even brought my squire back. You certainly have saved me quite a bit of effort."

"I am here to parley," Faust said.

"Parley? That is an odd way to say surrender," Timaeus said. Taking a deep breath, Faust pulled his pistol and leveled it at Michael's head. "What do you want?"

"I propose a trade, your hostage for mine," Faust said.

"How quaint that you hold a gun to your bargaining chip's head. But calling your bluff does nothing to resolve the situation. Regula, bring out the prisoner." One of the paladins, a woman with her dark hair braided down her back, turned and entered the church. After a few minutes, she returned, but not with Johann. The woman pushed Norbert von Arensfeld down into the street, his clothes in ragged tatters and his face bruised violet.

"Where is Johann?" Faust said.

"Who?"

"Johann von Tollkirsche, Markgraf zu Tholst. The man you captured as we fled from Elem."

"Oh!" Timaeus said, a sickening playful expression on his face. "I remember him now. The one with the broken leg?"

"What did you do to him?"

"Keep your head, Faust," Michael whispered.

"I slit his throat and left his corpse to feed the gluttons," Timaeus answered casually. "I admit, at the time, I thought he was just a manservant, the way he stood behind you at the negotiations."

What? What? No, this couldn't be right. It had to be a lie. Johann dead? Faust's hand fell to his side, shaking, the pistol rattling in his grasp. It had to be a lie; Johann couldn't be dead. "Had I known he was someone so important, I would have carried him with me. You barbarian patricians make excellent political tools. Isn't that right, Michael?"

A single gunshot rang out through the square, silencing the prelate forever. His body collapsed down to the street, chainmail clattering against stone as he slumped backward onto the steps of the church. Faust's hand shook as he held the gun level with where Timaeus' face had been. A thin wisp of smoke curled into nothing from the barrel. All he heard was ringing and the raging thrum of his own heart pounding in his chest.

Muffled words from all sides, muted gunshots, and the whisper of flames meant nothing to him. The rest of the paladins fell, and Laupen's militia streamed into the bloodstained square like vultures come to pick apart a corpse. Faust fell to his knees, the gun slipping from his fingers. Johann was dead, and he had avenged him. Arms wrapped around his neck from behind, a warm breath raking through his hair.

CHAPTER THIRTY-ONE

PETRA

Uhtric the Pardoned, Exaltations 11

Petra knelt down onto the cobblestone road and scrubbed hard at the bloodstains on the church steps. A good rain would wash all of it away, but with winter fast approaching, the likelihood of rain was getting too low to just leave it. Wendel loomed above her, trying his best to remove the unsavory splatter of what had been inside Timaeus' skull from the chapel's doors. The rest of the militia was helping except Kaspar, who was nowhere to be found.

"Great Harbinger, hear our prayers. Have mercy on these souls known to your kin, and see their souls brought to rest among the high dominions," said Traugott, praying over the piled corpses of the paladins. "Though they brought discord to our community, and we answered in kind, let our quarrels end with the blood of this life that we may be called comrades in the next."

"You're more forgiving than I am, old man, considering they wanted you in a pit," said one of the militiamen.

"We are all creatures deserving of grace. Even the accursed deserve last rites. Why should we treat the imperials any different?"

"If you say so," the militiaman responded. Petra scoffed just loudly enough that the barkeep turned and looked down at her, but he didn't make a fuss about it. She dipped her brush into the bucket of dirty brackish water and brought it dripping back onto the stairs. Wendel let out a strange noise as the door he was cleaning was pushed partway open then closed again. The other door swung open, and Michael stepped out.

His face was worn, and she knew he hadn't slept all night. He knew most of the bodies in the pile for who they had been in life, and he wasn't taking some of their deaths well. "Careful there, kid," Wendel said, getting a stifled yawn in response.

"Morning," Michael finally said, rubbing the circles starting to form under his eyes.

"Closer to noon, but good try," the barkeep said.

"Were you able to get any sleep?" Petra asked, leaving the brush on the stone as she leaned back to sit on her legs.

"A bit. Has Brother Traugott had the ceremony yet?"

"He just got through praying," she said. "Not sure how much they would have liked it, but you shouldn't worry about it."

"They can rest easy now," Michael said. "Though I do not envy them how they earned it."

"We've got men out in the woods collecting wood for pyres," Wendel said. "Figured that since we aren't animals, we'd give them a proper Gaersche burial."

"The Palidrians burn their dead too," Michael said.

"You still planning on heading back east?" Petra asked.

"Yes, I need to see to it that their ashes make it home to their families," Michael said. He was staring off toward the cart where the bodies were haphazardly piled. "And I need to find out just how deep this corruption goes."

"Whatever helps you sleep at night," Wendel said.

"I could say the same of you," Michael said, "but such pointless bickering is what got us here in the first place. I'll need a cart."

"Little lady here still has one on hand," Wendel said. "You can have it so long as you promise to take your surviving cohorts with you when you go."

"I have a cart?" Petra said, realizing a moment later that she did still have a cart here in Laupen. It wasn't a very good cart, what with its hastily made cage, but Michael wouldn't be transporting a raging bahkauv, so that shouldn't be too much of an issue. The barkeep opened his mouth, but she stopped him. "Shut up, I remember now. You can have it, Michael. No charge."

"Much appreciated," Michael said, rubbing a hand through his messy red hair. She would miss him. And she could not believe she thought such a thing.

"How's Faust?" she asked, trying to derail her thoughts.

"You can ask him yourself," Michael said a bit coldly, though with good reason, all things considered.

"I have my senses about me again if that is what you were wondering," Faust said, pushing his way past Michael to sit on the wet steps.

"That is debatable," Michael said.

"Spare me," Faust said. "You knew it could come to this."

"I did, but I had not imagined it would end quite so suddenly," Michael said. "In any case, Jeremias and I took care of the Freiherr's wounds. Sorry about your godfather." With that, he walked over to the cart to pay his own respects for the dead.

"I feel I made the wrong choice again," Faust said.

"Not in my book," Wendel said. Petra shot him a glare. "I'll shut up now."

"I can't really tell you I'd have done anything differently if it had been Heinrich and I thought I could pull off something like that. Timaeus was a monster wearing the skin of a man."

"I am more than well apprised of that," Faust said.

"When fighting monsters, you should never hesitate and never show any pity or remorse, because Confessors know they won't show any to us," she said.

"Of all the monsters let loose upon this earth, none are so dangerous as the ones born of man," Faust said.

"The line between man and monster is thin," Traugott said as he joined them on the steps of his chapel. "I cannot say I agree with your actions, but you need not become a monster in the pursuit of slaying them."

"You killed a monster, kid," Wendel said. "We killed all the rest of them. Don't beat yourself up over people you didn't pull the trigger on. Oh, and Brother Traugott, you might want to get a new robe before going inside."

"It wouldn't be the first time this chapel's had bloodstains in the carpet, and it won't be the last," the minister said. "Our ancestors slaughtered the Ershaen who resided in these lands before us, then their grandchildren's children slaughtered one another over who among them would rule it. People are ignorant and violent, often more so than the beasts that prowl the dark corners of the world. Yet, even the most bloodthirsty among them could find forgiveness."

"You can stop with the therapy now," Faust said.

"Fine, fine, just an old man trying to do the one thing he can," Traugott said. "Thank you both for getting me my chapel back. I would much rather live out my days here than in a cell in Wolfsstadt." Brother Traugott took his leave and returned to his home, the edges of his robe trailing a dark, wet stain behind him as he went.

"Have you decided when you're leaving?" Petra asked, returning to scrubbing while Faust sat beside her.

"I have." He stared down at his interlocked fingers.

"Are you going to tell me?" she said.

"I was hoping you would be the one to tell me," he said.

"What the hell is that supposed to mean? Wait, I thought you were going back to the Dornwald?"

"What is it you said last night in the bar? Something about not leaving things half-done? I do not see myself returning home for a long while yet, not when there are so many stones left unturned here in the Vahsland."

"So you want to come back to Kranzdorf with me?" It wasn't a terrible idea. At least, not when compared to the one to hunt down and rescue his dead godfather. That plan had been worse by a mile, but maybe just because it had been doomed to fail before it even started. "Okay."

"I can arrange to have money sent to you when we get there," Faust said. "Well, technically, sent to me, but I will pay you back for helping me with all this."

"Make it double. I'm already neck-deep in this shit as it is, I might as well help you shovel us out," Petra said.

"Deal. I would have settled for an introduction to the guild."

Michael left shortly after sunrise the next morning better rested than the night before but still ragged and a bit unkempt.

Freiherr Norbert, if she was remembering his name correctly, sat beside him on the driver's bench. The Laupen militia escorted Jeremias and Evander out and all but pushed them into the cage meant for another rampaging animal that had encroached upon their lives. They sat with their hands bound among the collected and marked urns of their comrades, though they looked far better than the lord of Elem had when he was their prisoner.

They were headed south first to Arien, where Norbert's extended family would take him in and put him up until they could reclaim and rebuild his holding. After that, they would go back east into the Herzland and report to the Viceroy in Stenwarl. Petra wasn't entirely sure it was a good idea to let Evander leave, but she didn't bother saying anything about it out loud. Faust saw through her.

"Think of it as a peace offering to Michael since he seems to respect the man for whatever reason," Faust had said as the cart started rolling. "It is the least that we, no, that I can do for him after how things turned out. He will also need the extra blade if anything attacks him along the way." Maybe Faust was right, but all she could think about when she looked at the inquisitor was her master's severed hand. It didn't matter that he'd had it reattached. Sometimes, you didn't get them all, but Heinrich had taught her to be thorough.

She and Faust said their final goodbyes to Wendel and Brother Traugott. Even Kaspar poked his head out of his hole to say farewell and good riddance. She still had no idea who the hell was actually in charge of Laupen, but it probably didn't matter all too much.

Passing by the Greifenflugel one last time on their way out, they left through the westernmost gate of the village as the sun rose behind them.

"So who's at the top of your list?" she asked.

"What list?"

"The list of people we need to deal with."

"Falvard, if we find him," Faust said, "but if not, Alwin Dahl seems the best place to start."

"Why Großmeister Dahl? I mean, he is a little weird and all, but you're a little weird too."

"I think Dahl is the one responsible for some of the recent werewolf outbreaks," Faust answered. "He may be using the Freikorps to collect specimens to experiment on, which would explain how Kalb knew how to cage and transport them at Elem. Have I not mentioned this before?"

"Maybe? We found those two vampires in that bunker, so Falvard was probably involved in that too. I wish we had questioned one of them, but whatever."

"That was more my fault than anything else," Faust said.

"You can make up for it," Petra said.

"I hope so," he said.

"I'm sure that when Erik and Master Taube get back to Kranzdorf, they'll be more than willing to help us. Cecilia might help too if she and Yorick are back. Her brother is one of Dahl's people, so that will give us an in with him if we need it."

"We will need to tread carefully." Faust pulled out the ring he'd kept from their hunt near Elem. He examined it for a moment, then handed it to Petra. "Both of the rings had the same insignia, likely the same as Falvard's, based on the description Erik gave. This shall be our north star."

"It'll be kind of hard to check every person with a signet ring for this exact image," Petra said, "but I'm sure we can make something work."

EPILOGUE

ERIK

Erik entered the crowded, smoke-filled tavern, scanning the room for a familiar face as he made his way toward the bar. He shouldered his way into a narrow bit of space where he could order a drink. Paying a few klein-thaler, he got his mug and drifted out amongst the crowded tables full of mercenaries and locals. He emptied his cup and left it on a table as he headed into a stairwell leading up to a handful of rooms in a tight hallway.

He hurried over to the window at the far end of the hall-way, opened it, and jumped through it into the alleyway where he had stashed his weapons. Arming himself, he poked his head out around the corner and saw a tall figure come out of the tavern pulling a hood up over his head. The hooded figure started walking in his direction; Erik ducked back into the darkness as it glided by.

He waited a beat before following, pushing himself out into the street and after his prey. When he looked back, their eyes locked, and they both started to run through almost-empty streets across dirt roads between poor houses and general stores. Erik could have fired a shot, but he wanted it to be clean. He continued pursuing the man on foot, waiting for the right moment.

The figure ducked into an alleyway up ahead, and Erik pulled out his true silver bayonet as he drew nearer. He spun around the corner, jumped up to kick off of the far wall, and pushed his weight knee-first into the man's chest. The figure's hood slid back from his head as he landed on his back, Erik's knee pressing hard into his ribs. He coughed, fangs baring out of his open mouth.

"Hello again, Brother Falvard," Erik said, pressing his blade against the vampire's neck where it began searing his skin. "I have a few questions for you."

"Piss off," Falvard said, growling as he tried to pull himself away from the blade.

"Now, that is certainly not how a priest should talk. But then again, you never were a priest, to begin with, were you? Who do you work for?"

"You can't really think it will be that easy, can you?" the vampire said.

"Of course not, but I have all night," Erik said, stabbing the tip of the blade into Falvard's shoulder. "Go ahead, scream, let everyone in town come and see your burning flesh. No? I guess I need to try harder then." His blade cut deeper into the vampire, catching on bone. Tears welled in the creature's eyes as their amber hue flickered into a shade that matched the blood dripping from his wound.

"You'll kill me regardless of what I tell you," Falvard wheezed hoarsely.

"True. But what changes is how fast or how slow I make it happen. Talk."

"We are all dying a slow death anyway, mortal," Falvard said. "Your torture is nothing compared to vitiation."

"I find that hard to believe coming from an immortal monster."

"Believe whatever the hell you want! We're as immortal as the damned Nachzehrer, rotting away in our own deathless skin!"

"Interesting," Erik said, twisting his bayonet. "I suppose that explains the feral vampires we occasionally find. But you still haven't answered my question. Who do you work for? Is it the Sanguine King?"

"The Sanguine King? A fairy tale at best. If he even is real, then he abandoned us," Falvard said through manic, pained laughter. "Damned us to become vitiates because he didn't deem us worthy. Why would I serve someone like that? Father Jericho promised us salvation." The vampire's eyes went wide, and in one last act of desperation, he clamped his teeth shut hard, biting off his own tongue. Erik pulled his blade from the creature's shoulder and jammed it deep into his throat, piercing into his spine.

Falvard, if that even was his real name, went slack as one last bloody gurgle left his lips. Only then did Erik pull his bayonet loose. With his free hand, he took out his canteen of holy water and poured it over the blade, the cursed blood sizzling like oil in a hot pan. He poured the rest over the body, watching with muted pleasure as it shriveled like a prune.

Father Jericho was a new name. He had heard plenty of vampires make reference to the first of their accursed race, their Sanguine King, but none had ever cursed him before today. Nor had any of them mentioned the term "vitiation," though he had seen something that matched its description well enough. Maybe it was all nonsense, but Falvard seemed convinced enough of it in those final moments.

Whoever this Father Jericho was, he had his roots buried deep into the soils of the Gaerschland. No matter how long it took, Erik would find and kill him, but only after he dragged him out into the light of day and tore every secret from his lips. Falvard had done his part in making this civil war worse, and even now, the flames were spreading to every corner of the realm. To what end? Salvation for the vampire race?

Those were questions for later. Baseless speculation would only distract him from the next step. Now that Falvard was dead, he could go searching for Petra and the two young princes and drag them back home before either of their fathers devoted forces to the war. He could still fix this.